This book is dedicated to my sister,
Laufey Ýr Sigurdardóttir

I would like to thank the following people for their
assistance with gathering information for this book and for
their general willingness to help:

Audur Ásgeirsdóttir, nurse
Grímur Hergeirsson, police inspector
Hálfdan Steinthórsson, ray of sunshine
Kristín Jóhannsdóttir, museum curator
Magnús Bragason, hotel manager
Thröstur Johnsen, entrepreneur

Pronunciation guide for character and place names

NB The stress always falls on the first syllable in Icelandic.

Ari – AH-ree

Ásta Jónsdóttir – OW-sta YOHNS-doh-teer

Breki – BREH-kee

Brimurd – BRIM-urth

Dóra – DOH-ra

Ellidi Jónsson – ED-lith-ee YOHN-sson

Erla – AIRD-la

Gaui – GOH-yee

Geir – GAYR

Grímur Marinó Steindórsson – GREE-mur MAR-in-oh
   STAYN-dohr-sson

Gudrún – GVUTH-roon

Gugga (Gudbjörg) – GOOG-ga (GVUTH-byeurg)

Hafnarfjördur – HAB-nar-FYURTH-ur

Halldóra – HAL-doh-ra

Heimaey – HAYM-a-AY

Heimaklettur – HAYM-a-KLET-tur

Hellisheidi – HED-lis-HAY-thee

Hnallthórur – HNADL-thoh-rur

Hótel Vestmannaeyjar – HOH-tel VEST-man-na-AY-ar

Idunn – ITH-un

Ína – EE-na

Karó (Karólína) – KAA-roh (KAA-roh-LEE-na)

Landeyjahöfn – LAND-ay-a-HUBN

Leifur – LAY-vur

Már – MOWR

Marta Bjarnhédinsdóttir – MAR-ta BYAD-hyeh-thins-
  DOH-teer

Móri – MOH-ree

Ragga (Ragnheidur) – RAG-ga (RAGN-hay-thur)

Ræningjatangi – RYE-ning-ya-TOWN-gee

Reykjavík– RAY-kya-veek

Sigga (Sigrídur) – SIGG-ga (SIG-ree-thur)

Stefán – STEH-fown

Stórhöfdi – STOHR-huf-thee

Thorlákshöfn – THOR-lowks-HUBN

Trausti – TROH-stee

Túngata – TOON-gat-a

Týr – TEER

Chapter 1
Day 1 – Thursday, 23 January

There had been little to see on the crossing but angry, grey waves. Trausti had come up on deck, not to enjoy the view but to blast away his seasickness. He clung to the rail, eyes closed, face raised to the merciless pelting of the snow. They were sailing into the wind, which gave the harmless flakes the force of hail. Yet, remarkably, this natural acupuncture worked. He felt better, no longer on the verge of throwing up, and his headache, which had made it almost impossible to think, was beginning to recede. Belowdecks, the air was thick with the pervading stench of vomit from passengers who had been upset by the motion. Trausti decided to stay out here until the ferry docked in the islands.

He raised a sheltering hand to his brow, then opened his eyes and made out the vague shape of land approaching through the veils of snow. They'd almost reached their destination. Turning, he peered through the big windows into the saloon where his friends were hunched miserably in the armchairs. It occurred to him to go in and fetch them, but he immediately abandoned the idea. None of them had wanted to come out on deck with him and they were unlikely to have changed their minds. They'd said they couldn't face standing up, despite his promise that the fresh air would revive them. Besides, they were afraid of losing their seats as the ferry was packed – so full that they'd only been able to secure four tickets. Trausti had been forced to hide under a heap of coats on the back seat of the car. Once they were on board, it hadn't been a problem as he'd been able to merge into the throng. Just as well, since he couldn't imagine what it would have been like to be stuck on the car deck with the ship rolling and pitching like this.

When he returned his gaze to the scene ahead, the rocky cliffs at the entrance of Heimaey harbour were no longer vague shadows. The ferry was drawing rapidly closer and before Trausti knew it they were sailing past the sheer, pockmarked precipice of Ystaklettur with the cave at its foot. He thought he caught a glimpse of the marine pen in Klettsvík cove, which was apparently home to two beluga whale sisters these days, but neither broke the surface to watch the arrival of the ship. Perhaps they weren't there or they'd grown blasé about all the vessels coming and going past their pen. But there were plenty of other sights worth seeing, like the spectacular Heimaklettur rock, rearing up on his right, and the raw expanse of the 1973 lava flow to his left.

It was all perfect and he wouldn't have changed a thing. Not even the gruelling two-and-three-quarter-hour voyage. The original plan had been to take the ferry from the nearer port of Landeyjahöfn, which offered a much shorter crossing of only thirty-five minutes. But Ari, who'd bought the tickets, had received a text message that morning notifying him that, due to inclement weather, the ferry would be going from Thorlákshöfn instead. This hadn't made much difference to the overall time taken; it had just meant a shorter drive from Reykjavík to the port, followed by a longer crossing. In any case, their visit to the islands wasn't the sort of thing they could postpone.

The change of port hadn't been the only obstacle fate had thrown in their path. They had almost been forced to abort their trip when it turned out that there was no accommodation to be had on the islands for love or money. It hadn't occurred to them that the town on Heimaey, the only inhabited island, would be as full of visitors now in January as it normally was at the height of summer. But the Icelandic government had called a conference on the future of the fishing industry and decided, in their wisdom, to hold it in the Westman Islands, the little volcanic archipelago off Iceland's south coast. Trawler operators and a host of other people employed in the fisheries sector had flocked there from all over the country, with the result that all the hotels, guesthouses and holiday apartments had sold out in no time, like the ferry tickets. Normally, this only happened during the famous outdoor festival that was held on Heimaey over the August bank holiday. The ratio of sexes on the tightly packed ferry was very different on this occasion, however, as was the atmosphere on board. Wherever you looked, there were men whose grim faces suggested an awareness that their vision of the future was unlikely to coincide with that of the government.

Fortunately, Ari had saved the day for Trausti and the others by pulling strings to sort them a place to stay. And not just any place. Instead of occupying separate rooms at a hotel, they would all be accommodated together in a newly renovated holiday let on the Stórhöfdi headland. There they would have the kitchen, living rooms and all the other amenities entirely to themselves. Every bedroom came with an en-suite bathroom, and the set-up sounded almost perfect. The only hitch was that there were four bedrooms and five of them. But Leifur, the third male member of the group, had solved the problem by saying he didn't mind sleeping on the sofa.

Trausti had been relieved when Leifur volunteered, as he'd assumed it would fall to him. The owners of the property weren't supposed to know that one of them would be sleeping on the sofa, and Trausti, as a much cleaner, tidier type than Leifur, was less likely to give himself away by leaving a mess. It was out of the question that either of the girls should sleep there, for reasons that were never discussed. And since Ari had fixed them up with the house, it went without saying that he had a right to a bedroom.

Trausti peered in the direction of the headland that rose up at the southern end of the island, but couldn't make out their house. He couldn't wait to see it, as it wasn't every day that he got a chance to stay in a property attached to a lighthouse. It had been home to the lighthouse keeper on Stórhöfdi until his retirement, by which time both lighthouse and weather station had been automated. A group of investors had now taken the house on a long lease and done it up, sparing no expense. Ari knew one of them through his job as an economist at a major bank, and the man had taken pity on him when he heard about the friends' accommodation woes. All credit to Ari for sorting this out, especially since no one else had stayed at the newly renovated property yet. Not even the investors had had that pleasure. There were plans to formally christen the place once the worst of the winter storms were over, but, until then, the investors probably didn't want to run the risk of being blown off the cliff.

Another big bonus was that the friends were getting the place for free. Trausti was doing a postgraduate residency in rheumatology in the US, and although this mainly involved working in a hospital, he was on a low salary. The hourly rate was probably no better than what a teenager would make working at a drive-in burger joint. Trausti had little money left over at the end of every month and the flight to Iceland had been extortionate, especially as he'd been forced to buy a ticket at short notice. Three nights at a hotel would have made even further inroads into his savings, so he welcomed the fact that the only condition attached was that they should look after the house and leave it clean and undamaged. The landlords must have assumed there wouldn't be much to worry about on that score when they heard the purpose of their trip: mourners on their way to attend a funeral could be trusted to behave themselves.

As the ferry made its slow approach to the docks, Trausti glanced back through the saloon windows. His friends were getting to their feet and Sigga beckoned him to hurry. He smiled at her and waved back, then let go of the rail and made his way inside. He hoped his smile hadn't been inappropriately wide for the sad occasion; he didn't want to betray how much he was looking forward to the weekend. With any luck, the others, like him, would feel that life goes on and, once the funeral was out of the way tomorrow, would be prepared to let their hair down and enjoy the reunion. But it wasn't something they could discuss. *Hey, why don't we go wild and throw a proper wake once Gugga's in her grave?* After all, you couldn't know beforehand what the mood would be like. It had to be spontaneous.

Trausti followed his friends down to the car deck where they got into their vehicles. He wished they could all have travelled together but it hadn't been possible to cram themselves and their luggage into a single car. And at least this way no one was condemned to sit in the middle of the back seat. They were all tall, with the exception of Sigga, but she would never have accepted a decision based purely on build. Which meant that being squashed in the middle would inevitably have been

Trausti's fate and he'd have spent the rest of the weekend trying to get the kinks out of his legs. No, it was better like this. He was allotted the back seat of Ari's smart electric vehicle and Sigga sat in the front. Ragga got a lift in Leifur's estate car. The vehicles were parked side by side and Trausti nodded at Ragga when their eyes met. She smiled at him, then turned back to face the front, while he continued to stare at her profile for an embarrassingly long moment.

'What's this crap? Can't you get away from advertising anywhere?' Ari gestured irritably at a flyer that was tucked under one of his wipers.

Trausti looked around, wondering at this advertising campaign, but couldn't see any other flyers on the nearby vehicles. 'Is it a fine?'

Ari was even more affronted: 'A fine? What for? Failing to put money in the ferry's parking meter? Driving too fast on board?'

'Maybe they clocked me?' Trausti hoped not. The others might expect him to pay the fine seeing as he was the stowaway, and it was bound to be much steeper than the normal fare. At the airport he had taken out all the cash he reckoned he could afford to spend on this trip, to stop himself getting carried away. An unforeseen fine would wreck his budget.

'Fucking fascists.' Ari undid his seatbelt, opened the door and reached for the flyer. He read it while he was still halfway out of the door, then dropped it on the deck before getting back in again. 'What a load of bullshit.'

'What was it?' Sigga sounded subdued, as though she was still fighting off nausea.

'Just some crap. Not a fine, though.' Ari fastened his seatbelt again and gripped the steering wheel with both hands. '*Come on*. When are we going to get out of here?'

'Any minute now.' Trausti had noticed writing on the flyer. 'What did it say?'

'Just some bullshit, like I said. "*Go home. Don't stay here.*" Something like that. Probably aimed at one of the politicians. From an angry fisherman who got the wrong car.'

With a squeaking and grating of metal that reverberated around the car deck, the big ramp was lowered and the cars started to move. Ari heaved a sigh of relief and Trausti gave up trying to read the flyer from the window. Turning back to the front, he was again careful to restrain his smile of happy anticipation in case Sigga or Ari glanced in the rear-view mirror. He didn't want them to think he was weird.

Right now there was nowhere in the world he would rather be than here in the Westman Islands with his friends. It was the only gang he had ever belonged to and he had been missing them terribly. They'd accepted him from the very first day, apparently oblivious to the personality traits that his fellow pupils at school had found so hopeless. As he'd never worked out what was wrong with him, he hadn't been able to correct it, though he'd done everything in his power to ingratiate himself with his classmates. But no sooner had he changed one thing about himself than they'd unpicked some other negative aspect of his character. He'd grown so accustomed to being bullied and ostracised that it had taken him a long time to relax his defences and accept that his new friends were exactly that – friends. Not enemies in disguise who would show their true faces the moment he dared to lower his guard.

Unless that was *exactly* what they were? If Trausti was totally honest with himself, his motivation for making this trip partly related to a niggling fear on this front. So many things remained unsaid among the five of them and he wanted to be there in case they surfaced during the reunion. He knew that none of the others would speak up for him – he would have to do it himself. But he was being paranoid. He reminded himself that in all the time he had known them, these people had never been anything other than friendly to him.

They had met in their first year at university in Reykjavík, moving into the same corridor in the student residence at the same time. They were all from the countryside, forced to start again from square one socially. You could say that it was being lonely in the city that had brought them together, rather than any similarity in outlook or interests, but the strange thing was that they had got on very well in spite of that. Acrimonious quarrels had been rare and none of them had really rubbed any of the others up the wrong way. Of course, there had been tensions at times, but they had always blown over. They had been a bit like a tightknit group of siblings.

Although it was ages since they had last met up, once on board the ferry they had slipped effortlessly into their old roles, despite the general atmosphere of misery and seasickness. It was hard to maintain any kind of pretence when you were struggling to keep down your breakfast, and the awkward small talk that had characterised the drive from Reykjavík to the port at Thorlákshöfn had soon been replaced by openness. They'd all gone their separate ways after graduation, getting jobs in their chosen fields, and adopted new roles, in new social circles. It was to be expected that over the years they would have changed and matured. Trausti had been afraid they wouldn't be able to recapture their old group dynamic after this dispersion, but his worries had proved unfounded – like the majority of the worries that plagued him. So far, at least, he hadn't seen any signs that they weren't exactly the same people, just a few years older. Perhaps this had something to do with the fact that none of them had settled down or become parents yet, although they would all be thirty this year.

The most conspicuous development since Trausti had first met them was in their fashion sense. Certain members of the group were noticeably better dressed than they used to be. Ari appeared to have put on his work suit that morning out of habit, then had second thoughts and removed his jacket, pulling on a jumper over his shirt instead, only to walk out to the car still wearing his shiny office shoes. Sigga's clothes were now prominently labelled with logos that Trausti assumed belonged to big fashion brands. Even her belt buckle was made up of two entwined letters. She worked as a solicitor at a large legal practice and during the drive to the port she had been at pains to assure them that she was getting on well. Her outfit had clearly been chosen to make a statement, trumpeting her success to everyone she met. Ragga's dress sense appeared to have evolved as well, from quirky to sensible. Gone was the small gold ring she used to sport in one nostril, leaving only a tiny scar that no one would notice unless they were looking for it.

While Trausti's style hadn't changed as much as the others', even he had adapted his look. The hospital had a staff dress code. In the two years and more that had elapsed since he'd moved to the US, neatness had become his instinctive guiding light in matters of clothing. He wasn't as smart as Ari, though; more like a discount version of his friend the banker. Only Leifur hadn't altered one bit. He still looked like the roadie of a band that hadn't quite made it, in his worn T-shirt, the picture on the front faded almost to invisibility, jeans and a grubby anorak. Oddly, this fact made Trausti happy. But then he would have preferred it if everything had remained the same.

That was impossible, of course. People's dress sense could fluctuate with the dictates of fashion, their age and profession, but nothing could alter the fact that one of their group was missing.

The pleasant sense of peace and contentment that had been stealing over him vanished in an instant, replaced by a knot of fear. Trausti closed his eyes and pushed away the uncomfortable memories, doing his best to swap them for those associated with happy times during their student days. But the bad memories refused to budge. He was kidding himself if he thought they could ignore what had happened. His breathing grew faster and he felt the onset of a crippling dread, a sense that they were somehow on an overdue collision course with destiny. Trausti forced himself to get a grip, to slow his breathing. He was no longer in danger of having a panic attack but still couldn't shake off the feeling of trepidation. He tried to distract himself by focusing on the risk of a possible fine and ducked back under the coats in case an alert employee on the car deck was counting the passengers in the vehicles as they left. But this did little to lighten his mood. To make matters worse, he now spotted his phone lying in the footwell. It must have slipped from his pocket when he squeezed himself down there as they boarded the ferry. Trausti had noticed it was missing during the crossing but assumed he must have left it in his hand luggage. It would have been better if he had. Even in the dim light under the coats he could see that the screen had shattered, and the phone didn't respond to any of his attempts to switch it on. He must have trodden on it, perhaps both when getting out and getting back into the car. As if it wasn't bad enough that the screen was broken, the phone itself was no longer flat but bent.

Ari drove out of the ferry and up the ramp onto the docks. Once Trausti was confident that the coast was clear, he sat up and inspected his broken phone. Again he tried and failed to switch it on, then shoved it in his pocket, hoping it would recover. Being stranded without a phone left him feeling exceptionally vulnerable but there was no way he could afford a new one. His mind began playing a reel of scenarios in which he would need his phone to call for help. Instead of looking forward to the weekend ahead, he was again assailed by anxiety. He thought of the message that had been stuck under their wiper. Had it definitely been a case of mistaken identity, as Ari had said? Or could it have been aimed at them?

Surely not. That couldn't be right. *Go home. Don't stay here.*

None of them looked round or checked the rear-view mirror as they left. They never saw the figure walking onto the empty car deck, picking up the flyer, and watching as they drove away into the falling snow.

Chapter 2
Day 5 – Monday, 27 January

For once there wasn't a breath of wind. A storm was forecast for that afternoon, but it was typical that the weather should be fine in the early hours of the morning, when there was almost no one awake to enjoy it. On the way here, she had seen only one person out and about, a man walking across the fields of the Breidabakki property, where hobby farmers had stabling for horses and sheep. She had no interest in either, fortunately, as it was a pastime that required getting up at the crack of dawn every day to feed the animals.

Ásta got out of the car and slammed the door. Her dog, Móri, barked and leapt up and down on the back seat, indignant at being left behind. He was convinced she'd forgotten him and that if he could only make her notice, the mistake would be rectified. But that wasn't going to happen. She didn't want to lose him in the darkness. Not now, when she had no idea what to expect.

Instead of driving out to Stórhöfdi, as originally planned, she had pulled in to the side of the road. At first, she'd thought the sun was rising in the east, beyond the narrow neck of land that connected the Stórhöfdi headland to the rest of Heimaey. But that couldn't be right; it was still far too early. As she got closer, she had realised that the bright glow wasn't on the horizon but appeared to be coming from Brimurd, the stony beach below the road on the eastern side of the isthmus. Despite being in a hurry, she thought she'd better stop and investigate. Underneath, though, she knew she wasn't acting out of curiosity but out of a desire to put off her errand. If she didn't get a grip on herself, there was a risk that once she got back in the car she'd simply turn tail and go home rather than finishing what she had set out to do.

Now that Ásta was standing outside the car, she became aware of a smell that gave away the source of the glow. Straining her eyes, she thought she could make out smoke rising into the black sky. Something had been set alight. She crossed the road gingerly, making for the slope down to the beach. The night frost had turned the thin layer of snow on the tarmac into a hard, slippery casing, and the last thing she wanted was to fall over, break her leg and lie here, alone and freezing, until someone eventually came by. It was likely to be a long wait out here. Once she was safely across the road, she relaxed a little. The familiar crunching of snow under her feet broke the silence and the clouds of steam emanating from her mouth competed with the smoke in the air.

Remembering the name of the rocky spit – Ræning-jatangi or 'Pirates' Point' – Ásta hesitated a moment and hugged herself, trying to ward off a sudden shiver. This was where the corsairs had supposedly come ashore during the famous 'Turkish Raid' of 1627, during which they had killed or carried off many of the islanders to be sold in the slave markets of Algiers. It wasn't that she was afraid of encountering a band of men armed with scimitars; what scared her was the realisation that now, as then, the area was empty of people. That's how the pirates had managed to come ashore unseen all those centuries ago and that was why she would be in trouble now if the arsonist responsible for the fire took it into his head to attack her. Ásta drew a deep, steadying breath. But as the icy, smoke-filled air entered her lungs, her dread intensified.

She told herself to stop being an idiot. No doubt it was just some rubbish burning. People came up with all kinds of dodges to save money, and burning rubbish under cover of night would save paying for waste disposal. The only hitch with this theory was that she couldn't see a vehicle anywhere, though no one would lug a load of junk out here on foot. Ásta peered down the slope. To her relief, there was no dark figure silhouetted against the glow.

From where she stood it was impossible to work out what was being burnt. The bonfire appeared to be quite large, though the flames weren't rising that high. Ásta turned away from the beach and scanned the surrounding area but in the dim moonlight she still couldn't see any sign of the person who'd lit it. She supposed it wouldn't be that hard for someone to hide behind a rock – but why would they want to? She was no suit-clad James Bond figure; she was Ásta Jónsdóttir, dressed in a rather uncool onesie under her grubby coat, and this was the Westman Islands, not the set of some action movie. As common sense reasserted itself, she decided to move a bit closer and see what was burning. After that, she would drive out to Stórhöfdi, finish what she had set out to do, then hurry home. All without giving her-self time to think, so her doubts wouldn't have a chance to sap her resolve.

Though bare of snow, the slope down to the beach was covered with seaweed. Ice gleamed here and there in the moonlight. Ásta picked her way down with great care. Having reached the stony beach in one piece, she started towards the glow. The fire had been lit in a narrow cleft at the foot of the steep, sandy slope, as far above the waterline as possible. Since it would have taken a spring tide to extinguish the flames, the choice of location must have been deliberate.

Ásta was close to the bonfire now but the flames were so blindingly bright in the darkness that she still couldn't see what was burning. Once her eyes began to adjust, though, she gradually made out a black shape. Even then, she didn't scream or fall over backwards, just clamped both hands over her mouth and stared, transfixed with horror. Over the crackling of the flames she became aware for the first time of the soft boom and hiss of the waves below. Her face was burning in the heat where a moment ago it had been freezing. The smell had altered too – she could detect the reek of petrol. The spectacle had sent her senses into overdrive.

The thing burning there was a body. The shape lying on top of the heap of wood was unmistakable. It was impossible to tell whether it was a man or a woman because it was pitch black, but it definitely wasn't a doll or mannequin. It was flesh, not plastic that was burning. Arms, legs, torso, and the head that was turned towards her, jaws slack, eye sockets like two even blacker holes in the black face.

After a moment, Ásta realised that she was screaming into her hands. It didn't take an expert in first aid to see that this person was beyond help – and had been for a long time. Slowly, Ásta began to back away from the bonfire, unable to tear her gaze from the head with its halo of flames. Time seemed to stand still; every step seemed to take hours. At last, Ásta wrenched her eyes away and turned. But once she was facing the direction from which she had come, she did a double-take, registering belatedly that she had glimpsed something out of the corner of her eye. Something bright, half hidden behind a rock, out of place in the dark landscape. Could it be a piece of plastic blown there by the wind or, worse, someone who had seen her? If so, would they come after her? She had to know. It would be too late if she found out only when she felt a blow to the back of her head.

Ásta peered into the gloom, poised to flee. If there was somebody else here on the beach, it went without saying that they must have lit the bonfire. She had lowered her hands from her mouth, so her next scream rang out unchecked as she spotted a figure sitting beside a large boulder, apparently watching the fire. She couldn't make out the person's features under the large hood pulled down over their face, and the shimmering heat haze caused by the flames made it impossible to tell if it was a man or a woman.

Ásta took to her heels. Her only thought was to get back to the car and away from here. To fetch help.

After she had clambered hastily back up the slope, sliding and stumbling over the slippery seaweed, Ásta finally dared to snatch a glance over her shoulder. There was nobody in pursuit. She peered towards the place where she thought the figure had been sitting, but the glare from the bonfire made it hard to discern anything in the gloom. That must explain why she hadn't noticed anything originally on her climb down to the beach. The anorak-clad figure could well have been sitting there ever since she arrived.

Ásta strained her eyes and eventually, with a rush of relief, made out a red coat. As far as she could tell, the person was still sitting there, glued to the macabre spectacle. Then it occurred to her that maybe it was just the anorak she was seeing and the person had shed it in order to move faster. The thought sent Ásta racing away again. Keeping her eyes fixed on her car, paying no heed to the treacherous road, she slipped and fell forwards onto her hands and knees on the icy tarmac.

Her knees and grazed palms were agony but she forgot her pain almost instantly, distracted by the sound of an engine approaching along the road to her left. She swung her head in that direction, ready to throw herself aside if a vehicle was heading her way.

The source of the noise seemed to be much closer to her than she had initially thought – and smaller too. Considerably smaller.

It occurred to Ásta that she might be dreaming.

Still on hands and knees, she watched in stunned bemusement as a robot vacuum cleaner trundled past and continued zigzagging down the road in the direction of the town. She watched its slow progress for a few moments, until she recalled that she was in a hurry to get out of here. Scrambling to her feet, ignoring her stinging knees, she fled to the car. When she reached it, she pulled the key from her coat pocket with hands that were shaking so badly that she almost dropped it. To add to her distress, Móri was barking wildly and flinging himself against the window in the back. After a moment's fumbling she was inside and locking the door behind her. She started the engine without pausing to wipe the tears and sweat from her face. Móri stopped barking, wormed his way between the front seats and tried to get on her lap. She pushed him onto the passenger seat since there was no way she could drive with thirty kilos of ecstatic joy in her arms.

The car was facing away from town, so Ásta had no choice but to turn round on the narrow road, a feat that proved beyond her in her panicked state. She stamped too hard on the accelerator and the car shot forwards, then backwards as she braked violently, rocking as if it were a cocktail shaker. Ásta quickly abandoned the idea, afraid she would end up driving off the road. Appalling though the thought was, she would have to continue in the direction she had been going, as far as the small parking area by the beach, and turn there. It would only take a moment. Ásta breathed slowly in and out until she was calm enough to grip the wheel and press the accelerator again. If anyone loomed up from the beach and threatened her, she would run them down.

She leant forward over the steering wheel, nose pressed to the windscreen. She didn't dare go fast in the icy conditions, aware that in her panic she was bound to react the wrong way to a skid. Then, remembering that her phone was connected to the car's dashboard computer, she switched it on so she could ring the police hands-free. Small though the population was here on Heimaey, the local station had a twenty-four-hour service, and it shouldn't take them more than ten minutes to reach her. She yelled at the phone to ring the emergency number, 112.

But it's hard to do two things at once under pressure. Ásta leant so hard against the wheel that she inadvertently hit the horn. The blare of it gave her such a shock that she stamped on the accelerator, drove out onto the dirt track and spun the car like a rally driver, then shot away without sparing a moment's thought for the icy tarmac.

Which turned out to be a mistake.

Chapter 3
Day 1 – Thursday, 23 January

Trausti had ceased to notice the howling of the wind outside. He'd become inured to it in a remarkably short time. Stórhöfdi was reputed to be the windiest place in Europe and, since their arrival, he'd seen no reason to dispute that claim. It was the southernmost inhabited area in Iceland, and apart from the narrow spit that connected it to the island of Heimaey, the treeless headland was completely surrounded by sea. There was no shelter at all out of doors.

The gale had lost none of its force since they'd emerged from their cars in the parking area in front of the house. Sigga and Ragga, who weighed less than the men, had struggled to keep their balance. Sigga's loose blonde hair had stood on end as she teetered her way unsteadily towards the house, and it had crossed Trausti's mind to take a photo of her before he remembered that his phone was broken. He would never have managed it anyway, as he was too busy trying to stop himself being blown off his feet. Still, no harm done: Sigga would only have forced him to delete it. She was usually impeccably turned out but at that moment she resembled a clown – a clown who had turned up sick to work. Her face was still pale green from the ferry crossing.

Even the blustery conditions on Stórhöfdi could do nothing to dampen their elation at being restored to dry land.

If anything, the effect was exhilarating, helping to scour the salty sea air from their lungs and the sour taste from their mouths. It had also blown away the cloud of foreboding that had descended on Trausti during the short drive from the harbour. The red wine they had knocked back once they'd settled in had erased the last vestiges of their suffering.

There was a lingering smell of fresh paint and sawdust inside the house. Trausti didn't know what the interior had looked like before but it was clear that all the doors and windows had been replaced, the walls re-plastered, the kitchen modernised and the number of bathrooms multiplied. At least, he doubted the lighthouse keeper would have had much need of four. There was no mains water supply but rainwater was collected in a concrete tank and piped into the house. It was a mystery to Trausti how this arrangement was consistent with a modern holiday let, but perhaps the landlords could get away with it because the house wasn't going to be permanently occupied. Between the times when guests indulged in showers like there was no tomorrow, there would presumably be weeks, if not months, for the tank to be replenished before the next round. Trausti gathered that the builders weren't quite finished, though the furniture was all in place and there were pictures on the walls. If there were still some final touches required, it was hard to see where. The kitchen appeared to be fully equipped, the tall glass-fronted dresser in the dining room was full of wine glasses, there were towels, bathrobes and soaps in the bathrooms, and the beds were made up in the bedrooms. Everything was brand new and of the finest quality, yet the effect was somehow effortlessly cosy.

If Leifur had feared that he'd have to sleep on an old sofa with broken springs, he needn't have worried. 'This is awesome, Ari. Awesome.' Leifur lay back on the soft down cushions of the sofa in the living room where they were sitting – one of two in the house. He put his feet up on the coffee table, took a mouthful of wine and a slow smile spread across his face. 'Awesome,' he repeated.

Compared to the parties they used to hold in their tiny student flats, this was paradise. In the old days they had made do with sitting on the bed, office chair or floor, the space so cramped they'd barely had room to change their minds. The wine was a big improvement too, glass bottles with corks replacing the budget cartons, and sophisticated matching wine glasses in contrast to the ill-assorted collection of tumblers and mugs they had drunk out of as students. There was a lot more booze as well – the bottles they had contributed, including Trausti's carefully selected mid-price wine from Duty Free, almost covered one of the kitchen counters. The only person who had stuck to the spirit of their student days was Leifur, who had slapped down two crates of beer and two bottles of Ópal schnapps, a menthol-flavoured vodka. But his loyalty to the past didn't extend any further than that since he too had opted for wine when Sigga brought out the glasses from the dresser.

'Feet off.' Ari bent forwards and jabbed at Leifur's feet. His socks were unevenly worn, one greyer than the other, with a hole in the toe. 'We've got to look after the place.'

Leifur grudgingly removed his feet from the coffee table, though he plainly thought it was ridiculous. But his bad moods never lasted long. He grinned, revealing red-stained teeth. 'I screwed up. I should have become an investor.'

Leifur had studied computer science. Before turning green and excusing himself on the ferry, he had been telling them of his dissatisfaction with work. The revelation hadn't come as any surprise to Trausti. Leifur simply wasn't cut out to be a programmer. He was far too slapdash – the very last person you'd employ to identify bugs in a system or perform any other task requiring precision. He was the type who opened beer bottles by smashing the necks if he couldn't find a bottle opener. Trausti had never understood why Leifur had chosen to go into IT, or, indeed, how he had managed to graduate. But it was also typical of Leifur that he succeeded somehow in blundering through any obstacle in his path, whether it was an exam or a snowdrift in a car park. Still, if he were to change profession, the world of finance and investments would never do. He'd be as badly suited to them as he was to programming. Trausti, for one, wouldn't trust Leifur to invest his money, even if he had any to spare.

'Oh, Trausti, you couldn't give me a refill, could you?' Sigga handed him her empty glass, confident of a positive response. It didn't matter that they were both sitting down. He was on his feet before she'd even finished speaking, the muscle memory from their student days clearly still in good working order. He had always jumped to it when Sigga asked for something. It wasn't that he fancied her, as the others no doubt believed. Perhaps it was because Sigga simply wouldn't take no for an answer. Normally she barked out orders, but when she asked a favour, she always did so nicely, with such gratitude that it wasn't as though she was taking his obligingness for granted.

Ari and Sigga had always been the leaders. They took all the big decisions for the group and it was usually their suggestions that prevailed even when the others came up with conflicting proposals. It had been Ragga's suggestion that they go to the Westman Islands to attend Gugga's funeral. Then Ari had come up with the even better idea of turning it into a proper reunion.

On graduating, Ragga, Sigga, Ari and Leifur had moved out of the student residence, one after the other, until only Trausti was left. There had been solemn promises to keep in touch, but despite their best intentions they had quickly dropped out of contact. The group chat had been active in the beginning but was used less and less as time wore on. At first, Trausti had the feeling it had been set up so that they could keep tabs on each other in case any member of the group decided to clear the air. But gradually these worries receded. By then, though, the chat had become practically dormant. Now and then it sputtered into life again, but Trausti suspected he was the only one who felt a twinge of excitement whenever he received a notification. The others had settled into their new lives, at home in Iceland. Unlike him, they hadn't had to go abroad to continue their education.

Trausti had read medicine, which required the most years of study. Sigga had gone straight on to do a Master's following her law degree but had moved out of the hall of residence after graduating and rented a flat in the private sector. The others had either made do with their basic BAs or taken a year off before going on to do postgraduate degrees. Trausti, meanwhile, had continued living in the student residence for a further two years after all his friends had left. It had been lonely, but thanks to his almost non-existent social life, his marks had improved dramatically towards the end. One of his tutors had even drawn special attention to the fact. Trausti would have been a lot more gratified if the man hadn't added that he had risen from the bottom, almost to the top. He would rather not be reminded that he'd got the second lowest marks of all those who had passed the entry test. It was typical of him that he couldn't even manage to come bottom, given that he'd failed to shine. Being worst was definitely cooler than being second worst.

When the news of Gugga's death reached them, Sigga had started a new group chat on the grounds that she couldn't bear to be part of a group that included a dead person. In the run-up to the trip, there had been more messages in the new group than there had been in the old one in the entire four years since Trausti had graduated. Perhaps that had made their reunion easier, preventing awkwardness when they finally met up again in person. No one had dropped any hints about having the conversation they had been avoiding, but Trausti couldn't be sure that the subject wouldn't come up once they were together. So saying pass wasn't an option, but he was also genuinely excited about seeing them again. Apart from the shared shitshow in their past, they were his friends. The only good friends he'd ever had. But since they were more socially adept than him, the group was less important to them. That was why he hadn't confided in them that he was travelling all the way from the States just to see them. Instead, he had pretended that, by pure coincidence, he'd been coming over to Iceland anyway for a short visit home. He was afraid the others might feel sorry for him if they knew the truth. Not that they had any reason to; he was actually regarded as quite promising in his specialist field, despite the dunce label that had clung to him for most of his time as an undergraduate in Iceland.

Trausti fetched the half-empty bottle and refilled Sigga's glass. He also topped up Leifur's almost empty one, but Ragga put a hand over hers, which left Ari with the rest. Trausti didn't mind as he wasn't much of a drinker. He sat down again, half hoping that no one would suggest opening another bottle. He was so tired that all he really wanted now was to go to bed, succumb to his jetlag and fall asleep. The time difference wasn't helping and he wanted to be wide awake tomorrow for the sad occasion. He didn't want to be caught yawning during Gugga's funeral or become weepy from sheer exhaustion.

Ragga smiled at him and Trausti returned the smile, hoping his teeth weren't as wine-stained as Leifur's. At one time he'd had a crush on her, being irresistibly drawn to her quiet demeanour and thoughtful expression. He'd also been charmed by her boyish haircut at a time when most young women seemed to have long hair. He had interpreted her decision to go short as meaning that she was different from other people and therefore more likely to understand him. But his hairstyle psychology hadn't been put to the test as he'd never acted on his feelings. He still had no idea whether the attraction had been mutual. Instinct told him it hadn't, which made him heartily relieved that he'd never made a move, only to be rejected. Besides, even if they had got together, they'd almost certainly have split up when he moved to America. Ragga had studied mechanical engineering and now worked for one of Iceland's utility companies on the renewal of the distribution network supplying natural hot water for geothermal space heating. Trausti couldn't imagine anything more boring but Ragga's face had shone when she'd described her job to them during the ferry ride. As far as Trausti knew, there was no natural hot water in the state where he lived in the US, so she could never have been as happy there as she appeared to be here in Iceland.

The glass in the floor-length window beside the sofa bowed slightly inwards under a renewed onslaught of wind. Trausti took another sip of wine to celebrate the fact he was snug indoors, then turned his head to stare out into the darkness. Sigga was reminiscing about the time Leifur had wrecked one of the communal dryers at the student residence by using a jar of garlic powder instead of a tennis ball when he was drying his down jacket. The jar had opened as it was rattling around in the drum and the powder had got into the mechanism, with the result that no one had been able to use the dryer again. But Leifur hadn't seemed to mind smelling like garlic bread every time he put on his coat to go out. They all smiled at the memory and Trausti joined in. Then immediately stopped smiling, worried yet again that it might be inappropriate. Until the funeral was over, they were here in the islands to mourn Gugga. He thought about her, trying to imagine how she would look if she were alive and among them now. Would she have changed more than the others? She had been a year older than them, already turned thirty when she died. But one year wouldn't have made much difference. She had probably been as scatty and chaotic at the time of her death as she had been as a student.

Gugga had been an activist, perpetually fired up about one cause or another – generally the trendy issue of the day. But her zeal wasn't enough to prevent her from oversleeping more often than not when she was supposed to turn up to a protest. Nor did she have any qualms about abruptly switching to a new pet cause. Her attempt to be active in student politics had been similarly short-lived: she had put herself forward for the student council, then failed to follow it up. It had been no surprise to her friends when she didn't win any support in the election. She hadn't seemed that disheartened by her defeat, though, as her attention had already moved on to something new. She hadn't even bothered to turn up at the polling station to cast a vote for herself.

Trausti hoped Gugga had managed to find some focus after she moved out of the student residence – for her own sake, if nothing else. She had read sociology and seemed genuinely interested in the subject; at least she'd never toyed with the idea of switching courses, which was unlike her. This made it all the more odd that she should have left without graduating, just when she was so close to her goal, but in retrospect perhaps it wasn't so surprising. Her mother had been engaged in a gruelling battle with cancer and, after her death, things had started to go downhill for Gugga. Maybe Trausti and his friends could have made more of an effort to help her, but at the time they had all been up against it. Most of their waking hours had been taken up with lectures, exams, assignments and revision, and any that were left over had been devoted to letting their hair down rather than providing pastoral care for their mates.

This wasn't a very cheerful train of thought and Trausti determinedly pushed it away. Shifting himself into a more comfortable position on the sofa, he tried to savour the moment. He reminded himself that there was nothing odd about wanting to meet up with old friends and have a few days' break from the pressure he was under back in the States. Unlike the rest of them, he would have to make up every single day of his holiday, which meant he faced the prospect of working flat out for several weeks without a break when he got back to the hospital. He could only hope it would be worth it, despite this lingering sense of dread.

'Didn't Gugga always talk about wanting to be buried in some family graveyard in the east when she died? Back when we were at uni, I mean?' Sigga took a sip of her wine. 'I wonder what happened to that idea. She talked about it like it was Père Lachaise in Paris.'

'Probably doesn't even exist. She was such a ditz.' Apparently Leifur hadn't heard of the rule about not speaking ill of the dead.

'That's not fair, Leifur. She died young. She probably just assumed she'd make it through to old age. Maybe she thought

27

she'd jinx her chances of survival if she started making burial arrangements.'

'Speaking of graveyards and burials, I hope you brought some black clothes, Leifur?' Ari put down his glass. 'And I don't mean dark jeans and a heavy metal T-shirt.'

Judging by Leifur's expression, the thought hadn't even entered his head. But Sigga cut in before he could answer, thereby letting him off the hook: 'Do you think we could have changed anything? Could we have saved Gugga?' She drawled slightly as she enunciated these words and her jaw appeared slacker than when they'd first sat down. No change there from when she was a law student: two drinks and it was as though her words had grown tails, taking that much longer to leave her mouth.

'What are you on about?' Leifur scowled. 'What the fuck could we have done? Gugga died of cancer, remember? Were we supposed to . . . what . . . find a cure?'

Trausti suppressed a sigh, knowing that any minute now he'd be dragged in. It's what always used to happen when the subject of illness came up. The group regarded him as the best qualified among them to pronounce on such matters. The others were in a similar position when it came to their chosen disciplines: Sigga was expected to know everything about courts, laws and regulations; Leifur was asked about anything related to computers, software or AI, though he knew next to nothing about the latter; Gugga was supposed to be the expert on refugee matters and social issues. Ari was their economics expert and made to answer for the Central Bank's policy on interest rates. And they had tried to make Ragga into the spokesperson for civil engineering, industry and energy companies, but she had mostly just shrugged and refused to be drawn in, especially if the exchange was heated.

Sigga looked aggrieved. 'Of course not. I wasn't talking about a cure. I just meant that people tend to hang on longer if their mental health is good. But Gugga can't have been happy.'

Leifur had sunk down into the soft sofa but now he sat up straighter, his irritation plain. 'What makes you so sure she was unhappy? We don't know anything about it. I'm willing to bet she was perfectly happy.' Realising how stupid this sounded, he added: 'Given the circumstances, I mean.'

Sigga shook her head, her blonde hair lifting as if in a breeze. The movement was a little exaggerated, like her drawling speech. 'You all saw her message.' Sigga lowered her gaze. 'She said she'd been diagnosed with pancreatic cancer and asked us to visit her in hospital. But none of us went, even though we knew she had nobody else.' She looked up and shifted her gaze around the group, not even attempting to hide the implied accusation.

Misfortunes tend to travel in groups. Gugga's father had died two years previously, leaving her an orphan. She was an only child and had no close relatives, which had left her without any kind of support network. That was when she had popped up in the group chat again, wanting to meet up, but nothing had come of it, any more than the hospital visit she had later pinned her hopes on.

Ari rolled his eyes. 'How were we supposed to know it was so serious?'

The subject of medicine had been raised. Sigga turned her gaze on Trausti, then gesticulated at him, to indicate that this was where he came in. Which he did, with utmost tact, ensuring that no one's feelings would be hurt by his answer. 'Cancer of the pancreas is almost always very serious, but of course you weren't to know that. And I was abroad and couldn't get back to Iceland.' He stopped himself from asking why none of them had bothered to google the disease. One look at the results would have removed all doubt.

'Well, we're here now. Not everyone would be prepared to travel this far for a funeral. I'd say we count as bloody good friends and that this makes up for our earlier failure.' Ari appeared to be trying to convince himself. It might have worked if Ragga hadn't felt compelled to expose his attempt to gloss over their shoddy behaviour.

'Attending a funeral doesn't make up for failing to visit someone on their deathbed,' she said. 'Funerals are for the mourners. The body in the coffin couldn't care less.' She drew a sharp breath through her nose. 'We were shitty friends.' She shrugged her slender shoulders. 'But it's too late to change that now.'

While Leifur emitted the sort of exaggerated groan he had reserved in the old days for the times when the girls brought up the subject of feminism, Trausti noticed that Sigga's eyes had narrowed and she seemed to be squinting at the shelves on the wall. He tried to work out what had caught her attention, but all he could see was a stack of board games. Perhaps she was going to suggest they play Monopoly to lighten the atmosphere. But it turned out she had something else in mind.

'Why don't we get out the Ouija board?'

Their reactions were predictable, as they were all fairly down-to-earth types with little patience for nonsense, especially of the spiritualist kind. Sigga couldn't make herself heard over Leifur and Ari's snorts of disgust. Ragga and Trausti didn't say a word until the other three had shut up. Then, much to everyone's surprise, Ragga spoke up in favour of Sigga's suggestion.

'I'm in. After all, it can't do any harm.'

Once she had spoken, the other three changed their minds, one after the other. Perhaps it was the wine. Or perhaps they felt anything was better than beating themselves up about how they had let Gugga down on her deathbed. Before they knew it, they had moved with their glasses of wine to the dining table and were seated around a commercial American version of a Ouija board, consisting of an array of letters and numbers and the words 'Yes' and 'No'. Sigga had dimmed the lights until they could barely see a thing but the mood still fell far short of the solemnity that was appropriate at such a moment. Giggles and general light-heartedness kept bubbling to the surface. Nobody believed they were about to commune with the dead. Trausti was mainly interested in guessing which of them would be responsible when the letters started to be spelled out. It was inevitable that one of them would take the bait.

They placed their fingers on the planchette, a tear-drop-shaped indicator with a clear window. Sigga demanded silence, then asked if there was a spirit present. As Trausti had predicted, the indicator was soon moving fast over the board. It proved harder than he'd expected to identify who was manipulating it, though. It could be any of them. Trausti looked at each of his friends in turn, trying to figure out which one was the culprit. But they all seemed equally likely and he got a sinking feeling that they might have joined forces to mess with his head. He brushed it aside and switched his attention to watching as the answers were spelled out.

'Are you dead?'
Answer: YES.
'Did you live in this house?'
Answer: NO.

'Did you drown off Stórhöfdi?'
Answer: NO.
'Were you a man or a woman?'
Answer: W O M A N.
'Did you die young?'
Answer: YES.
'Do we know you?'
Answer: YES.

Sigga jerked back her hand and the planchette came to a halt. 'This isn't cool. Whoever's messing about, please stop. There's nothing funny about bringing Gugga's death into a silly game.'

In the short silence that followed, Trausti became aware of the shrieking of the wind outside. The noise was almost a whistling now, as if the wind were seeking an audience, frustrated that there was no one out there to witness its magnificence and force. But the eerie sound couldn't compete with Leifur's raised voice as he blurted out: 'Bullshit!' He had apparently undergone a change of heart and now wanted to carry on with the game: 'We know loads of other people who've died. Celebrities and so on. Let's keep going. I want to see how this joke ends.'

Reluctantly, Sigga returned her finger to the planchette with the others and resumed her conversation with the imaginary spirit:

'Were you famous?'
Answer: NO.
'Did you die in an accident?'
Answer: NO.
'Did you die of an illness?'

The planchette didn't move. They all exchanged glances and Trausti noticed that Ragga was frowning. He thought she was staring at Ari and guessed that she suspected him of being behind this. After a brief pause, Sigga continued:

'Do you have a message for us from the afterlife?'
Answer: YES.
'What is it?'
Answer: H I.

'*Hi?*' Ari shook his head and laughed. 'Whoever's taking the piss, please – you can do better than that.'

Sigga shot him a quick frown and carried on with her inquisition:

'Hi back. Do you want to tell us something?'
Answer: I M C O L D.

It was Leifur's turn to laugh. 'Well, there we have it. Clearly, the soul isn't in hell.'

Ignoring his joke, Sigga asked:

'What's your name?'

Ari laughed again as the letters spelled out: *G U D* . . . 'Whoever is doing this, could you have been a little more original? And why the full name Gudbjörg and not just Gugga?'

He smiled mockingly at Sigga, but his amusement was short-lived, once the planchette stopped and the name was revealed in its entirety.

Answer: G U D R U N.

Sigga took a gulp of wine, then pushed herself away from the table.

'That's enough.' She got to her feet, looking round her friends who were sitting in silence, mesmerised by the little window in the planchette. Through the magnifying glass, the last letter of the name was perfectly clear.

The temperature in the room dropped and Trausti felt a shiver run down his spine. His worst fears had been realised.

In the old days none of them would have dreamt of bringing up that name from the past just for the hell of it. Not under any circumstances. Trausti pictured again the corridor at the university's hall of residence; the door to his flat, and the doors to the flats belonging to Ari, Sigga, Ragga, Leifur and Gugga.

And at the end – the very end of the corridor – the door to Gudrún's room. Even the mental image made him feel nauseous and claustrophobic.

Something terrible was going to come from all this.

Chapter 4

Day 5 – Monday, 27 January

Air terminal was rather a grand name for the glorified shed on the edge of the runway. It served a small airline with no more than a couple of light aircraft at its disposal. There was a reception desk, a set of scales for weighing luggage and a few seats for passengers awaiting departure. The shed also boasted a vending machine offering fizzy drinks and snacks, but no one had bought anything as there was free coffee on offer. At that time of the morning, sweets and Coke couldn't begin to compete with caffeine.

The cardboard cup had cooled down to the point where Idunn no longer had to keep shifting it from hand to hand. She stared into it for a moment, then looked up at the clock on the wall with an inward sigh. She had delayed too long. It was too late now to stand up and announce that she was feeling unwell and wouldn't be able to go after all. Her suitcase had vanished into the plane and in a few minutes the waiting group would be herded on board as well. If she dropped out now, it would take time to find a replacement – and actually, there was no one else in Iceland with the knowledge or experience to step into the breach. As someone who lived for her work, Idunn was usually happy to think she was indispensable – but not this time. If there had been another pathologist in the vicinity, she would have said at once that she couldn't attend.

Her replacement wouldn't even need to be that qualified, just experienced enough to take good photos, conduct themselves properly at the scene and arrange the transferral of the bodies back to Reykjavík where Idunn could take over and perform the post-mortems. And it wasn't just that she was the only person capable of the job – in truth, she really wouldn't want to miss out on it. It was only the necessity of visiting the islands that she was dreading.

Idunn squared her shoulders. This wouldn't do. She was too strong a person to crumple under the weight of self-inflicted fear. The problem was all in her head, but because she had ignored it for years, it had assumed the proportions of a sky-high, unscalable barrier. She reminded herself that in reality the barrier was no more than a threshold a few centimetres high. Easy-peasy to step over, if only she set her mind to it. She took a mouthful of tepid coffee but it did nothing to boost her courage. She was still wrestling with the longing to walk out of here, get in her car and drive away from the situation.

'It's no more than a short hop. Really just straight up and down again.' The young detective Karólína, known as Karó, sitting beside her had noticed that something was wrong. She was in uniform, the peak of her cap pulled down over her mild brown eyes. The first black woman ever to be employed by the Icelandic police, she had proven herself to be a damn good detective. Everything Idunn could have wished for in a colleague, in fact: level-headed, thoughtful and smart. 'You're scared of flying, aren't you?' Karó added.

'No. Not in the slightest,' Idunn answered truthfully, disappointed with herself for failing to put on a normal front. It shouldn't have been a stretch for her. After all, she was naturally taciturn and unimpressed with life, which wasn't a difficult impression to convey. 'Why do you ask?'

Karó shrugged. 'Oh, just . . . you seem a bit stressed.'

'No, not at all.' Idunn hastily clamped her knees together to still the trembling in her legs. She hadn't noticed it until now and would have done better to ignore it. By her abrupt movement, she had only drawn Karó's attention to this involuntary sign of anxiety.

An awkward silence followed, broken eventually by Karó. 'Unbelievably enough, this will be my first visit to the Westman Islands. Not quite how I'd pictured it, but there you go. How about you? Have you been there before?'

Idunn released a breath and concentrated on trying to appear casual. 'Yes. But a long time ago.' All perfectly true. What she omitted to mention was that she'd been born in the Westman Islands and lived there until just before she was confirmed. She also left out the bit about still having family on Heimaey – two half-siblings and a father. Siblings she had nothing in common with and a father she had encountered only once since her parents had split up. He'd attended the ceremony when she'd graduated in medicine. Uninvited. The reunion had been anything but amicable and conspicuously lacking in hugs. If she had a choice, she'd never set eyes on him again, but this work trip risked complicating things. The town on Heimaey was so small that there was every chance she would run into him. It was this thought that was causing her so much unnecessary grief right now.

Karó didn't ask any further questions, just turned back to watch a young woman from the airline preparing to announce boarding. They could probably have dispensed with the formalities as this was no scheduled flight; the police had chartered the plane at short notice. The only people on board would be the Reykjavík CID and crime scene investigation teams, and Idunn herself, from the University Hospital's pathology department. She recognised most of the faces but knew only two by name, the detectives Karó and Týr. She hadn't yet decided whether it was a good or a bad thing that they would be travelling to the islands with her. In this instance, it might have been preferable to be able to get on with her job without the presence of people she knew.

She was particularly keen to avoid spending much time with Týr, the problem being that she was sitting on information regarding the death of his mother. He had a right to know the truth, but there were times when it was better to remain ignorant. He appeared happy enough, and relaxed too, as if he'd come to terms with his past, that the people he'd always believed to be his parents were in fact his aunt and uncle.

Týr had only discovered this recently, during an investigation into an axe murderer. Idunn had also been assigned, and had drawn attention to an older case because of certain similarities regarding the choice of murder weapon. Týr had simply joined the dots. He was not the biological son of the people he knew as his mother and father, but the offspring of a tragic murder victim and the man who had supposedly killed her.

His aunt and uncle had taken him in as a small boy after his father had attacked and murdered his mother with an axe. The big, ugly scar on Týr's forehead was the result of that attack. A far cry from a tumble from a tricycle, as Týr had always been told. His father had apparently come to his senses enough to stop short of killing his four-year-old son, though the reason for that would never be known. The man had taken his own life while on remand awaiting trial and sentencing.

But after reviewing the evidence in the files, Idunn now had doubts about Týr's father's guilt. The man's confession, made at the time of his arrest, was inconsistent with Týr's mother's injuries. Although the father had confessed to the deed, he wouldn't be the first man in history who had told the police what they wanted to hear during questioning. The investigation hadn't been dropped immediately after he was discovered dead in his cell, but for understandable reasons it had never gone to trial. The police had eventually concluded that Týr's father must have been guilty as they had no other suspects and, after all, he *had* confessed. In the circumstances, it wouldn't be surprising if the investigators had overlooked or chosen to ignore an inconvenient detail, or regarded it as a misunderstanding that would have been clarified during questioning.

Therein lay Idunn's dilemma. If she shared her reservations with Týr, he would be back at square one; any peace he had made with his past would be destroyed, yet he would have little chance of getting to the bottom of what had really happened. Wouldn't it be kinder, then, to spare him this unsettling revelation?

Their eyes met and Idunn hastily dropped hers. She hoped he wouldn't interpret this as unfriendliness. It was anything but. She was unusually well disposed towards him and Karó. They were both calm and composed types, and could be trusted not to start jabbering away whenever an unexpected silence fell. She got the impression that for most people she interacted with, silence was like a glowing ember that had to be put out before it could catch fire. Idunn, in contrast, was happy with her own thoughts and hated being forced to take part in conversations where the only purpose seemed to be to create hot air.

Luckily, the group in the waiting area this morning seemed in no mood to chat. Apart from exchanging the odd word, they stared at their phones, sipped their coffee or gazed out of the windows. The subdued atmosphere was due to the reason for their trip to the islands. A murder investigation was never an occasion for celebration. No one felt inclined to laugh or joke. Although they had received scant information so far, the gravity of the case was not in doubt. Two people were dead – apparently it was unlikely to be from natural causes – and a third was in a critical condition after crashing her car, her life now hanging by a thread.

The phone had rung early that morning, just as Idunn stepped out of the shower. She'd had to come here via the office to fetch the tools of her trade, which had left her with little time to get ready beyond dragging on her clothes and chucking a change of outfit and a toothbrush in her bag, just in case. The radio had been issuing warnings about the planned closure of the Hellisheidi mountain route out of Reykjavík, due to a storm – a storm that could easily shift southwards and ground all flights later that day. Having grown up in the Westman Islands, Idunn knew that at this time of year there was no guarantee they would be able to leave again this evening. And that only increased the risk that she would come face to face with her father. Regrettably, he wasn't as keen as her to avoid a meeting. On the contrary, he'd made active attempts to end their estrangement in the past.

The young woman came out from behind the desk and announced their flight, then walked over to the only gate in the little terminal. The police team filed after her. Idunn realised that if she wanted to get out of the trip, now was her last chance, but, as if of their own accord, her legs carried her inexorably towards the gate.

The 'gate' was no more than an exit to the tarmac where the passenger plane was waiting. The door of the plane was open and the inbuilt steps had been lowered. The moment they were on board and the door closed behind them it would be too late for Idunn to plead illness. The thought made the door and steps momentarily appear to her like a tongue lolling out of a gaping maw that was about to swallow her up. Even as this melodramatic image formed in her mind, she came to her senses. It would be fine. She would go to the islands, do her job and leave again. If she bumped into her father, so be it. She could use the flight to rehearse what she would say to him.

But the journey proved too short for that. The plane took off and landed again before Idunn had succeeded in coming up with a single devastating put-down to use against the man who hadn't given a shit about her when he and her mother split up. Even though he had known better than anyone that her mother wasn't capable of looking after so much as a pot plant. It hadn't required medical training to realise that her mother was struggling with the kind of severe mental problems and personality disorder that made her an unfit caregiver. Despite still being a kid, Idunn had taken on the role of adult as soon as the two of them had moved to Reykjavík. It had been a sink-or-swim situation, a role taken on out of necessity rather than any kind of desire for responsibility.

A bitter but invigorating wind greeted Idunn as she disembarked and she reminded herself that she had turned out well – against all the odds. The past couldn't be changed, no matter how unfair it was, but there was no need to drag it around like a weight round her neck. Sadly, this voice of common sense didn't help much. While they were waiting for their luggage and equipment to be unloaded, Idunn kept her back turned to the entrance in case her father happened to walk in.

But when she heard the door of the terminal opening, it occurred to her that she'd rather be forewarned than surprised by a sudden tap on the shoulder. At least that would give her time to take refuge in the toilets and wait for him to leave, avoiding an unpleasant scene. Luckily, her humiliating plan wasn't put to the test. The people entering the terminal were a heavily pregnant girl and a young man with his arm around her shoulders. Idunn watched them, guessing the reason for their presence here, on the evidence of their sad but loving goodbyes. The Westman Islands had no obstetrician or surgeon who specialised in caesareans: if there was any risk of complications, pregnant women had to go to Reykjavík well before they were due in order to give birth there. In practice, often alone. Realising that she'd been staring at the young couple for an embarrassingly long time, Idunn turned back to wait for her luggage.

Once their bags had been loaded into the vehicles provided by the local police, they set off. Their first port of call would be the police station, to dump their stuff before continuing to the crime scene. A duty officer from the islands led the way, while Idunn rode with a member of the CSI team. She couldn't remember his name, though she got the impression that she ought to know who he was since he hadn't seen any need to introduce himself when they got in. While he was droning on about the bad weather forecast for that afternoon, Idunn stared out of the passenger window, watching the familiar town pass by. Little had changed in the decades that had elapsed since she'd last set eyes on it. Apart from a block of flats that had gone up near the harbour and the odd house that had been painted a different colour, few new places had been built or old ones torn down. It was as if time had stood still, in stark contrast to the frenetic pace of change in Reykjavík, which was becoming ever more built-up, until the glimpse of an empty plot was merely the sign of an imminent development.

When Idunn caught sight of her childhood home, she couldn't stop herself from twisting in her seat to get a better look. In that brief glance she had seen that the large house had acquired a conservatory, and the garden had been fenced in and smartened up. This must be the second wife's influence, as Idunn's father had never taken much interest in his immediate surroundings. As far as her father was concerned, the house's sole purpose was to protect his family and belongings from the elements. All he cared about was waking up safe and dry in the morning so he could focus on running his fishing business. But seeing the house again only emphasised the stark contrast with the tiny one-bedroom flat Idunn and her mother had moved into after her parents' divorce. True to form, Idunn's mum had taken the bedroom and left her daughter to sleep on the sofa in the living room. Idunn had had to make up her 'bed' every evening and start every day by removing the bedding from the sofa. She had moved into her own place the first opportunity she got.

In hindsight, it was a miracle that Idunn still managed to harbour any feelings of love for her flawed, defective mother. Maybe it was because the compartment for hatred in her brain was full to the brim with the animosity and resentment she felt for her dad.

'See something?' The officer at the wheel had clocked her interest.

'No. Just a cat.' Idunn hastily returned her gaze to the road ahead and sat still as a statue, even when the driver jumped out to drop their bags off at the police station. He must think her weird, but never mind. Most people thought that anyway because of her decision to become a forensic pathologist.

The police station was located in a sort of industrial estate, where she remembered there used to be a carpentry workshop. The old station had burnt to the ground in the late eighties. Someone had neglected to remove a lighter from a repeat offender before throwing him in the cells, with the result that he had set his mattress alight. Fortunately, thanks to the prompt action of the officer on duty, no one had died in the blaze, and even the owner of the lighter had been brought out safely.

From the station, they headed straight to the scene, and Idunn breathed easier as they left the outskirts of the small town. A convoy of police vehicles was such a rare sight on Heimaey that the few souls who were out and about on a weekday couldn't fail to notice them. And although it was ridiculous to think anyone would recognise her after all these years, some people were unusually good at faces. She couldn't be sure she wouldn't be spotted and that word wouldn't get back to her father. It was a relief when the houses petered out and all they could see was a treeless landscape of fields containing the occasional horse. Once they pulled up in the parking area by Brimurd, the beach on the eastern side of the narrow neck of land connecting Stórhöfdi to the main island, Idunn was able to put the past out of her mind. The job she was here to do left no room for other thoughts.

There was quite a crowd of vehicles by the time their convoy had joined the cars of the local police already at the scene. Not far off, on the other side of the road, another car was lying on its roof. Idunn took this to be the vehicle that had rolled over with a woman on board. Through a piece of extraordinary good luck, the woman had put through a call to emergency services just before she lost control of the car, so they had been able to locate her using her phone coordinates. Apparently she hadn't managed to say a word; all the call handler had heard were her screams accompanied by crashing noises. It was just as well for her that she'd called when she did, as she had been in no fit state to do anything as she lay in the wreckage afterwards, and there was no way of knowing when another car would have passed by. It wasn't unheard of for people to die when they crashed in remote spots like this – from blood loss, exposure or dehydration – before help could arrive.

Below them on the beach was a white CSI tent that Idunn assumed had been erected over one of the corpses. She opened the boot of the car and took out her case of instruments, then donned her protective overalls and slung her camera around her neck. She was only interrupted once, when the local police inspector came over to introduce herself. She was a tall, grave-faced woman who said her name was Ína. She appeared to be in her early forties like Idunn.

They exchanged a few words, after which the woman stepped aside. She didn't go far, however, just stood back and watched as Idunn got ready, then returned to join her once Idunn had closed the boot and set off down towards the beach. It was clear that Ína intended to accompany her, and although Idunn preferred absolute peace to work in, she could understand. In terms of gathering information, Idunn was the most important person at the scene right now, and Ína was in charge of the investigation. The CSI team were gearing up to start collecting specimens, which might eventually provide useful clues, but as these would take time to analyse, there was little to be gained from them at present. Whereas Idunn's preliminary examination of the bodies could at least provide some immediate insights, though they were unlikely to be earth-shattering.

Inside the tent of thin, white nylon an unpleasant reek of burning hung in the air. Idunn had been ready for this, as she'd been told that an attempt had been made to burn one of the bodies. There it lay, in the middle of the tent, pitch black and unrecognisable, on a bed of charred wood and shingle. Idunn noticed splashes of some pure white substance spattered here and there around the macabre scene, though none were visible on the body itself. They must have melted, as the corpse was still radiating a little heat. Idunn gathered that the person who had arrived first at the scene had put out the flames with a fire extinguisher, which explained the white stuff. She turned to the police inspector standing in the tent flap. 'Where's the other body?'

'It was found nearby.'

'Is it far?' Idunn hadn't noticed any other tent on the beach.

'No. Not at all. A hundred metres or so. We'll measure the exact distance before we erect a tent over it.'

Idunn raised her eyes from the blackened corpse to the inspector's sombre face. 'Has this body been touched at all?'

Ína shook her head. 'No. At least, not by us. Or by the man who was first on the scene. I spoke to him myself and he didn't mention it.'

'Who was he?'

'The driver of the ambulance that was called out to the car crash. He spotted a fire on the beach, grabbed an extinguisher, ran down here and put it out while the others were cutting the woman free from the wreckage. Mind you, the bonfire was already dying down by then. He rang us immediately afterwards. He didn't touch a thing.'

Idunn frowned. 'And you believe he was telling the truth?'

'Yes. Why, do you doubt him?'

Idunn didn't answer that, as it must already have been clear to the inspector that the question was redundant. 'Is it possible that he tried to resuscitate the victim? Attempted CPR?'

The inspector raised her eyebrows incredulously, then jerked her chin at the charred corpse. 'The man's been driving an ambulance for nine years,' she said drily. 'I doubt he'd have thought he could produce a sign of life from that.' Then she shrugged. 'But who knows? We'll question him properly later. Perhaps we'll learn more then. Why do you ask?'

Idunn looked back at the corpse. 'Because the position of the body is odd. Not what I would have expected. The victim's lying perfectly straight, arms by their sides and legs flat. Normally, when bodies burn, they curl up into what's known as a boxer pose. With knees and elbows bent, hands to their chest and clenched fists. Like a boxer.'

'So? What does it mean if it's not like that?'

'I haven't a clue. Yet.' Idunn removed the cap from her camera lens and took a photo. She checked the screen to make sure the result was satisfactory, then began making a record of the scene. Usually she kept up a running commentary while doing so, documenting what she saw, noting anything that roused her interest or that she wanted to bear in mind during the post-mortem. But this time she could hardly get a word in edgeways, thanks to the inspector.

'Is it a woman or a man?'

Idunn snapped a picture. 'Don't know. The internal examination will clarify that.'

'But which is more likely?'

Idunn rolled her eyes, confident that the inspector wouldn't notice as she had her back to her. 'I don't like making guesses. As you can see for yourself, there are no obvious visual clues. You'll have to wait for the post-mortem.' She shifted position and bent down, then resumed her snapping. After a moment, though, she relented. 'If I had to guess – and I stress that I don't want to – I'd say it was a woman. Or a boy. An adolescent, that is. Based purely on the size, though that in itself doesn't tell us much. There are plenty of small men and big women out there.'

The information gave her a brief respite which she used to good effect, taking photos and recording observations in the hope that there wouldn't be any more interruptions. But her luck was out.

'It's fairly obvious – isn't it? – that this woman or boy was already dead when they were set alight?'

Idunn lowered her heavy camera to her chest and felt the strap around her neck take the strain. She should never have let herself be badgered into speculating. 'Let's get one thing straight: we can't be sure it's a woman or a boy, OK? Don't take anything for granted until the question has been settled beyond doubt. You're asking me to make guesses again.' The inspector looked a little discomfited at this, and Idunn again experienced a twinge of sympathy, a fact she blamed on the circumstances. Not on the grim sight in front of her, but on being here, in the islands. She had been a sensitive child, and it was as if returning to her roots had revived part of her former self. She took pity on the inspector. 'I doubt the victim was alive. If they had been, the body wouldn't be in this position. It would probably be lying face down, as a result of having tried to crawl towards the water.'

Ína didn't seem particularly reassured by this information, but at least she shut up, allowing Idunn to complete her examination in silence. She didn't share the other aspects that were puzzling her with the inspector, as she didn't understand them herself, and the last thing she wanted was to indulge in further speculation. For one thing, as far as she could tell from the half-open mouth, the teeth were missing.

The tent filled up with people after Idunn had requested the help of the CSI team to lift the body off the cooled pyre and prepare it for transport. Once it had been placed in a body bag and securely zipped up, the technicians carried it on a stretcher to the ambulance to be conveyed to the airport. The plane that had brought the police team to Heimaey was still on standby, and Idunn requested that the body should be airlifted to Reykjavík without delay. She still had a fair amount of work to do at the scene and didn't want the corpse to be left lying around unsupervised at the terminal. She rang her office and arranged for an employee of the pathology department to be at Reykjavík airport to receive it.

This done, Idunn closed her case and asked Ína to escort her to the second body. They stepped out of the tent and Ína directed her round behind it, in the direction of the spit of land known as Ræningjatangi. Another tent had now been erected there, large, lopsided and out of place among the boulders at the foot of the slope. As they walked, Ína apologised for its appearance, explaining that they only had the one CSI tent at the station, so they had been forced to improvise. This had involved fetching the marquee normally used for the Island Festival and hastily pitching it over the evidence. It was the first time they had needed a tent in all the years the inspector had been working here. It was more than three decades since the last murder in the islands and probably never before had two CSI tents been needed at once.

Idunn nodded, feigning interest, as Ína went on talking about the low crime rate in the islands and supporting her claim with statistics. When Idunn opened the tent flap, the inspector's words faded to a background buzzing in her ears. The sight before her eyes was so disconcerting that she took a step backwards. For a moment she thought the person in front of her was a member of the public who had wandered in there by mistake and taken a seat. But then she realised that this was the second body, sitting propped up against a boulder, as if the person had taken their last breath in that position.

A capacious hood almost completely hid the face, revealing only a delicate chin and bluish lower lip. The size of the figure's trainers suggested it was a woman.

'How strange.' Idunn had spoken aloud, without meaning to address the inspector. But now that she had started, she might as well go on. 'You'd think she'd sat down there to enjoy the view.'

Idunn continued to stare into the tent, only turning when Ína tapped her on the shoulder. 'That's what I thought. But look.' The inspector pointed towards the other tent. 'Before the tents went up, she didn't have a view of the sea but of the bonfire. And the other body.'

Idunn glanced round at the other tent, then back inside the one they were standing by. As far as she could tell, Ína was right. She stepped inside the flap, put down her case and set to work.

Chapter 5
Day 2 – Friday, 24 January

There was a pitifully small number of mourners at the church when they arrived. They couldn't even console themselves that more people would turn up, since they were late and the service was about to start. It wasn't that they'd overslept; they'd woken at the crack of dawn, but precisely because they'd got up so early, they'd felt they had all the time in the world. Then suddenly it was only half an hour until the service was due to begin and they'd had to get ready in a rush, with the result that the outcome left a bit to be desired. The knots on Trausti's and Ari's ties were crooked; clothes were buttoned up wrongly. Sigga had smudged her lipstick while applying it in the rear-view mirror in the car park outside the church; it was a bit bright for the occasion, too – if there were rules for that sort of thing. Trausti was unshaven and, being dark-haired, his stubble made it look as if he'd come straight to church after clubbing all night. He had been reprimanded for this at the hospital; they worked him like a slave, then scolded him when it had an adverse impact on his appearance. But this time he couldn't plead the excuse that he'd left his razor at home and hadn't been expecting to be ordered onto night duty straight off his day shift.

No one had said a word about the disastrous Ouija board session when they drifted downstairs that morning. Just as well. The joke had misfired so badly that Trausti didn't know what there was to say. He didn't feel capable of bringing it up. The others must feel the same. He had lain awake for hours, trying to work out which of them could have manipulated the planchette to spell out Gudrún's name like that. Surely no one who knew the story would dream of doing such a thing? Or was this part of someone's ulterior motive to . . . what? He couldn't come up with anything remotely plausible to finish this thought.

His immediate suspicions had fallen on Leifur, who could be thoughtless. But it was out of character. Leifur's sense of humour was cruder; not in the sexual sense, just unsophisticated. For him, there was nothing funnier than sneaking chilli powder into the food of his neighbour at dinner, or putting clingfilm over the toilet bowl. The business with the Ouija board had been different. It had been more akin to mixing glass shards into cookie dough.

It must have been Ari or Sigga – unlikely as it seemed – as it simply could not have been Ragga. She would never have dragged up Gudrún's name like that, not in a million years.

But then none of them were the type to make such a crass error of judgement, especially not when they were trying to be funny. But people weren't always what they seemed. No matter how well you thought you knew someone, there was always room for surprises.

As they sprinted to the church, they looked back to see if Leifur's car was on its way but the streets were empty. Predictably enough, he had forgotten to bring a suit – if he even owned such a thing – but he'd done his best, wearing black jeans and a black T-shirt. Contrary to Ari's predictions, the shirt wasn't emblazoned with the name of a heavy metal band, but it still wasn't smart enough, so Ari had ordered him upstairs to fetch a jacket of his that he could borrow. Then he had yelled after Leifur that he could follow them in his own car; they were already late and there was no need for them all to arrive after the service had started.

'Hadn't we better go in?' Sigga asked when they reached the church door and there was still no sign of Leifur. They went inside, and were handed service sheets in the porch before entering the nave. They'd been intending to sit unobtrusively at the back, but as most of the pews were empty, this plan had gone out of the window. It would be absurd to sit that far away from the action when there were so many free places at the front.

It wasn't the first funeral Trausti had attended. Both his grandfathers had died a few years back, and when he sat down on the hard wooden pew, he was inescapably reminded of those occasions. The attendance had been sparse then as well, since, according to his mother, the older a person was when they died, the fewer mourners there were left to see them off. In contrast, churches were usually packed to overflowing when the deceased was a young person. A rough count of the heads in front of them suggested that Gugga's funeral was the exception. In addition to the four of them, there were only about twenty people in all.

The service was simple but beautiful, like the church. Trausti's gaze kept straying up to the white ceiling studded with golden stars. In his opinion, it was the church's finest feature and perfectly suited the mood. He paid little attention to what went on at the altar, and let the prayers, readings and liturgy wash over him. But he pricked up his ears when the vicar gave the eulogy, with a brief summary of Gugga's life. While he was listening, he studied the photo on the front of the service sheet, which appeared to have been taken when Gugga was a student. At least, she looked exactly as he remembered her: long, mousy hair tied back in a ponytail, a band of freckles across her nose and cheekbones, slightly slanting eyes, a flippant smile, one eyebrow dead straight, the other arched like that of an old-fashioned mime artist. He even recognised the jumper she was wearing.

Her short biography went some way towards explaining the poor turnout. Although Gugga had grown up in the Westman Islands, neither of her parents had been from local families. Her father had been from Reykjavík and her mother from a remote farm in the east of Iceland. What's more, Gugga had moved to the mainland to attend sixth-form college and lost touch with the pupils from her old school. Consequently, there were no relatives or close childhood friends to fill the church. Any college friends would presumably have had to make the long trek from the north of Iceland, as Gugga had gone to sixth form in Akureyri, and, as far as Trausti could remember, she hadn't made any close friends at university in Reykjavík apart from the five of them. Although he didn't believe in life after death, he was extremely glad they'd decided to attend. Their presence helped to flesh out the small congregation and made it less glaringly obvious that the deceased had enjoyed a limited social life.

Trausti thought glumly that his own funeral would be no different if he were to drop dead right now. He had relatives but they were scattered around the country and, apart from his immediate family members, he had only sporadic contact with them. He couldn't help wondering if his friends would bother to make the trip to the East Fjords if he were buried in his childhood home. He wouldn't bet on it. Perhaps he should mention to his parents that he would rather have a quiet funeral, to spare them the humiliation of an empty church.

Trausti was startled out of these melancholy thoughts by the vicar saying something that took him completely by surprise. It sounded as if Gugga had gone into rehab about a year ago. The vicar's tactfully vague phrasing made it hard to guess whether she had been battling alcoholism or drug addiction. Perhaps both. Gugga had not only drunk heavily as a student but dabbled in drugs too. Trausti sighed inwardly. Clearly, life hadn't treated Gugga kindly since she'd dropped out of university and moved away from Reykjavík.

The eulogy came to an end and was followed by an alternating sequence of hymns and prayers until the vicar finally announced that a reception would be held in the church hall and all those present were welcome to attend. As the service drew to a close, the members of the small church choir went over to the white coffin and lined up on either side of it, now taking on the role of pallbearers. The vicar processed alone down the aisle in front of the coffin, then the mourners began to file after it, heads bowed, joining the short procession one by one as the coffin passed. Trausti expected to see Leifur sitting at the back, having sneaked in after the service had begun, but there was nobody there. Paranoia quickly set in. Where the hell was he? They had made the trip over to attend this funeral, so his absence now was odd to say the very least. Could Leifur have wanted the opportunity to be alone in the house to set something up? If it had been him fooling around with the Ouija board, he might well have something else in store for them. And if so, it would probably take things a step further.

When they emerged into the cold air, the friends exchanged glances. None of them knew whether they ought to go to the graveside or head straight to the reception. But when the rest of the congregation set off towards the church hall and it appeared that no one else was going to follow the vicar and the coffin, the decision was taken for them. They had no choice but to accompany Gugga on the last stage of her journey.

Trausti was assailed by a sense of unreality as the coffin was lowered into the grave. While the straps were being pulled up again, he stared down at the shiny white lid at the bottom of the hole and couldn't stop thinking about the fact that Gugga was lying under there. Before evening, the grave would be filled in and their friend would literally have vanished off the face of the earth. For good. Feeling suddenly dizzy, he shuffled from foot to foot to keep his balance, afraid he might fall into the grave. The wind stung his cold cheeks, helping to revive him and remind him that this wasn't a dream. It was real. Nobody was immortal; not Gugga or any other member of their group – including him.

The vicar hadn't said anything in his eulogy about where Gugga had been working. Nor had he talked about her illness, mentioning only that she had died suddenly after a short stay in hospital. It had emerged that she had moved back to the islands after her father's death, though there had been no mention of why, whether it was for work or possibly even love. If it had been the latter, the relationship presumably hadn't lasted, as there was no sign of any grieving partner. Besides, a partner would hardly have made a beeline for the reception without attending the interment. And as it was the custom for colleagues to pay their final respects, no doubt more people would have turned up to the funeral if Gugga had been working here on Heimaey. Trausti guessed she had been unemployed. It was only to be expected if she had been in a bad way from drug addiction or alcoholism. Perhaps she had decided to move to the islands after being diagnosed with cancer, to make the most of the natural beauty. If so, he could understand that.

Her doctors would no doubt have been straight with her and, knowing she didn't have long to live, she would have abandoned any idea of trying to work. After all, nobody went to their grave saying they wished they'd worked harder.

Glancing at his friends, Trausti read in their eyes the same fear of doing the wrong thing. None of them were familiar with funeral etiquette. As it was only them and the vicar left – the pallbearers had melted away once the coffin was in the grave and the straps had been drawn up – they couldn't follow the example of more seasoned mourners. In the event, they got through the ritual without disgracing themselves, making the sign of the cross over the coffin and murmuring in the right places, and no one tripped and fell into the open grave.

During the short walk to the church hall, the vicar enquired about their connection to Gugga. He no longer cut a remote, formal figure; if he hadn't been wearing his cassock and carrying a Bible, he would have seemed like any other normal bloke. Curious about other people and up for a casual chat. As usual, it was Sigga who answered for the rest of them. Out of politeness, she asked in return whether the vicar had got to know Gugga after she moved back to the islands. He answered that he hadn't known her well, though he'd spoken to her on a couple of occasions.

At this point, Trausti saw his chance to ask a question: 'Did she move here for work?'

The vicar smiled at him indulgently, as if humouring a child: 'Er, no. Gugga didn't have a job. That would never have been possible.' He didn't explain why not, just seemed to take it for granted that they would be up to date with what had been going on in her life.

He was wrong. Since graduating, they had pretty much lost sight of her: they hadn't got in touch to ask her news and she hadn't volunteered any. On the rare occasions when Gugga had posted anything on the group chat it had tended to be no more than a thumbs-up to other people's posts or some bland emoji. Admittedly, she had tried to get them to meet up with her after her father died, but they'd all been too busy and their responses had been shamefully lukewarm. About six months later, she had announced that she'd moved into her parents' house on Heimaey but that she was desperate to get back to Reykjavík. In order to do that, though, she would need her friends' help. This time, the response had been a deafening silence.

In retrospect, they should have asked how she was doing, shown an interest in her life. Especially when she had broken with habit again back in November, messaging them to say she had been admitted to the University Hospital with cancer of the pancreas and would appreciate a visit. Trausti wished he'd sent her a private message, asking about her prognosis, but he hadn't got round to it. Pancreatic cancer was a horrible disease and the chances of survival were slim. Besides, he'd been too busy with his studies to ask questions about her diagnosis. And Gugga was the type who googled things. If he'd got involved, she was bound to have bombarded him with questions about various alternative treatments that only got patients' hopes up for nothing. He didn't have time for that, nor did he want to be the one who kept extinguishing every spark of hope.

The standard buffet awaited them in the church hall: a warm savoury bread pudding with ham and asparagus, a prawn-sandwich cake, canapés, and a variety of cream cakes, chocolate cookies and coffee. It was plain that the caterers had been expecting a larger turnout; pretty much every guest could have sat at their own cloth-laid table with a whole cake or dish to themselves. The congregation had thinned out even more after leaving the church, and those who had continued to the reception had already piled their plates high with food. They glanced up when the group of friends walked in, then immediately returned their attention to the refreshments. All, that is, apart from a young man and woman who were sitting together at a table. They went on staring, then started exchanging whispers. Trausti hoped they weren't close friends of Gugga's who would know that her old uni mates hadn't even bothered to visit her in hospital.

They found a table, sat down and took off their coats. Then they went to the buffet and helped themselves, largely in silence. Trausti was the only one who went back for second helpings. The girls were unimpressed by the old-fashioned offerings and Ari had piled so much onto his plate the first time round that he was still eating. While Trausti was carefully cutting himself a thin slice of the prawn-sandwich cake – though thick enough to get some of the cucumber garnish – an elderly woman swooped down on him. She introduced herself as Halldóra. Trausti responded with his own name.

'It was all so sudden, so sad.' Halldóra shook her head sorrowfully. 'You'd think death had it in for some families. First Marta, then Geir and now Gugga. The whole family wiped out.'

'Yes. It's terribly sad.' Trausti recognised the names of Gugga's parents. He had seen them on the gravestones next to hers. Presumably there would be few people around to tend to their plots now that Gugga had gone, let alone to tend to hers. When he stopped to think about it, though, there had been a newish bunch of flowers on her mother's grave, which suggested that someone must care about the family. 'Were you related to her?' he asked.

'Oh no, dear. We were neighbours before I downsized. I used to live next door to her parents, in the house Gugga was living in towards the end. What about you?'

'No, we weren't related. We met at university.' Trausti indicated the table where the others were sitting. 'She was part of our group of friends. We've come over from Reykjavík.' He saw no need to mention that he had undertaken a far longer journey himself, as it wasn't any of her business.

'So you're one of her friends. Of course. I should have guessed.' The woman smiled at him. 'She told me about you – talked about you all so fondly; about how much it meant to her that you came to see her. She was over the moon that you'd visited her in hospital when she was in Reykjavík.'

Trausti couldn't make head or tail of this. 'Visited her?' The woman must be muddling them up with some other group of friends. People Gugga had met after leaving university, perhaps. Because none of the others had said anything about going to see her, and he certainly hadn't. 'I think that must have been someone else, I'm afraid. We didn't realise how serious things were until it was too late.' Thank God he hadn't told the woman he was a doctor doing his postgrad studies abroad.

The woman gave him a kindly smile. 'No one could have known. It was all so sudden. Terribly bad luck. No one could have predicted that she would die.'

Trausti disagreed with her there, but before he could say a word, the woman continued:

'She must have been talking about one of you. She was so happy. It had been just like meeting up in the old days, she said. And she talked so warmly about how much your friendship meant to her.'

'Did she mention any names?'

The woman thought. 'No. Not that I can remember. She didn't go into details, just said how grateful she was to have a visit, especially as she hated being bedbound. And she didn't know many people in Reykjavík. Things were a little better after she was transferred to the hospital here, since this was her home and there were a few familiar faces, at least.' The woman surveyed the almost empty hall. 'Not many, as you can see – but a few. Sadly, most of the mourners are staff who looked after her at the local hospital, or else people like me who had some connection to her parents. But there are one or two friends. And your party, of course.'

The woman helped herself to the savoury bread pudding before continuing. 'Not everyone warmed to Gugga. And she moved home rather late in the day. She'd have done better to come back while her father was still alive and work for his business or something. He could have done with some help. He was never the same after his wife died, a shadow of his former self. It would have worked out better for Gugga, too. If she'd been here to help him, she'd have integrated more with the local community and got to know some people. She hardly had any childhood friends left here, though I think a few of them turned up to the church.'

Trausti had little interest in hearing about the attendees at Gugga's funeral. 'Did you say she was bedbound?' he asked, puzzled. He was finding it harder and harder to get a handle on Gugga's illness.

'Goodness, yes. They were such bad breaks. But they were healing well. Then . . . you know. Life's just not fair some-times.'

Trausti wished he could borrow one of his friends' phones and look up their old group chat. Had he missed something? He couldn't remember hearing anything about an accident or broken bones. It could be that Gugga hadn't mentioned them, regarding her injuries as trivial in comparison to her cancer. Perhaps the disease had been discovered by chance while she was in hospital for another reason. That was a common enough occurrence. 'Was the cancer very advanced by the time it was diagnosed?'

The woman regarded him with surprise. 'Cancer? Gugga didn't have cancer. Not as far as I'm aware.' Seeing Trausti's look of astonishment, she smiled at him kindly again, as if he was a bit slow on the uptake. Then she put down her plate and reached into the bag on her shoulder. 'Listen, I've got a spare key to Gugga's house. Her father wanted me to keep one in case he got locked out, even after I moved house. And I hung on to it after he died. It came in handy when Gugga went into hospital and she asked me to water the plants for her. Why don't you take it? You and your friends should drop by her house before you leave. Take something to remember her by. There are no legal heirs, so goodness knows where most of the stuff will end up. I've been asked to help clear out the house and I know she'd have been happy to think that some of her belongings would end up with friends. You can return the key to me once you're done.'

Trausti accepted the key, reflecting on how unusual this kind of small-town trust would be in the big city as he was memorising Gugga's and Halldóra's addresses. He was too dazed to decline the offer, though he had absolutely no desire to take anything that had belonged to Gugga. He had enough trouble trying to fit his own stuff into his shoebox of an apartment in the States. Besides, for him memories didn't have to be associated with tangible objects, though it was possible the others might feel differently. And, anyway, he wasn't sure he wanted to be constantly reminded of Gugga and how they had failed her at the end.

The woman patted him on the shoulder and reached for a napkin, then said goodbye and that she'd see him later, before returning to her table.

He was left standing there with a plate of cake, the key and a perplexed look on his face.

Chapter 6
Day 5 – Monday, 27 January

It was every bit as bad as Idunn had feared: they were stranded on Heimaey. While she was examining the body found sitting on the beach, the weather had deteriorated until it was barely possible to stay upright in the blast. The tents the police had erected over the bodies weren't up to the job and had to be taken down early. It was either that or lose them out to sea. Although this didn't inconvenience Idunn too badly, it had a serious impact on the work of the CSI team. The Island Festival tent had managed to withstand the strain as long as Idunn required its shelter, but by the time she'd finished it was leaning at a drunken angle and flapping wildly. Meanwhile, the crime scene investigators had to contend with the full force of the gale. Although no one put it into words, they were all thinking about what might have been blown away. They kept glancing at the angry sea as if expecting to see some vital piece of evidence being tossed around in the breakers. But if the wind had snatched up any clues, they had either sunk or drifted off, because they certainly weren't to be found at the scene.

No footprints showed up on the stony beach, and where the shingle gave way to sand, the waves had erased any possible tracks. No murder weapon had been found. No cigarette stubs, clothes, shoes, scraps of paper, leftovers of food, cups, vomit, blood or anything else that might provide DNA or the perpetrator's fingerprints. Or any explanation of what had happened here.

Nevertheless, before Idunn left the area, the CSI team had been rewarded for their pains by the discovery of several long blonde hairs scattered among the rock pools. Although it was impossible to say when they had got there and whether they were related to the case, they were carefully collected and bagged up. At first sight, the hairs appeared to be missing their roots, as if they'd been cut off. Extracting mitochondrial DNA in this case would be expensive and success couldn't be guaranteed, but if nothing else the hairs could be used for comparison purposes if any future suspects with long hair tried to deny having been at the scene. Analysis could also reveal whether the hair had been dyed, the owner had taken specific drugs or, indeed, whether they were human. Given the length of the hairs, Idunn was fairly sure they couldn't belong to an animal, unless they were from the mane or tail of a horse, but in that case she would have expected them to be much coarser.

The other piece of evidence was an empty petrol can. It had been lying where the waves lapped the beach, as though it had been thrown away only for the sea to return it to land. At this, the Reykjavík team were greatly cheered, convinced it had to be connected to the blaze. The locals, on the other hand, were more cautious, pointing out that Heimaey was home to any number of small fishing boats carrying similar petrol cans that were liable to fall overboard. Idunn had said nothing, privately convinced that the can was linked to the bonfire, bearing in mind the reek of petrol in the tent that had been hurriedly erected over the cooling pyre. If they were lucky, fingerprints might turn up on the handle of the can, though presumably the person who threw it in the sea would have wiped them off first. Then again, since the arsonist hadn't had the brains to take the precaution of filling the can with seawater to make sure it sank, it was clear the police weren't dealing with a criminal mastermind.

According to the CSI team, after Idunn left the area they'd found nothing that shed any further light on the incident. They had dismantled the bonfire, one charred piece of wood at a time, and discovered the remains of what appeared to be books among them. They were too badly burnt to tell what kind of books they were, though the few words still legible were in English. The ashes had also yielded two metal springs of the type found in spiral-bound notebooks. There was no way of knowing whether the books and notebooks had had any particular significance for the person who'd started the fire; perhaps they had just been used as extra kindling. Several small round objects, believed by forensics to be beads from a bracelet or necklace, had also turned up in the ashes, but whatever they had been strung on had disappeared, either burnt up or melted, like the paint on the beads – if they had originally been coloured.

It would have suited Idunn if they had found a putative murder weapon – assuming a weapon had been involved: of course, people could easily be killed without one. The dead woman sitting among the rocks had displayed no visible injuries from a knife, firearm or blunt instrument. Nor did she appear to have been strangled. Meanwhile, the corpse on the bonfire was too badly burnt for any signs of this type of injury to be detected. It was possible, however, that the charred remains of fabric Idunn had found on top of the body could be concealing a stab wound or bullet hole. To find out would require a more detailed examination than any she could carry out on the beach.

As she had grudgingly conceded to Inspector Ína, Idunn was inclined to believe that the body on the fire had also been female. It couldn't have been a fully grown man because it was too light for the loss of weight to be explained by the evaporation of all the water it contained or the melting of the subcutaneous fat. For that to happen, the skin would have to tear, but, as she had observed at the scene, there were no signs of splitting or tearing. Idunn didn't think they were dealing with the body of a teenager either, as toothless adolescents were rare in Iceland. But since even an average-sized woman should have been heavier than this corpse, she had to admit she was stumped. All she could think of was that it might be someone who had suffered drastic weight loss due to a serious illness. This, in turn, led her to wonder whether the person's death could in fact have been from natural causes. But, if so, how on earth had the body ended up on a pyre on the beach? All would be revealed in due course, with a bit of luck. But they wouldn't get any answers today – or tomorrow, for that matter, if the weather forecast was to be believed – since the burnt corpse had already been flown to Reykjavík, while Idunn was stuck here on Heimaey.

The other body was still in the Westman Islands, temporarily stored in the hospital morgue. Idunn had accompanied it there herself, removed the clothes and conducted a preliminary examination in the presence of Inspector Ína, who had asked if she could hitch a lift with her. She'd claimed that she was worried about her mother, who was in hospital and not answering her phone, and wanted to seize the chance to look in on her at the same time. Idunn suspected this was a pretext and that the inspector was actually trying to ensure that the pathologist from the big city wouldn't scornfully reject her presence. It was obvious that Ína wanted to observe the preliminary examination, but as the woman had no experience of murder cases, Idunn hadn't dared take her eyes off the body for a second, to prevent any accidental DNA contamination. She would just have to trust that her instructions for the handling of the burnt corpse had been followed to the letter during its transferral to the plane and from there to the University Hospital in Reykjavík.

It was dark in Idunn's hotel room. Thick curtains blocked out the feeble winter daylight and only the small bedside lamp was on. Her first action on entering the room had been to draw the curtains. Foolish as it was, she felt better knowing that no one could look in the window. It didn't matter that the streets were empty thanks to the storm, and that passers-by were unlikely to stare at the hotel in the hope of spotting movement inside. She simply felt more comfortable knowing that no one could see in, as it reduced the chances that her father would get wind of her presence.

The compartment of Idunn's brain in which her blackest thoughts were stowed now slid open, releasing a burst of mocking laughter. How naïve she was. Of course her father would have realised that she was in the islands. A police operation wouldn't pass unnoticed and he was well aware that she was the only pathologist in the country. He would be perfectly capable of joining the dots. At that moment a loud rap on her door almost made Idunn jump out of her skin. Her wet hair was wrapped in a towel after her shower and all she had on was a hotel bathrobe. She had no intention of getting involved in an argument with her father dressed like this, even if it was only through a crack in the door.

'Who's there?' Idunn was furious to hear a slight wobble in her voice. 'I'm busy,' she added, more firmly.

Karó's voice carried through the door: 'We're going to get something to eat. Do you want to join us?'

Idunn let out a breath, mainly from relief but also from embarrassment at not having answered normally. 'I think I'll pass. I don't particularly want to go out again in this weather.' She hoped the loud rumbling of her stomach wasn't audible through the door. The truth was she was famished, though she hadn't realised this until she heard the mention of food. No way was she setting foot outside the hotel, though.

'There's a restaurant downstairs – Einsi Kaldi. It's pretty good. You wouldn't have to go outside.'

Idunn dithered. 'Is there a bar?' The discovery that the minibar in her room was empty had been a major blow.

'Yes, I think so.'

Idunn didn't need any more encouragement. 'I'll be down shortly.'

The restaurant had large picture windows, which meant the diners were on display to any passers-by. And as there were no more than a couple of dozen streets in the little town, it was inevitable that the few people who ventured out in the storm would have to go past at some point.

Idunn had pulled on her clothes before she was properly dry from her shower and kept having to wriggle to stop them sticking to her body. By the time she stepped out of the lift, things had mostly sorted themselves out, apart from her back where her shirt would continue to cling to her skin until her hair was dry. That would take a while, since it was thick, curly and far too long. This was due to her reluctance to go to the hairdresser's and risk having to keep up a constant flow of chatter with the person wielding the scissors

It was a relief to see that the team from Reykjavík were occupying the largest table in the restaurant and that there was no room for her. What she craved was food and wine, not company. The others immediately started budging up to make space but she told them not to bother, pleading a headache, and instead chose a small table further inside the restaurant where she could sit with her back to the window.

But her wish to eat alone was thwarted by Karó and Týr, who left the big table and moved over to join her, each bringing their drinks: his an orange juice, hers a soda water. Only one person at the other table had a beer; the others were all sticking to water or soft drinks. But Idunn didn't let this stop her from ordering a glass of white wine the moment the waiter appeared. She was in her forties and had long ago got over the feeling of being obliged to follow the herd.

'How soon can we get out of here? Has anyone said?' Idunn asked, though she had a feeling she already knew the answer. She had checked the next day's forecast on three different websites in the hope of seeing the faintest chance of getting home. But the comparison had only made her even more despondent. The Hellisheidi mountain route between the port at Landeyjahöfn and Reykjavík was still closed to traffic and wasn't expected to open until tomorrow evening at the earliest, or possibly not until the following day. If the storm continued like this, the outlook wasn't hopeful.

Týr got in first: 'There's a small chance of a window opening up tomorrow afternoon. Between two areas of low pressure.'

The waiter appeared with Idunn's glass and she took a mouthful before replying to his enquiry about what she'd like to eat. As soon as he had vanished into the kitchen, she turned back to Týr and Karó, realising she was glad they'd joined her. Now she would be able to distract herself from obsessing over her father and his betrayal by discussing the investigation with them. 'Has there been any progress in identifying the intact body?'

Karó shook her head. 'No. No one from the local police recognised her. Of course, she wouldn't be looking quite herself, but still.'

'Has no young woman been reported missing?' Idunn took another sip of wine, a little smaller this time, having learnt from experience that the first mouthful was always the best. The wine's charm diminished as the level in one's glass went down. 'Here or anywhere else in the country?'

'Not here, though they're looking for two women in Reykjavík. But the description doesn't fit. Nor does the age, as far as I can tell. The missing girls are both under twenty. And both are addicts.'

'This woman's older, I agree with you there.' Idunn pictured the dead woman's face with the fine laughter lines at the corners of her eyes – lines that the woman may not even have noticed yet. 'But a notification could still come in. She hasn't been dead long. Perhaps no one's missed her yet.' Idunn stopped herself from mentioning that rigor mortis hadn't set in and the body temperature hadn't dropped to match that of its surrounding environment, indicating that the woman had been dead a relatively short time before her body was found. Their food was about to arrive any minute, and Týr and Karó might be queasy about such details. 'Although I don't have much to go on,' Idunn said instead, 'I doubt the woman had substance abuse problems or was homeless. Someone will notice she's missing.'

Týr squared his shoulders and puffed out his chest a little: 'We'll have established her identity before there's any need for that.'

Idunn had already notified the police's official Identification Commission about the two bodies. She herself was a member of the commission, which convened whenever unidentified bodies or human remains were discovered. Their remit also covered air crashes, shipwrecks and natural disasters. Fortunately, the commission wasn't often required and Idunn didn't expect the job to take long this time. There was every likelihood that they would quickly track down the names of the deceased. 'Yes. No doubt.' She was careful not to smile. She didn't doubt the ability of the police to solve the case and understood Týr's impulse to uphold the honour of the institution. 'There can't have been many non-locals or tourists in the islands at this time of year, so you should have an easy job of it.'

'As a matter of fact, the town was packed with visitors.' Karó extracted the cutlery from her napkin, obviously impatient to start her meal. 'There was some fishery congress or conference being held on Heimaey. Loads of people involved in the fishing industry had congregated here from all over the country. The woman could have been part of the conference, though most of the attendees had left. There was a handball game, too; ÍBV against the Hawks. The ferry's last trip was at ten yesterday evening, but a few people may have stayed on. Voluntarily or not. It would have been touch and go if they'd tried to make it to the ferry after the game. Apparently it didn't finish until after 9 p.m.'

'Which team won?' Idunn unwrapped her cutlery from the napkin too, to be ready as soon as their food arrived. 'I mean, would the Hafnarfjördur fans have been in the mood to celebrate afterwards or would they have hurried off home?'

'The home team won.' Týr glanced towards the kitchen, then turned back, disappointed, when no one emerged bearing plates. Evidently he was starving too. 'But there's an Automatic Number Plate Recognition camera by the ferry that photographs all the cars as they embark and disembark.

It registers the number plates and keeps a record of all the vehicles. The plan is to check the numbers of the cars that arrived before and during the weekend, and compare them to those that departed with the ferry to see if any non-local vehicle failed to leave. Though, of course, the fact that a car left again wouldn't necessarily tell us whether all the passengers were on board. What's more, there's no requirement to give the names of the passengers when you buy tickets, so we can't compare lists of individual arrivals and departures.'

Idunn nodded. 'What about passengers on flights? Their names are recorded.'

'It's been confirmed that everyone who'd booked a flight turned up for it. It'll take longer to go through the ferry records. Naturally, it complicates things that so many people flocked to the island at the weekend. All we know so far is that the bodies could be either locals or visitors who were here in connection with the fishing congress or the handball match.'

'Or foreign tourists,' Karó chipped in, adding: 'Apparently there are a few here at the moment, strange though it may seem.'

'Do you think it was a tourist?' Týr asked Idunn. She was the only one at the table who had seen the intact body up close.

Idunn shrugged. 'No idea. There was nothing in her coat pockets but a packet of chewing gum. Both her clothes and the gum could have belonged equally to an Icelander or a foreigner.' She left it at that. Gone were the days when Icelanders could be distinguished from foreigners by their appearance alone. The nation had become more diverse, as Karó demonstrated. But as this newfound diversity was a recent phenomenon, people were still getting used to it and were liable to make ridiculous statements out of pure thoughtlessness. Idunn had no intention of falling into that trap. They wouldn't prise anything out of her in relation to the woman's possible nationality, or whether she looked Icelandic or not. There was no such thing as a typically Icelandic appearance.

'What about the other body?' Karó asked. 'Did you learn anything at all?'

'No. Nothing I'd trust myself to stand by. The picture will become clearer once I get back to town and can start the internal examination.'

Silence fell. Neither Karó nor Týr appeared eager to have details about the autopsy as an appetiser. Which was fine, because Idunn meant what she said. Her observations had revealed several things that she didn't yet understand and it would be irresponsible to discuss them at this stage. The most perplexing problem was that of the body's posture. Muscles and sinews were supposed to contract in contact with fire, so why hadn't the corpse's limbs bent at the joints? Could there have been something heavy weighing it down as it was burning and drying out? If so, why? And who had subsequently removed it? Unless it had burnt to ashes.

She had muted her phone but at that moment the screen lit up. Seeing who was ringing, she sighed under her breath but resisted the temptation to turn it face down. Instead, she groaned, stood up and took the call once she was out of earshot. 'Hi, Mum.'

'Where are you? Why haven't you visited? I need you to come.' Her mother's voice was shrill and Idunn immediately regretted picking up. She was obviously in one of her moods and Idunn really didn't want to have to deal with this at the moment.

'What's wrong, Mum?'

'Everything. Everything's wrong. The sink's leaking, the radiators aren't heating up properly and the upstairs neighbour had a party last night and I couldn't sleep for the racket.'

'Well, why don't you go for a rest now? I assume the party's over.' Knowing her mother's penchant for overdramatising things, Idunn would bet her life savings on this so-called party having been very civilised, if there had actually been a party at all.

'I can't. I've got this terrible headache. Can you come over? I'm worried I might be having a brain aneurysm.'

Idunn groaned again, silently this time. Her mother's headache was just that. A headache. 'I can't. I'm away on a job.'

'So you're just going to let me die, then? After all I've done for you?'

Idunn had to suppress a bitter laugh at this skewed vision of their relationship. 'You're not going to die. But if you think you need a doctor, go and see one. Go to A&E. I'm stuck here; I can't get to you.'

'Stuck where? Why are you stuck?'

Clearly, her mother hadn't been following the news, not that this surprised Idunn. Her mum was only interested in things directly related to herself. 'I'm stuck due to bad weather. In the Westman Islands.' As soon as the words had left her mouth, Idunn regretted disclosing the location. It was bound to set her mother off and, sure enough . . .

'What? Are you nuts? Haven't you forgotten how your dad left us high and dry for that stupid whore? How could you go and visit him after what he did to us? How many times have I told you that your father's an evil bastard?'

'A million times would be my guess.' Idunn needed to hang up before her mother went off on a tirade about the woman her father had been having an affair with in Reykjavík.

Idunn had only ever heard her mother refer to her father's mistress as 'the whore', and, as far as Idunn knew, nothing had come of her father's relationship with the woman after their divorce was finalised, so she sometimes suspected the affair might have been a figment of her mother's imagination. Her mum had a tendency to misinterpret situations and events, but she would never back down and admit it, even when her conclusions proved totally incorrect. Even now, decades after their divorce, she still hadn't forgiven Idunn's father, but then Idunn was in no position to preach to her mother on that score. She was too bitter at him herself for that. 'Listen, I have to get back to it. I'm here for work, as I told you, not to visit anyone.'

'Oh, sure. Work's more important to you than I am. Always has been, always will be. But you'll regret not helping me when you get back and find me lying dead on the floor.'

'What part of me being weatherbound do you not understand? I can't come. *Can't*, not don't want to. Go to A&E like everyone else.'

Before her mother could get in another word, Idunn hurriedly said goodbye and hung up.

She returned to her dining companions without providing any explanation of the phone call. 'Do we know any more about the woman who crashed her car? Whether she's linked to the case at all?' The instant Idunn had finished speaking, it occurred to her that the woman might have gone there to remove whatever it was that had been weighing down the burning body.

'No. Not yet,' Karó replied. 'She's arrived in Reykjavík and is being kept in an induced coma. Her name's Ásta Jónsdóttir and she's local. With a clean record. She's never cropped up on the police database in any capacity. It seems she's never been anywhere near a criminal case. She has a job and lives alone with her dog.'

'Where is it now? The dog, I mean.' Idunn saw from their expressions that her apparent concern for the dog came across as odd and inappropriate, given that two people were dead and one in a coma after being badly mashed up in a car crash.

'The dog was in the car when it rolled,' Karó said. 'It was badly injured. But I don't know what happened to the poor creature after it was patched up. I expect it's being looked after by friends or relatives.'

The kitchen door opened and their eyes immediately flicked towards it. The waiter came out bearing two plates but unfortunately he was starting with the big table, which meant they would be at the back of the queue. Idunn thought she would go mad from hunger as the delicious smell of food wafted over to them.

When she finally got her supper, it didn't take her long to grab her knife and fork, though she had the grace to glance at Týr and Karó before taking the first bite: 'Bon appétit.' She also managed to refrain from cramming a vast load onto her first forkful. But before she could get it to her mouth, Týr jerked his chin at her, indicating something behind her. Idunn became aware of a presence at her shoulder.

She put down her knife and fork.

It could only be the one person she would give anything to avoid. Everyone involved in the investigation was seated at the two tables, and there was no one else in the Westman Islands who had any claim on her. She cleared her throat politely, took a deep breath and turned her head.

'Hi, Idunn. I heard you were in town.'

Chapter 7
Day 2 – Friday, 24 January

The funeral refreshments hadn't agreed with Trausti. He'd overindulged in cream, sugar and mayonnaise, unable to hold back, since the various bread dishes were unknown in America, as were the elaborate gateaux, known in Icelandic as *hnallthórur*, filled with real whipped cream. Now it felt as if his stomach was full of rocks, as if he hadn't only gobbled down the food but the plate as well. On top of that, he was feeling a bit disorientated from his conversation with Gugga's old neighbour, Halldóra. What he'd learnt was proving as hard to digest as the food. He still hadn't told his friends what she'd said. He couldn't get the words out.

Instead, he had sat at the table in silence, working his way through a mound of second helpings. From time to time, he'd scanned his friends' faces, trying to work out which of them could have visited Gugga in hospital and lied about the fact. Because none of them had admitted to responding to Gugga's plea. Perhaps they'd all gone. But, if so, why not be open about the fact? There was something going on, and the thought made him uneasy. The business with the Ouija board hadn't helped either. But no matter how hard he tried, he couldn't figure out what was happening, who was behind it or what the hell that person's motive could be.

'Are you OK?'

Trausti glanced up to see Sigga watching him. Her normally smooth brow was puckered with concern and her large eyes were narrowed. They had been back at the house on Stórhöfdi for some time but no one had noticed how silent and withdrawn he was until now. That told its own story about his status within the group; no one could exactly call him the lynchpin.

Trausti squeezed out a smile. 'Yeah, sure. I've just eaten too much.'

Sigga locked eyes with him as if she were cross-examining a witness in court. 'No. There's something wrong.' She frowned. 'Are you pissed off that we were so late to the funeral? And that Leifur was a no-show?'

Her question struck him as odd. After all, he had been just as late getting ready as the rest of them, and he wasn't the type to get worked up or throw a fit when things didn't go according to plan, whatever Sigga seemed to think. The reason for Leifur's absence from church hadn't elicited any particular response from Trausti, who wasn't sure whether he had made up his lame excuse for not attending. According to Leifur, Ari's jacket had turned out to be far too small for him, so he had decided to pay his respects to Gugga by having a quiet beer at the house instead. He had still been wearing his black T-shirt when they returned, and the moment he turned his back to them they got an eyeful of the inappropriate picture that should, by rights, have been on the front. Clearly, he had reversed it to appear more respectable, so perhaps it had been for the best that he hadn't come along, whatever his true reason for staying behind.

'No. I'm not pissed off.' Trausti was going to leave it at that but then saw from Sigga's expression that he would have to be more convincing. 'There's just a lot to think about, that's all. I'm feeling a bit confused.'

'What about?'

Gradually the others stopped talking and turned their attention to him. This was as good a time as any to report his conversation with Gugga's neighbour. Or at least share part of what she'd told him. 'I spoke to a woman at the reception, an old neighbour of Gugga's parents, and according to her, Gugga didn't have cancer. She died from something completely different.'

'What?' The exclamation jumped from person to person around the living room. Their astonishment seemed genuine.

'Hang on . . . what did she die of, then?' Leifur asked, when the echo had faded.

'I don't know. The woman mentioned broken bones.' Trausti felt like an idiot as soon as he'd said it. The chances of a young person dying from a fracture were almost zero if they were receiving medical attention. 'It was all a bit vague. She took it for granted that I already knew the whole story.'

'Can you die of a broken bone?' Ragga, ever the logical engineer, wasn't going to let him off that lightly.

'Of a broken neck, obviously. Or a broken skull.' Leifur was quick to reply.

Although Trausti regarded Leifur as the least qualified of all of them to work in healthcare, he had in fact hit on the right answer.

Looking pleased with himself, Leifur raised his beer can in a toast and took a generous slug.

'It didn't sound like a broken neck or fractured skull from what she said. I got the impression she was referring to the pelvis or a badly broken leg, maybe. Possibly both, since she mentioned broken bones in the plural. But neither of those injuries would be fatal in a young patient.'

'It didn't occur to you to ask the woman about it?' Ari was the only one still wearing his funeral outfit, complete with crooked tie. The others had changed into more comfortable clothes, which in Leifur's case had simply meant turning his heavy metal T-shirt the right way round.

'I suppose I should have but I was just so thrown.'

Sigga chipped in: 'Isn't it possible that the woman got it wrong? I mean, who would say they had cancer if they'd just broken a bone? Like we wouldn't have noticed if we'd gone to visit Gugga in hospital?' Sigga raised an arm and started waving it in circles. 'Oh! Are you in plaster? Of course. That makes sense; it's a well-known treatment for cancer.' Her arm fell back to her side. 'For goodness' sake, the woman must be gaga or something. Because Gugga wasn't an idiot.'

Trausti wasn't sure whether she expected him to respond to this, so he decided not to. He had learnt during his medical studies that it was better to keep his mouth shut unless he had something clever to say. He hadn't detected any signs of senility in Halldóra, but then they hadn't spoken for long and strangers don't always pick up on the clues at first when someone is suffering from dementia. It was perfectly possible that the woman had been muddled and that Gugga had died of cancer, with all her bones perfectly intact.

The silence was abruptly broken by the shrill ringing of a phone and they glanced at each other, puzzled. Ragga was the first to work it out. 'It must be the phone downstairs. The landline.'

None of them made any move to get up and answer. The ringing continued, impossible to ignore, ominous in its persistence. Soon they were all growing restless. Sigga waved at Ari. 'You answer.'

'Me?' Ari looked indignant. 'Why should I?'

'Because it's your friend's house,' Ragga reminded him. 'It must be for him. If anyone wanted to get hold of us, they'd ring our phones.' She gestured towards the stairs. 'You'll have to answer. We don't even know your friend's name.'

Ari gave in and went downstairs. The ringing stopped and they heard him say a few brief words. Then he fell silent and came back up, though they hadn't heard him say goodbye, which seemed odd. Although Ari could be rude and brash with them, he was never less than polite to others. When he reappeared, he seemed a little shaken, as though he'd received bad news. Trausti hoped they weren't about to be chucked out of their accommodation and forced to return to Reykjavík early. Now they'd got the funeral out of the way, the wake was supposed to begin – the part of the weekend he'd been looking forward to.

'Who was it?' Sigga was the first to ask the question on all their lips.

'I don't know. Some idiot. A prank call.'

'A prank call?' Sigga pulled a face. 'Do they still exist?'

'Apparently.' Ari returned to his seat.

Leifur swallowed a mouthful of beer, belched, then asked: 'What did the caller say?'

'Just some rubbish. It doesn't matter.' It was evident to all of them that Ari was shaken. His reluctance to share the message with them suggested that it had been personal. Trausti's first thought was a girlfriend, stubbing out their relationship like a malodorous cigar. But then Ari had claimed he wasn't seeing anyone at the moment. For some unsettling reason, Trausti suspected that the call had something to do with himself.

When no one else said anything, Sigga resumed their previous discussion, addressing herself to Trausti. 'Anyway, you should be able to ask around at the hospital. About Gugga's illness, I mean. You're a doctor, so they'll answer your questions.'

Trausti wondered if he should explain that it wasn't that straightforward. Just because he was a doctor, that didn't mean he had any right to see Gugga's medical records. But instead of muttering about patient confidentiality and data protection laws, he put his hand in his pocket and brought out the key Halldóra had given him. 'By the way, the neighbour gave me a key. She invited us to go round to Gugga's house and choose something to remember her by – if we wanted to.'

The group stared as if hypnotised at the key he was waving. While their attention was fixed on the very ordinary ASSA key, Trausti searched each of their faces in the hope of working out which of them was hiding something. He couldn't get rid of the feeling that there was a traitor in their midst and that he could consider himself lucky if it was only one of them.

Ari broke the silence: 'Weren't you planning to tell us?'

'Sure. I just hadn't got round to it yet.' Trausti put the key back in his pocket. 'Perhaps there's something at Gugga's house that might explain what was wrong with her. If we really want to go there.'

Ari folded his arms across his chest, knocking his tie even more crooked. He didn't comment on the idea that he might want a memento of Gugga; none of them did. But then Trausti couldn't imagine that anything she had owned would appeal to Ari the banker. His expensive new electric car, overly smart clothes and highly polished shoes didn't give the impression he'd care much for a 'No Borders' poster. But, oddly enough, he didn't protest or raise the kind of objections he normally would when any of them made a suggestion.

'Like what?' Ari asked. 'What could we find that would explain what was wrong with her? Not that I'm against the idea of going.'

'Well, medication, for example.'

Sigga looked at Ragga and their gazes locked for a moment. The sight was a familiar one to Trausti; they'd always been like that. Gugga too. The girls seemed able to exchange information with no more than a glance. He envied them. He didn't know if it was a gender thing or if they were simply closer than the boys. Ari and Leifur were good mates and all that, but his relationship with them went no further. If they wanted to communicate with each other, they had to go ahead and voice what they were thinking. He wished the same applied to Sigga and Ragga as he badly wanted to know what was going through their minds.

'Let's do it.' Sigga spoke as if issuing an order, not a suggestion for them to mull over. She had always been brilliant at that. At barking out terse orders: *Let's eat. Come on. Stop it. Let's dance.* And they usually obeyed without a murmur. Apart from Ari, that is, who always had to drag his heels. But this time even he seemed happy to go along with the plan.

They arrived at the address to find a small detached bungalow with a concrete basement level. It wasn't as well maintained as the other buildings in the road, but then that was to be expected. Gugga had never been particularly practical herself and presumably hadn't been able to afford painters and decorators. She must have been living on unemployment benefits, which wouldn't have left her with any money to spare. Trausti had no idea how much she might have inherited from her parents. If he remembered right, her mother had worked at a nursery school and her father had a small business hiring out earth-moving machinery, which, if Gugga was to be believed, had been in financial difficulties. It was unlikely that they had left her much. The small car parked in front of the garage looked hardly worth the deposit, and the mini digger in the drive appeared to be rusted up, which seemed to confirm Trausti's assessment of the situation.

They had all squashed into Leifur's car and the slamming of the doors as they got out echoed in the empty residential street. They hovered on the pavement, eyeing the gloomy house. It was no surprise that the lights should be out, but there was something so off-putting about the black windows that none of them were eager to go inside.

'And you said we can just take whatever we like?' Leifur asked, attempting to lift the mood. 'Bloody good deal if you ask me.'

Sigga gave him a hard jab with her elbow. 'We can take something to remember Gugga by. Not just anything we fancy. You're not walking out of there with a game console or a TV.'

'Why not?'

Sigga had evidently read him right.

They continued to bicker. Leifur wanted to know where the line was; why one inanimate object should be judged better than another to commemorate somebody, and why he himself wasn't allowed to decide on a suitable keepsake. Sigga parried his points adroitly, a skill she must have learnt in her job as a lawyer, since Trausti couldn't recall her being particularly good at rational argument in the old days. She used to support her points by insisting 'Yes, it is,' or 'Well, that's just how it is,' which he doubted would prove particularly successful in court.

None of the others intervened in their pointless quarrel. They just stood there, staring at the house, until Trausti gave voice to what he assumed they were all thinking: 'Do we really want to go inside? The idea makes me feel a bit uncomfortable. At best, it's like we're being nosy; at worst, it's like we're breaking in.'

Ari's response was typically short and to the point: 'We've got a key. We were invited. No reason to make a drama out of it.'

Leifur, abandoning his argument with Sigga, joined in: 'I agree with Trausti. It seems a bit creepy when you stop to think about it. Like entering a tomb or something.'

'If you don't want to come in, you can wait outside.' Ari didn't sound remotely hesitant.

At that moment, a chilly gust of wind made up their minds for them. Sigga hugged herself against the cold, then barked out a command: 'Inside.' As usual they all jumped to obey, even Ragga and Leifur.

They piled in front of the door, forgetting that Trausti had the key. As always, he'd been overlooked and found himself at the back. Perhaps it was the cold or the turmoil of emotions inside him, but for once he lost his temper. Rather than snapping at them when they stepped aside to let him through, however, he inserted the key in the door, then paused. Looking round at them, he asked: 'Did any of you visit Gugga in hospital?'

'No. As you're well aware,' Sigga replied. 'We've already discussed this and we all feel bad about it. Don't start trying to guilt-trip us even more.' She shook herself to stay warm. 'Open the door.'

'You can't answer for everyone.' Trausti looked round at the others. 'Did one of you go?'

They all denied it. He could read nothing but puzzlement in their faces. Perhaps it was a little overdone in some cases, but he couldn't see any other signs of dishonesty or clues that one of them was lying.

Maybe Halldóra, the old neighbour, really was a bit senile, confused about Gugga's illness. About the visits she'd received. That had to be it. The simplest explanation was usually the right one.

He turned the key in the lock, opened the door and a waft of warm, stale air flowed out to meet them.

Chapter 8
Day 5 – Monday, 27 January

Idunn was deeply regretting the food she'd had to abandon untouched and, even more, the glass of wine left behind on the table. Knocking it back would have helped to make this reunion more bearable. It had been a mistake to bring her uninvited guest up to her room, but the presence of her colleagues had made talking in the restaurant impossible, and if they'd sat in the lounge, the girl on reception would have been able to hear every word. But, in that case, at least Idunn would have had the option of fleeing and locking herself in her room when she'd had enough. She'd blown her chance of that. Still, there was one consolation; the visitor now sitting on her bed, prattling away nineteen to the dozen, could have been even more unwelcome: it could have been her father rather than her half-sister.

Idunn's eyes strayed to the minibar. There was a faint chance the hotel staff might have replenished it while she was downstairs. But Alexandra's voice dragged her back to the real world, in which the evening shift wouldn't know by telepathy that an empty minibar needed restocking. She tried to focus on the vacuous chatter issuing from Alexandra's mouth, which sounded like the sob story of a young woman with strictly first-world problems. Idunn's half-sister didn't exactly come from a deprived background. On top of that, she had youth, health and beauty on her side. The only thing she lacked was intelligence, a conclusion Idunn had drawn from the content of Alexandra's social media. She had sneaked the occasional look at her half-sister's posts and a quick scroll through Alexandra's photos had revealed nothing but a cringeworthy succession of designer labels, TikTok dances and posed selfies. In fact, it was only thanks to this nosiness that Idunn had recognised Alexandra at all when the girl materialised at her side in the hotel restaurant. Otherwise Idunn would have taken her for a stranger, since she had avoided all contact with her half-siblings: Alexandra, and her brother, who was a couple of years older.

Idunn chose this moment to interrupt. She had allowed the girl to prattle on, pretending to listen while waiting for the flow to dry up, when she'd been struck by a sudden thought: 'Why have you got a suitcase with you?'

Alexandra broke off. Her big blue eyes widened under their carefully plucked brows. 'Because I'm coming with you. To Reykjavík. Like I was just telling you.' She beamed as if informing Idunn that she'd won the lottery. 'Remember? I'm going to stay with you. Just to start off with. Until I find a flat of my own.'

'Uh . . . no.' Idunn didn't even try to disguise how preposterous she found this idea. Not to mention how incredibly presumptuous it was of Alexandra. That was typical of spoilt kids like her: they assumed that getting what you wanted was a law of nature. Well, Idunn was sorry to have to disabuse her, but there was no avoiding it: 'You're not moving in with me,' she said firmly. 'It would have been politer to ask first, but it wouldn't have made any difference, because it's not happening.'

The look of shock on her sister's face would have done credit to an actor in a soap opera. 'But I sent you a message!' Alexandra exclaimed. 'I've sent you loads of messages but you never answer. You don't even bother to read them.'

Idunn was not going to have this conversation. She had zero interest in any sort of relationship with her half-siblings. As far as she was concerned, they were strangers. The fact they shared some DNA was irrelevant. 'How did you know I was here?' she asked.

'Everyone knows a dead body's been found and that the police always stay at Hótel Vestmannaeyjar when they're in town. And you're the only pathologist in the country. I do keep up, you know.'

If Alexandra had been capable of working this out, the same must surely be true of their father. Perhaps he was walking into the hotel reception at this very moment and Idunn would find herself throwing a teetotal party for three in her room. The idea made her sick to the stomach. 'Look, you've got to go. I'm not going back to Reykjavík this evening, anyway. So just go home. This is a single room and you can't stay here.'

'I'm not going home. I've already told you that.'

Idunn dimly recalled that during her self-pitying rant Alexandra had described a fight with her parents. Something about them refusing to buy her a flat in Reykjavík on the grounds that she was too young to leave home and far too young to live alone in the city. 'You can always go home, Alexandra,' Idunn said. 'It's not like we're living in the Viking age, when families had feuds. People make up.' Then she tried softening her tone in case a gentler approach would have the desired effect. 'Anyway, you need to finish school, take your leaving exams. Not quit with half the year still to go.'

The hurt expression on Alexandra's face made her look even younger than she was. The mascara, lipstick and plucked eyebrows seemed incongruous with her childish features. 'But I've already passed my leaving exams,' she protested. 'Back in December. I invited you to my party but you never replied. You didn't even bother to read my message, any more than the others I've sent you. You—'

Alexandra was interrupted by a loud knocking on the door. Idunn leapt to her feet, hoping the powers that be had sent someone to rescue her from this situation. It turned out to be Karó.

'We've finished supper and we're about to have a quick meeting. Ína's here with her people. Do you want to come along? Your food's still on the table, by the way.'

As a rule, Idunn was no great fan of meetings, but this one was a heaven-sent opportunity and she'd have gone along even if it had been about some tedious update to the privacy laws. 'I'll be down in five.' She had only opened the door a crack, to prevent Karó from seeing inside, but this precaution proved futile since Alexandra now came up behind her and yanked the door wide open.

'Hi!' Alexandra insinuated herself into the gap beside Idunn, holding out her hand and introducing herself, adding that she and Idunn were sisters.

As Karó took Alexandra's outstretched hand, Idunn made a valiant attempt to control her features. Underneath, she was seething with rage. When Karó smiled and commented on the strong family resemblance, it was the final straw. Idunn and this half-sister of hers had nothing in common, least of all their looks. 'I'll be down in a minute, Karó,' Idunn said crisply. She shut the door and rounded on her sister as soon as she thought Karó was out of earshot. 'I don't want to find you here when I get back from my meeting. Go home.'

The food and wine had met each other halfway, so to speak, as the fish was now cold and the wine warm. But Idunn didn't let this stop her from emptying both her plate and her glass while she was listening to the briefing. Little of what was said had any direct relevance to her, since it was mainly about assigning the various jobs that needed doing. But she pricked up her ears when the talk turned to the chances of them making it back to Reykjavík the following day. When the inspector explained that the outlook was bleak, Idunn drained her glass. And when Ína added that if the forecast was correct, it was pretty much out of the question, Idunn waved to the waiter and ordered another glass. Apparently, the prospect didn't look good for the day after either. Idunn wasn't the only person to groan at this point.

No sooner had the waiter placed a new glass in front of Idunn than Ína finally directed a question at her. Not the best timing but it couldn't be helped. The inspector wanted to know whether, following her initial examination of the bodies, Idunn felt able to shed any light on the circumstances, the cause of death or the identity of the victims. Ína was in fact perfectly up to speed with what had emerged from Idunn's examination of the intact body, but apparently she would rather those present heard it directly from the horse's mouth. Before the meeting, the inspector had thanked Idunn for allowing her to observe, and Idunn had asked in return how Ína's mother was doing. Praise and thanks invariably made her squirm and she preferred to deflect them if possible. What's more, she suspected that the inspector's concern for her mother had been no more than a pretext. Ína had replied briefly that her mother was fine. Apparently she hadn't been answering her calls because she had unwittingly muted her phone. Idunn wished privately that her own mother would do the same. Messages from her were piling up in Idunn's inbox.

She embarked on a dry enumeration of the facts. 'I can't say much at this point. There were no visible injuries that could explain the cause of death – on either body. That said, the female sitting among the rocks did display marks on her ribcage consistent with an attempt to administer CPR, though they could have a different explanation. At any rate, it's clear that if she died sitting up, it wasn't due to the attempt at resuscitation, because CPR is only performed with the subject lying flat on their back. But I can't say anything conclusive about the nature of the marks at this stage. With regard to the time of death, it looks to me as if the woman died only hours before we arrived at the scene, and I should perhaps mention that the timing of the car crash, according to the emergency line records, would fall within that period. But my calculations are based on the assumption that the woman died in situ, in the open air, rather than indoors somewhere and that she was subsequently moved. That's it, although it may be worth noting that the woman had nothing in her pockets except chewing gum. There was a noticeable odour of menthol from her mouth, which could be linked to the gum, but could equally have another explanation, possibly even relating to the cause of death. I took a blood sample which will be sent off for analysis. We'll know more in due course.'

All eyes were on Idunn as she continued: 'With regard to the body on the bonfire, I can say very little because it's so badly damaged. The time and cause of death are both unclear. The clothing has been reduced to burnt tatters fused to the skin, but I did glimpse some small pieces of metal on the torso, possibly the remains of a zip. They were lying too high up to have belonged to a pair of trousers. I also saw signs of similar bits of metal on the chest, so it's conceivable the victim was wearing a zip-up jacket. They don't appear to have been wearing shoes, though; at least, I'd have expected to see the remains of the shoes on the feet if they had been. Similarly, I couldn't detect any trace of clothes on the underside of the body, but as it was lying on its back, the fabric could have burnt to ashes or the remnants could have dropped into the fire. Any plastic buttons would have melted. And if there was anything in the pockets that could have helped with identification, that's been destroyed too. All I can say is that I'm hoping to be able to provide more substantial findings post the MRI scan and autopsy. Which obviously won't be any time soon.'

The police inspector nodded, her expression sombre. 'Would you be able to perform a post-mortem on the body that's still here at the hospital? To hurry things along?'

'Well, there's no legal requirement about where a post-mortem has to take place,' Idunn replied, 'so it's conceivable. But you'd need to request permission from the next of kin. And that's going to be a bit tricky, seeing as we don't have an ID on the victim yet. In cases like this, a court order is required.'

'It won't come to that. We'll find out who the victim is and get permission from the family.' The inspector sounded sure of herself. Idunn thought this was partly from an unshakeable belief in the investigative process, partly an attempt to boost morale. Everyone present was tired and dispirited after a long day. No fingerprints had been found on the petrol can, so they had little, if anything, to go on; only two victims who had yet to be named.

Idunn shrugged. 'Assuming you can get permission, it's possible I could perform the post-mortem here. The other one will have to wait until I get back to Reykjavík, though, as there's no one else qualified to do it. But we may have more information about the body tomorrow if they get a move on with the scan. They don't need me for that.' Idunn had already decided to send the burnt body for an MRI scan. Since this would have to be done before she wielded her scalpel, it would be as well to get it out of the way now, while she was marooned in the islands. 'But I didn't bring any instruments with me,' she continued, 'so I hope there's a good DIY store here, or the post-mortem will have to wait.'

Most of those present looked puzzled, as if they thought she'd finally lost the plot. Perhaps they pictured her sawing up the body on a workbench. Or even in her hotel room. 'I need tools that I doubt they'll be able to supply at the hospital,' she elaborated. 'I mean, obviously they'll have scalpels but I'll need more. Saws, shears and so on.'

The inspector grimaced and hastily changed the subject. 'We've received an update on Ásta, the woman who crashed her car near the scene. She's been operated on and is being kept in an induced coma for the time being. The doctors still don't know if she'll regain consciousness or remain in a coma when they try to revive her tomorrow. We'll just have to wait and see. However, her clothes stank of smoke, so they're currently being analysed. It would be a pretty big coincidence if she'd been near some other bonfire apart from the one on the beach. Until we learn otherwise, we should assume she's linked to the incident in some way. Perhaps only as a witness. Perhaps as the killer. Or a third victim, trying to escape. If nothing else, she might be able to provide us with the names of the deceased.'

This time Idunn suppressed the urge to ask what had happened to the dog.

As the investigators were either from the islands or temporarily stranded here, there was nothing to prevent them from taking a closer look into the injured woman's circumstances. According to the inspector, the wrecked car had been towed to a garage. It might contain evidence that would shed light on the case, provided the woman had been involved somehow. But since she was alive – for the moment, at least – there was no role for Idunn in all this. If she didn't get authorisation to conduct an autopsy on the intact body, she faced a day or two of enforced idleness, spending every waking hour plagued with anxiety about accidentally bumping into her father. The thought was unendurable. 'You didn't answer my question,' she broke in. 'About the DIY shop. Can I buy tools here in the islands?'

Inspector Ína turned back to her, evidently not too pleased at being interrupted mid-flow. But she was a polite woman. 'I wasn't sure if you were being serious. But yes, you can. The shop opens at nine tomorrow morning. Or possibly ten.'

Idunn thanked her and scribbled down the address. Then she tried to focus on the meeting, though admittedly this became increasingly difficult as the level in her glass went down. Not that it mattered much, since the dry recital of the facts available so far was of zero relevance to her.

The meeting broke up at last. Idunn exchanged a few words with Karó and Týr. Then, feeling the conversation had gone on long enough, abruptly rose to her feet and said goodnight. She was tired and wanted to make herself scarce before Karó started asking questions about Alexandra. Her half-sister was the last thing Idunn was in the mood to talk about right now. Complicated, painful and sordid family secrets were best kept locked away; there was no call to discuss them with all and sundry.

Outside her room, Idunn closed her eyes in a brief but fervent prayer that Alexandra had obeyed, gone home and stopped kidding herself that she was going to move in with her sister. If not, Idunn thought, she would threaten to call the police and have her forcibly ejected from her hotel room. Alexandra need never know that the threat was hollow: the very last thing Idunn wanted was to draw the attention of the local police to her private affairs. Still, with any luck her room would be empty and she wouldn't have to resort to bluffing. She opened the door.

Inside, she was met by Alexandra, smiling from ear to ear. 'Hi!'

Idunn clung to the door handle, wondering whether to close it again, go downstairs and book herself a different room. Then she spotted her camera – in her sister's hands. 'What are you doing?' she exclaimed in tones of outrage.

'Nothing.' Alexandra put the camera down on the bed. 'I was bored. I was only looking. I haven't damaged it.'

Idunn snatched it up. 'This is my work camera. You'd better not have been taking pictures of yourself.'

'Taking pictures of myself? Selfies, you mean? With this clunky thing? You've got to be kidding.'

Idunn didn't trust her: the camera had been switched on. Peering at the little screen, she expected to be confronted with Alexandra's face, wearing a pout and a wide-eyed look. But she was wrong. Idunn met her sister's eye. 'Have you been looking at the pictures on here? Are you out of your mind? They're part of a murder investigation. They're not for posting on Instagram.'

'But . . .' Alexandra looked remorseful. 'My phone was out of battery and your charger lead is the wrong kind. I was bored, so I decided to see what you'd been photographing. I didn't know it was your work camera.'

Idunn glanced back at the screen and noticed that the shot wasn't the last she had taken at the scene. 'I see you've scrolled through them in spite of that, long after you must have realised they weren't snaps of my Christmas holiday.'

'I did realise. But I just couldn't stop myself. I've never seen anything like that before. Never seen a dead person, only dead fish.'

Idunn rolled her eyes. Yet part of her understood what had compelled her sister to keep scrolling. Horror has its allure – for those who are unaccustomed to it and don't have to cope with the fallout.

'Sorry. I'll forget everything I saw.' Alexandra hesitated. 'Only . . .'

'Only what?'

'I don't think I'll be able to forget the woman I recognised.'

'The woman you recognised?' The only pictures on the camera were from the scene Idunn was currently working on. She always wiped her memory card clean as soon as she had downloaded the photos onto her hard drive at work. Which meant there was only one woman it could be, since there was no way Alexandra could have recognised the burnt body. Idunn scrolled to a photo of the dead woman sitting by the rock, in which her frozen features were clearly visible. She turned the screen to her half-sister. 'This one?'

Alexandra looked at the picture and nodded. 'Yes. I've seen her before. But I'll try to forget I saw the photo. I promise.'

Chapter 9
Day 2 – Friday, 24 January

An eerie atmosphere met them in the deserted house. There was a thin layer of dust over everything in the hall and a cobweb in one corner. The lightbulb, in keeping with its surroundings, emitted only a feeble yellow glow. It was like being invited to a Halloween party, Trausti thought. All that was missing was a pumpkin and a plastic bat dangling from the ceiling.

An untidy heap of post, newspapers, advertising flyers and magazines covered the floor inside. As they collected them up, they kept an eye out for anything that might be connected to Gugga's illness, but they couldn't spot any correspondence from the University Hospital on the mainland or the local one here in the Westman Islands; no invoices from A&E or for X-rays of broken bones; no envelopes bearing the logo of an insurance company either, which you'd have expected if Gugga had been involved in a car crash or work-related accident. But this didn't necessarily mean anything, as those letters could have arrived earlier or been sent by email.

Inside, they found a very ordinary home. No designer furniture, artworks by big names or expensive household appliances. But no cheap tat either. The furnishings fell somewhere between these two extremes. A typical middle-class home, furnished well before the millennium. Tidy, but neither minimalist nor fussily overdone. No doubt the owners had gone out of their way to make it cosy, yet in spite of that the atmosphere was unsettling; a feeling no doubt arising from the knowledge that the people who had lived here were all dead. Their house would be sold, their home broken up, their possessions scattered to the four winds, the majority no doubt ending up at the dump or a charity shop. It was almost like travelling back in time. Outside, life went on, but in here it had stopped. The dead pot plants were evidence of that. It appeared that the old neighbour, Halldóra, had given up watering them – perhaps when Gugga died. Because what would be the point? If no one wanted second-hand possessions, it would be hard to find a home for an overgrown yucca plant.

It was all so depressing that Trausti would have given anything to be outside in the open air.

They walked through the rooms, one by one, inspecting the possessions Gugga and her father had accumulated over the years. Trausti didn't know which was worse: the things that had obviously been Gugga's, like the colourful half-knitted jumper on the sofa, or the ones that must have belonged to her father. There were model ships all over the house and most of the walls were hung with rather mediocre paintings of boats. Trausti thought it unlikely that these had been Gugga's. At least, he couldn't remember her taking any interest in the sea or fishing during her student days. The furniture and the books on the shelves looked as though they'd been chosen by her parents too. He spotted the *Emergency Callout* collection, a series about daring sea rescues, and countless other titles relating to ships or fishing, none of which would serve as a fitting memento of Gugga. But this didn't prevent Leifur from picking up the largest of the model ships as if intending to walk off with it.

'You can't take that.' Even the normally quiet Ragga was plainly shocked by the inappropriateness of his behaviour. 'It's part of a collection. It might have been left to someone in a will.'

'But we were given a key and Trausti was told we could take anything.' Leifur tightened his grip on the model.

'We were invited to take something to remember Gugga by. That ship doesn't count.'

Sigga, it seemed, agreed with Ragga. She went over to Leifur, carefully removed the model from his arms and put it back in its place. 'Don't be an idiot. Do you want us to be charged with theft?'

Leifur shrugged and they continued their exploration, though Trausti noticed him casting a covetous glance at another model on a chest in the bedroom hallway.

All the doors opening off the hall were shut. The first they tried turned out to be the workshop where Gugga's father had built his models. There was a half-finished ship on the table, surrounded by tools, pieces of wood and sawdust. Above it on a shelf was a jar of paintbrushes; the liquid it had once contained had evaporated, leaving behind a matt residue. A faint smell of turpentine lingered in the air. They closed the door, as there was nothing for them in there.

In the bathroom, on the other hand, most of the contents seemed to have belonged to Gugga, which was no surprise, given that her father had died two years previously. Although Gugga had left his workshop untouched, it would have been odd if she hadn't removed his razor and other items from in here. There were various lotions and cosmetics on the counter by the sink, as well as a brush containing a lot of long mousy hair, enough for a fair-sized clump. Ari picked up the brush, turning it over in his hands. 'That's a sign of cancer, isn't it? Losing your hair?'

They all looked to Trausti for his medical opinion. 'Yes, if she was having chemo.'

Sigga took the brush from Ari and examined it. 'This is just like my brush and I'm not on chemo. If you have long hair, it's not unusual to shed some.'

Leifur made a face. 'Ugh. How about cleaning your brush after you use it, Sigga?'

She answered by tapping him with the brush and he recoiled as if she'd thrown a sick bag at him. 'Now you're going to get nits,' she mocked. 'Better change your T-shirt.'

While they were bickering, Ari opened the cabinet on the wall beside the mirror. 'Whoa!' he said.

Trausti, standing in the doorway behind the others due to lack of space, could nevertheless see what had elicited Ari's reaction. The cabinet contained three shelves, one of which was crammed with all kinds of pills.

The others moved aside to let Trausti through. He picked up each packet, bottle and blister pack in turn, reading their names as the others stood by in silence for once. After replacing the last one, he looked round at them. To him it was obvious that if Gugga had been to rehab for drug addiction, the treatment hadn't worked. But he didn't want to say so aloud out of consideration for her. After all, it was no longer relevant. He frowned, wondering how best to sum up what he had deduced from the stash of pills. 'There's not much here to indicate cancer,' he said eventually. 'They're mostly strong painkillers, antidepressants, sleeping pills and so on. You might expect some of these to be prescribed for patients who are critically ill, but not in these quantities.' When nobody said anything, he continued: 'Some could have been prescribed by a doctor to alleviate the sufferings of a cancer patient, but there are no drugs here of the kind you'd normally expect to see if someone had pancreatic cancer or was undergoing treatment. I'd have thought there should be anti-nausea medication, for example. And Valtrex to prevent shingles. But there's nothing like that here. I suppose it's always possible that she took them with her when she was admitted to hospital, though.'

Ari stared into the cabinet. 'No cancer medicine? You know – the kind that makes people's hair fall out?'

'Chemo, you mean? No. But that's usually administered intravenously. In hospital. So that's not necessarily significant.'

Sigga folded her arms across her chest. 'What about broken bones? Could she have been taking painkillers for those?'

'Well, yes and no. There are far too many pills and the doses are way too strong. I can't see how antidepressants would fit in with that scenario either. They would be more consistent with cancer, especially the aggressive kind. But, of course, she could have had mental health issues, unrelated to whatever it was that killed her.'

'So, in other words, you're saying she could have had cancer or broken every bone in her body? Or neither?' Sigga sounded exasperated and again Trausti felt like a witness she was cross-examining. He didn't bother to respond, as he'd already made it abundantly clear that the medicine cabinet didn't provide the information they were after.

They filed out of the bathroom, closing the door behind them. There were two doors left, both of which led to bedrooms. One had obviously belonged to Gugga, the other to her father. None of them had any desire to enter the latter's room. It was plain that nobody had slept in there for a long time and, in any case, they had no interest in Gugga's late father. Ari and Leifur were reluctant to linger in Gugga's room. They merely stepped in, glanced around, then backed out again, saying that being in Gugga's bedroom made them feel like perverts.

That left Trausti, Sigga and Ragga. None of them knew exactly what they were supposed to be doing or evinced any desire to start opening drawers or rummaging through shelves. They just stood there without speaking, surveying the room. It was so small that there wasn't much to see. A single bed, neatly made, stood against one wall. Trausti guessed it had been Gugga's when she was a girl. No adult would buy themselves a single bed nowadays. The white-painted desk also appeared to date from her adolescence, judging by the name of a long-forgotten band, popular fifteen years ago, written in felt pen on the top. Each ornamental letter had been carefully drawn in a different colour. Trausti felt a brief pang for those days of being young and impressionable. Like most people, he had long ago ceased to be filled with the kind of passionate enthusiasm that drove one to express it by scribbling on the furniture.

On the desk was a laptop, a pile of loose papers and some writing materials. Trausti plugged in the laptop, opened it and turned it on. But it was password protected so he couldn't get in and look around for any information of interest.

A book lay face down on the bedside table, open at the point Gugga had reached. She'd almost finished it when she left this room for the last time. There was also a wardrobe and a large bookcase containing a variety of books and ornaments.

'We'll have to take something.' Sigga broke the silence. 'Or it's like we only came here to snoop. If nothing else, we need to be able to tell the neighbour what we chose when we return the key to her.'

Trausti hadn't planned to do anything but hand the woman the key with his thanks. In his opinion there was no call for them to report back to her on what they'd taken. Especially as he didn't actually want anything. Sigga had always been an expert at over-complicating things, interpreting situations in a way that subsequently hardened into fact, at least in her own mind. Aware of this, he had the sense not to contradict her. Instead, he considered taking a pen from the desk, just to placate her.

'And we'll need to put some thought into our choices,' Sigga continued. 'So we can tell her why we took what we did.'

So much for his idea of settling for a pen. He didn't have the imagination to come up with a plausible explanation for why he would associate Gugga with a cheap, mass-produced biro. He followed the girls to the bookcase and watched Sigga open a white jewellery box. It contained necklaces, including a silver cross, a heart and other pendants hanging from slender gold or silver chains. Several rings too, some of them no doubt Confirmation presents. Trausti couldn't remember Gugga ever wearing jewellery.

In one of the compartments there was something white, wrapped in clingfilm. Ignoring the jewellery, Sigga lifted it out and unwrapped the clingfilm to sniff at the contents. 'Whoops.' She wrapped it up again and stuck it in her pocket.

'Is that what you're choosing?' Trausti asked. Maybe he'd get away with taking a pen after all.

'No. I'm just removing them so they don't accidentally fall into the hands of some kid. Or I might keep them. But not in memory of Gugga.' She gave him a withering look. 'Don't pretend you don't know what they are.'

But Trausti didn't know; he hadn't got a proper glimpse. It was Ragga – ever direct – who came to his rescue: 'They're joints.' While Sigga was still looking scornful, Ragga turned to Trausti and asked: 'Isn't cannabis supposed to help alleviate the pain associated with cancer?'

'Some people claim that. But since most users don't have cancer, that doesn't really tell us anything about Gugga's illness.'

Sigga went on rootling around in the jewellery box. She removed the top tray, revealing a large compartment underneath, which contained more than just cheap costume jewellery. There was a light-brown lock of hair, tied with a yellowing ribbon that had once been white; a tiny box with a child's milk teeth inside; a small collar with a bell on it that must have belonged to a cat, and various other treasures. A few photos, too, of a woman holding a little girl, presumably Gugga. It didn't take a genius to guess that the woman was her dead mother. There was another picture of the same woman in a white bridal gown with a bouquet of flowers, standing next to a man in a black suit. Presumably Gugga's parents on their wedding day.

Underneath all these was a small white envelope of the type that would hold a card, perhaps one that had accompanied a gift that had meant a lot to Gugga. Sigga opened it carefully and peered inside, then grimaced and drew out a tiny plastic Ziploc bag that she showed to Trausti and Ragga. In the bottom of the bag was some white powder that Trausti assured them had nothing to do with cancer or broken bones. He wasn't born yesterday.

Sigga licked her finger and dipped it into the bag, but before she could touch the tip of her tongue to the powder, Ragga grabbed her hand. 'Are you crazy? Put it back! It could be anything.'

'Yeah, right. Like what? Rat poison? In a jewellery case?' Sigga's tone was mocking but, even so, when Ragga released her grip she wiped the powder off her finger onto her trouser leg. Then she slipped the bag into her pocket with the cling-film-wrapped joints.

'You'd better be taking that to throw it away. Promise me you'll throw it away,' Ragga said. She sounded frantic.

Trausti suspected that Sigga wasn't being sincere when she assented. He watched her replace the upper tray in the box. The click of the lid sounded unnaturally loud in the silent house and Trausti suddenly realised that he couldn't hear any sound from Leifur and Ari. As they weren't usually the self-effacing type, it occurred to him that they might have lost interest and gone to sit outside on the doorstep. He felt a strong urge to follow their example. The air inside the house was stale as the windows obviously hadn't been opened for ages and the stuffiness was getting to him. Sensing the beginnings of a headache, Trausti thought the sooner he got out of there, the better.

'There's nothing here from the time when we knew Gugga.' Sigga went over to the wardrobe and opened it. 'Like we'd be interested in her Confirmation presents or sticker books from when she was a kid.'

Trausti thought privately that none of Gugga's worldly goods had any relevance to them. But he didn't voice this opinion aloud, just watched as Sigga peered inside the wardrobe. Neither he nor Ragga made any move to go over and see what she'd found. He had no interest in women's clothes, especially not clothes that had belonged to a dead person. The girls seemed to have forgotten the whole purpose of their visit, which had been to find out what had been wrong with Gugga and could have led to her death. When they'd failed to find an easy answer to that question, they had become distracted.

It seemed that Ragga was thinking the same as him: 'Why don't we just take a necklace each? They're not valuable heirlooms but they're not embarrassingly inappropriate either. Haven't we seen enough?'

Sigga muttered something and reached up to the shelf above the tightly packed hangers on the clothes rail. She brought down what appeared to be a heavy cardboard box, then turned to them with a look of triumph. 'There you go! Marked "University of Iceland". What were you two complaining about?'

Trausti relieved her of the dusty box and set it down on the desk. Judging from the weight, it must be full of books, presumably textbooks in which whole paragraphs had been marked with yellow highlighter. If so, the box was a godsend. He could just grab a textbook, thereby fulfilling his duty to select a memento, then go and join Ari and Leifur outside. The subject of the book was irrelevant. If Ragga and Sigga wanted to carry on searching for something more suitable, that was up to them.

He turned out to be right. The box contained textbooks and several spiral-bound notebooks or diaries, labelled with the years when they'd been at university, including one from the year when Gugga had dropped out of her degree – the year when everything had fallen apart. He lifted them out to get at the thicker, more substantial textbooks underneath, and was still holding them when Ari appeared in the doorway. There was a wild expression on his face and he gripped the door frame with both hands, as if to stop himself from falling.

'You need to see what we've found in the cellar.'

Chapter 10
Day 5 – Monday, 27 January

Idunn listened as Alexandra repeated her story about the woman who had been found dead on the beach. The girl seemed to be enjoying herself more now that she was surrounded by gravely attentive police officers than when she'd had an audience of one furious half-sister. She was making an effort to provide a coherent account and, oddly enough, this grated on Idunn even more than if the girl had made a hash of it. From time to time, though, Alexandra would sweep her hair back from her face with an exaggerated hand gesture, tilt her head coyly on one side or blink with heavily mascaraed lashes, reminding Idunn that her opinion of her half-sister wasn't that wide of the mark.

She'd had to grit her teeth as she introduced Alexandra to the group who had stayed on after the meeting. When the girl had appeared behind her during supper, Idunn had immediately whisked her away, which must have seemed odd to the others, especially as she hadn't referred to the incident in the meeting afterwards. This time, Idunn had tried to gloss over the nature of their relationship, merely introducing the girl by name and explaining that she was a local. But Alexandra had chipped in proudly that they were sisters. This had provoked Idunn into blurting out that they were actually only half-sisters – with the emphasis on *half*. The moment she'd said it, Karó and Týr flashed her odd looks, and she felt the blood rushing to her cheeks. She wasn't usually this petty but she was mortified at having her private family affairs on display like this.

She had every right to be annoyed. Thanks to Alexandra's nosiness, she couldn't get away with a brief introduction. Instead, she'd been forced to explain that Alexandra had seen a photo of the dead woman on her camera. It had been an unforgivable breach of protocol. Members of the public – even if they were related to investigators – were not supposed to have access to evidence of any kind. Idunn couldn't even plead extenuating circumstances as she had left her camera lying around in full view. So far, though, it seemed she was the only one who regarded this as a disgrace. Inspector Ína hadn't even given her a disapproving glance when Idunn explained what had happened.

'So, you saw this woman here in the town? And she came over to speak to you?' The man who asked was one of the CSIs from Reykjavík. He had already asked a number of questions but apparently needed to hear everything twice.

'Yes. Like I said, she came out of a house on Túngata. This was on Friday. Just before seven. And she was with some other people. Another woman and three men. Or it may have been two. I'm not quite sure. They didn't come over.'

'And you're certain she's not local?'

The Westman Islanders in the group smiled at this. Heimaey was the only inhabited island and the town had a population of just over four and a half thousand people, most of whom knew each other by sight. But Alexandra merely answered politely: 'Yes. Quite certain. I've never seen her before. And she was asking the way. If you live here, you know your way around.' There was no hint of sarcasm in her voice. 'Unless she'd only just moved here. Or one of her friends had. The woman who used to live in the house died recently, so maybe one of them has bought it.'

This part of the story was new to Idunn. All Alexandra had told her was that she'd seen some people coming out of a house on Túngata. Perhaps this was proof of the persistent questioner's shrewdness. It seemed witnesses were like tubes of toothpaste and you could always squeeze out a smidgen more, long after you thought they were empty.

A local police officer chipped in at this point: 'I know the place you're talking about. It hasn't been sold yet but there's going to be an open house for prospective buyers on Thursday. Maybe the people you saw were being given a sneak preview.' He added, slightly sheepishly: 'My wife and I are house-hunting.'

Týr, who had been listening in thoughtful silence, now spoke up: 'You said you'd noticed the people and had been watching them when the woman came over to speak to you. Was there something unusual about their behaviour or appearance that attracted your attention?'

'Yes, there was. They were acting really strangely.'

'In what way?'

Alexandra paused to think. 'Their behaviour just seemed so weird. They burst out of the house like it was on fire, almost falling out of the door. One guy had his hand over his mouth like he was about to throw up. Or that's what it looked like to me. Maybe he was just trying to stop himself laughing.' She paused, then went on: 'When they saw me watching, the woman came over and asked where they could find a bakery. But she hesitated before she said "bakery", like she was trying to think of what to ask. The whole thing was really strange.'

Idunn wondered if the toothpaste tube that was her half-sister had been reduced to producing hot air now, because none of these details had been in the account Alexandra had given her a few minutes earlier. And witness statements were notoriously unreliable. People's experiences were influenced by a number of factors, and memories could easily become confused. Then again, Idunn hadn't waited to ask any questions, just chivvied Alexandra downstairs to pass on the information to the others. Perhaps the girl's story hadn't changed and Idunn had only heard the main points up in her room.

'Did you see where they went after that? Was it in the direction of the bakery?'

Alexandra shook her head. 'They got in a car, but they didn't drive away. I looked back before I went round the corner at the end of the street. They were just sitting there. They weren't on their way to any bakery. I think . . . I had a feeling they were just waiting until I was out of sight.'

Ína took out her phone, tapped at it, then handed it to Alexandra. 'Was this woman one of them?' The picture on screen was of the woman in the car crash.

Alexandra shook her head. 'No. Though I recognise her. I can't remember her name but she's local. She definitely wasn't one of them.' Alexandra handed the phone back. 'Anna? Is her name Anna?'

'No. Ásta.' The inspector returned her phone to her pocket.

There were a few more questions, mostly relating to the car. Had Alexandra seen it before? Did she happen to notice the number plate and could she remember it? To which the answers were no, no and no. Asked if she remembered what type of car it had been, she said simply: 'A white car'. Since no manufacturer yet had been enough of a genius to use this as a brand name, the questions kept coming. Was it a saloon car, an SUV, a two-door, four-door or estate car? The conclusion was that it was almost certainly an estate car. With an unspecified number of doors – though minimum two, of course.

The inspector, apparently agreeing with Idunn that this was enough, forestalled any further questions. 'Thank you very much, Alexandra. We'll be in touch tomorrow and get you over to the station to give a formal statement. And maybe also to look at footage of vehicles that arrived recently on the ferry. You might recognise the car when you see it.' If Alexandra could identify the vehicle, they would be able to read the number plate and the follow-up should be easy.

Ína took Alexandra's phone number, then asked her to pass on her greetings to her father. Of course she did, Idunn thought bitterly. Of course the inspector knew who Alexandra's father was. And if she hadn't already been aware that Idunn was the daughter of one of the biggest trawler operators in the islands, she was now. Ína must realise that Idunn and Alexandra couldn't possibly share a mother: Idunn's father had traded in his wife for a younger model, and his new wife would have been at primary school when Idunn was born. Idunn had never met her; she'd been invited to the wedding but her own mother had ripped the invitation to shreds the size of its component atoms. Not that her mother blamed the new wife for her divorce: she was a local girl from the Westman Islands, whereas the hated mistress had lived in Reykjavík. But this fact hadn't made any difference to Idunn's mother's bitterness about the wedding.

The local police now headed off, vanishing into the storm that was raging outside, and the CSI team retired to their hotel rooms. That left Idunn, Alexandra, Karó and Týr. Idunn was prepared to wait the others out, then see to it that Alexandra went home: she had no intention of having this discussion in front of witnesses. But Týr and Karó showed no signs of going anywhere. Alexandra didn't budge either, just stood there with them, as if she found it perfectly natural that she should be part of the team. Idunn wouldn't have been surprised if her half-sister had started sharing investigation tips with them, picked up from crime series she'd seen on TV. But the girl didn't go that far, just contented herself with gazing at Týr and Karó in turn, and nodding from time to time.

Idunn wasn't sure what her colleagues made of this, though she suspected that they were merely waiting politely for her to get rid of Alexandra. Until, that is, Týr turned to the girl and asked if she had known the owner of the house the group had come tumbling out of.

'No. Not really. The woman who lived there had been away on the mainland for years. She was the daughter of the old couple who used to own the house, but she was much older than me and didn't have a job, so you never really saw her around. I heard she was a bit weird, actually.'

'In what way?'

'She never said hello to anyone and didn't seem to want to live here. She used to smoke joints openly in the garden. She'd just sit there, staring at the cemetery across the road. That kind of weird. I don't understand why she didn't just move back to Reykjavík. That's what I'd have done in her situation. But her father was a weirdo as well, apparently, so maybe it ran in the family. Maybe the people I saw were related to them and crazy too.'

As Idunn didn't want to encourage Alexandra to linger, she refrained from pointing out that being eccentric didn't run in families. Instead, she returned the smile of the barman who was back in his place. He raised the bottle of white wine with an enquiring lift of his eyebrows and Idunn nodded. She definitely needed another glass and felt a little more human once she had one in her hands. And even better after the first mouthful.

The second didn't slip down quite as smoothly because Alexandra started to speak just as Idunn was on the point of swallowing: 'I can help you, if you like. Ask around about the woman. I know everyone in town.'

Týr's answer saved Idunn from choking on her wine. 'Er, thanks but don't worry; the police have got that covered. It's kind of you to offer, though.'

This had gone far enough; Idunn would have to intervene. 'I think you should go home now, Alexandra,' she said. 'You'll need to give a statement tomorrow morning and this storm's not going to get any better. You don't want to get trapped here at the hotel.'

Instead of looking awkward and hurrying off home, Alexandra said, undaunted: 'No. I'm staying here, remember? I'm coming to Reykjavík with you guys.'

The silence that fell in the aftermath of this statement tested the resolve of both sisters. In the end, Idunn was forced to admit defeat. It was her colleagues' obvious discomfort that did it. They couldn't help noticing the sisters' strained exchange and fake smiles. Clearly Alexandra didn't give a damn what they thought – but Idunn did. And this lost her the battle.

But not the war. Over her dead body were they going to share a room. Ordering Alexandra to come with her, Idunn went to reception and booked the girl a room. The expense meant nothing to her. She was on a good salary and had few outgoings, so the balance in her account only grew at the beginning of every month. Besides, she thought, her money had rarely been better spent than on getting rid of her half-sister. Even if it was only for the rest of the evening.

Alexandra entered the lift, smiled at Idunn and wished her goodnight, then asked what time they should meet for breakfast. Luckily the doors closed as she spoke, sparing Idunn the necessity of answering. Raising her glass, Idunn toasted her own reflection in the shiny steel doors. A bleep from her phone announced that Alexandra had followed up her question with a message, but it didn't cross Idunn's mind to read it.

Týr and Karó were waiting in the restaurant. They stopped talking when Idunn walked in. She pretended not to notice and offered no explanation for the scene with her half-sister. As far as she was concerned, family matters were best kept hidden away at the back of a drawer. A locked drawer. It may have been broken into, but that was a temporary blip. It wouldn't be a problem to shut them away again – as soon as she was out of here.

'We've got to get back to Reykjavík tomorrow evening,' Idunn said in a heartfelt tone. Then, without waiting for her colleagues' reactions, she changed the subject: 'What do you make of the people she saw?'

Týr shrugged. 'It's a good start. But all it really tells us is that the victims were here in town. Or at least the woman who was found sitting by the rocks was. But we knew that already. I mean, in what universe would a perpetrator go to the trouble of transporting the bodies to a spot as small and remote as Heimaey in order to dispose of them? It's probably a bad idea to start talking out of my arse at this stage, but I'd be very surprised if the killer or killers weren't the men Alexandra saw.'

Karó agreed: 'Absolutely. If not, surely they'd have reported that two members of their party were missing?'

'What about Ásta, though – the woman in the car crash?' Idunn asked. 'She could be our killer. She's local, and according to Alexandra she wasn't part of the group. We can't take it for granted that the perpetrator was one of them.' Idunn felt it was worth reminding them of this. She had pointed out during the meeting that Ásta had probably been in the area when the woman on the beach died, but she'd got the feeling that the others had dismissed this as purely hypothetical. Which was true, of course. The time frame for the death was still wide open.

Týr and Karó conceded that this was a possibility, but that did nothing to deter them from coming up with wild theories. The investigation had barely got off the ground yet and they knew next to nothing apart from the fact that two people had been found dead in bizarre circumstances. Karó seemed to read Idunn's mind: 'Is there any chance the other victim could have ended up on the fire by accident?'

Týr frowned. 'How do you mean? That it was a just a bon-fire and someone had the bad luck to fall into it?' He smiled. 'Maybe the woman sitting by the rocks witnessed the acci-dent, had a heart attack and dropped dead. Case closed.'

Karó was not amused and Idunn sympathised. She didn't enjoy being the butt of sarcasm either, even when it wasn't intended to be malicious. 'Stranger things have happened,' she said. 'But in this instance, I don't believe it was an accident. Not because such a thing couldn't happen, but because, judg-ing by the smell, someone had poured petrol over the body. It's far more likely that they set fire to it with the intention of destroying evidence or because the perpetrator was opti-mistic enough to believe they could make the body disappear. Though I don't for one minute believe that would have worked since the fire wasn't hot enough. I'm also fairly sure the victim was already dead when they were set alight.'

Not long after this, the conversation ran out of steam. With so little information to go on, they were reduced to empty spec-ulation. Karó was the first to announce that she was going to bed and the others followed suit. Idunn tossed back the rest of her wine, wondering if this would be a good moment to ask Týr for a word. Then, reflecting that the wine was bound to have taken the edge off her judgement, she decided to leave it for now. She didn't want him to be misled by the alcohol fumes and slurring speech into dismissing what she was saying as drunken nonsense. It was a good rule of thumb never to have confidential chats when under the influence. The tragic fate of Týr's mother, and Idunn's suspicions that his father had not in fact wielded the axe that had killed her, would have to wait.

Once she was back in her room, she scrolled through the photos from the scene again. They were more interesting than the foreign TV stations that pumped out the same news stories round the clock. The camera screen blunted the true horror by reducing the pictures to tiny images.

She studied them frame by frame in the hope of receiving a revelation that would help her understand what had happened, but it brought her no closer to the truth. She felt confident in her ability to determine the fate of each body separately, as if they were two unrelated cases, but she couldn't connect them. The best she could come up with was that the woman by the rocks had been the killer and that she had taken her own life when she recognised the hopelessness of her situation. By an overdose, at a guess, since there was no evidence that the woman had used a knife, gun or noose.

The main argument against this was that there had been no smell of petrol on the woman's hands, which meant she could hardly have been responsible for igniting the blaze.

In the end, Idunn abandoned the attempt and switched off the camera. Once she was in bed with her eyes closed, she surprised herself with an unexpected thought: it was a mercy the photos on the little camera screen had diminished the horror of the scene since it had spared Alexandra from seeing the worst. Idunn's eyes flicked open in astonishment. This had nothing to do with any feelings of affection for the girl, she assured herself. She would have felt the same with regard to any young person. She didn't care about Alexandra and, when she got back to Reykjavík, her half-sister would vanish from her life again. Satisfied with this conclusion, Idunn closed her eyes and went to sleep.

Chapter 11
Day 2 – Friday, 24 January

Trausti couldn't now recall which of them had been the first to bolt up the cellar stairs, making for the front door. He couldn't remember who had come next either, though he did know that it had only been a fraction of a second before there was a general stampede. Now they were standing on the steps outside the front door, gasping for air. All except Ari, who put his hands on his knees, leant forwards and retched, then clamped a hand over his mouth to stop himself vomiting. No one said anything: words were inadequate to describe what they had just witnessed. Of course, there was no excuse for Trausti, with all his medical training, to have lost his head like that, but he had been just as pathetic as the others, whose jobs largely revolved around paperwork and computers. He didn't know if it was the mass hysteria that had got to him or the predicament they were in, but he was disappointed in himself, to say the least.

The cellar had been cold and dimly lit; the narrow windows high on the walls were shuttered and the only illumination was the brownish glow cast by a dirty, low-watt lightbulb hanging from the ceiling. The dust floating in the air only enhanced the feeling that they were standing in an ancient potato store. That and the musty smell. Why Ari and Leifur had gone down there in the first place was anybody's guess, though Trausti wouldn't put anything past Leifur. Perhaps he'd thought there would be more model ships down there that he could smuggle out to the car without the others noticing. He couldn't have expected to find anything valuable, like a new game console. You only had to peer down the stairs to see that the cellar housed nothing but dusty old junk, the smaller items stored on a rickety set of shelves, the larger ones lined up against the wall.

But what immediately caught Trausti's attention was the long, wooden box or crate, which looked as though it had been roughly knocked together by hand, occupying the middle of the room. Neither Ari nor Leifur could be persuaded to tell the others what was inside; they just pointed towards it with their noses buried in the crooks of their elbows. Trausti, Ragga and Sigga were forced to discover for themselves. At first, they just stood there, staring at the crate, then, after a moment, Sigga prodded Trausti and said: 'You open it.' So it fell to him to lift the lid, which wasn't that unreasonable, seeing as he had the most experience of dealing with grisly sights. He didn't for a moment suspect that all his training would be in vain.

He raised the lid and peered inside. In the feeble illumination of the lightbulb, it took him a while to work out what he was seeing. To begin with, he took the contents for coarse, white sand, but on closer inspection he made out dark shadows that suggested there was something underneath. The surface wasn't as smooth as he'd first thought, either. Whether this was because Ari and Leifur had been digging around in it, he didn't know, but he guessed they must have been, given the violence of their reactions.

Trausti turned and saw that they were hanging back. Noticing how keen they were to stay well clear, he got cold feet. Could there be scorpions or some other poisonous creatures in the sand? That would explain their shock. Leifur was so phobic about spiders that he had once asked Trausti to remove one from his student flat. 'Is there something alive in here?' he asked.

Ari produced a rattling sound in his throat. 'No. Definitely not.' He shuddered, then added: 'Try rummaging around.'

Trausti had 'rummaged around' in various things since starting his medical studies, but always with gloves on, aided by shiny steel instruments. Now, in contrast, his hands were bare and he couldn't bring himself to stick them in the sand. He glanced around in search of a tool he could use, and spotted a hammer. Using the handle, he started pushing the coarse sand aside. The white grains crunched as they rubbed together, in a manner that was oddly unlike sand. He was tempted to pinch a few grains between finger and thumb and rub them together, but he told himself it didn't matter what the substance was, only what it was concealing.

Trausti probed deeper with the handle and soon encountered resistance. He tried to clear away the sand but the grains kept trickling back. Then he struck plastic and unthinkingly grabbed it and eased it out. It turned out to be a freezer bag. It was opaque with age but he could tell that it contained something soft. Not wanting Sigga and Ragga to think he was a wimp or over-fastidious, he unzipped it and peered inside. To his relief, the bag turned out to be stuffed full of blonde hair. Remembering how revolted Leifur had been by the hairbrush upstairs, he guessed that this was what had made the boys retch. Trausti held it up to show the others. 'God, you two are squeamish!'

'Not that.' Leifur pointed impatiently at the crate. 'Just stick your hands in and dig. That's what I did.'

Ragga came to Trausti's rescue. 'But you didn't know in advance that there was something nasty in there. That's hardly the same, is it? Why don't you just put us out of our misery and tell us what to expect?'

Neither Ari nor Leifur answered. Trausti shook his head, held his breath, and got down to work. Turning the hammer round, he used the claw, which proved more effective. This seemed like a good thing – until he uncovered what it was that Ari and Leifur had seen. From the white sand, the lower part of a face emerged – a chin and an open mouth. Trausti recoiled, staggering backwards, then, getting himself under control, he borrowed Ragga's phone and, hand shaking, used the torch to get a better view. He had to be sure he wasn't seeing things; that it really was a person and not some weird dummy or sex doll.

Inside the sand-filled mouth cavity he glimpsed teeth that no self-respecting dummy- or doll manufacturer would have signed off on. Instead of being fixed in the gums they were loose in the mouth, still partly wired together with what appeared to be braces. Hooking the wire with the claw of the hammer, he extracted it from the mouth and saw that he had been right. The teeth, some broken, others missing, were glued to a set of braces. He had only known one person who wore braces, apart from a few classmates when he was in his teens. A chill spread though his veins.

'Find the arm. It's lying against the side of the crate closest to you. Check out the bracelet.' Leifur's voice was hoarse.

Trausti rooted around with the hammer in the place where he judged the arm should be. Immediately encountering an obstacle, he started digging as well as he could. First a thin, desiccated arm appeared, then he saw the wrist. And the bracelet. He stared, transfixed, at the familiar, multicoloured beads, threaded on a cord that encircled the wizened flesh. The hammer dropped from his nerveless fingers. Ragga and

Sigga were standing either side of him and their strangled cries rang in his ears.

It was as if time stood still. Trausti realised he was holding his breath. His heart was pounding in his chest and although he longed to scream, his body refused to follow orders. Even his worst fears hadn't come close to imagining this. Gudrún had been like an invisible presence, overshadowing the entire reunion. He had tried to suppress all thought of her when agreeing to the get-together but her ghost had been there from the moment he met the others again. The Ouija board had brought all these fears to the surface. Now the nightmare had taken physical form.

The next moment, all five of them were charging for the door.

There could be no doubt: the body in the crate belonged to their old friend Gudrún who had vanished from the student residence one January night, six months before she was supposed to graduate in chemistry, and had never been seen again.

For years he had done his best to avoid thinking about her. Now he had no choice but to face his fears.

Gudrún had been from the west of Iceland. She'd never been a fully paid-up member of their gang but had danced around the edges, joining in with some activities but not with others. Considering how loosely she had been associated with them, it was astonishing the way her disappearance had convulsed their world. In the aftermath it had been as if a dark fog had descended on their corridor. Trausti used to catch himself walking rapidly along it, averting his eyes from the door to Gudrún's empty flat. It had been a relief when a fresher had moved in at the start of the new academic year in the autumn. By then, Trausti had been the only one still living there; all his friends had left.

Gudrún had gone missing at the beginning of the last term when they were all still living in the student residence. The remainder of the term had been blighted by sadness and depression, and the formerly fun-loving gang had completely lost their mojo. Gone were any high spirits, inventiveness or desire to shake up their mundane existence. Everything but their studies had been put aside. In Gugga's case, her studies had gone the same way as her social life; instead of burying herself in work like them, she had quit her degree course and moved out. Trausti had always assumed this was connected to the death of her mother, shortly after Gudrún's disappearance, but now that Gudrún's body had turned up here in Gugga's cellar, things appeared in a very different light.

Trausti concentrated on breathing. It was all he was capable of right now. Chest heaving, he scrutinised each of his friends' faces in turn, wondering which of them was behind this. It couldn't be a coincidence. Not when you added it all up: the Ouija board, the old neighbour's account of the visit Gugga had received in hospital, the puzzling vagueness about Gugga's cause of death, and now that macabre thing in the crate. Could they all have conspired to stage an elaborate hoax for his benefit? No. Impossible. He knew a human body when he saw one, whether it was alive or dead. And the thing in the crate was no special effect from a horror film, no prank or stunt. It was a corpse. His friends weren't trained actors; they could never have faked such convincing reactions. But why had they made him touch the crate and the body? Were they trying to incriminate him and make him the fall guy? Had he walked into a trap by coming here?

It was Sigga who eventually broke the silence: 'What *was* that? It can't really be . . . ?' She broke off, her eyes wide and staring. Her gaze flickered to the right, then to the left, then back again, as if searching in vain for something normal to fix on, but the ordinary suburban street offered nothing that could erase the sight in the cellar.

None of them made any move to finish Sigga's sentence. Ari was still retching, Ragga appeared to have fallen into a trance, and Leifur was behaving as if an insect had crawled inside his collar. When he took a brief pause from his shuddering, it wasn't to confirm that it had been Gudrún in the crate. Instead, he said: 'Let's get out of here. Leave. As soon as possible. Get off this bloody island.'

Ragga jerked her chin towards the road, murmuring: 'Act normally. We're being watched. Don't look.'

They all turned in unison to look in the direction she had indicated. A young blonde woman, or perhaps girl, was standing on the pavement on the other side of the street, a few doors down. She was unquestionably staring at them, but then that wasn't surprising. They must have looked like a bunch of lunatics. Leifur began fidgeting again and said in a panicked voice: 'She's seen us. She'll be able to describe us. What are we going to do?'

Level-headed as ever, Ragga took the initiative. 'Try to act normally, for Christ's sake. I'll talk to her.'

'And say what?' Sigga asked.

'Anything. Anything that'll make us seem like ordinary tourists.' Ragga waved to the young woman and set off across the road towards her. The young woman waved back hesitantly, looking as if she was considering running away. But she stayed where she was and waited for Ragga to reach her. They exchanged a few words, then the young woman pointed down the street, apparently giving Ragga directions. After that, Ragga came back to join the others and the young woman continued on her way.

'Come on. Let's get in.' Ragga ushered them impatiently towards the car. As they started to obey, she added: 'I asked where we could find a bakery, so we'll at least have to pretend to be going there. It was all I could think of. She keeps turning round. She's still watching us.'

They climbed into the car, one after the other, and sat there in silence until the young woman had rounded the corner. Before she vanished, she glanced back one last time and saw them sitting, as if turned to stone, in the car that no one had started.

'I can't face going to a bakery.' Ari was no longer retching but his face was drained of colour.

'No one's going to any bakery.' Ragga sounded resolute and angry. 'We're going to sit here and discuss this until we come to a sensible conclusion.'

'Conclusion?' Ari echoed, as if hearing the word for the first time. 'What are you talking about? We all know who it is. That's the conclusion.' He folded his arms across his chest, making a face like a petulant child. 'Let's go. Let's pack up and go home before it's too late. I have absolutely no desire to get mixed up with the police. None whatsoever. I've had my fill of that and I can't go through it again. I work in a bank, for Christ's sake. I won't be doing myself any favours if I keep having to miss meetings because I've got to go and be interviewed by the police. We're not students any longer, with no one giving a shit whether we turn up to lectures or not. Fuck. I don't know about you guys but I'm going places at work. There's no way I'm going to jeopardise my chances of promotion. Absolutely no way. Can't you see how bad this will look from the police's point of view?'

Trausti agreed with Ari in one sense. It did look terrible. They had been suspects at the time Gudrún went missing, having been the last people to see her alive on that fateful evening they would all rather forget. But when her body was discovered in the cellar – which it inevitably would be, sooner or later – they would find it hard to explain why they had fled the scene without reporting it. His DNA was bound to be inside or near the crate now – the others,' too. If they really had touched the crate as they claimed . . . Through the car window, he noticed the young woman peering round the corner. She had obviously found them so suspicious that she'd lingered to see what they were up to. He was sure she would remember them when the story of the body in the cellar hit the news. He coughed to get the others' attention. They were also watching the girl, who now finally disappeared from view. 'I vote we ring the police,' he said. 'That *we* do it ourselves. Before that girl has a chance to. It would look much better if we did it first. Why don't we just tell them the truth? That we found the body by chance and haven't a clue how it ended up there. We don't need to say that we believe we know who it is. The police will have to find that out for themselves. If you ask me, it's the least bad option in the circumstances.'

To his surprise, Ragga failed to back him up. She was supposed to be the sensible member of the group. He'd been ready for Leifur, Ari and Sigga to drag their feet, but he'd been sure Ragga at least would see the light.

'We can't ring the police.' She was sitting behind the wheel and now twisted round to meet Trausti's eye. 'None of us can afford to get caught up in a criminal investigation and be constantly forced to dash out of the office to attend interviews, as Ari pointed out. Don't tell me you've forgotten what it was like? And, by the way, didn't you say you had to fly out to America on Monday? Go straight back to work? You can forget about leaving the country if we call the police. It'll take more than half a day for them to deal with this.'

Trausti was silent. He was still shivering with the shock of what had occurred and had to force himself to focus on the here and now. What Ragga said was as reasonable in its way as his own suggestion. Common sense could take different forms; it depended on your point of view. This was one of those moments when he wished life would intervene and settle the question for them. But of course that wasn't going to happen. The street was as quiet as when they'd arrived and there were no signs or portents in the heavens. The police didn't suddenly appear with lights flashing and sirens wailing. Perhaps that in itself was a sign that they should do nothing hasty. Just sit tight. On balance, that was probably the best option. He didn't want to think about what it would mean for his career if he had to call the hospital in America and explain that he wouldn't be back in time for work.

Ragga held out her hand. 'The house key. I'll return it. Where does the woman live?'

As Trausti was trying to fish the key out of his pocket in the cramped conditions of the back seat, Ari grabbed his arm. 'Hang on a minute. Don't give it back just yet. Maybe we should go back inside and destroy any evidence that we were there.'

'I'm not going back in there. Not under any circumstances.' Sigga was breathing raggedly beside Trausti, her voice trembling, near to tears. 'Anyway, how come Gudrún's body isn't a skeleton? We're talking, what? Six . . . no, seven years. What's going on? And how in God's name did the body end up there? Did Gugga bring it over? If she did, where was it before she brought it to the islands?'

Leifur ran his hands agitatedly through his thick mop of hair, scratching his scalp as frantically as if he had nits. 'We don't know. Nobody knows anything about it except Gugga, and she's dead. The answers died with her and we'll never find out now.'

Ragga started the engine. 'Let's go back to Stórhöfdi. Sit down and have some coffee. Or wine. Anything. And try to think this through coolly before we make any rash decisions. Otherwise we'll only make matters worse, as we know to our cost. The decision can wait a bit longer.'

She didn't need to say any more. None of them could object to that. If only they had paused to think before they'd acted seven years ago, they wouldn't be in this mess now. Ragga pulled away, turned out of the street and headed back in the direction of Stórhöfdi.

Chapter 12
Day 6 – Tuesday, 28 January

Although it was crowded in the small house, nobody talked much. Everyone was busy searching for clues that might explain what the dead woman on the beach had been doing here with her companions. The investigators were working on the basis that Alexandra's account had been correct, though there was little evidence so far to support her story. On the other hand, they hadn't found anything to disprove it.

The CSI team had mostly finished on the ground floor and were now occupied with the garden and cellar. They had been sent in as soon as the search warrant came through. A set of keys had been acquired from the estate agent, who said they hadn't lent them out for any private viewings, thereby knocking on the head the idea that the dead woman and her friends had been prospective buyers. Nor was there evidence that anyone had been staying in the house. There were two bedrooms, one with a double bed, the other a single, neither of which had been used recently. The amount of dust on the cover of the double bed suggested that it hadn't been disturbed for a very long time. The single bed, though less dusty, still looked as if it hadn't been slept in for a while.

However, someone had clearly broken in through the back door. And an even more compelling piece of evidence that the woman and her companions had been up to no good was that all the door handles had been wiped clean, along with various other objects and surfaces. In addition, the floors seemed to have been hoovered or swept. The investigators concluded from this that the group, or possibly another individual who'd entered the property subsequently, had wanted to obliterate all trace of their presence. Given the thick layer of dust over everything else, it was hard to come up with any other explanation for the patchy cleaning. Why else would the efforts have been so haphazard – an object here, one section of a table or shelf there? And who in their right mind would wipe the handle of the front door when they left the house?

The CSI team's main task was to ascertain whether the murders could have taken place on the premises. So far nothing pointed to that. There were no signs of blood or a struggle or that a corpse had been lying there, emitting bodily fluids that would be almost impossible to clean up effectively enough to evade detection by ultraviolet light or luminol spray. But, as Idunn was well aware, that on its own wasn't enough to rule anything out. Neither of the bodies had displayed any visible stab or gun shot wounds, so their deaths were unlikely to have involved much loss of blood. Some murders were tidier than others; some killers were better prepared and wiser to the methods of the police.

As the house wasn't regarded as a sensitive site, the detectives had been admitted to the ground floor as soon as the CSI team were done. Idunn hadn't originally intended to look around since the property didn't appear to be relevant to the deaths of the bodies on the beach: her role was solely to find out how and when death had occurred.

But when Karó had phoned to ask if Idunn wanted to see inside the house, then go to lunch with her and Týr, she had changed her mind. The address wasn't far from the hotel and

with the snow coming down this heavily she was unlikely
to run into her father on the way there. Besides, the prospect was far more appealing than her plan to sneak down
to the hotel restaurant and skulk in a corner, in the hope
that Alexandra wouldn't see her. Eating breakfast with her
half-sister had been more than enough for Idunn. She was
convinced Alexandra had been lying in wait for her, as the
instant Idunn sat down with her slice of toast, the girl had
materialised, smiling brightly, as if the two of them went
better together than skyr and cream. Idunn had been saved
by the appearance of Týr, who had come and joined them
at their table. He had kept up a conversation with Alexandra, something Idunn had been incapable of. She had done
no more than fake a smile or nod when required. Týr had
even offered to escort Alexandra to the police station where
they wanted her to look through footage of the cars that had
recently come over on the ferry. He had added kindly that
she had nothing to worry about, and Alexandra had thanked
him profusely for this reassurance. Before Týr arrived, Idunn
thought sourly, the girl had been yacking on about how much
she was looking forward to it.

As soon as Idunn had finished breakfast, she excused herself on the grounds that she had to go upstairs and work. She
had been as good as her word, and dealt with all the tasks she
could do remotely, armed only with a laptop. This had mostly
involved liaising with the Identification Commission, giving
the other members a status update, and discussing the next
steps for establishing the names of the deceased. As one of the
victims had been recognised from a photo, there was no reason to pull out all the stops at this stage. For the time being, it
would be enough for Idunn to keep the commission informed
of any developments.

Alexandra had knocked on her door to announce that they'd postponed her appointment to go through photos of cars, so she was at a loose end if Idunn felt like doing something. Idunn had politely explained through the door that she was busy. As further evidence of Alexandra's total failure to grasp the nature of their relationship, the girl had answered cheerfully that they would see each other later, then. Not if she could help it, Idunn thought. She'd rather go on working in her room until she keeled over on her keyboard.

Towards lunchtime, she found herself running out of jobs and becoming wildly impatient for the go-ahead on the autopsy of the young woman. Once the results of the MRI scan of the burnt body came in, she would be drowning in tasks again, but until then there was frustratingly little she could do. She had called one of her assistants to ask about the scan and learnt that it wouldn't now happen until tomorrow morning. The machine was completely booked up today. Once the call was over, it wasn't only disappointment about the delay that rankled with Idunn. She could have sworn she'd detected relief in the man's voice when she told him she was still weatherbound in the islands. His concern had rung rather hollow too when he'd asked whether they would be back the day after tomorrow. She reflected that it shouldn't really come as a surprise. She doubted she was the most popular boss in the world. Although no one could accuse her of being unfair or a tyrant, she was dry, unsociable and rarely in a good mood. She never attended work parties and shunned anything that could be classed as a social life with her colleagues. Those emails went straight in the bin. No wonder the coffee room invariably emptied when she looked in. The desks in the department were never as busily occupied as when she felt like a coffee. She just hoped her staff weren't enjoying her absence so much that they were failing to get anything done.

Determinedly banishing these thoughts, Idunn brought her mind back to the present. She surveyed the modest living room they were standing in. The furnishings were very ordinary and nothing jumped out at her. Nothing of relevance for the investigation, anyway. There were several model ships which couldn't possibly be of relevance to the murder. Idunn turned to the local officer, an older man who had bent down to examine one of them. 'Did the occupant collect them or make them?' she asked

The officer straightened up. 'The man who used to live here was a model maker. Not a professional, just a gifted amateur.'

As the daughter of a trawler owner, who had frequently accompanied her father on board in her youth, Idunn knew her boats better than she cared to admit. She appreciated the level of detail – the rails, companionways, masts, nets, lights, rust stains and even the odd tiny coil of rope – all lovingly recreated. It seemed obvious that the craftsman had been to sea himself. 'Was he a fisherman, then?'

The man shook his head. 'No. He was a machine operator. Used to drive a fork-lift on the docks and had a mini digger of his own. Hired out his services as a private contractor. Took care of snow clearance for a couple of trawler companies. The church was a client of his too.'

Idunn, keen to avoid a conversation about local trawler operators, hastily changed the subject. 'What about the daughter? The one who lived here until recently?'

'She didn't work at all, as far as I know. She was an invalid.' The man caught Idunn's eye meaningfully. 'If you can call it that.'

Idunn didn't like hints and insinuations. If people would only speak their mind, life would be a lot more straightforward. 'What do you mean?' she asked bluntly.

Looking a little embarrassed, the man replied: 'Well, she wasn't exactly what you'd call ill. She had problems with drugs and alcohol. We once had a run-in with her when she was sent some cannabis in the post. She claimed it was for medical use, to help with pain and depression, and that she'd bought it online from one of those Facebook dope dealers, but she refused to reveal the name of the account. We let her off with a fine. Those accounts are always changing names anyway, so there's not much point trying to pursue them from this end.'

'So she had a substance abuse disorder?' Many people found it hard to grasp that addiction was a disease, but Idunn wasn't about to waste time arguing with the old policeman about something that had long been recognised within the medical community. In her experience, people rarely changed their minds, however compelling the proof.

'I suppose you could say that.'

'And how did she die?' Idunn wasn't going to hazard another guess. An individual wrestling with an addiction could die from anything, just like other people.

'Overdose. She had an accident and was badly smashed up. While she was in hospital, she managed to get her hands on some drugs. Whether the overdose was deliberate or accidental is hard to say.'

Idunn twigged. 'Was her name by any chance Gudbjörg?'

The police officer nodded. 'That's the one. Known to all as Gugga. She was the daughter of the couple who used to live here.'

Idunn had conducted the post-mortem. There couldn't be many young women called Gudbjörg, admitted to hospital with multiple fractures, who had died of an overdose in the Westman Islands. Like the internet, Idunn forgot nothing. A high concentration of fentanyl had been present in the young woman's blood, along with pregabalin, ibuprofen and diazepam. The last three had been prescribed by the hospital, but no one there would admit to having given the young woman the opioid. Idunn had concluded that the cocktail of drugs had proved lethal thanks to the addition of fentanyl, as tests on the dead woman's hair had revealed that she had almost no history of using it, which meant she would have had little resistance to such a hefty dose.

Idunn hadn't come to any firm conclusions about how the woman had taken the drug. There had been no tablets among her stomach contents, but that wasn't particularly surprising, given her past drug use. Opioids in tablet form were prolonged-release pharmaceuticals, whereas addicts typically ground up pills and took them in other ways to get a more immediate hit. The fact the woman hadn't swallowed them in pill form suggested that she had taken them intentionally. But her purpose remained unclear. Autopsies could reveal a number of things but they rarely provided answers to all one's questions. Had Gugga taken the drug with the intention of ending her own life or had she just wanted to get high? And how had she got hold of it? Had she brought it with her when she was originally admitted to hospital or had a visitor smuggled it in to her?

The young woman had initially been treated at the University Hospital in Reykjavík, having been airlifted there after a bad fall on Heimaklettur, the rock by the entrance to the harbour on Heimaey. That was odd in itself, as the accident had happened in November, when the weather was hardly conducive to clambering around on sheer cliffs. What's more, the woman definitely hadn't been the outdoor type, all of which seemed like a compelling argument that she had been intending to throw herself off the north face of the cliff into the sea. The drop was a big one and there was no real question of how it would have ended. Ironically, though, her life had probably been saved by the fact that she had slipped and fallen while climbing one of the ladders on the way up. Yet when she was capable of talking again, Gugga had flatly denied that she'd meant to do anything other than walk up to the top to enjoy the view.

Idunn remembered the stories she'd heard as a child about sheep tumbling over the cliffs on Heimaklettur or on the small, uninhabited islands of the archipelago where the flocks were put out to grass in summer. Their bodies were rumoured to explode when they hit the surface of the sea, and the thought had given her nightmares as a little girl. She used to walk around staring at her feet in summer to avoid looking in the direction of Heimaklettur or the outlying islands. But that was a long time ago. Idunn reckoned she could pinpoint the day when she had toughened up and smothered all feelings of sentimentality. She had her father to thank for that. If he hadn't turned out to be such a shit, she might be in the University Hospital now, patting the shoulder of a living patient, rather than wandering around the house of a dead woman.

No fentanyl had been found when Gugga's hospital room was searched, so however she had come by the drug, she must have used all of it. According to the University Hospital in Reykjavík, it was inconceivable that she could have stolen the drug while in their care as she had been unable to get out of bed the entire time she was with them. After transferring to the islands hospital, however, she had been capable, towards the end of her stay, of dragging herself around with the aid of a walking frame. Nevertheless, a stock check had revealed that no pills were missing from the hospital's controlled-drugs cupboard, so she couldn't have got hold of them there. The possibility couldn't be entirely ruled out that she had been administered the fentanyl by mistake and that another patient had been given her medicine, but this was regarded as implausible. For one thing, she would have had to cotton on to the mistake and grind up the pills once she was alone. For another, the concentration in her blood had been higher than any doctor would have prescribed in a single dose.

The least plausible scenario was that someone had deliberately given her the drug with the intention of murdering her. The woman didn't have any legal heirs or any enemies, according to those who knew her. Nor had she received any visitors during the days immediately preceding her death. And there had been very few in the weeks before that. The only drugs-related item she had among her possessions when her hospital room was searched after her death was a bottle of CBD capsules and another of vitamins for strengthening nail and hair growth. It was unclear who had brought her the bottles but it must have been one of the tiny handful of people who had come to see her. According to the local hospital in the islands, she had brought them with her from Reykjavík.

'I remember the young woman,' Idunn said now. 'It happened very recently, didn't it?'

The police officer nodded: 'Yes. At the beginning of this month.'

'I did her post-mortem. Tell me, has anything more come to light about where she got hold of the opioids?'

The policeman shook his head. 'No. But we sent everything we found among her possessions for analysis, in case any of the capsules in the bottles she had with her could have been used to smuggle in the drug. We haven't had the results yet.'

The case would hardly be regarded as a priority. Even if it turned out that the capsules were packed with ground-up fentanyl, it would never be possible to determine whether Gugga's death had been an accident or suicide.

Idunn saw no reason to continue the conversation, as what more was there to say?

But the police officer seemed unwilling to leave the subject. 'I wouldn't be surprised if this case turned out to hinge on drugs. I expect those people were searching the house for them. Maybe they fell out when it came to dividing up the spoils. That's one theory the connection to this house has thrown up.'

Idunn merely nodded. Even if this conjecture proved right and it had been a case of an argument that had got out of hand, the nature of the quarrel would have no influence on her verdict about the cause of death. She searched her mind for something to say. Judging by the police officer's expression, he was expecting her to accept the conversational ball: *your turn.*

Týr came to her rescue by entering the sitting room, apparently looking for her: 'Would you like to see what sort of things they appear to have handled?'

Idunn didn't have any real interest in this, but anything was preferable to continuing the present conversation. Týr led her from room to room, pointing out the objects that bare patches in the layer of dust showed had been touched or moved. He explained that there were no fingerprints on any of them as they had all been wiped clean. Nor had any trace of blood been found on them. This came as no surprise to Idunn since none of the items in question would be suitable as weapons: a jewellery box, some model ships, books, cosmetics and other random stuff. Nothing particularly sharp or heavy.

After being cleaned, it appeared that everything had been returned more or less to its place, except in one instance where a sizeable object was missing from the table just inside the entrance hall, judging by the bare patch in the dust. Of course, it could just have been wiped as part of the general clean-up, but the rectangular shape suggested that something had been removed. It was possible that the people Alexandra saw had stolen it, or that it had been used as a murder weapon. After all, Idunn reminded herself, she might still detect injuries on the burnt body during the post-mortem, and most killers would have the sense to dispose of the murder weapon. Idunn was more curious to know what the object was than what had become of it. For it to have been the murder weapon, it would have to be heavy but lacking in sharp edges, so that it could have been used to bash the victims over the head. Neither body had displayed any visible head trauma, but the autopsies might reveal internal injuries beneath the scalp. Idunn doubted this would be the case with the woman who had been sitting by the rocks, from the cursory examination she'd already made of her, but it couldn't be ruled out.

After this, Týr led Idunn to the cellar stairs and pointed down them. It was the same story there. 'According to the CSI guys, a large object has recently been removed. Whoever cleaned the floors everywhere else clearly forgot about the cellar as it's covered in what appears to be coarse salt.'

'When you say large, how large do you mean?' The word in itself conveyed little to Idunn.

'Two metres by one metre. Approximately.'

Too big to count as a likely murder weapon, then. Idunn's interest waned, though she tried not to show it. 'A sofa?'

'No. Too narrow. And apparently it didn't have any legs. It was something that sat flat on the floor.'

'A box?'

'Possibly. Odd shape, though.'

They were both silent as they peered down the steps. There was little point descending in order to stare at a bare patch on the floor. It was easy enough to see it from where they were standing, in spite of the dim lightbulb, as Týr hadn't been lying about the salt on the floor. If anything, he had understated the extent of it. A thick layer of it lay strewn over a wide area around the bare patch, with small heaps dotted here and there. It looked as if a huge sack of the stuff had burst down there.

Týr pushed a lock of hair away from his face, inadvertently revealing the livid scar on his forehead. Idunn looked away so as not to be caught staring. It was obvious to anyone who knew him that he tried his best to keep it hidden. Presumably he wanted to avoid awkward remarks or questions about the fact his father had hit him with an axe. Idunn could well understand that he didn't want to talk about it. He'd been less self-conscious when she first met him and he'd been under the impression that it had simply been the result of a childhood accident. It occurred to Idunn that this might be an opportune moment to tell Týr of her discovery in relation to his mother. They were alone and there was no one to overhear. Maybe she should go ahead and get it over with. He had a right to know. Never mind that he'd finally come to terms with his family history. If his acceptance of his past was built on sand, it would be better to make him aware of the fact.

But no sooner had she opened her mouth than Týr resumed what he had been saying, robbing her of the chance: 'One theory is that, if it's a crate, it may have contained drugs.' He turned to her and smiled. 'If so, it would be a mega bust, because you could fit a hell of a lot in a container that size – assuming it had deep sides and wasn't flat. Alternatively, I suppose it could just have been a sheet of cardboard.'

Idunn was flooded with relief. Fate had granted her a reprieve: the conversation would have to be postponed yet again.

As there was nothing more to see, Týr switched off the light and proposed that they find Karó and go and get some lunch. It was nearly two and he was starving. Idunn agreed enthusiastically. Her stomach had started rumbling.

Her insides abruptly fell silent when Týr added that Alexandra would be joining them and that she must be fed up of waiting by now.

Chapter 13
Day 2 – Friday, 24 January

It was bone-chillingly cold in the house on Stórhöfdi. Some-one had left a window open and the gale from the sea must have been blasting in unhindered ever since they'd left. The air was so damp that it felt, if anything, warmer outside than inside the house. They'd closed the window immediately but it was taking a long time for the place to warm up again.

Of course, their goosebumps and shivers may have had another cause. Shock. They all seemed on the brink of becoming catatonic with it, and Trausti was no exception. He tried to see if any of them were faking it but it was no use. He was in no fit state to judge as he was having enough trouble just breathing, without trying to diagnose his friends' psychological condition as well.

He nearly jumped out of his skin when a gentle hand touched his shoulder. He spun round, no doubt looking as if he expected to see a zombie standing behind him, but it was only Sigga. She could almost have passed for a zombie, though; cheeks streaked black with mascara, wildly tousled hair and blotchy skin. She had kept up a deafening wailing and sobbing all the way back from Gugga's house. Since Trausti had been sitting next to her on the back seat, even clamping his hands over his ears hadn't helped much. His ear on that side was still ringing, trivial though this was in the circumstances.

Sigga took his hand and pressed a glass into it. When his fingers instinctively tightened round the cold crystal, she let go. 'Drink.'

Trausti obeyed, filling his mouth with alcohol, too dazed to tell whether it was brandy or whisky. It didn't matter. The spirits burnt their way down his throat and seemed to help. If they were strong enough to stop Sigga's incessant howling, they were bound to do him good as well. He took another sip and the world seemed to come into sharper focus as he stood there in the kitchen doorway, facing into the dining room.

Ragga, Ari and Leifur were sitting round the table, all distractedly looking in different directions: Ragga out of the window, Ari at the wine glasses in the dresser, and Leifur down at the tabletop in front of him. They seemed as shell-shocked and disorientated as Trausti felt. The same was true of Sigga, who now returned to his side, carrying two brimming glasses in her hands. She placed them in front of Leifur and Ari, ordered them to drink, then vanished back into the kitchen to fetch a glass for Ragga. When she reappeared with it, she had clearly given herself a top-up at the same time.

Ragga didn't touch her drink. Instead, she asked the question that was burning on all their lips, keeping her gaze fixed on the window as she spoke: 'How the fuck did Gudrún end up in Gugga's cellar?'

Nobody spoke. They had no answers. It was clear, though, that Gudrún couldn't have got from the student residence in Reykjavík to the Westman Islands under her own steam the evening she vanished. Unlike the people who had noticed she was missing at the time and mounted a search for her, the five of them had known in their heart of hearts that Gudrún hadn't gone anywhere of her own accord – let alone all the way to the Westman Islands.

After a long silence, Leifur knocked back his drink in one. He blew out a breath and wiped his mouth with the back of his hand, then slammed his glass down on the table and said: 'We're not complete idiots, are we? Of course Gugga brought her here. It can't have been anyone else.'

Ari spoke up next, but it wasn't to agree with Leifur or to speculate about how the body had got there: 'I don't know about you guys but I'd started to convince myself that it never happened; that we'd just imagined it or misinterpreted what we saw.'

Trausti knew what he meant. Almost from the first day, he had been inclined to go with that explanation too, although he'd never fully succeeded in deceiving himself. That day when he'd woken with a splitting headache, nausea and only a patchy recollection of the previous evening. The snatches he could recall had filled him with dread and reluctance about trying to rake up the rest. Instead, he had been grateful for his amnesia and hoped it would wipe the evening from his brain. But it didn't work like that. He could still remember far more than he wanted to and those memories persisted. He had tried banishing them to some dusty corner of his brain but to no avail. Every now and then they would ambush him, but never for long enough to force him to be honest with himself and confront what he had done. Or not done. It was too shameful.

'Oh, it happened all right. We can't all have the same false memory,' Ragga said drily, in her down-to-earth voice. She sipped the spirits and made a face. 'Gudrún died. She vanished. And now she's turned up. In a crate in a cellar in the Westman Islands.'

'Has she, though? Has she?' Sigga sounded as if she was losing it again. They all turned to look at her. She didn't resume her wailing, just added in the same, brittle tone: 'The person in the crate can't be Gudrún. She'd be a skeleton by now, wouldn't she? Wouldn't she?'

All eyes flicked to Trausti. The question related to medicine, which was his area. He hadn't been intending to contribute anything to the conversation; in fact, he'd been scanning the room for the quickest escape route past the table and up to his bedroom. He wanted to be alone behind a locked door, safe from this group of people he no longer trusted.

'Is she right, Trausti?' Ragga prompted.

He stared at the red-gold liquid in his glass. 'Yes. If the body had been lying in the open air. But not if it had been kept in a freezer, for example. Or buried in a bog.'

This seemed to annoy Ari: 'A bog? What bloody bog?'

Trausti experienced a flash of anger. He had simply been answering as conscientiously as he could. 'I'm a doctor, not an expert in dead bodies – any more than you are.' This last part wasn't strictly true as he had at least taken a course in forensic pathology as an undergraduate – a course that definitely wasn't offered to students in the economics department. But as his momentary anger subsided, his thoughts became clearer. 'The body was buried in sand or some other type of mineral. Salt, maybe. That could have had an influence – perhaps dried it out and delayed decomposition.'

'Then why didn't you say so straight away instead of talking some bullshit about bogs?'

Trausti chose not to answer Ari. He had long ago read an article about some bodies that had been discovered in a bog in Britain. Although the people appeared at first to have died comparatively recently, they had turned out to be hundreds of years old. In his confusion, Trausti's mind had produced this fact. Stress and panic obviously messed with one's memory centres and caused them to throw up random information that was of absolutely no use in the present circumstances. But, damn it, he was a human being, not a computer hard drive.

'Stop fighting, you two. We need to focus on the practicalities.' Once again, Ragga's was the voice of reason. Sigga seemed on the verge of collapsing like a marionette. Ari was buoyed up on a tide of rage. Leifur seemed to have lost the ability to speak. It had crossed Trausti's mind to wonder if he himself might be having a psychotic episode. Maybe none of this was really happening. He had an impulse to react like his grandmother used to whenever they got bad news and ask if anyone was hungry. Ragga was the only one who appeared to be herself. She folded her arms across her chest and said composedly: 'We need to talk. Calmly, without getting worked up.'

Had the moment finally arrived? Were they actually going to talk about the evening Gudrún had disappeared? Up to now, Trausti had only ever discussed it in private with individual members of the group. They had never all sat down together and thrashed out what had happened, arranging their fragmented memories in chronological order in an attempt to get to the bottom of the mystery. Once the police had got involved, several days after the party, the friends had been warned not to discuss the case with the other witnesses. This had taken it off the agenda. It probably hadn't occurred to the police that the friends would actually obey their orders, but the truth was that none of them had wanted to talk about it, and the police had given them a valid excuse to block it out and get on with their lives.

Trausti began to feel anxious. Did he really want to know what had happened or should he just make his peace with the little he remembered? It wasn't much but maybe more than enough.

What he knew for a fact was that they'd held a party in Ragga's flat. Mixed far too strong a punch. Gudrún had left the party first, complaining that she didn't feel well. She had certainly appeared to be very drunk. The rest was hazy at best.

Sigga was the first to speak. 'There's nothing to talk about. None of us remember anything apart from snippets.'

Trausti got a grip on himself. If they didn't have the conversation now, they never would. 'You know,' he said, 'we might not be in such a mess now if we'd sat down at the time and methodically gone over the events of that evening.'

Sigga seemed annoyed. 'There are no events to go over. We all suffered blackouts after drinking that punch.'

Trausti had never been so drunk in his life. He'd almost given up alcohol for good in the aftermath. On the rare occasions when he let himself think back to the state he'd been in, he felt as if he'd been split in two, into a physical self and a disembodied brain. Whenever he moved, his physical body had been a little ahead of his brain, which had done its best to follow, like a younger sibling struggling to keep up. It had been a horribly disorientating experience, and because everything had been so strangely off-kilter that evening, he had almost managed to dismiss the Gudrún business as part of his general confusion.

Ragga seemed to be on the same page as Trausti. 'We all remember something, right? Maybe if we piece our memories together, we'll be able to work out the sequence of events. I mean, it's unlikely we all retain the same fragments, isn't it? Who knows, maybe we can get a clearer picture of what happened. Clearer than the one we have now, anyway. So, who remembers leaving the party? Or going into Gudrún's room?'

'Oh, for God's sake.' Ari sounded angry. 'We all slipped away from the party at one point or another to fetch something from our rooms or use our own toilets when the one in Ragga's flat was occupied. Nothing suspicious about that, is there?'

'I never slipped out.' Ragga kept her tone relaxed and calm. 'The party was held in my room, remember? I was hosting it. Does anyone remember what order you left in or what time it was? Or if you went into Gudrún's room?'

None of them could say exactly when or why they had nipped out, Trausti included. He did know that he had gone into Gudrún's room, though he had no intention of sharing the fact. It was too painful and private. He had no idea what had made him do it, nor did he want to revisit the memory. If the others had similar stories to tell, they too kept quiet.

Trausti stared at the tabletop in front of him. When he spoke, his voice was flat. 'We all remember what really matters, I think. We all have a vague memory of discovering Gudrún in bed. And coming to the conclusion that she was dead.' He paused here for dramatic effect, although none was needed. 'I don't think anything else matters really. But does anyone remember why we went in to check on her?'

It had been towards the end of the party when they had all crowded around her bed. But no one could recall why they had gone in to see her. They all avoided each other's eyes as the scene he was referring to was intensely painful to rake up. But, reluctant as he was to think about this part of the evening, it was vividly imprinted on Trausti's memory. He closed his eyes and tried to push the unwanted images away. It was one thing to talk about it, another thing to picture what had awaited them in Gudrún's room.

Trausti resumed: 'OK. Can anyone remember who suggested we come back next day to check if she was better, instead of phoning for an ambulance straight away?' The replies from the group were all the same, a murmured chorus of 'no'.

'What does it matter?' Ari asked, his voice unnaturally loud all of a sudden. 'It was just an epic piece of drunken bullshit. We all thought it was a good idea at the time. Even you – Trausti, the medical student.'

Trausti felt his face flushing and looked away from Ari's angry gaze. Ari, taking this as a sign to continue, added: 'It makes no sense to drag this up. Let's just shut the fuck up about it and try to enjoy ourselves. That is what we came here for – right?'

Ragga ignored Ari's outburst and returned to the point. 'Do any of you remember why we went into her room? I don't.'

Trausti didn't either and the murmured replies of the others indicated that the same went for all of them.

Ari groaned. 'Seriously, guys. Let's change the subject. I do not want to dwell on that moment. I've tried hard to forget it. Please don't start going into gruesome details.' For the first time on this trip, Trausti detected a pleading note in Ari's voice. 'Let's talk about something else. *Please.*'

Ragga went on as if she hadn't heard Ari. 'We can't kid ourselves now that Gudrún had simply passed out drunk in her bed. We have to face the truth. Our pathetic excuse that she could have come round later that night, walked out of her room of her own accord and disappeared, is obviously a joke. However much we wanted it to be true at the time.'

Trausti had tried to salve his conscience by imagining this scenario many times, but had failed, though he would give anything to believe it.

Sigga wasn't about to give up, though. 'Well, I'm not so sure. Maybe it did happen. We don't know anything for a fact. Unless any of you can remember something concrete?'

Trausti only had a few lingering fragments he could share, but they were of no consequence, so he kept his mouth shut. It was safer, as he didn't want to accidentally blurt out something that had to be a false memory. It was something he badly wanted to forget, to expunge from his mind so he couldn't even recall it himself, let alone share it with the rest of the group.

In the memory, he had been standing alone in Gudrún's room, watching her lying there.

'I agree with Sigga.' Ari's voice was almost back to normal. 'Gudrún could well have left on her own that night. Maybe she came over here with Gugga, died here and somehow ended up in the basement. Stranger things have happened.'

But Ragga seemed determined to stick to the facts. When she spoke again it was plain that she had faced up to what the others had known subconsciously all along: 'Come on, guys. Gudrún died the night of the party. And we failed her because we were totally wasted.'

And now the day of reckoning had come.

'Well, if that's true, then Gugga must have taken the body. Brought it over here. Nothing else makes any sense.' Sigga sounded shrill, as if she was about to crack.

'Gugga didn't go home to the Westman Islands until quite a while after the party,' Ragga pointed out. 'Two or three weeks, at least. Don't you remember? Her mother was in hospital in Reykjavík, for an operation. It wasn't until after she died that Gugga went back to Heimaey with her father to prepare for the funeral. Where was Gudrún kept in the meantime, assuming you're right and it was Gugga who brought her here?'

It was a valid question but they couldn't come up with any valid answers. The others started suggesting various dark corners in the student residence, none of which were plausible:

the bike store, the laundry, the bin shed and the reading room – all spaces that the other residents had access to. Nothing could have been hidden there, particularly not something the size of a body.

'Couldn't she have hidden the body in her room?' Sigga didn't sound convinced even though it was her own suggestion.

It was Leifur who now intervened to blow this ridiculous idea out of the water. 'You have got to be joking. Don't you remember how small the student flats were? The only hiding place would have been under the bed and I don't buy that for one moment. Nobody would want to sleep on top of a dead body.'

'There would have been a mattress between them.' Sigga seemed determined to dig her heels in. 'I think it's perfectly possible.'

Trausti felt the need to jump in. 'The smell would have been unbearable and it would soon have spread to the corridor. Do any of you remember a terrible smell back then?'

No one did.

'What about the storerooms?' Sigga seemed to have temporarily recovered her equilibrium as she chipped in with this suggestion. 'There were storerooms in the cellar, don't you remember? One per flat.'

Trausti had completely forgotten this detail and it seemed the others had too. None of them had owned anything beyond what they needed, as they were young and had only just left home. Trausti's storeroom had stood empty throughout his years in the hall of residence, and the same was bound to be true of the others, who had lived there a much shorter time than him. He vaguely remembered being shown a cupboard-like space in the basement when he was originally given the keys to his flat. If he wasn't mistaken, though, it would have been difficult to cram a body into the tiny space, and besides, it had been separated from the others by bars rather than walls. Since it was possible to see into all the storage spaces through the bars, they wouldn't have made a very suitable hiding place for a body. 'Couldn't you see inside them?' he asked aloud.

Sigga, who obviously thought she'd hit on the answer, as if it were a fun puzzle they were trying to solve, looked deflated. 'Yes, but . . .'

'Who ever went down there? No one, I bet.' Ari seemed eager to grasp at the solution this offered. 'Gugga could have stuffed Gudrún's body in there and covered it with a sheet. No one would have noticed. Those storerooms were never really used.'

'What about the smell you mentioned, Trausti?' Ragga seemed determined to bring them back down to earth. They were clutching at straws to find an explanation; after all, it was only human to be frustrated by unsolved mysteries, but she was right to force them to face the facts. There was nothing to be gained by kidding themselves. 'How could Gugga have lugged her down there, then got her out again? Then transported her to the Westman Islands, all without being seen? Could she have taken a taxi with the body? Gugga didn't own a car, remember?'

The answer eluded them. After a brief search on her phone, Ragga dug up an obituary for Gugga's mother, which confirmed that her funeral had taken place more than a month after Gudrún's disappearance. That completely ruled out the possibility that Gudrún's body had been concealed in Gugga's flat or storeroom at the student residence, let alone anywhere else in the building. The smell would unquestionably have betrayed the hiding place.

Sigga opened her eyes wide once this had been established. Her voice held a note of relief and optimism as she asked: 'Couldn't this mean that we were right all along? That Gudrún was OK and left of her own accord? Could she have taken herself to the islands somehow?'

Leifur had contributed little to the proceedings up to now, focusing on his glass instead, but Sigga's naïve words seemed to rile him. 'Yeah, right. Gudrún had stopped breathing, if you remember? Now you're saying she started breathing again and took it into her head to go over to the islands. Then what? Did she decide to go to sleep in a crate full of sand in Gugga's parents' cellar, having wandered into it by chance? Of all the cellars on Heimaey?'

Sigga turned bright red. Trausti knew her well enough to be sure that her heightened colour was a sign of anger, not shame or embarrassment. From the poisonous look she shot at Leifur you'd have thought a cockroach was sitting in his chair. Her wild hair and smudged make-up only enhanced the effect. 'Of course I didn't mean that,' she said. 'But maybe there was nothing wrong with Gudrún and we were all so out of it that we misinterpreted what we saw. Gugga could have lent her the keys – later that night, after the rest of us had gone to bed. Maybe Gudrún woke Gugga and asked if she could go and stay at her house. Gugga's parents were in Reykjavík for her mother's operation and the house was empty, so perhaps Gugga said yes. It's perfectly possible that Gugga had forgotten all about it by next morning. I mean, none of us could think straight at the time.'

It was possible and Trausti felt briefly cheered at the thought before reality hit again. There had to be another explanation. He took a sip from his glass, noticing that the level had already gone down perceptibly. The tremor in his hand was causing tiny ripples in the surface of the liquid. He continued to drink while Sigga and Leifur argued. By the time he'd emptied his glass, he was growing exasperated by the quarrel, which Ari and Ragga had now got sucked into as well. Why were they so fixated on how Gudrún had got to the islands? Why weren't they trying to figure out how she had died? He desperately wanted to know what had killed her, but at the same time he was afraid of the answer. Losing his temper again, he put an end to the rapid, angry exchange of words by going over to the table and banging down his glass. The thick-bottomed tumbler made a loud noise. 'I want to know,' he said into the sudden startled silence. 'Which of you was pissing around with the Ouija board? It can't have been a coincidence that Gudrún's name came up, then the very next day we stumble across her body. Either one of us orchestrated the whole thing or Ouija boards genuinely work. Which I don't believe for a minute. If you ask me, somebody in this room knows a lot more than the rest of us about what's going on.'

The silence stretched out after Trausti had finished speaking. He hadn't yelled or spoken sharply but used his normal level, unexcited tone. This didn't seem to have detracted from the impact of his words, though. After a long moment, he went on: 'I also know that somebody visited Gugga in hospital, although none of you are admitting to it. And I find it all too likely that it was the same person. So, I'm asking: which one of you knows more about this than you've been letting on?'

He would have done better to wait before asking the second part. They all started talking in unison, swearing they hadn't visited her, and the Ouija board was forgotten, though Trausti was actually more interested in knowing who had been behind that. It stood to reason that whoever it was must have known about the body in the cellar, and therefore, logically, how it had ended up there. If not, it would be an absurd coincidence. He supposed it might be possible to discover the identity of Gugga's visitor by other means, such as finding out which ward Gugga had been on and asking the staff. Or questioning Halldóra, the old neighbour. She might know more than she appeared to. He was glad now that he hadn't asked about the other thing that was bothering him – the note under their windscreen wiper on the ferry. They had all disappeared from view at some point during the nearly three-hour crossing, so theoretically any of them could have put the note there. It had to be the same person in all three instances. The question was, who? And, perhaps more importantly, why?

He became aware again, through the numbing haze of alcohol, of how cold it was in the house. An image flashed into his mind of Gudrún's face as she lay in bed that evening when they had all barged into her room. Between her parted lips there had been a glimpse of white teeth and braces, and from one corner of her mouth a trickle of bloody foam. He had been pushing this picture away for so many years that he had forgotten that detail, if he had ever remembered it before. But he couldn't recall giving it any thought at the time as they had clustered around her bed. He'd been entirely taken up with trying not to fall flat on his face. Now, though, despite the spirits he'd drunk, he was better informed, no longer a third-year medical student.

There weren't many reasons for people to vomit up foam: an epileptic fit, poisoning or rabies. He could rule out rabies, and she hadn't been having an epileptic fit the first time he'd walked in on her. Besides, the foam produced from the mouth during epileptic fits didn't contain blood and wasn't as common a side effect as people believed. That left only one possibility: poisoning.

How could it have happened? They had all drunk the same punch, eaten the same meagre refreshments. Crisps and dips provided by Leifur, and one cupcake per person from Gugga, decorated with white icing and a small red star on top, as if they were attending a children's birthday party. Salted nuts from him and a sticky cheese dip from Sigga. But only Gudrún had got ill. Critically ill.

Earlier this evening, Trausti had been feeling slightly detached, as though he weren't fully present in the moment. Now that this sense of unreality had gone, he missed it. Because, like it or not, he was here. Here with his old friends in a remote house, battered by the wind and almost completely surrounded by the raging sea. Outside, the light was failing and before long the headland would be engulfed by darkness. Sooner or later, once this pointless conversation ended, they would have to go to bed. Would he be able to sleep, knowing that one of the friends sharing the house with him could have poisoned Gudrún? Unless she had unwittingly poisoned herself? She had been studying chemistry and although he found it implausible that chemistry students would walk around with dangerous toxins in their pockets, it wasn't unthinkable. Especially bearing in mind that, for once, she had been as shit-faced as the rest of them.

At that moment he was shocked out of his thoughts by the ringing of the phone downstairs.

Chapter 14
Day 6 – Tuesday, 28 January

The storm was supposed to be dying down. The Hellisheidi mountain route to Reykjavík would remain closed for now but elsewhere the forecast was looking brighter. This news was enough to keep Idunn going through lunch. There was a very real prospect that they could be home by this evening and her sufferings would be at an end. Instead of prepping for an autopsy at the local hospital, she would hopefully soon be floating above the clouds, clutching a plastic cup of airport coffee, on her way home. Then normal life could resume; her familiar existence, free of her half-sister and father. If Alexandra managed to get a seat on the same plane, or popped up in Reykjavík in the next few days, so be it. Once Idunn was on her home ground, she should have no difficulty in shrugging the girl off.

Matters were complicated at the moment by the fact that Alexandra had managed – by some inexplicable means – to strike up a friendship with Týr and Karó. While there were various downsides to this from Idunn's point of view, there was also one major upside: the trio could chatter away together, leaving her to eat in peace. From time to time, though, she was startled into glancing up from her food, unable to believe her ears. Her sister's shallowness came as no surprise but it was a serious blow to hear Týr and Karó talking with such interest and insight about vacuous reality shows like *Love Island* and *The Bachelor*. Though even that hadn't been as bad as hearing Alexandra's response to their questions about her future plans. She was going to take the entrance exam to study medicine at the University of Iceland and was set on qualifying as a doctor like her big sister. At this point Idunn had choked and Karó had to thump her on the back. Idunn's throat was still sore and, if she was honest, so was her heart when she saw how hurt Alexandra had been by her reaction. Although Idunn didn't want her half-sister in her life, she wasn't ill disposed towards her. But that didn't alter the fact that the girl would be wasting her time taking the entrance exam. She didn't have a hope in hell of passing it.

This incident dampened the atmosphere at the table, the happiness in Alexandra's eyes was extinguished and she prodded silently at her food while Týr and Karó kept up a flow of conversation to try and lift the mood. They seemed relieved when the time finally came to settle the bill and leave. Idunn hastily said she would pay for Alexandra, by way of a peace offering, but Alexandra handed the waiter her card, saying that she could look after herself. Luckily, this strained moment was interrupted by Karó and Týr receiving simultaneous notifications that they were to go to the police station for a quick meeting. Idunn had muted her phone but when she checked it there was only one message. From her mother. In no mood to read it, she shoved her phone back in her pocket.

'Since I don't need to go along, I think I'll pop over to the hospital and prepare the body for transport,' she told the others. In fact, there was no urgency. All Idunn needed to do was reassure herself that the body bag was still tightly closed before it was transferred to an ambulance to be conveyed to the airport. But while she was there, she could use the opportunity to examine the dead woman's clothes and see if any clues could be gleaned from them. Anything would be better than hanging around in her hotel room where the time would crawl by with agonising slowness.

Even Alexandra seemed to realise that this was a parting of the ways. She said a friendly goodbye to Týr and Karó, and gave Idunn a curt nod, her expression still wounded, before walking away. To Idunn's frustration, the girl didn't appear to be heading home but back to the hotel, where she seemed determined to stay until Idunn left for Reykjavík. Clearly, she still had every intention of accompanying her big sister to the city like an unwelcome souvenir of this visit. Idunn watched her figure disappearing into the swirling maelstrom of whiteness and sighed. Why could life never be simple?

The walk to the hospital cleared her head. Battling the full strength of the gale, squinting against the stinging snowflakes, Idunn had no time to think about anything but keeping her balance and finding her way. It wasn't far but by the time she reached the back entrance, she was so out of breath that she felt as if she had hiked the length and breadth of the island. She rang the bell and waited impatiently, hopping from foot to foot and trying to shield herself from the blizzard. A young male nurse finally let her in and stepped back as Idunn set about stamping the snow off her shoes and brushing it off her shoulders and head. Then, still shaking the rest off her clothes, she introduced herself and explained why she was there. The nurse, unfazed by the mess, introduced himself in turn, saying that his name was Már, then went off to check whether he was allowed to let her into the locked mortuary suite.

Having obtained authorisation, Már unlocked the door to the post-mortem facilities and asked if she'd like some help. She accepted his offer. He opened the refrigerated store and

Idunn noticed that the body count had risen. When the bag containing the woman from the beach had been placed inside it, the fridge had been empty. But now there was another corpse, wrapped in a white sheet, an embroidered cross over its face. There was still capacity for four more bodies, but that was unlikely to be required.

The nurse clearly felt compelled to explain the presence of the new body. 'An old woman died here at the hospital yesterday evening. But there was no mystery in her case – she was ninety-five.'

Idunn wondered if he seriously thought she'd want to see this body too, in case there was anything untoward about the death. She just smiled at him and didn't bother to explain that she was here to do one job only and wasn't on the lookout for any more work. Death was an inescapable consequence of being born and there was no need to call her in every time someone in Iceland kicked the bucket.

She asked Már about protective clothing, then followed him to a storeroom which turned out to contain everything she needed. She noticed that whenever she took something off the shelves, he followed her example. When they were both standing there with an identical pile of equipment in their arms, the young man, noticing Idunn's puzzled expression, explained: 'I'm going to assist you. I'd like to. For a bit of a change.'

She didn't object. It was rare to encounter someone with a genuine interest in her field. Regrettably, though, she wasn't planning to do anything particularly exciting; just satisfy herself that everything had been properly secured and check again to see if she could find any clues on the body to facilitate identification. If, by an irony of fate, she had to stay on the island long enough to conduct the post-mortem here, this young man might make an excellent assistant. All the same, she fervently hoped it wouldn't come to that, for her own sake.

After getting into their protective overalls, gloves, masks and goggles, they manoeuvred the steel trolley with the body bag on it into the post-mortem suite next door to the cold store. Together, they heaved the bag onto a long steel table with a sink at one end. The facilities weren't bad; Idunn had worked in more primitive conditions. The dead woman's clothes were in a row of sealed plastic bags on the table by the wall, waiting to be sent to Reykjavík for analysis. They didn't appear to have been touched since Idunn had brought the body in yesterday evening. At the time she had been so tired that she had only performed a cursory search of the pockets to see whether the clothes contained any ID, plastic cards, a phone or anything else that might provide a clue to the name of the deceased. She had found nothing but a packet of chewing gum, though it was possible she might have overlooked something. After all, she had been working on the assumption that she would be going straight back to Reykjavík the following morning and would be able to do a more systematic examination there. Fatigue and anxiety about being here in the islands might well have affected her powers of observation.

Idunn fetched the bags of clothes and began by removing the coat and spreading it out. A powerful reek of smoke was released, which suggested that the dead woman had originally been much closer to the bonfire than where she had been found. Neither Idunn nor Már recoiled. She inspected the coat while Már watched intently. But, as Idunn had established the day before, the pockets were empty and she couldn't find any other clue to the woman's name. Gone were the days when people used to label their outdoor clothes – if adults ever had.

Idunn examined the collar anyway but found nothing of interest. The manufacturer was no help either, as it was a popular type of down jacket from the Icelandic 66°North brand.

However, Idunn did spot something she hadn't originally noticed. She stood back to allow Már to take a look. On the lower part of the coat was a blonde hair. It was very short, but, as far as she could tell, it included the root. In her haste to get away from the hotel, she had forgotten to bring her camera along, so she had to rely on her phone. After photographing the hair in situ, she bagged it and labelled it for forensics. You never knew if the hair might be significant. The colour didn't match that of the dead woman, and anyway it was too short to be hers. If Idunn had to guess, she'd say it belonged to a dog or some other animal – but forensics would settle that question.

'Amazing.' The young man didn't appear to be speaking ironically. In fact, he seemed to find the process fascinating and had been listening attentively while Idunn explained what she was doing.

'Maybe.' She smiled at him behind her mask. 'There's not much chance this hair will be important, but you never know.'

They returned the coat to the bag and Idunn methodically went over the rest of the clothes. Nothing new came to light until she spotted another short hair on one trouser leg. That ended up in a specimen bag too. All she had got for her pains were two short hairs, but that was better than nothing.

Next, Idunn turned to the body itself. Már helped her remove it from the bag. The woman lay naked on the slab, her blank face white. Idunn glanced at Már. There was no sign that the nurse found the experience unsettling, but then he would presumably have been faced with dead people before. 'Do you recognise her?' Idunn asked.

He shook his head. 'No. I've never seen her before. But that doesn't necessarily mean much. I'm not from the islands. If she *was* local, though, she can't have been living here in the last few years. I'd have seen her around if she had.'

Idunn hadn't been expecting any other answer, but in a small country like Iceland it was best to be on the safe side. The dead woman could have been a relative, acquaintance or even friend of the young nurse. While that would have solved the problem of identification, it would also have disqualified Már from assisting Idunn any further.

The nurse was studying the dead woman's face. 'She's young. Relatively speaking.'

'Yes, she is. Around thirty, at a guess. It's hard to tell which side of thirty, but I certainly wouldn't put her under twenty-five.'

Már raised his eyebrows, his goggles lifting with the movement. 'She could be around my age, then?'

'Possibly. People mature at different rates. It's impossible to determine age by appearance alone. Except maybe in the case of children.'

Már seemed saddened by this, though it was hard to read his face behind the mask. Presumably he hadn't been a nurse for long enough yet to develop the thick skin that all health-care workers need to grow in order to cope with life's injustices. 'Do they know who killed her?'

Idunn shook her head. 'At this stage we don't even know if it was murder. It's very probable in the case of the burnt body that has been sent to Reykjavík, but, as far as this woman's concerned, everything remains to be clarified. She may even have been responsible for killing the other victim. It's anybody's guess.'

Idunn began to examine the front of the body, coming to the same conclusions as before. There were no ligature marks on the neck to suggest strangulation. No wounds on the abdomen or limbs. Apart from the bruising on the woman's chest, there were no signs of any attack or defence injuries. Nor were there any puncture marks from needles, or other evidence of self-harm. The hands were sealed in plastic bags to preserve any material that might be under the nails, so Idunn omitted them from her examination. She had taken a careful look at them during her preliminary inspection and hadn't noticed so much as a scratch. The woman wasn't wearing any rings and there were no paler marks to suggest any had been removed from her fingers, but there was a healed piercing in one of her nostrils.

While she was engaged in her examination, Idunn explained the process to Már, pointing out that it was rare for someone this young to die outside hospital, without displaying any potentially fatal wounds. That was why she had wanted to make doubly sure that she hadn't missed anything. The cause of death was almost certainly something else, though. Poisoning, for instance. Though it couldn't be ruled out that the woman had died of natural causes, like a heart attack. With any luck, the post-mortem would make that clearer.

They turned the body over onto its front. This had to be done with extreme care and Idunn noticed with approval how painstaking the nurse was. He seemed not only to grasp instinctively what was required but to be genuinely interested too. Idunn longed to ask if he'd ever thought of moving to Reykjavík, but stopped herself. Hospitals were fighting over nurses as it was and she would earn the undying enmity of the staff here if she poached a valuable employee. She didn't want to take the risk, despite her resolve never to return to the islands if she could help it. Anyway, the question was academic because it wasn't as if she could appoint a new assistant without the system gearing up to go through some complicated, time-consuming official process. And she felt happiest when the system was dormant. Quite apart from which, the ability to smooth out articles of clothing and turn bodies over would hardly count as adequate tests of a candidate's suitability. She obviously wasn't thinking straight.

Idunn forced herself to concentrate on the task in hand. She surveyed the body from the back of the head to the heels. 'Nothing to see here. No injuries and no tattoos.' She probed the scalp with her fingers, feeling for signs of a fractured skull or swelling. 'The head seems intact too.'

She observed that the skin on the back of the body looked different from yesterday. Now it was a light-red colour, as if sunburnt. An oddly intense pink, in fact, apart from the large, pale patches on the shoulder blades, buttocks and mid calves, on which most of the body's weight had been resting.

'What does that mean?' Már too had noticed that the skin looked different on the back from on the front.

'The body was discovered in a sitting position. When it was brought here, the skin colour was pretty normal. Hardly any observable livor mortis, which means it must have formed after the body was transferred here to the mortuary and laid on its back. The pink patches are quite extensive, which suggests the body hadn't been sitting on the beach for very long before it was discovered. In other words, the blood hadn't started collecting in any great quantity at the lowest points of the body.'

Már stared at the back of the corpse. 'How can you be sure that there isn't bruising that is being obscured by the livor mortis?'

'I can't be sure. Not by examining the body with the naked eye. But when I checked it yesterday, the skin was unblemished, with no evidence of bruising, so I can be fairly confident that there isn't any. Everything will become clearer once I can get going on the internal examination.'

Idunn took a few photos, hoping her phone wouldn't alter the colours too much. The red appeared oddly vivid, but there could be a number of reasons for that. The first to occur to her was poisoning, since certain substances were known to turn the livor mortis strange colours. She had seen very few examples of this with her own eyes, but the possibility of poisoning had to be taken into account in this instance due to the absence of injuries. What made it less likely was that there had been no foam in the mouth or nose of the dead woman. Nor had any vomit been found in the proximity of the body. In a case of fatal poisoning, Idunn would have expected to see one or both of these indicators. But the blood sample she had taken yesterday would help to remove all doubt.

All would be revealed in due course, when the toxicology results came back. Tomorrow morning, she would be able to get to work in her own lab, taking all the samples she regarded as necessary and focusing on getting to the bottom of the mystery. Free from the constant anxiety about bumping into her father or having to come up with ways of dodging Alexandra.

'Tell me something. Do you by any chance remember another young woman who was in hospital here and died at the beginning of the month? She'd suffered multiple fractures and internal injuries as the result of a fall. Her name was Gudbjörg.'

'Yes, I remember her well. Gudbjörg, known as Gugga. Why do you ask?' Már frowned. 'Was she connected to this death in some way?'

Idunn didn't want to reveal anything that wasn't already common knowledge. Although many locals must have noticed the police activity around Gugga's house, Inspector Ína hadn't yet issued a statement to the press. 'I'm only asking because I conducted her post-mortem and it raised some questions that remain unanswered. I assume the police will have spoken to the staff here, but sometimes not everything is reported. To me, I mean.'

Már nodded. 'I can try to answer any questions you might have, but you would do better to talk to the staff who were responsible for looking after her. I did a few shifts in her ward – night shifts mostly – but I didn't attend to her regularly. Going by the few times we spoke, she seemed very nice, though. She was in pain and everything, but she managed to be positive in spite of that. She said she was incredibly grateful not to have to go home, if I remember right. She said she found it impossible to sleep there.'

'Why?'

'I didn't ask. Should I have?'

'No. Not necessarily.' Idunn went on to ask if he had noticed anything to suggest that Gugga might have been on the point of relapse. Although the mask made it hard for Idunn to read the young man's expression, she got the sense that he was suddenly unsure.

'Look, I don't know quite how to answer that. She was suffering and kept pestering me for painkillers. Strong painkillers. But her medical records mentioned that she'd been in rehab and that every effort should be made to avoid giving her opioids. So she wasn't given any – not by me, at least. But whether she wanted them for her addiction or to alleviate her pain, I couldn't tell you.'

Next, Idunn asked about evidence of depression, but Már said he wasn't the right person to answer that. He couldn't enlighten her as to whether Gugga had had any visitors either, as he'd mostly been on night shift as he'd mentioned. But he supplied Idunn with the names of several staff members on Gugga's ward, and said he thought that one of the nurses, Dóra, and a doctor called Breki would be the best placed to answer her questions. They had been the main people responsible for attending to Gugga during the day.

Idunn thanked him, though she doubted she would take any further action. She had only asked on the off-chance. On second thoughts, it had been over-optimistic of her to think she would learn anything useful. Sometimes you just had to accept that there were no answers to be had.

While they were returning the corpse to the body bag, there was a loud knocking on the door. Már went to see who it was and reappeared with Týr in tow. He didn't come into the examination room but stood in the doorway, his face grave, and told Idunn she would have to come with him. Her presence was required.

That never boded well.

Chapter 15
Day 3 – Friday Night – 24/25 January

Trausti had finally got off to sleep. It had taken hours for his brain to stop racing, the way it used to on the night before an exam. New thoughts would surface while he was still trying to process the existing ones, sending his mind into turmoil. He couldn't work out what mattered and what didn't, let alone get to the bottom of what was really going on. The phone downstairs had started ringing again, and although the sound was only a faint echo, it was impossible to ignore. To Trausti's ears the sound seemed menacing and it was driving him increasingly frantic. Since the first two calls, it had become increasingly hard to block it out or convince oneself that it was just a prankster, as Ari kept insisting. Ragga had answered the second time and her version of what had been said definitely didn't fit with the idea that it was just kids fooling about. She couldn't remember the exact words, only that the caller had asked twice whether the knowledge that the day of reckoning was nigh was keeping them awake at night. When Ragga had asked who was calling, the person had hung up.

Leifur, dismissing Ari's theory that it was a nuisance call, came up with the suggestion that it might be a builder or other tradesman, angry that he hadn't been paid. It was a good idea, persuasive enough to give them an excuse to shrug off the problem, since they had more serious things to worry about. None of them paid any attention to Ragga's objection that the voice had sounded more like an old woman – too old to be a tradesperson. They didn't want to hear it, as Ragga's input made it harder to grasp at the straw Leifur had offered them. Trausti, for one, really needed to quell his darker suspicions that the phone calls were actually intended to threaten them, that someone had found them out. Once Trausti was lying in bed, he had found himself wondering if it could have been Halldóra, the old neighbour from the funeral reception. But surely he hadn't told her where they were staying? In the end, he had gone downstairs to check the small screen on the landline phone. In spite of his tiredness and distracted state, he had managed to locate the call log. The repeated calls that no one had answered all turned out to have been made from the same number that had rung when Ragga answered. He opened Leifur's laptop, which was lying on the dining table, and looked the number up in the online directory. He knew the password because he'd borrowed the computer earlier to log in to the group chat. Sigga had insisted that they delete the latest thread as a precaution, and as Trausti's phone was broken, this was the only way he could do it.

While he was calling up the telephone directory, he spotted Ari and Leifur through the window, sitting outside on the deck. They had their backs turned and Trausti was glad. He wasn't in the mood to talk to them; he just wanted to work out what the deal was with the phone calls so he could get to sleep. At first it occurred to him that the guys might have taken refuge outside to escape the relentless ringing, but the thick clouds of smoke rising above their heads suggested that they were enjoying a cigar. He stood for a moment, watching them, and through the window he heard the low murmur of their conversation. He wondered if they were talking about him. Could Leifur and Ari be in cahoots? It seemed unlikely. Trausti couldn't imagine the two of them agreeing on anything other than it being time for a drink. Dragging his thoughts back to the phone calls, he hurriedly entered the phone number into the directory and discovered that it was registered to a fisherman. The address didn't match Halldóra's. There was no woman registered with a number at that address, but of course it wouldn't be too difficult for a man to imitate an old woman's voice.

Trausti also checked to see who owned the number of the original phone call that Ari had answered. That did turn out to belong to a woman, but she too lived in a different street from the neighbour Trausti had met at the reception, and she wasn't a tradesperson either. She was listed as a teacher. Both the man and the woman had quite common names, but when he looked them up online, he discovered that they were old; the man was in his seventies, the woman in her eighties. Nuisance calls were unlikely to be a popular pastime among their age group.

After dithering for a while over whether to return their calls and ask what the hell they were playing at, Trausti eventually went ahead and did it. But the phone rang unanswered in both cases. He hurried back upstairs, only narrowly avoiding Ari and Leifur, as he heard the door to the deck opening just before he closed his.

Increasingly agitated by the phone calls, Trausti had lain in bed, staring at the freshly painted ceiling that was intermittently lit up by the lighthouse beam on its endless revolutions. In the end, the flashes had soothed him enough for his head to clear. Just before he finally dropped off, he had persuaded himself that none of his friends were out to get him. It was irrational to think they were. But try as he might, he couldn't entirely shake off the suspicion that they weren't to be trusted. The secrets and lies between them all fuelled his distrust, and until whoever was behind what was going on came clean, they were all suspect. If he was being reasonable, though, any serious threat had to be an external one. None of his friends could be making the phone calls, for one thing. Besides, it was absurd to think he might be in some kind of physical danger. He had always steered a careful course through life, at pains not to provoke anyone or air any controversial opinions – on the rare occasions that he held any. So it stood to reason that he couldn't have angered anyone, let alone given them cause to hold a grudge against him. This sense of menace must be a result of the grotesque events of that day. No doubt the location was a factor too. He had lived so long in the big city in America that he was unused to being in such close contact with the elements, let alone staying somewhere as remote and wind-swept as this house, surrounded by impenetrable darkness.

He was in the middle of a dream, which slipped away like water through a sieve when he was rudely awoken. Ragga was standing over him, shaking him roughly by the shoulder. On his bedside table, a small alarm clock was shrilly bleating away like a smoke alarm in overdrive. It must be three in the morning. He had borrowed the alarm clock from Sigga as his phone was still refusing to switch on. Of all of them, he'd guessed that she was the most likely to travel with a back-up, as she was always prepared for the worst – anything from a power cut to the end of the world. He had set an alarm but for once hadn't even stirred despite the racket it was making. The sound must have infiltrated his dream but he couldn't remember what role it had played there. Reaching for the clock, he saw that it was now ten past three. He switched off the alarm and fell back onto his pillow.

'We're leaving. Get dressed and come down. No hanging about.' Ragga reached out and for a moment he thought she was going to caress his cheek but her hand continued past his head to the switch on the wall behind him. A reading lamp clicked on, hurting his eyes, and Trausti raised a hand to shield them. Ragga gave him another shake and said: 'Hurry up.' Then she left his room without closing the door behind her.

Resisting the urge to switch off the light and go back to sleep, Trausti braced himself, sat up and swung his legs out from under the warm duvet. It wouldn't be a problem; he was used to waking up after too little sleep. He was also used to starting the day by jumping in the shower but there was no time for that now. He dragged on his clothes, but the moment he straightened up properly, he realised how badly he'd needed that shower. He still felt groggy with sleep.

The others were waiting downstairs, blinking blearily, though Leifur was visibly in the worst state. Ragga seemed the most alert. Trausti would have given anything for a coffee but didn't dare mention it in case they thought it was a good idea. It would only delay the evil hour, and it was best to get this over with. The sooner they set off, the sooner they would be back and he could return to bed and try to forget about this crazy nocturnal adventure.

'Right. About time.' Ragga stood up, blew out a breath, and picked up a bag from the floor. It contained the cleaning products and cloths they had found in a store cupboard the previous evening, after they had taken the decision to obliterate all signs of their presence from Gugga's house. To reduce the risk of being seen, they had voted to go in the middle of the night. Only Trausti had regarded it as a bad idea but he had been overruled. His argument that it was far more suspicious to go round at night than during the day had been dismissed by the others. But in his view it was still valid. If a neighbour had insomnia and happened to look out of the window, they were bound to remember the group, maybe even make a note of their number plate. Whereas by daylight people didn't usually pay much attention to what other people were doing, as long as they behaved normally. Not that it could be taken for granted that they were capable of that, judging by the way they had succeeded in arousing the suspicions of a passer-by the day before.

Leifur was the last to rise to his feet. He held on to the back of his chair and swayed unsteadily. Trausti noticed the wine glass on the table in front of him, which looked as if it had recently been emptied. 'You're not drunk, are you, Leifur?'

'Nah.'

He wasn't fooling anyone.

Sigga made a face. 'He's been boozing all night. Him and Ari.'

Trausti looked from Leifur to Ari. So they hadn't gone to bed after smoking their cigars. Ari didn't appear to be in quite such a rough state, but that was no surprise. He had more self-control and rarely got completely wasted. It happened, but not often. He was too concerned about his image. Leifur, on the other hand, had never had any self-discipline. He always jumped in at the deep end, whatever he did. 'There's no point you coming with us, Leifur,' Trausti said. 'You'd better stay here.'

But, as is often the case with drunks, rational arguments made no impression on Leifur. 'I'm coming too. There's nothing wrong with me.' The way he slurred didn't exactly help his cause.

Trausti opened his mouth to object but Ragga got in first: 'We've already been over this and I have no intention of repeating the conversation. If you hadn't overslept, Trausti, you could have had your say. It's pointless arguing about it. He's determined to come.'

This was going to be even more of a shitshow than Trausti had feared when he went to bed. The chances that Leifur would take care while cleaning, and leave behind fewer traces than he had the first time round were slim at best. Trausti resolved to follow him every step of the way around Gugga's house, to make sure their clean-up wouldn't be rendered completely futile. It meant he wouldn't be much use himself, but that couldn't be helped.

Before going out to the car, Ragga asked if they all had their gloves. They'd found only one pair of rubber gloves in the house, but as everyone had come dressed for winter, they had decided that leather gloves and one pair of mittens from their luggage would serve just as well to prevent fingerprints. Ragga checked the pockets of Leifur's coat herself to make sure he was telling the truth as he nodded with exaggerated movements of his head.

The town was perfectly quiet as they entered it. For once, there was no wind, and a thin veil of fog lay over everything, dimming the streetlights. The higher they got, the thicker the fog became. Perhaps it was just low cloud, sitting on the island, but whatever the cause, the weather was to their advantage. Fog muffled sound and reduced visibility.

When they got out of the car, they were careful to close the doors quietly. Trausti kept an eye on Leifur, who was most likely to forget himself and slam his door. Leifur, noticing this, leaned in towards Trausti, his finger raised to his lips, making a loud shushing noise. Presumably this was intended to demonstrate that he was perfectly on the ball. But the strong blast of alcohol merely confirmed to Trausti that his friend was pissed out of his skull.

Before Ragga opened the front door, they all donned their gloves, and again Trausti was alarmed by the state of Leifur, who seemed unable to get his fingers into the right holes. In the end Trausti had to help him on with them like a kid at nursery school. The mittens would have been easier to put on him but Leifur couldn't be trusted not to tear them off in frustration and leave a trail of fingerprints around the house.

After they had eased the front door shut behind them, they paused in the entrance hall, none of them making a move. Trausti guessed the others were thinking, like him, that this whole enterprise was unbelievably stupid. All apart from Leifur, who was probably wondering where the toilet was or whether he'd be able to find something to drink.

Ari yawned, then whispered, as if they were still standing outside in the street: 'Wait a minute, how were we planning to do this?' They had carefully gone over their plans yesterday evening, recalling in detail which rooms they had entered and what they had touched. Perhaps Ari was drunker than he appeared. Or just very tired. The third possibility was one Trausti was reluctant to contemplate but, try as he might, he couldn't help wondering whether Ari hadn't been paying attention to their discussion because he'd been busy hatching his own plans for the visit. But why he should do that was beyond Trausti.

He had to admit that Leifur deserved some credit for stopping them yesterday when they'd been about to google on their phones how best to destroy fingerprints and biological traces. He had fetched his laptop and used a VPN to search without leaving a trail. Not that they'd learnt much from this, as all the websites he'd found had been American and recommended products that were only available over there. Even if they could find the equivalents from Icelandic manufacturers, they wouldn't be able to go to the shops and stock up on bleach and hydrogen peroxide. People were bound to notice. The cleaning products they'd found in the holiday house had all turned out to be environmentally friendly. Unfortunately, protecting the environment and preventing global warming weren't priorities for those whose sole purpose was to destroy biological traces. None of these products contained the chemicals required for the job. Nevertheless, they would have to do.

In the end, they had convinced themselves that it wasn't DNA so much as fingerprints that were the main problem, but that didn't stop them from using their phone torches to illuminate the floor and other surfaces in order to find and remove any hairs they might have left behind. Flakes of skin would hardly matter. The most important thing was to get rid of the most obvious evidence that they had been in the house. That would do. It would have to do.

Before they left the hall, Ragga distributed cloths to the group, then sprayed them with cleaning fluid. 'The idea is to wipe everything we touched. Each and every one of us.' Ragga looked pointedly at Ari as she continued: 'As we agreed. Remember to turn on as few lights as possible. And switch them off again as soon as you move on to the next room.'

Just then, Trausti came the closest he had ever been to suffering a heart attack when an unidentifiable noise started up somewhere in the house. It sounded as if it was coming from the sitting room, which was only a few steps away. His heart was going like the clappers and there was a sharp pain under his ribs. Judging from the others' expressions, they were equally thrown – all except Leifur, that is, who didn't seem to have noticed. He was too fascinated by the cloth in his hands, gazing at it in wonder as if he had no idea where it had materialised from.

'What was that?' Sigga whispered, her eyes almost completely round with fear. 'Is there somebody there?'

None of them knew the answer to that. The sound came again, a low humming and a quiet click, as if someone had tapped a pencil on a tabletop. 'Let's get out of here,' Sigga said, but her order didn't carry its usual authority as she was forced to whisper. 'Now.'

Leifur opened his mouth and Trausti reacted fast, clapping a hand over it and stifling whatever he had been about to say. The odds were overwhelming that Leifur would forget to whisper. Still with one hand over his friend's mouth, Trausti raised a finger to his own lips and shushed him quietly. Then, taking Leifur's shoulder in a light grip, he pulled him carefully with him as he backed towards the front door. This turned out to be a mistake. Leifur lost his balance and bashed his shoulder against the wall. Trausti's hand wasn't enough to smother the resulting yelp of pain.

The noise was like a dam bursting. They all stampeded into the entrance hall, jostling to get out, abandoning any idea of being stealthy. It was too late now. While Sigga was fumbling with the latch, Trausti glanced round and saw the cause of the alarm. 'Don't open it,' he said at normal pitch.

The others turned, astonished, but their tension eased when they saw the movement on the floor behind him. 'Christ. Are they trying to kill us?' Ari blew out a breath. A robot vacuum cleaner was busy dancing its zigzag progression across the parquet. There was nobody else in the house; the gadget had simply started up in obedience to its timer.

When they had recovered from the shock, they filed one after the other into the rooms they had entered on their previous visit. Trausti gripped Leifur's shoulder when he showed signs of wandering off. 'Better stick together,' he said.

Leifur obeyed without a struggle. He seemed to have sobered up a bit but his eyelids were drooping. Trausti decided it would be best to begin in the bathroom. It was small enough that he would be able to keep a close eye on his piss-artist of a friend while he was wiping clean the pill bottles, blister packs and any other surfaces they had touched.

'I feel sick.'

Leifur made no protest when Trausti steered him to sit down on the toilet seat.

'Try to focus on something else.' Trausti opened the medicine cabinet, his thoughts going to the Ritalin it contained. That would perk Leifur up a bit, but, on second thoughts, a perky Leifur was probably the worst thing that could happen in the circumstances. It would only make him even more unpredictable.

'Like what?'

'Anything. Think about Gugga. Remember the old times with her.' Trausti wiped a pill bottle with his cloth, replaced it, then picked up the next.

'Gugga. She was all right. Mind you, she could be a bloody bitch at times.'

'I don't know. Aren't we all a mixture of good and bad? Isn't the most important question which weighs heaviest in the end?' Trausti glanced at Leifur, who made a face as if he had no idea what Trausti was on about. 'Just focus on her good points.'

'Yeah. Right.'

Leifur lapsed into silence and Trausti shot him a look to make sure he wasn't about to topple head first into the bath or something. But in spite of rocking to and fro, he seemed not to have lost his balance. The rocking was rhythmic, rather than inadvert. Leifur stopped and blew out a breath. 'I can't do it. I just keep remembering her going on and on about her mother. How ill she was and how much pain she was in. It was a real downer when you were trying to have a laugh.'

Trausti remembered that period in Gugga's life. Every time she had a drink inside her, she was like a broken record. As Leifur said, it had been a real mood killer. Trausti had borne the brunt of it because he was studying medicine, and he'd sometimes had to smother a yawn. She'd ranted on about pain and hospital services and Icelandic law. Why shouldn't her mother be prescribed cannabis if it would make her feel better? Why couldn't she get to choose when she'd had enough and wanted to die? What would come after death? Of course he'd had no answers to any of these questions, since he was only a student, focused on what might come up in the exams rather than the big existential questions. 'Gugga was having a hard time. You must see that.'

Leifur ignored this. 'She was a bitch to Gudrún too.'

Trausti wiped clean the last pill bottle and turned his attention to the blister packs and packets. It came back to him now that Leifur used to fancy Gudrún; although he had never admitted as much, it had been blindingly obvious to the others. Still, Leifur was right about Gugga's attitude to Gudrún: Gugga was always picking on her or talking about her behind her back. They had been like chalk and cheese: Gudrún rather earnest and not much of a party animal; Gugga always up for a laugh. Instead of simply accepting their differences, Gugga had never been able to let it go if Gudrún declined an invitation because she didn't feel like joining in or preferred not to drink.

Now, confronted by all these drugs and with more experience under his belt, Trausti had a better insight into the reason for Gugga's inability to leave Gudrún alone to enjoy her healthy lifestyle. Gugga had taken it as personal criticism or felt that Gudrún despised the rest of them. Clearly, Gugga had been well on the way to developing a dependency on drugs or alcohol – or both. And, as is common with those wrestling with the demons of addiction, she was determined that everyone else should join in the fun. That way it was easier for her to kid herself that her behaviour was normal.

'I reckon Gugga killed Gudrún.' Leifur started to take off his gloves.

Trausti swooped to prevent him. 'We don't know that. If Gudrún died that night, it was probably from natural causes. Or alcohol poisoning. She wasn't used to drinking, so she wouldn't have known her own limits.' Trausti had no intention of confiding in Leifur about the suspicions he'd had the night before. The last thing the friends needed now was for Leifur to start rambling drunkenly about poisoning and murder. 'She could have choked on her own vomit,' he continued. 'Maybe she just passed out drunk and we misinterpreted the situation.' This was far too complicated for Leifur to follow in his befuddled state. Trausti wondered if he ought to add something to simplify matters. Then he realised that it didn't matter: Leifur probably wasn't even listening. But it turned out he was wrong.

'Gudrún hardly drank a thing. She had two glasses max.' Leifur raised two fingers. 'Two.'

He must be mistaken. Trausti's memories of the later part of the evening were worryingly hazy, but some things stood out pretty sharply. Oddly enough, Gudrún had been in high spirits, which was quite out of character for her. As a rule, she had been serious and slow to smile, though he suspected that was partly out of embarrassment about her braces. But that evening he remembered her beaming round at them all. She had to have downed a fair amount of booze. Perhaps not enough to give her alcohol poisoning, but there was no question that she'd needed help getting to bed. So it stood to reason that she had been drunk. What other explanation could there be? Trausti was about to close the medicine cabinet, when he paused, his gaze arrested by all the pills. Maybe Leifur was on to something.

Could Gugga have had access to this many drugs in the old days? Could she have been so ill disposed towards Gudrún that she'd slipped something into her punch to get rid of her? The idea was ludicrous. Gugga had repeatedly nagged Trausti to tell her which drugs her mother could take to put an end to her suffering. Indeed, she'd begged him for help in getting hold of the necessary pills, which made it highly improbable that she'd already had access to them. Trausti had ducked out of all such conversations, which hadn't been that hard, as Gugga had usually been totally wasted by the time she brought up the subject. It was easy enough to change the subject when you were talking to a drunk. Unless it had all been an elaborate ploy on Gugga's part? Perhaps her mother hadn't wanted to put an end to her life at all. Most people didn't opt for that way out, however wretched their sufferings, regarding any sort of life as better than none. After all, there was nothing awaiting them after death but the eternal void. Was it possible that those absurd conversations had actually been about Gudrún, not Gugga's mother?

No, out of the question. Trausti had a vivid memory of Gugga's descriptions of the dreadful ordeal suffered by her mother, who'd had squamous cell carcinoma, a type of skin cancer that had attacked her mouth and throat. The treatment had deprived her of all her enjoyment of life, ruining her appearance and making it almost impossible for her to eat. It was only too believable that she wouldn't have wanted to go on living in that state. Especially since the surgeons kept having to remove more and more of her face and neck. The drugs Gugga had nagged him about had unquestionably been for her mother. That would have been infinitely more important to Gugga than any desire to poison Gudrún just because she found her a bit boring. Gugga had even approached some of the others in the group with the same request when Trausti proved obdurate. Ari had once shoved her away when she started describing her mother's illness in the hope of getting him to help her. He had always been terribly squeamish. The fact Gugga was offering to pay generously for the pills wouldn't have made any difference.

Trausti closed the medicine cabinet and told himself to stop indulging in pointless speculation. The very idea was mad. Gugga hadn't been some kind of psychopath. She hadn't bumped Gudrún off. There had to be another explanation for how the body had ended up in Gugga's basement. He wiped the area around the sink and cabinet door, though he didn't think anyone had touched it. 'One question, Leifur.'

Leifur started violently. He had been nodding off. 'What?'

'Did you visit Gugga in hospital?' Trausti couldn't understand why he hadn't thought to ask before, since Leifur was in no state to lie convincingly.

'Nah. Why would I have visited her? What for?'

'OK, then tell me this. Was it you who was steering the pointer on the Ouija board? For a joke.'

'Nope. Not me. Maybe it was Gugga. You know, her spirit – from beyond the grave. Or something.' Leifur rubbed his face with a gloved hand. 'Wow. That would be cool.' He yawned, then began to slump slowly sideways.

Trausti straightened him up and gave him a light slap. His glove softened the blow and Leifur only half opened his eyes. 'Man, this party is shit,' he muttered.

Leifur was right about that. Having reassured himself that every surface and loose object they'd touched was clean, Trausti heaved his friend to his feet, switched off the light, then, wiping the door handles inside and out, closed the door to the bathroom. He led Leifur to the next room, which was Gugga's bedroom. There they found Sigga and Ragga hard at work wiping all the bits and pieces from the jewellery box. They assured Trausti they had it covered and told him to go away. Leifur had other ideas, however, pleased to have found company that was more to his liking. He took up position between the girls, draped his arms over their shoulders, and hung his full weight between them, declaring them to be wonderful.

Trausti scanned the room, trying to remember what he'd touched. Recalling the box of books, he went over to the wardrobe where he had replaced it. 'I handled several of the books in here. Have you cleaned the box and its contents?' He realised he didn't trust them to do it, since it was only his fingerprints on the box. 'No worries, if not. I can do it.'

Sigga gave Leifur a shove before he could pull her and Ragga over. 'No, we'll take care of that. The best way you can help us is to take Leifur away. Please.'

There was no getting around it; Trausti couldn't refuse and insist on cleaning the books and box himself. He would just have to remember to do it later, before leaving. He dragged Leifur out of the room with him and started looking for other things to clean. For a moment, he actually contemplated tying his friend to a chair as he could get almost nothing done while he was constantly having to keep an eye on him. But with a bit of adroitness, he was able to achieve something. He drew the line at cleaning the model ship Leifur had tried to carry off, though. There were too many fiddly small parts and it would be impossible to wipe them all with the cloth in one hand while fending Leifur off with the other. Drink didn't seem to have done anything to lessen his interest in the model. In the end, Trausti decided to take the ship with them. It couldn't be helped. At this news, Leifur rediscovered his good mood and declared that Trausti was a great guy and his best friend. Then he started rambling on about how they should meet up more often and vowed to come and visit Trausti in America. It would never happen, but this wasn't the moment to tell Leifur that. Tomorrow, Trausti would remind him of what he'd said and add that the best way to cut your alcohol intake was to try to realise all the plans that had seemed so brilliant when you were pissed.

Trausti felt a huge weight off his shoulders once they had finished the cleaning. Before leaving the house, Sigga interrogated Ari about whether he'd definitely wiped the banister on the cellar stairs as well as the door knobs. Wearily, Ari confirmed that he had and added that he'd had such trouble with the crate that his gloves were full of splinters. It was no joke trying to wipe fingerprints off rough, unfinished wood.

Next, Sigga rounded on Trausti, frowning at the model ship he was carrying. Before she could start interrogating him, he decided to turn defence into attack. He was too tired to go around kow-towing to her any more. 'What about the cardboard box? The one with the books in it. Did you clean that?'

They'd forgotten, of course. Everyone except Leifur groaned. Before anyone could suggest that they did it now, which would mean further delays, Trausti said quickly: 'Let's just take the box with us. Like the model. We need to get out of here now.' In the end, they grabbed the robot vacuum cleaner too, in case it had hoovered up anything incriminating that could be connected to them.

They made it out to the car, apparently unobserved. All the lights were still off in the neighbouring houses and they couldn't see any curtains twitching. Cautiously, they pulled the car doors closed and Ragga started the engine. Trausti got the impression she was trying to do so as quietly as possible, though of course this made no difference. The engine started with a booming roar as usual. Surprisingly enough, Leifur seemed to have noticed Ragga's caution. 'We should have used your electric car, Ari,' he observed, then leant his head back and fell instantly asleep.

He was right. That would have been a better idea. But then there were a lot of things they should have done differently. Both now and in the past. Like ringing the police as soon as they'd realised Gudrún was missing. And telling the truth about what had happened at the party. Then they wouldn't be up shit creek now.

None of them said a word as Ragga drove off into the fog.

Chapter 16
Day 6 – Tuesday, 28 January

Although the blizzard had let up, the gale Idunn had been battling against on her way to the hospital seemed in retrospect
almost like the waft of warm air from a heater in comparison
to what awaited her on Stórhöfdi. Týr and the policewoman
driving them spoke little during the short journey and Idunn
used the opportunity to send her mother a message, asking
how she was doing. She had zero worries that her mother had
died from a brain aneurysm and her intuition proved correct.
The reply pinged back at once: *Are you still with your father
in the Westman Islands?* Idunn didn't let herself be drawn but
simply replied: *Ring you tomorrow.* Then she switched off her
phone and stuck it in her pocket. She wasn't going to let herself
be dragged down into the black hole of her mother's obsession
with her father. She had quite enough on her plate with work.

On the way out to the headland, Idunn watched the
familiar landscape of her youth passing by. Once the town
was left behind, little had changed apart from a new sign-
post to a bird-watching hide about halfway up the road to
Stórhöfdi. She couldn't remember there being any facilities
for bird-watchers other than the bare hillside when she was a
child. But the biggest change was what had emerged from her
conversation with Týr as they were walking out to the car: the
lighthouse keeper, who used to be responsible for collecting

meteorological information and tagging birds, no longer lived on the headland. Private individuals had leased the keeper's house and completely renovated it as a holiday let. You could have knocked Idunn down with a feather. It would never have occurred to her that such a thing was possible.

Although the house would be considered ready for use by any normal standards, apparently the renovations weren't quite finished. Outside, the eaves and guttering on the roof still needed repairs, while indoors the burglar alarm had yet to be connected and the electricity circuit board needed labelling. Since the house wasn't supposed to be in use yet, it hadn't crossed anyone's mind that the people they were looking for might have been staying there. Yet it appeared they had. According to Týr, when the electrician turned up to finish his job, he had immediately noticed that the house wasn't as he had left it. There were shoes and coats in the hall that had previously been empty. On further inspection, it transpired that people had been sleeping there. There were suitcases in the dining room, dirty dishes in the kitchen, empty bottles and glasses littering the living areas, and used towels in the bathrooms. The electrician had rung the landlord and been informed that a group of visitors, who he didn't know personally, had borrowed the house for a couple of nights. The landlord said that, as far as he was aware, they were supposed to have left by now. The group had been lent the keys on condition that they would be out by Monday. Apparently they had assured him that they would be leaving on Sunday morning. The landlord added that he'd been aware the electrician was due to come in at the beginning of the week.

The electrician, who rented out a flat on Airbnb as a sideline, had heard that the police were appealing for information about a group of visitors, and that this was in connection with the recent discovery of a dead body. Immediately after hanging up, he had called the police station to report what he had found. The electrician had been told to go and wait in his car, touching as little as possible on his way out. When the police arrived and began their examination of the scene, they had discovered more than just a mess and some abandoned luggage: they had found yet another body.

There was a crowd of police vehicles outside the old lighthouse keeper's house on Stórhöfdi. They almost filled the gravel parking area, so the young policewoman driving Idunn and Týr's car had to use Tetris tactics to squeeze into a place. The number of vehicles suggested a major incident, as did the grave expression on Karó's face as she stood sheltering from the wind by the front door, holding her protective clothing at the ready. Týr hurriedly got out of the car to open the door for Idunn. She felt like a film star on the red carpet but knew that he did this only to ensure that the door wouldn't be blown off its hinges. She had dropped by the hotel to pick up her camera and other equipment, so Týr knew she would have her hands full.

After a struggle, Týr got the better of the wind and managed to close the car door again. They went over to join Karó, who handed Idunn a neat bundle of protective gear. 'Yet another body. Number three,' she said tersely.

Idunn nodded, unsurprised. She began pulling on the overalls. 'Alexandra said there were four or five people in the group she saw. So that would leave only one, or maybe two, alive, which should simplify the investigation if it does turn out to be murder.' Idunn wasn't being ironic, just stating a fact.

'Oh, believe me, unlike the others, this one is unquestionably murder,' Karó said. 'According to the man who lent them the house, there were four of them, so there should only be one left. Unless the man's remembered wrong and there were actually five.'

Idunn didn't ask any further questions. She wanted to approach crime scene and body with an open mind. She finished doing up her overalls and donned gloves and goggles. Then she hung the camera round her neck, picked up her case of instruments and blew out a breath. 'Ready. Lead on.'

The gale ripped at her overalls and Idunn had to plant her feet firmly on the ground to stop herself being blown off course. She raised a hand to her hood as it ballooned out with air, then lowered her head between her shoulders and trudged doggedly in Týr's wake. He made his way past the front door of the house, then round the side, past the wooden deck, to a small, ramshackle shed clad in corrugated iron. Týr had to shout to be heard over the wind: 'The body was found in here.' Fortunately, the front of the shed was in the lee of the storm, so the door could be opened without difficulty. 'We've rigged up a light in there but apart from that no one's been in. I'll wait out here.'

Idunn went inside and Týr shut the door behind her. She switched on the floodlight but it was far too powerful for the tiny space. Temporarily blinded, Idunn closed her eyes and waited for the bright spots on her eyelids to fade. When she opened them again, she searched for a switch to dim the light. Only then could she turn her attention to the task she had come here to perform.

The body was male. Quite young, at a guess thirty, like the woman they had found on the beach, but it was hard to tell with any certainty. His face was puffy and distorted. His swollen tongue poked out from between shrivelled lips and the whites of his dry, open eyes were red. This man hadn't died yesterday, or the day before. Through her mask, Idunn could smell the telltale odour of decomposition, and the colour of the flesh she could see strengthened that impression. All the indications were that the man had died before the woman on the beach. Possibly also before the burnt body, though in that case the time of death was an open question. But Karó had been right that there was no doubting the cause of death this time.

Around the young man's neck was a belt – a leather belt that had been pulled tight. The buckle was located exactly at the front of his neck, over the windpipe. It looked familiar, but then Idunn had seen countless similar buckles. It was a gold-plated logo, formed of two interlinked letters: D and G. Idunn was no fan of designer goods herself but assumed that a belt like that wouldn't come cheap. She based this assumption on the fact that the sort of people she had seen wearing these belts generally tucked their shirts into their trousers at the front to show off the buckle, even if they were allowed to hang loose at the back. She couldn't help wondering whether the location of the buckle in this case had been dictated by the same urge to show off the brand.

One thing was immediately clear. If the buckle was facing forwards, the killer had almost certainly been standing in front of the man. As far as Idunn could see, the leather strap had been threaded through the buckle. This meant that the buckle would have taken the strain and most likely been dragged round to face the person pulling on the belt. If the man had been throttled from behind, the buckle would have been situated at the back of his neck.

Knowing whether the killer had stood in front of or behind the victim could be significant – to test the credibility of any story they concocted if they were caught, for example. If they had stood in front of the victim, they would have been in very close proximity. Involuntary reactions to strangling were of two types: on the one hand, to clutch at the ligature and try to reduce the pressure; on the other, to claw at the face of the attacker when it became obvious that scrabbling at the ligature wasn't working. Consequently, the killer might be expected to display injuries. Possibly on the face.

It also gave an idea of the murderer's mentality or state of mind at the moment of the killing. Looking someone in the eye while they're fighting for their life, and continuing to exert pressure, is easier said than done. The victim would quickly lose consciousness from lack of oxygen but the pressure would have to be kept up for several minutes to result in death. And several minutes is a long time in circumstances like those. The killer would have had plenty of time to realise the consequences of what they were doing and loosen their grip. Yet that hadn't happened.

The dead man was sitting on the floor with his legs straight out in front of him, his back propped against some boxes that were stacked up by the wall. His head was slightly tipped back and had lolled towards his right shoulder. Idunn was fairly sure he hadn't died in situ. If, as she guessed, he'd been strangled sitting down, his legs should have been thrashing around all over the place, yet there were no heel marks on the floor. She deduced from this that the body had been moved to the shed after the event.

She crouched down and examined the man's neck, noting the conspicuous grazes made by scratching and clawing. She lifted first one, then the other of the man's hands, inspecting his nails. There appeared to be tissue under them – a mixture of skin and dried blood. She laid them carefully down again, hoping the perpetrator's DNA would also turn up there.

Then she picked up her camera and began taking pictures, simultaneously recording her observations on the audio file that accompanied every frame. She took care to leave absolutely nothing out and didn't stop until every square centimetre of the scene had been documented in the camera's memory. It was a luxury to be allowed to complete the process in peace like this, instead of having to put up with spectators disturbing her concentration. It wasn't unknown for her to be struck by a sudden insight while she was snapping away. The feeling was reminiscent of being on the point of falling asleep, when all obstacles to the free flow of her thoughts had been cleared. The view through the lens showed her the scene in miniature, enabling her to isolate specific details, instead of being forced to confront the full horror.

But despite the peace and quiet, she received no flashes of inspiration this time. Perhaps because there was no mystery. Strangulation was a common murder method and almost all the details were on display. The belt was still round the victim's neck and no obvious attempts had been made to destroy the perpetrator's DNA, although the location of the body in the shed suggested that the killer had wanted to conceal the deed. If so, the attempt was perfunctory, and an odd choice too, in view of where the shed was located. It wasn't far from a sheer drop into a rough sea, while just to the north of it there was a steep slope leading down to the cliff edge. It wouldn't have required much effort on the killer's part to lug the body there and roll it down the slope, then fill the dead man's pockets with stones and push him over the edge. The body would have been found eventually, but the murderer would have bought him- or herself some precious time.

Idunn took one last picture, then replaced the lens cap and pulled over her case of equipment. Opening it, she commenced her measurements.

*

'Thanks,' the inspector said to Idunn, who had just finished reporting her findings, emphasising that they were all pre-liminary but would be confirmed – and possibly modified – following the post-mortem.

'Anyway, I'm done here, and as far as I'm concerned CSI can take over.' Idunn peeled off her latex gloves and stuffed them into the pocket of her overalls. 'But first I'll need help getting the body out of the shed and onto a stretcher to be taken to the ambulance. I've prepared it for transferral.'

The inspector nodded. 'No problem. Will it be taken to the hospital?'

'No, to the airport. It'll be coming to Reykjavík with me. So will the other body from the morgue.'

'To Reykjavík?' Ína looked as astonished as if Idunn had said she was going to take it to a Confirmation party.

'Yes. I understood the wind was dropping.' Idunn looked out of the window. 'At least, it's improved a lot since earlier.'

'That's correct. Flights will have resumed. But I thought you'd been told that you won't be leaving immediately. We need your team here for now.'

Idunn felt as if she were in a rowing boat that had nearly reached the shore when it suddenly sprang a leak. But she controlled her features and tried not to let her feelings show. 'That's impossible, I'm afraid. I need to get back to Reykjavík and start the post-mortems. They can't wait any longer. I assume Týr and Karó will have nothing against staying on to help you but my talents are being wasted here.' She did her best to conceal her desperation.

But Inspector Ína wasn't backing down: 'We've got their names. The name of the man, Ari, who borrowed the house, and the others from the IDs and credit cards in the bags they left behind. They belonged to a man and a woman. Then the person who'd lent them the house gave us the name of a woman Ari had apparently mentioned when asked who else would be travelling with him. After that, we rang the woman's workplace and a colleague confirmed that she'd gone with a group of friends to the Westman Islands and hadn't turned up to work since. The person we spoke to mentioned a boyfriend, which we found odd since he hasn't reported his girlfriend missing, but when we phoned the man in question he downplayed the relationship. He said they were only in the early stages of dating and it wasn't very serious. He sounded credible. But, most importantly, we've got all the names now.' She paused and took a deep breath. 'There were four of them and none of them have returned from the trip. Well, of course, there may have been five, but so far we only have three bodies, which begs the question, where are the other one or two members of the group? The plan is to search the entire island tomorrow, so we'll need you on hand.'

'What about the ANPR cameras on the docks? Can't you use the images to check whether the other member or members of the party have left? So I'm not kept hanging around here for nothing.'

'Unfortunately, only a small number of the images are usable. The camera was facing into the wind and the lens was encrusted with snow for part of the period in question. The fact we can't see the car in the images we have doesn't tell us anything, but your sister went through them earlier and didn't spot the vehicle she saw, either coming or going, which means there's a possibility it's still on the island. Flights have been ruled out and no one could have swum to the mainland.'

Idunn wasn't ready to give up. 'The harbour is full of boats; someone could have hitched a lift on one of them. Or stolen a small motorboat.'

Ína shook her head. 'It would be impossible to steal a boat without somebody noticing. And since no one's reported a vessel missing, that rules out theft. Besides, the boats here aren't hired out as taxis to take people to the mainland. You can't just hitch a lift.'

'But what about the post-mortems? Aren't they more urgent?' Idunn had to give it one last shot, though she doubted it would work. The inspector didn't strike her as the type to back down.

'It was my understanding that the facilities here at the hospital are perfectly adequate. You said so yourself. We can get hold of the tools you mentioned and make sure you receive the necessary assistance. You'll be supplied with everything you need.'

There was little point in Idunn objecting since her own words had been her downfall. Self-inflicted woes were the worst. But she had to try. 'I've got other tasks awaiting my attention in town as well as the post-mortems, you know. I need to get back to the office.'

'Oh, I rang Reykjavík earlier, before making my decision,' Ína said. 'I spoke to the man who's covering for you and he assured me there was nothing they couldn't handle in your absence.'

Self-inflicted woes and Judas betrayals. It seemed there was no end to Idunn's trials that day. The inspector, considering the matter closed, walked off to have a word with the CSI team, who had nearly finished inside the house. A technician emerged with a model ship in his arms, similar to the ones Idunn had noticed at Gugga's house. Alexandra hadn't mentioned that the group had been carrying one of those, and Idunn was surprised the girl hadn't remembered such a striking detail. People didn't usually wander around with large model ships in their arms.

Another CSI came out carrying some clear specimen bags containing plastic bottles. Idunn thought they looked like the kind in which lighter fluid for barbecues was sold. All the pieces of the puzzle were falling into place. The technician put the bags in the police van with the model ship, then got in and closed the door.

Idunn was left standing there alone, staring into the middle distance. She puffed out her cheeks with air, then slowly released it. After that, she took off her protective overalls and freed her hair. It would be all right. She had managed to avoid her father so far and there was no reason why she shouldn't be able to continue doing so for another twenty-four hours. If she focused on the autopsies, she should be safe enough. No one could wander into the hospital basement.

She switched on her phone. There were six new messages from her mother. She decided not to open them. It wasn't hard to guess what they would say. Her mother was unstable and tended to spiral when things didn't go exactly her way. No doubt she was as upset that Idunn was in the islands as Idunn was herself. But, unlike her mother, Idunn knew how to keep a cool head. Instead of taking a deep breath, her mother would work herself up into a frenzy, imagining all kinds of ridiculous scenarios, until she hit a wall. The resulting crash would last longer than the build-up, and Idunn was resigned to having to take on the role of listening ear when she got home.

Great. Just great.

Her phone bleeped. Idunn checked the screen, expecting it to be another message from her mother, who had worked herself into a complete tizzy. It wasn't. Since Idunn didn't recognise the number, she thought it was probably safe to open the message. She was wrong: it was from her father.

The terse communication betrayed no hint of a desire for reconciliation or an apology for the way he had treated her. Clearly, he'd abandoned that tactic. Ever since Idunn had left home at twenty, she had received the occasional email from him, attempting to end their estrangement. When she didn't reply, he would give up and there would be a long interval of silence before he tried again. Sometimes he offered her money but she deleted those emails too without answering them. She didn't want anything from him, least of all something as impersonal as money. When he died, she stood to inherit quite a fortune, as legally it wasn't permissible to disinherit your offspring. She was thinking of donating it to charity. Doctors Without Borders, for example. Or – the biggest kick in the teeth of all for her dad – donating the lot to Greenpeace, the organisation she remembered him despising for their anti-whaling stance. Fewer whales meant more plankton for the fish to eat – and therefore more fish for him to catch. But even that act of vengeance would probably be wasted. The new wife would almost certainly sit on the money during her lifetime, and, since the age difference between them wasn't that great, Idunn might even die before her.

It wasn't really surprising, then, if he was curt and showed no sign of wanting a rapprochement. He had finally realised that he didn't need her. He had a new family and a new life. She and her mother had been no more than a practice run. An experiment that had gone wrong but had no doubt been instructive in its way. Although Idunn had suspected as much for a long time, it still hurt to see the evidence in black and white like this.

Is Alexandra OK? Can you persuade her to come home?

Chapter 17

Day 3 – Saturday, 25 January

Trausti couldn't get back to sleep after their return to the house on Stórhöfdi. He lay in bed, tossing and turning in search of a comfortable position. But whichever way he turned, his thoughts wouldn't allow him any relief. The storm raging inside his head made it ache. How could he have let himself become embroiled in this clusterfuck? What the hell was wrong with him?

In the end, he gave up the attempt and went downstairs. He was expecting to encounter some of the others as he'd heard the sound of voices rising from below while he was lying awake, but there was no one up. Perhaps that wasn't surprising since it wasn't yet seven. Anyway, the solitude suited him perfectly. He sat down on one of the sofas on the middle floor of the house and mindlessly watched the rhythmic beam of the lighthouse illuminating the dark morning. Dark, light, dark, light. The unceasing spectacle of the sweeping beam outside the window had a hypnotic effect on him and his eyelids began to droop. If he had been allowed to go on sitting there in peace and quiet he would have nodded off.

But Sigga appeared and came over to join him. She was wearing a capacious white bathrobe, like the one that hung in his own en-suite. Below it, her legs were bare and the low-cut neckline did nothing to hide her cleavage. He found himself wondering inadvertently if she was naked underneath. He himself was dressed, which was a good illustration of the difference between them. Although Sigga's ambition knew no bounds, she could relax when appropriate. It was a talent that had always eluded him. He had noticed the bathrobe in his en-suite but immediately begun creating mental obstacles for himself, like thinking the owners might want to christen the garments themselves. He had always been this way – afraid of taking up too much room or causing any inconvenience. Yet here he was, recently returned from what practically amounted to a break-in at the home of a dead friend, undertaken in order to destroy incriminating evidence and mislead the police. He might as well have donned the bathrobe. It was too late to avoid creating waves at this point.

'How can they sleep?' Sigga sank down on the sofa, reclining her head against the soft cushions. 'I'm completely shattered but I just can't switch off.' She turned to him and he saw the black circles under her eyes. 'Haven't you got anything with you? Like sleeping pills?'

Trausti shook his head. He was no fan of drugs and up to now had more or less managed without them. In particular, he steered well clear of sleeping pills because it was so easy to become dependent. The temptation was strong, especially since his gruelling residency had screwed up his sleep patterns. He often did twenty-four-hour shifts during which he could only snatch an hour's rest here or there, but he still found it hard to drop off when he finally got home. Pills weren't the answer, though; they only meant replacing one problem with another.

Sigga sighed and turned her head back to stare into space again. 'Oh well, it was worth a try.'

They were silent for a while, listening to the low snores carrying from the other sitting room where Leifur was sleeping it off. They seemed to be in sync with the lighthouse: dark, snore; light, snore.

Sigga emitted a sudden giggle. 'I've got a boyfriend. I wasn't going to tell you guys about him because it's still very early days, but it feels like there are already too many secrets between us.'

'Good for you.' Trausti didn't understand why she was bringing this up now. 'Is he a nice guy?'

'He's amazing.' Sigga gave another brief, humourless laugh, betraying a faint note of hysteria this time. 'I met him at work and it's his fault I can't sleep. His dream is to become a judge and if he had any idea what was going on here, he would drop me like a hot brick.'

Trausti couldn't help smiling. 'I see. I suppose visiting his girlfriend in prison might not be a very good look for a judge.'

Sigga jabbed him with her elbow. 'We're not going to prison. We've made sure of that.' She flashed a grin at him. 'Unless someone has reported us to the police and they lock us up for illegal cleaning.'

Trausti hadn't even thought about prison. His catastrophising hadn't got that far. In his case, the consequences would be disastrous enough if he simply failed to make it back to the US on time. How would he be able to explain that to his bosses at the hospital? They insisted on an official sick note every time he had to miss work. One of his fellow students had lost his mother and had to provide a copy of her death certificate before he could get leave to go home for the funeral. Trausti would not be popular if he waved a note from the Icelandic police saying that he'd been detained for questioning. That's if he was even permitted to re-enter the US. It was from dread of this happening that he had allowed himself to be roped into last night's foolish escapade.

'How long do you think we've got until someone finds the crate in the cellar?' Sigga wrapped her bathrobe more tightly around herself, clutching it to her throat as if she was cold.

'I don't know. Sooner or later someone's bound to go down there. The house will be sold and they'll need to clear it out. It'll be discovered then, if not before.' Trausti became aware of the same chilly draught as Sigga had obviously felt. He pulled over a woollen blanket that was lying folded on the arm of the sofa. It was so new that it still had the price tag attached. He hesitated out of the same scruples that had made him reluctant to use the bathrobe, then decided to follow Sigga's example. He offered her the blanket first but she declined it, so he wrapped it around his own shoulders. The price tag ended up at the back of his neck where it scratched his skin as if to remind him that he shouldn't be using it.

'We need to get out of here as soon as possible.' Sigga drew her feet up on the sofa and tucked them under herself. 'We can't risk being here when they find the body. There's a tiny, infinitesimal chance that our earlier statements will be regarded as sufficient and we won't be dragged back in for questioning. But if the police spot us wandering around here when the body's discovered, they'll definitely home in on us. I mean, Gugga's dead so it's not like she can answer their questions.'

Sigga had put her finger on the problem. Trausti experienced a sudden urge to leap to his feet, pack his things and jump in the car. He could change his ticket and fly to the US later today or tomorrow instead of leaving on Monday as planned. Never mind the cost. If he was abroad by the time the shit hit the fan, he would be well out of it. If the police wanted to question him, he could agree to an online interview and no one at the hospital need know a thing. The Icelandic authorities were unlikely to insist he fly home. After all, he hadn't done anything wrong. 'I'm with you. Let's leave by the next ferry.' If his phone had been working, he would have changed his flight and bought a new ferry ticket then and there.

Sigga pointed to the big window. 'The weather seems OK for once. It should be possible.'

Trausti had been gazing out of the window before she came down but hadn't even registered the weather. He'd been too fixated on the lighthouse. 'Good.' Yet again he regretted the loss of his phone as he was thwarted in his desire to check the forecast. Until he could be sure, he'd only fret about the possibility of another storm blowing up. To suppress these worries, he turned to Sigga: 'Can I ask you a question? You're a lawyer: won't the fact that Gudrún's body has turned up change everything? At the time, she was only officially missing and the investigation was allowed to peter out. But now it's clear that she didn't just disappear: she's dead.'

Sigga countered this with a question of her own: 'Let me ask you something. You're a doctor: will the police be able to tell how she died?'

Trausti looked at Sigga and wondered why she had brought this up. Was she worried about Gudrún's cause of death coming to light? And if so, why? But he couldn't tell from her blank expression whether she was worried or just curious. 'Yes. I'd assume so. But I can't be certain. It depends how she died and what sort of condition her body's in. I didn't examine it at all, just saw enough to make me want to get out of there.'

Sigga looked disappointed and Trausti dropped his suspicions about her motives. 'But the police must be able to tell. Please, humour me and say they will.' She caught his surprised expression. 'We didn't kill her, remember? So it would be to our advantage if they could work out what happened. Maybe she just had a heart attack.'

Trausti decided to spare her the knowledge that this was one thing that couldn't be established with any certainty after so many years, irrespective of the sand or salt the body had been preserved in. 'Are you quite sure that none of us did any-thing to Gudrún?' he asked. 'I'm not.'

'What do you mean?' Sigga shrank away from him, as if his suspicions were infectious. 'Of course I am.'

Trausti felt doubt rearing its ugly head again. Could Sigga's childish innocence be a pretence? 'Doesn't it strike you as at all odd that she should have ended up in Gugga's cellar if she died of natural causes? Who would bother to hide the body of someone who dropped dead of a heart attack?' When Sigga didn't answer, he said it for her: 'No one. No one would do that.'

'Well, I know for sure that I didn't touch her.'

There was no need to remind Sigga that they had all admit-ted that their memories of the evening Gudrún vanished were patchy in the extreme. 'Neither did I,' he said quickly instead. 'Gugga's the most likely suspect. But, like you say, it's too late to ask her now.'

Sigga released a long breath. After a moment, she said: 'I've had an idea.' She looked at him and he read in her eyes that he wasn't going to like what she had to say. He was right. 'Would you be prepared to examine the body?' Seeing the consternation on his face, Sigga added hurriedly: 'Just a quick look. Enough to see what she died of. It would help us to know. I mean . . .'

'No. It won't help us. It'll do anything but.' Trausti didn't know where to begin in listing all the arguments against this terrible idea. 'In the unlucky event that suspicion *is* directed at us, wouldn't it be better if we were in the dark? Would you trust yourself to act as if the cause of death came as a com-plete surprise to you?'

'Yes, actually.'

'Well, I wouldn't. No, it's totally out of the question. I'm not going anywhere near that house again.' The idea was so ridiculous that Trausti couldn't help wondering if it had been suggested as a ploy. Were they trying to trick him into incriminating himself further in this pathetic mess? If so, they could think again. He wasn't going to take the fall.

'I'd just feel so much better if I could be sure that Gudrún had died of natural causes. Because in that case we'd have nothing to fear.'

'Forget it.' Trausti felt a chill that the blanket did nothing to dispel. 'You saw the same as I did. Her teeth had been ripped out. The only reason I can think of for that is that someone wanted to prevent her from being identified. And that points to only one thing: that Gudrún didn't die naturally. She didn't have a heart attack or a stroke or a bowel obstruction. Surely you can understand that? Examining the body won't achieve anything.'

Sigga looked even more exhausted. Her shoulders sagged and she let go of the neck of her bathrobe and began picking at her cuticles instead. She had always done this when she was stressed as a student. At exam time her fingers used to have bleeding sores around the nails. 'Isn't there any other conceivable explanation? I can't picture Gugga pulling the teeth out of a corpse. Couldn't they have come loose and fallen out by themselves? As a result of decomposition or something?'

Trausti simply shook his head. He was too tired to keep up this pointless conversation. Nothing Sigga could say would change his mind, not even one of her single-word commands or prettily worded requests that were usually enough to propel him to his feet.

'We mustn't forget to return the key.' Sigga had apparently realised that it was useless to go on nagging him. She could be bossy and domineering but she was also clever; not the type to persist with an argument when she saw that it was a lost cause. 'That would be the final straw.'

'We can drop by on our way to the ferry. Chuck it through the letterbox if Halldóra's out or asleep.'

Sigga sat upright. 'Come on, I'll make some coffee. There's no point going to sleep now. If we get bored, we can start on the cleaning.'

The idea was no worse than any other, and she was right about the cleaning. If they were going to catch the first ferry, they'd better not hang around. Trausti let out a groan when he saw what awaited them: cans, bottles, glasses, a pile of washing-up, and floors filthy from their outdoor shoes. They would have to put the sheets on to wash and dry, then remake the beds. Wash and dry the towels, too. Maybe it was a bit optimistic to think they'd catch that first ferry.

The coffee revived him. His thoughts came into focus and the list of jobs no longer seemed as insurmountable as before. It didn't matter if they left with the first, second or third ferry, as long as they made it to the mainland today. He wouldn't catch the evening flight to the US but, never mind, he would just leave on tomorrow's plane instead. There was no way the police would react so fast that they'd be in touch just hours after the crate was discovered. It would take them time to identify the body and, to begin with, their sights would be focused on Gugga. Trausti and his friends would come under scrutiny eventually, but they wouldn't be a priority. He could afford to relax a little.

They were seated at the dining table, facing each other with the model ship between them. Strange to think he'd admired it at first. Now the sight of it made him agitated. 'We need to get rid of that.'

'Yes. And the box of books. And the robot vacuum cleaner.' Sigga took a sip of coffee, then smiled at him. 'Come to think of it, we could plug in the vacuum and let it take care of cleaning the floors. Then push the model ship out to sea and burn the books.'

'Or just take the lot to Reykjavík and dump them there. No one's going to miss them but it would be better not to draw attention to them by leaving them here. Sod's law, the model would sail into the harbour right under the noses of the police. It would be best if they thought no one had entered the house since Gugga died.'

'What about the neighbour? What's-her-name who lent you the keys?'

'When I drop them off, I'll tell her we didn't have time to go round. Then we'll just have to cross our fingers and hope she doesn't contact the police. She may not make the connection when the discovery of the body hits the news. With any luck, the fact the body's been there a long time means she'll have no reason to think we were involved.'

Sigga tried to pretend that she agreed with him but he saw through her unconvincing smile. Perhaps she was thinking about the young woman who had seen them spilling out of Gugga's house. He kept thinking about her himself. He took another mouthful of coffee but this time it failed to soothe his nerves. Would it be better to tell Halldóra that they'd briefly stepped inside the house, wandered around the sitting room, then left, or to lie that they hadn't been there at all? They would have to decide, then agree on a story. And they would have to do it before he left Iceland, because he had no desire to leave a digital trail by discussing it online. He hoped to God Leifur wouldn't wake up too hungover to take in the information, though the danger of that was all too real.

Trausti couldn't wait to be sitting on the plane, feeling the surge as it took off and broke its ties with Iceland. As soon as the seatbelt lights were switched off, he was going to order himself a stiff drink – the strongest spirits they were permitted to sell on board.

He realised he might never be able to move home as a result of this shitshow. He would be safer abroad, where in time he would gradually put the nightmare behind him. His parents would be sad and his younger brother disappointed, but it would be a far greater shock for the family if he was embroiled in a murder investigation. That mustn't be allowed to happen. His mum and dad were so proud of him that a disgrace like that would finish them off. He reflected wryly that his sister would get over it, though.

Sigga dragged him back to the present by reaching across the table and gripping his arm. 'Look. Headlights.'

Trausti turned and his heart missed a beat when he saw a car making its way up to the house. It stopped and for a fraction of a second Trausti thought the driver had realised they were going the wrong way and decided to turn round. Then he remembered the gate. A shadowy figure appeared silhouetted against the headlights, then vanished and the car started moving again. It stopped once more while the gate was being closed. There was no mistaking it – someone was coming to the house. Trausti found himself muttering obscenities under his breath. It stopped him screaming. All he could think of was the police. Coming to interview them. In which case it would be too late to agree on a story. He couldn't even make up his mind which version would be better to blurt out now to Sigga.

'Is that the police?' Sigga was clutching her bathrobe to her throat again. 'Oh my God. Surely they wouldn't be coming here this early in the morning unless it was something serious? What are we going to do?'

There was nothing they could do. There was no point switching off the lights and pretending no one was home. If it was the police, they would have seen the lights in the windows as they were approaching. Trausti forced himself to think rationally. The body in the cellar couldn't possibly have been discovered that early in the morning, such a short time after they had left the house. A far more likely explanation was that a neighbour of Gugga's had spotted them and followed their car to find out where they were staying. It hadn't occurred to any of them to check the rear-view mirror for signs of pursuit. A car with its lights off could easily have given chase; the driver could have seen where they were staying and reported their suspicious movements.

The police must have come to question them about their nocturnal visit to Gugga's house, under the impression that it had been a burglary. As Trausti squinted into the glare of the headlights, he tried to come up with an explanation plausible enough to make the police thank them for their time, apologise for disturbing them and go away again. But his mind was blank, his breathing shallow with panic. All he could think of was to say that they hadn't been able to sleep, so they had decided to use the time to fetch some mementos to remember their dead friend by, since it had been one of her last wishes. A ridiculous story – but that might actually work in their favour and make it more plausible. After all, people did much stranger things. 'Shit. The model ship!' Trausti stared wildly at the ship in the middle of the table. If the police saw that, any talk of mementos would be futile. They would be charged with theft. Then, when the body was eventually discovered in the cellar, one thing would lead to another. 'Shit.'

For once, Sigga showed that she could keep a cool head in a crisis. She sprang to her feet, grabbed the ship and dashed out of the room. When she returned, she said she'd stuck it in the utility room. In the sink, with some cloths spread over it.

They watched as the vehicle came to a halt and the blinding headlights were switched off. Only then could they see it in the glow from inside the house. It was Leifur's estate car. Did this mean it wasn't him snoring away in the other room? Had he gone out driving while drunk? If so, it was a miracle that he hadn't wrapped the car round a lamppost or driven off the road, or into the sea. Still, even a pissed Leifur behind the wheel would be better than the police. Trausti was so relieved that he couldn't breathe for a moment. But Sigga seemed angry rather than glad. 'Christ. What the fuck's going on?' She marched to the front door and wrenched it open, then switched on the outside lights. Trausti thought he saw Ari getting out of the driver's side and Ragga the passenger's. 'Are you out of your minds?' Sigga shouted. 'We thought you were the police. Where have you been?'

Ari was the first to enter the house. Not for the first time, he seemed extremely pleased with himself, chest puffed out, chin held high. 'Quit moaning. You should be thanking us. We don't need to worry about the police any more. We've taken care of that.'

Trausti froze and the relief that had flooded him on seeing that it wasn't the police was replaced by a dawning apprehension. What the hell had they done? Set fire to Gugga's house? An even worse scenario occurred to him. He went to the door, pulled on his shoes and didn't answer when Ari and Ragga asked where exactly he thought he was going. Instead, he marched, coatless, to the car. Peering in through the window, he noticed that the rear seats had been put down to create more space. What he saw there forced him to reassess the situation: his friends hadn't been out to incriminate him. What he was looking at proved that they were all equally fucked. He straightened up, running both hands distractedly through his hair. In the back was the wooden crate from the cellar.

Chapter 18
Day 6 – Tuesday, 28 January

It was too late to conduct a post-mortem. Not because Idunn wasn't prepared to work half the night if necessary – in fact, she'd have welcomed the chance – but for reasons beyond her control. There were formalities that had to be taken care of before she could start wielding her scalpel. It wasn't as though she was in the Wild West where the body could be dumped on the nearest table and she could roll up her sleeves and set to work. The police needed to contact the next of kin of those now resting in the hospital mortuary, and, until that had been done, Idunn would have to sit on her hands. On the bright side, at least she wasn't the one tasked with having those conversations.

The names of two of the deceased had now been established: the woman from the beach and the man from the shed on Stórhöfdi. Idunn had been right about their ages; both would have turned thirty this year. The woman, Ragnhildur, was a mechanical engineer; the man, Leifur, had worked in IT. It was hard to comprehend how things could have gone so wrong for two young people at such a promising stage of their lives. Mercifully, neither had children or were in a relationship. When this was pointed out, several members of the investigation team had avoided meeting Idunn's gaze, as though they assumed she must be devastated that she hadn't reproduced.

Especially as it was too late now. She didn't let their attitude get to her, any more than her childlessness, which was by her own choice. Having a partner and ensuring the survival of the human race wasn't everyone's ultimate dream.

The odds were that the burnt body had belonged to one of the two or three members of the party who were still unaccounted for. Idunn, reluctant to make a wild guess, simply didn't answer when she was pressed for an opinion about which of the two individuals named so far was the more likely candidate. Neither of them appeared to have been toothless, according to the pictures of them from social media she had been shown, but it was always possible that one had had bridgework. The second possibility was that the teeth had been removed to prevent identification, a theory which would also be consistent with the attempt to burn the body. Teeth and bones were usually preserved when a corpse was disposed of in this way. But the quick glimpse she had got of the victim's mouth cavity hadn't suggested that the teeth had been extracted just before it was placed on the pyre. Though it was always possible that the fire had destroyed the evidence. Anyway, further speculation was unnecessary since tomorrow's MRI scan would go a long way towards revealing the person's identity.

The low point of the day had without a doubt been when the storm had subsided and Idunn heard a plane come in to land and take off again soon afterwards. If life had been fair, she would have been on that plane to Reykjavík. Instead of staring moodily out of her hotel window at the Heimaklettur rock, she would be enjoying a last aerial view of the islands. Because she was sure of one thing: she was never coming back here. Still, although she herself hadn't been able to leave, with any luck the specimens of urine and blood from the woman

found on the beach should be on board, as she had requested
that they be sent for analysis as soon as possible.

She had successfully avoided Alexandra at the hotel. Idunn
guessed this wasn't so much skill on her part as the fact that her
half-sister was sulking. Instinct told her the respite wouldn't
last long. Alexandra seemed hell-bent on moving to Reykjavík
and Idunn appeared to hold the key to that dream. Which was
absurd, since Alexandra was perfectly capable of taking care
of herself – something Idunn had been forced to do when she
was much younger than her half-sister was now. As if that
hadn't been enough, Idunn had had to care for her mother,
too, whenever she had one of her episodes. It hadn't taken
Idunn long to realise that these *episodes* were timed precisely
for when she herself had plans. If there was an after-school
function she was looking forward to, or a party, her mother
would throw a fit on cue, claiming she was dying or threaten-
ing to kill herself, and Idunn would be compelled to cancel. It
was no wonder she had excelled at school. Being her mother's
emotional crutch had robbed her of a social life and this in
turn had given her plenty of time to study. Being poor only
amplified this. No money meant no going anywhere except
for a walk. Everything else involved some kind of expense.

So, in comparison, Alexandra didn't deserve her sympathy. At the end of the day, people in possession of bottomless
funds could always find a way. All Alexandra had to do was
talk her parents round to her point of view, then she could
rent a flat or even buy a property. She could even afford to hire
a cook to prepare her meals, for that matter. Idunn did not
feel obliged to get involved. Their father, the fishing baron,
was bound to fork out for his favourite daughter.

There was a knock at the door of her hotel room. Guessing Alexandra might have shrugged off her sulks sooner than

expected, Idunn cursed as if she'd brought it on herself by thinking about the girl. She was in no mood to talk to her half-sister and had no intention of opening the door to her. She called out: 'Who is it?'

The visitor turned out to be a young member of the CSI team called Stefán. He regarded her with surprise when she opened the door, saying he'd been trying to call her. Idunn lied that her phone was out of battery, but the truth was that she had switched it off after getting that message from her father. She had no wish to receive any more. It was bad enough dithering over whether to reply or ignore him, in which case there was a risk he might come looking for her. In the end, her failure to act had decided the matter for her. If her father was waiting in suspense for her response, he would have to wait a long time.

The young man shifted from foot to foot in the corridor. 'I just wanted to let you know that I managed to examine those hairs. We weren't allowed to go back to Reykjavík, so I asked if I could borrow a microscope at the hospital.'

'And?' Idunn couldn't imagine how information acquired with the use of a microscope could be of any interest to her. The hairs had nothing to do with the cause of death, though they could conceivably be used to track down the guilty party. But that wasn't her job.

'They were dog hairs.'

'Right, I see.' Idunn couldn't tell what the young man expected her to say. He was new to the job and still eager to prove himself. 'Thank you.'

Stefán seemed to sense Idunn's limited enthusiasm for his information. 'I thought maybe you'd want to know. In case you found bite marks on the body.'

If Idunn had been the type, she would have smiled at this point. He couldn't know that there were no bite marks on the body or that she was perfectly capable of telling the difference between the bite of a dog and that of a human – or pretty much any other animal. She didn't need dog hairs for that. 'Thanks. I'll bear it in mind.'

But he hadn't finished. 'The woman, Ragnhildur, didn't own a dog – as far as I'm aware. So they're probably not hairs she brought with her to the islands. Which means they could be from the killer's dog.'

Since the killer was most likely to have been one of the party, this theory was of little significance. The group had not, to Idunn's knowledge, had a dog with them. But the young man meant well, so Idunn was careful about how she phrased her reply: 'Yes. It's possible. Hopefully it'll come to light in due course. If so, the evidence of those hairs could be vital.' She refrained from adding that it all depended whether the woman had known the killer, in which case the hairs could have ended up on her clothes by innocent means. If she hadn't, and it proved possible to trace the hairs to a particular dog, they might be important. She doubted it, though.

'The woman who crashed her car near the scene had a dog with her. A golden retriever. Which would be consistent with the hairs.'

Idunn's interest was finally roused. She had been so preoc-cupied with her own predicament while he was talking that she had completely forgotten about the car crash victim's dog. Even though it wasn't her job to solve the murders, she was naturally interested in the events leading up to them and it was a safe bet that the accident was linked to them in some way. It would have been an unbelievable coincidence if not. But whether the woman was the murderer, a witness or a prospective victim attempting to flee was impossible to tell at this stage. For the dog's sake, Idunn hoped she wasn't the perpetrator. Pets weren't allowed in Icelandic prisons. 'By the way, has the woman regained consciousness yet?'

'Yes. She's conscious, but in no fit state to be questioned. I understand they might be allowed to talk to her tomorrow. Only briefly, but still.'

'Does she have any connection to these people? Has that been clarified yet?'

'No. Not as far as I'm aware. But they may have found a link. I haven't talked to the rest of the team yet. They're at the police station, having a meeting.'

Idunn merely nodded. This conversation had gone on long enough. She didn't want to get trapped in a pointless discussion of the investigation, especially not in the hotel corridor. 'You'll report on this when they get back, I assume. The business of the dog hairs.'

'Yes. Will do. I was also supposed to pass on the message that we're meeting downstairs for supper in half an hour.'

'Thanks. I'd better get back to work, then.'

The door closed, leaving Idunn alone in her hotel room again, with nothing but the silence, her laptop and the view of Heimaklettur. But instead of sitting down at the small desk, she decided to use the time before supper to have a quiet tipple in the bar. She'd exhausted the tasks she could complete on her computer and she had no interest in the TV schedules. She'd run out of online distractions too. She'd been browsing aimlessly, uninspired by what she found, before eventually giving up and closing her laptop. There was nothing left but to sit on her bed, stare into space and brood on her problems. If this situation didn't call for a drink, she didn't know what did.

Idunn picked up her camera, crept out of her room and eased her door shut. She opted to take the stairs down from the third floor, for fear, foolish as it was, that the dinging of the lift bell would reach Alexandra's ears. Her precautions paid off and the bar turned out to be just as she wanted it: empty.

She chose a table in the corner at the back of the dining room and settled down with a glass of white wine. Before switching on her camera, she took a mouthful of her drink and waited for her worries and tiresome thoughts to recede. It didn't work. She turned her attention to the photos instead. If she immersed herself in those, there would be no room for intrusive thoughts. Work could be even more effective than alcohol when she needed to distract herself.

Idunn scrolled to the pictures of the burnt body. It would be good to have them fresh in her memory when she got the results of the MRI scan. She'd been in too much of a hurry to examine the body on the beach as well as she'd have liked. You couldn't reason with the weather gods and postpone a storm in order to carry out a vital examination at a crime scene.

The photos didn't really tell her anything new. She just became more convinced that the body had been barefoot, and dressed in front but naked behind when it was consigned to the fire. Logically, then, the burnt material on the front of the body must be the remnants of a blanket or some other type of cover. A partially or fully naked victim often indicated a murder aggravated by sexual assault, but Idunn couldn't ascertain that from the photos and it was highly improbable that she would be able to detect it from an internal examination either. The fire would have destroyed the evidence. She couldn't even distinguish the body's gender from the burnt genitals, which were also covered in black lumps of material. Once she conducted the post-mortem she would get a better view, but by then the MRI scan would have determined the question of gender. If it was a woman, her internal sex organs ought to be intact.

Idunn scrolled on, pausing at the photos of the body's chest and the glimpses of metal here and there that she had taken for a zip. That wasn't consistent with the idea that the body had been covered by a blanket. The longer she pored over the photos, the more her original conjecture bothered her. The small screen size hampered her ability to see, but there was something about the metal that wasn't consistent with a zip. No matter how she tried, though, she couldn't come up with any better idea. She was itching to get on with the post-mortem when she'd be able to scrape off the lumps of burnt cloth.

Stefán from CSI now appeared in the dining room, smiled at her and, coming over, sat down opposite her. His eyes lingered on her glass of wine a moment too long for Idunn's liking. She took a gulp, rather larger than she was accustomed to. If he wanted to disapprove, she'd give him ample reason to. 'Any news?'

Stefán, recovering from his apparent disapproval, shook his head. 'No, apart from the fact that I found out the dog's still alive.'

The news cheered Idunn, though it was of little significance for the investigation. Stefán misinterpreted her smile as meaning she was excited about the implications. 'I was worried it had died and been cremated. In that case it might have been hard to find any hairs for comparison.' Seeing that Idunn's smile had faded, he added: 'Dogs and other pets are usually cremated when they die. But, like I said, this dog survived the accident. It was operated on and is recovering. I'm going to ask someone to bring me a sample of its fur so I can compare it to the hairs I found.'

Although Idunn was happy for the dog's sake, she couldn't help inwardly sighing over having to endure Stefán's company. Switching off her camera, she took another big slug of wine and forced herself to smile: 'Well done.'

Chapter 19
Day 3 – Saturday, 25 January

The wind had picked up in the early morning and swept the clouds from the sky before retiring, satisfied with its work. Though the moon wasn't full, its cold light was bright enough to reveal the outlying islands rearing out of the black sea. Trausti gazed at the view, trying to purge his mind of everything but the breathtaking beauty before him. He was afraid his head would explode if he didn't. The sight of what Ragga and Ari had brought back with them had sent him blundering off into the darkness, desperate to get away. There weren't many places to flee to on the exposed headland. His steps had led him round behind the house and down the slope to the very brink of the cliff, with its dizzying drop to the sea far below. Here, the house was out of sight and there was nothing to remind him of his friends or the reckless stupidity that had characterised this trip.

There was no escaping his own thoughts, though. He no longer suspected his friends of trying to make him the scapegoat for Gudrún's death. Instead, he was now wrestling with the idea that one or more of them must be trying to cover up their own guilt by getting rid of any evidence that might incriminate them. Why couldn't his mind give him a reprieve, even if it was only for a few minutes?

He took a deep breath and focused on the dim shapes of the islands. In the pale glow of the moon they seemed as unreal as his own situation. He wrapped his arms around himself, suddenly aware of the biting cold. The shivers that now assailed him were a sign that he was calming down and no longer in the mood to scream at the top of his lungs. In the stillness, he heard the waves crashing on the rocks at the foot of the cliff and he edged closer to peer down at them but it was impossible without leaning out over the abyss. He hesitated. In normal circumstances he would have backed gingerly away, but safety wasn't at the forefront of his mind right now. Part of him couldn't help wondering what it would be like to jump – to plummet into the icy sea and feel it closing over his head as he sank and the world vanished from view forever.

'Trausti! Come away from the edge.' Ragga's cry cut through his thoughts. It was as if she'd read his mind.

He turned, not even trying to hide his disillusionment. He'd always regarded her as the voice of common sense, the one to call things to a halt at the height of the game, before the friends could get into foolish scrapes. But now she had let him down. It seemed he didn't know her as well as he'd thought. For all he knew she could have been responsible for Gudrún's death.

'Come back inside. Talk to us.' Ragga had to call out to be heard from the top of the slope. Clearly she didn't dare venture as close to the edge as him.

'I'm fine here.' Trausti turned back to the sea. He hoped she would go away and leave him alone.

'It was the only thing to do, Trausti. You just got a shock. You'll soon realise we were right. Trust me.' Ragga's voice was tinged with despair and he wondered if she had really imagined that he would welcome this rash act of theirs. If so, she was a lot stupider than he'd thought.

'Go back inside. I want to be alone.'

'I'm not going anywhere. Talk to me.'

It wasn't easy to call out in a whiny tone but Ragga managed it. Whining had always got on Trausti's nerves. He didn't usually show it, but now he couldn't see any reason to conceal his irritation. Rounding on her again, he snapped: 'There's nothing to talk about. Leave me alone.'

His words had the opposite effect from what he'd intended: Ragga now started inching her way down the slope. She didn't speak again until she reached his side, then clutched frantically at his shoulder when she realised the precariousness of their position. 'Christ, Trausti!'

He resisted the urge to shake off her grip. If he did, there was a risk she'd plunge over the edge. That was all they needed. Instead, he glared at her, willing her to let go. The moon cast an unearthly light on her face, accentuating the sadness of her expression. The beam from the lighthouse made little difference beyond briefly lending her cheeks a yellowish sheen. Her downcast brown eyes appeared black and her lashes glistened with tears, as though she were weeping quicksilver. Trausti's fury melted away. He had never been able to hold on to his anger for long. Whenever he lost his temper, his habitual equanimity would reassert itself almost before he knew what was happening. 'How could you do it?' His voice held a defeated note.

Somewhat to his surprise, Ragga didn't try to blame it on Ari. 'It was the only solution. I just didn't realise it until earlier this morning, when I couldn't sleep.'

'The only solution?'

'It'll solve all our problems. You must see that.' The quicksilver tears had gone from her lashes. Since they hadn't trickled down her cheeks, they must have been sucked back into her tear ducts. 'Everything will be like it was before. Nothing will change and our life can go on as normal.'

Trausti frowned. 'Speak for yourself. Failing to report a body is one thing; I could probably live with that. But moving it is another matter entirely. Don't you realise? We've made ourselves complicit with whoever hid her in the cellar in the first place.'

Ragga didn't let go of his shoulder but her face hardened. 'Complicit with who exactly? Gugga? She's dead, so she's not here to tell anyone what happened. And what body? There won't be any consequences if nothing's found at the house. That's the point. Now we can stop worrying about whether we overlooked something when we were trying to clean up. Or whether that girl who saw us will ring the police. Or the woman who lent you the key, for that matter. Not to mention whether we've left traces of our DNA in that sand in the crate. We all opened it and looked inside. Maybe we shed skin cells or hairs in there? What do we know? And there's no getting away from the fact that we were with Gudrún the evening she went missing. None of us are experts in forensics – maybe it's still possible to link us to the body using our DNA from seven years ago. You must have realised that? It makes no difference that we didn't do anything wrong. Who will believe us? This way at least we can leave the islands without any worries. No body, no problem.'

Trausti was silent and the roar of the breakers reasserted itself. Ragga's reasoning was logical enough, but that didn't alter the fact that removing the body was wrong, and that, to his mind, rendered her arguments null and void. A new thought occurred to him. What about Gudrún's family? Were he and his friends really planning to deny her next of kin closure, just in order to sleep better at night themselves? 'Didn't it even occur to you that Gudrún's family have a right to know what happened to her?' he asked. 'Her mother? Her father? Her brother and sister?'

Ragga's reaction implied she hadn't even thought about that angle. She opened her mouth and in the dim light it resembled a black hole in her pale face. As is the nature of black holes, it emitted nothing, and she closed it again without uttering a word. Trausti shook his head and turned away from her. How was it possible that she and Ari could be so short-sighted? 'It's too late to return the crate today. People will be waking up and there's a good chance you'll be spotted.' He had no intention of going with them. 'You'll have to wait until tonight.'

Ragga found her tongue again. 'Or not.'

Trausti spun round so fast he almost lost his footing. It was only thanks to Ragga's quick reflexes that he didn't topple over the cliff. His escape had been so narrow that she kept hold of his coat even after he'd recovered his balance. She started backing up the slope, pulling him with her and he yielded. As soon as they reached safer ground, she let him go. Not that they were really safe even here; if one of them tripped and fell, they would roll down the slope and over the cliff. It would just take a little longer than plunging straight over the edge. 'What do you mean?' Trausti demanded. 'Didn't you listen to what I said about Gudrún's family? You've got to put the crate back where you found it.'

Ragga was looking beyond him, at the distant islands. 'Her mother's dead and her siblings are younger than her. They're bound to have got over it ages ago.'

Though Trausti had lost count of all the times he'd thought about Gudrún's parents and wondered how they must be feeling, he had never dared to look them up online or on social media to spy on them. It was news to him that Gudrún's mother had died. 'How do you know she's dead?' he asked.

'I saw the obituaries. She died of a heart attack, I think. It didn't say so in as many words but you could read between the lines. It happened two years after Gudrún vanished, so it had nothing to do with that. We need to stay grounded.'

Trausti gulped. 'Did it say how they were coping – her family, I mean? Following Gudrún's disappearance?'

'Yes.'

'And? How were they?'

'How do you think? Her disappearance was desperately hard for her parents. It goes without saying.'

'What about her siblings?' Trausti wasn't going to let Ragga off that lightly. He had to make her understand the consequences of what she and Ari had done. Only then would her eyes be opened to the inhumanity of leaving Gudrún's father in the dark. 'Did it say?'

'No. There was only a brief mention of them, but I got the impression from what it said that they were doing OK. They were both at university. Gudrún's disappearance clearly didn't destroy their lives, however much they must have suffered as a result of it. Isn't that obvious?'

Gudrún used to talk to Trausti most when she attended their parties. He was the quietest and probably also the best listener in the group. Remembering the warm way Gudrún had talked about her younger brother and sister gave him a pang. He had pushed away the thought of them all these years. Her brother had dreamt of becoming a dentist and her sister had been planning to study fishing technology. They had both lent Gudrún all their savings to help her out when she was broke and she'd been worried she wouldn't be able to pay them back.

He doubted those debts had been repaid by the time of her disappearance. 'Did it say what they were studying?'

'No. I don't remember.' Ragga gave him a puzzled look. 'Does it matter? The main thing is that the family have all had time to get over their grief by now.'

Trausti closed his eyes and rubbed his forehead. 'What are you trying to say? That the damage is done and there's nothing more to be said – is that it?'

Ragga met his gaze. 'I'm going to be frank here and consider this objectively. If we evaluate the feelings of all the people who would be affected by the discovery of her body, it's clear that the outcome would be better if it never turned up. It won't make Gudrún's family feel much better. Think about it. They must already have accepted that she's dead. OK, they could bury her, but what would that actually change? How often do people visit the graves of their dead relatives?'

Her attitude left Trausti speechless. He had no idea how conscientious people were about visiting their relatives' graves. Presumably it varied. But the coldness and lack of empathy in her voice shocked him. She no longer seemed like the Ragga he'd known. As a result, he had no idea what she might be capable of. For all he knew she could even be in league with Ari. The two of them could have a shared secret they wanted to hide.

Ragga continued in a clinical tone that reminded him of the senior doctors at the hospital giving their assessments of critically ill patients. 'Unquestionably the worst outcome for us would be if the body was found. So the logical conclusion is that it would be worse for the body to turn up than for it to stay lost. The latter outcome would be preferable, not only for us but for Gudrún's family too. That may sound harsh but you have to face facts. I, for one, can't think of a more practical way of approaching the problem.'

'Logical conclusion? Practical way of approaching the problem? How can you talk like that?' Trausti's head swam. Was Ragga a sociopath? His brain couldn't take any more of this.

'You know what I mean. As a doctor, you must have had to make decisions based on choosing the least bad option.' Ragga gestured with her hand as she came up with an example. 'Like the choice between amputating a limb or allowing someone's cancer to spread. Or deciding whether conjoined twins should be separated if it's uncertain that one of them will survive. Or whatever. This is that kind of moral dilemma.'

'I don't have to decide anything like that at work,' he replied. 'Besides, patients are always involved in decision making. If we take the example you mentioned, Gudrún's father and siblings ought to have a say. And what do you think their choice would be?'

Ragga, who had always been a quick thinker, came straight back at him with: 'What about conjoined twins? Aren't they usually too young to decide for themselves? Let's focus on that example. Imagine that her father and siblings were newborns – conjoined twins. You couldn't ask their opinion in that case.'

'Shut up about conjoined twins,' Trausti said. 'This has absolutely nothing to do with that kind of dilemma.' Turning, he looked up the slope behind them. 'I'm out of here.' Anything was better than standing on top of a cliff in the freezing cold, having this crazy argument with someone he used to respect.

A smile flickered across Ragga's face, not from happiness but from relief. Perhaps she had been afraid he might still throw himself off the cliff. 'Good idea. I'll put some fresh coffee on. Then we can sit down and discuss this rationally.'

Evidently she still believed she could persuade him to change his mind. There was no chance of that. He didn't care what happened. The others could clean up the mess they'd made. Working out how to do so was their problem. He didn't want to be mixed up in their guilt. He would face the music from a safe distance, abroad. 'I'm leaving,' he told her. 'I'm going back to the mainland.'

He set off fast up the steep slope and heard Ragga toiling along a little way behind. The climb was too strenuous for talking and he was grateful not to have to listen to her insisting on the merits of her and Ari's terrible idea. When he reached the top, he paused to catch his breath. A thought struck him. Before striding off towards the house, he looked round at her and asked: 'Just how were you planning to get rid of the body? Take it on the ferry with you and dispose of it somewhere on the way back to Reykjavík?'

Ragga held up a hand to indicate that she was still recovering her breath. Then she answered without seeming angry or affronted: 'We haven't worked it out yet. But we'd thought of putting rocks inside the crate, nailing down the lid and throwing it in the sea. From the cliff where you were standing.'

'What if the crate hits the rocks on the way down and is smashed to pieces before it lands in the sea? What then? Don't you think the police will come looking for us if Gudrún's body washes up by the golf course? Or on the beach where Stórhöfdi joins the main island?'

'Like I said, we haven't made up our minds yet.' Ragga was still calm, though she appeared hurt by what he'd said. 'Instead of trashing all our ideas, maybe you could help us find a solution?'

Trausti didn't dignify that with an answer. Instead, he strode off towards the house and pretended not to hear when

Ari and Sigga called out to him as he stormed past the dining room. He went straight up to his bedroom and locked the door to give himself breathing space in which to pack. But he needn't have bothered as no one knocked or tried the handle. With every garment he folded and put in his case, his determination and the certainty that he was right were eroded a little further until by the time he was ready to chuck in the last pair of socks, his position had softened.

Was he making a terrible mistake that would jeopardise his future dreams? Instead of becoming a consultant rheumatologist, would he end up removing verrucas and blowing the noses of snotty kids? Would he come to regret his decision to do the right thing? If he was honest, he knew that he would be overwhelmed with regret. Feeling utterly defeated, he sank down on the side of his bed, still holding his socks. Which was better, to live your dream life gnawed by guilt or to live out your life with a clean conscience at the cost of sacrificing all your professional ambitions and job satisfaction? He was gradually coming round to the idea that he could live with a bad conscience. If he applied Ragga's logic, he could add into the equation the critically ill patients he would one day help – assuming he completed his specialist training. Whereas the podiatry treatments he would be reduced to offering if he had to give up his ambition would hardly balance the equation.

One of the ten principles of medical ethics flashed into his mind. He was supposed to show integrity and responsibility in his life and work. It had never occurred to him that it might prove difficult to follow this rule. Could he get away with bending one of the principles a little, so long as he carefully adhered to the other nine?

Trausti's vacillating thoughts were interrupted by the door handle moving. When the door turned out to be locked, there was a loud banging. Trausti went to open it, prepared to tell Ragga that he wanted to be left alone, but he was faced with a much seedier figure. Leifur had to cling to the door frame to stop himself swaying. His hair was rough, his eyes bloodshot and there was a white streak of dried saliva from one corner of his mouth. He looked as though he'd slept in his clothes. His voice, when it emerged, was as rough as his appearance. 'Have you got any Alka-Seltzer?'

Trausti didn't have anything like that with him but he invited Leifur in for a drink of water. Steering his friend as he had at Gugga's house, he sat him down on the bed while he filled a glass from the tap. 'Here. Drink this.'

Leifur took it in trembling hands and drained it in one go. Trausti refilled the glass and Leifur drank down half, then wiped his mouth with the back of his hand and said: 'I think I'm dying.'

Trausti sat down next to him. Leifur didn't actually appear to be at death's door. 'You'll survive. Trust me.'

'I just threw up.'

Leifur had no need to tell him that as his sour breath gave him away.

'That'll have done you good. You'll get over it sooner.'

'God, I want to go home.'

'Tell me about it.'

'I'd happily jump on the first ferry but I don't think I'll be up to going until this evening.'

Leaving by the first boat was no longer Trausti's plan either. Since there was little chance of the body being discovered that day, he was no longer in quite such a hurry. If he relented and agreed to help his friends, he wouldn't be taking the evening ferry either. They would have to wait until nightfall to dispose of the body in such a way that it wouldn't be found for years. Decades, preferably. He was strongly opposed to the idea of transporting the crate back to the mainland on board the ferry. It would be just their luck if customs decided to do a drugs search on board and their dog sniffed out the contents. By far the best plan would be to leave the body behind in the islands. That way, if it was discovered at some later date, he and his friends were unlikely to be suspected as they had next to no connection to the place. The investigation would home in on Gugga, as was only fair.

It seemed that Leifur, like Ragga, could read his mind. 'I still can't get over the fact that it was Gugga who bumped off Gudrún. I swear Gugga's lucky she's dead because, if she wasn't, I'd kill her myself.'

Trausti took this with a pinch of salt. It was one thing to threaten to murder someone, but quite another to go through with it. 'I don't suppose we'll ever find out what happened.' He realised that in saying these words he had come to a decision. The police wouldn't reopen their investigation into Gudrún's disappearance unless new evidence came to light. Like her body, for example.

'Ever since we got here I've been having dreams about Gudrún,' Leifur said. 'That's why I couldn't sleep. I keep waking up with a jolt.'

'You'll get over it when you're home again. I don't think anyone in the history of the world has dreamt the same dream all their life. It probably means you're processing the loss. That's a positive step.'

'But they're real nightmares. Horrible. I don't know whether I'm remembering something that actually happened or it's just my brain inventing shit. The dreams are always about that party.' Leifur raised the glass to his lips again and emptied it. This time he managed it with only one hand, which suggested he was probably going to survive.

'I expect it's a mixture of both. You remember snatches, then, when we sleep, our brain fills in the blanks.'

Leifur considered this. 'I hope so. But I'm not convinced.'

Trausti went silent. He wished the party and what had followed had all been a dream – or a nightmare, rather. Every single action he and the others had taken, or had failed to take, had been so illogical that it might as well have been. After finding Gudrún unresponsive in her bed they had simply retired to their own flats, only to wake up next day and discover that she was nowhere to be found.

That's when they had made their second, and probably biggest, mistake. They'd been too hungover to raise the alarm and had instead convinced themselves that they must have misinterpreted the events of the night. Gudrún would turn up. Several days later, at her parents' insistence, the police had been notified. The friends had all been interviewed. It had been clear by then that things looked very bad indeed for them. *Why didn't you call an ambulance that night? Why didn't you report next day that Gudrún had vanished? Or in the following days? You could have launched a search for her but instead you kept quiet. Why?*

Stupidity and drunkenness were not considered valid excuses. So they had adapted their stories. Not by lying exactly, but by leaving out the most important part. *We threw a party, Gudrún went back to her flat and that's all we know.* It was obvious to all of them that the police suspected there were omissions in their statements, but in the end the investigation had tailed off and they were no longer called back for questioning. They were off the hook. Or so they'd thought . . .

Now that the body had turned up, the half-truth they'd told was bound to come back to haunt them – if the police found out, that is.

Trausti recalled now that Leifur had hardly contributed at all to the discussion the previous evening, when, after finding the body in the crate, they had tried to reconstruct the night of the party. Could he be in possession of the missing pieces of the puzzle?

'Do you remember any of your dreams?' he asked, with a sick feeling in the pit of his stomach.

'More than I want to.' Leifur closed his eyes and massaged his temples, but it didn't seem to alleviate his hangover. 'In the dream I go into her room. She's lying there asleep. I try to wake her but she doesn't stir. Then I pull the duvet off her. She's naked from the waist down and her legs are spread in a V shape. I cover her up again. After that the dream takes off in another direction.'

Once again, Trausti found himself thinking that they should put the crate back in the cellar and let the police examine the body. Leifur's description implied there had been a sexual element, almost certainly non-consensual. In his own painful but hazy memory of visiting Gudrún's room earlier that night, she hadn't been in any state to consent to sex. The duvet had been partly spread over her, so he didn't know whether she had been dressed or naked underneath. He had tried desperately to forget the visit and what had transpired but Leifur's story made him think it might be even worse than he remembered. On his second visit, the terrible one with the others, she had still been covered up. If they had taken the duvet off her, his memory of that part had gone. For all he knew, she could have been dressed or naked.

The most likely explanation was that Leifur's unconscious mind had invented these details in his sleep. That seemed most plausible and Trausti felt his initial resolve to do the right thing begin to crumble. Maybe the path of least resistance was the way to go. Simply let the others decide, stay on another night and help dispose of the body. He was too tired to argue and knew in his heart of hearts that he lacked the conviction to persuade them to change their plans.

He wished he could believe Sigga's laughable theory that Gudrún had come to the islands of her own accord. But no matter how hard he tried, he couldn't kid himself. And yet he let himself go with the flow.

Chapter 20

Day 6 – Tuesday, 28 January

'Don't you want your ice cream?' Stefán, the young CSI, was still sitting across from Idunn, having stayed put even as the rest of the Reykjavík team started drifting into the restaurant. She wasn't sure why he had sat tight instead of moving over to the table with his CSI colleagues. It could hardly be because she was such scintillating company. And he didn't look particularly excited about sitting with Týr and Karó either. Idunn guessed that the attraction must be Alexandra, who had appeared and taken the seat beside her as if nothing was wrong.

'Be my guest.' Idunn pushed her bowl with the scoops of melting ice cream over to the young man. She hadn't touched it. She'd felt like it when the waiter took her order but couldn't understand what she'd been thinking of when the desserts arrived.

'Unless you'd like it?' Stefán asked Alexandra, turning pink, suddenly anxious that he might have pushed in front of her in the ice-cream queue. As Idunn's half-sister, Alexandra naturally had first claim to her leftovers.

'No, thanks. I'm full.' Alexandra smiled at him and the young man was visibly relieved.

Idunn sighed under her breath over her dining companions and turned to Týr. Karó had stepped outside to vape once she'd finished eating and her head could be seen through the large windows of the restaurant, accompanied every now and then by big white clouds of steam as she exhaled. If it weren't for the two uninvited guests at the table, Idunn would have seized the opportunity to speak to Týr about his mother. Or about the investigation. Instead, she was forced to waste her time making general chit-chat. 'Is there any chance of us going home tomorrow?' she asked.

'Your guess is as good as mine. Although the island's not large, they'll need to search it from end to end. After all, the whole place fills up with tourists in the spring. They'll want to see the puffins without any risk of stumbling over skeletons on their way to the bird-watching hide.'

Idunn bit back the observation that if the winter contin-ued to be this cold, the remains were bound to be a lot more grisly than mere skeletons, especially if they were lying out-doors. Noting that Alexandra and the young man were now deep in conversation, she judged it was safe to ask a couple of questions about the progress of the case. 'Do they think the missing person or persons are still on the island, then?'

'Probably not. They've found ferry bookings bought using a card in the name of one member of the group. Tickets for two cars and four passengers. The outward tickets were used on Thursday to travel from Thorlákshöfn to Heimaey, but the return tickets were not used on Sunday. However, new ones were bought first thing on Monday morning, though only for one car and four passengers this time. There's no foot-age of their arrival, but the camera lens had been cleaned by the time the lone car left the island. Although the faces of the people inside can't be seen, there were clearly only two of them. Which suggests there were five altogether, since we have three bodies. Having said that, the passenger could have been a local, perhaps an accomplice of the driver. Or maybe the driver had offered someone a lift.' Týr shrugged. 'Things will become clear eventually. The mountain roads over Hellisheidi and Threngsli were impassable on Monday, so when they got back to the mainland, they must have driven home to Reykjavík via the southern coast road. Footage is being collected from the few CCTV cameras they'll have passed. We're slowly getting there.'

'What about the other car?'

'It's turned up. And it's the one Alexandra saw. A white estate. They found the same kind of salt in the boot and on the floor as CSI discovered in the cellar. In other words, it seems the vehicle had been used to move the box, or whatever it was, that had been stored down there. Presumably the people went back inside the house as soon as Alexandra had gone, fetched the box from the cellar, then made their getaway. I expect the search of the island for survivors or more bodies will draw a blank. They're all either dead or they've left the island by now. No one else has been reported missing.'

Idunn nodded. The population of Iceland was small and at present almost everybody was accounted for. There were few missing persons on the police's books. 'Does that mean we can go back to Reykjavík, then?' she asked hopefully.

Týr's expression was not promising. Nor was his answer. 'I gather Ína's thinking about it. But it sounds to me like she believes it would be better if we hung around a bit longer. Better safe than sorry and all that.'

Idunn forced a smile to give the impression that she was resigned to the fact. She wasn't. 'Where did the car turn up?'

'In the car park at the wholesaler's on Ofanleitisvegur, right by the airport. More than four kilometres from Stórhöfdi. Unfortunately, there's no CCTV footage of it being parked, so they still don't know who was driving, but, according to the staff at the wholesaler's, it was there when they came to work on Monday morning. The most likely scenario is that one or more members of the group left it there. Though why is anybody's guess.'

Týr called the waiter over and ordered a coffee. Being younger than Idunn, he could still tolerate caffeine in the evenings. She couldn't and declined. Then, to her own surprise, she also declined the offer of another glass of wine. One was enough. More than enough. To her chagrin, she read from Týr's expression that he was as surprised as she was at her decision to abstain. Clearly, it was time for a lifestyle change.

Alexandra's phone rang and she glanced at the screen, made a face, then asked them to excuse her, adding that she wouldn't be long. Idunn hoped this was an optimistic assessment, as Alexandra's absence would provide them with an opportunity to speak more plainly about the investigation and what had emerged from the meeting with Inspector Ína. 'Do we know any more about the group's links to the woman – Gugga – who used to live in the house on Túngata? Or did they just break in?'

'No, they knew her. Apparently, they used to live in the same student residence in Reykjavík, on the same corridor.'

'How did you find out so quickly?'

'They turned up in the police register. All of them. The four from the group and the dead woman who lived in the house. All in connection with the same case. We've also found out what they were doing here in the islands: attending her funeral. The vicar has confirmed that four of her university friends were at the ceremony. He couldn't fail to notice them because it was such a poor turnout.'

'What was the case they were involved in? Drugs?'

'No.' Týr broke off when the waiter appeared with his coffee. He took it and thanked him, then picked up the story again once the waiter had gone. 'A missing person case. Unsolved.'

Idunn's brows shot up. 'Were they suspects?'

'Yes and no. The missing girl was a friend of theirs. She lived on the same corridor. They were the last people who admitted to seeing her on the evening she vanished. But as there was no sign of anything untoward, there was no compelling evidence that they'd had anything to do with her disappearance. Their witness statements were a bit vague, though. They'd been at a party together and had clearly drunk a hell of a lot because they only had a hazy memory of the night's events. But they all agreed that the missing girl had left early as she wasn't much of a party animal. That fact was confirmed by other people who knew her.'

'So what do the police think happened to her?'

Týr shrugged. 'They don't know. Her phone, all her cards and her outdoor clothes were found in her flat, and it was clear that she hadn't packed for a journey. But it looks like she'd taken her duvet with her, as it was nowhere to be found. As she hasn't been seen since that evening, it's thought she ended up in the sea. After all, the university campus isn't far from the shore. There's no knowing whether she was drunk and recklessly decided to go for a swim or fell out of a boat and it wasn't reported. That was the best the police could come up with at the time.'

Idunn vaguely remembered seeing the news. Photos of a young woman, issued with an appeal for information from the public. Idunn hadn't taken much of an interest at the time, assuming the girl was sure to be found eventually, either alive or dead. In the latter case, Idunn would have to acquaint herself with the background, since the body would end up on her slab.

She could remember hoping that this wouldn't happen. Later, she'd just taken it for granted that the young woman must have turned up. 'Did they ever consider that she might have taken her own life?'

'Yes, but that theory was quickly dismissed. She had financial difficulties – she'd got into debt – but then what student hasn't? And there was no history of depression or previous suicide attempts. Mind you, people sometimes succeed first time.' After a moment's pause, Týr continued: 'Of course it was also considered possible, though unlikely, that she might have gone out for a walk and encountered some nutter. A rapist or someone who killed her, whether by accident or deliberately. That she was hit by a car and the driver hid her body, for example. That's what her parents believe – or rather believed. Which is understandable, given that she wasn't depressed or the type to do anything stupid – like going for a swim in the sea in the middle of the night in January. But the fact she hadn't taken her coat contradicted the theory that she'd gone for a walk. The weather was cold when she went missing. Still, who knows? Maybe she wrapped the duvet round her shoulders instead of wearing a coat. She'd been at a party, after all – with the very people we're investigating. And, according to them, she was wasted.'

Idunn was familiar enough with the condition herself to know that buttoning up a coat and remembering to look both ways before crossing the road were not necessarily the first things that would spring to mind in that situation. She'd never actually gone for a walk wearing a duvet as a cape but that wasn't saying much. Any theory was equally valid when nothing could be proved. 'What do you think?' she asked.

'Basically, anything could have happened. We only know one thing for certain: she vanished without a trace. She wasn't picked up on CCTV and the only witnesses were too drunk even to tell the police what time it was when she left. But it's possible that things will be explained now. In fact, I'm confident they will. At the time there was nothing to point to drugs but that might change if it turns out that this woman Gugga's cellar was used to stash illegal substances. With any luck, we'll find the drugs when we track down the members of the group who went back to the mainland.'

Týr paused to take a mouthful of coffee. Idunn didn't say anything until he put down his cup. He seemed well informed about the old case, although he couldn't have been involved in the original investigation as he had still been living in Sweden at the time. 'You know quite a lot about it,' she remarked.

'Yes. We went over the old case files at the meeting earlier.'

Idunn was momentarily silent, her thoughts flying to the mysterious body on the pyre. 'Can I ask you something? Were the young woman's teeth missing? All the front teeth in her upper and lower jaws, as well as the first molars?'

Stefán from CSI had been listening as he shovelled down the ice cream, but now that he had finished, he piped up: 'Do they think the old case is linked to the one we're investigating now, then? Could the burnt body be the missing girl?'

Evidently, the fact that the burnt corpse was missing its teeth wasn't a secret, but then there was no need for it to be kept from the rest of the investigation team. 'Nobody knows. I was only asking.' Idunn looked back at Týr in the hope of getting an answer to the question Stefán had interrupted.

'No. She had all her teeth.' Týr glanced over at the entrance to the restaurant as the door opened and Alexandra came back in, then said hurriedly: 'The missing girl wore braces. So, logically she must have had her teeth.'

Idunn was itching to continue the conversation but she'd lost her chance. Alexandra had taken her chair again. 'Sorry I was so long.'

'Did you read my message?' Alexandra's blue eyes were fixed on Idunn's. Idunn had given up waiting for the girl to leave so she could continue discussing the case with her colleagues. But when she herself got up and left, Alexandra had followed her to the lift. Idunn had been about to berate the girl and order her to stop following her around, when she changed her mind. This might actually be a good solution after all. As soon as Alexandra was safely in her room, Idunn could sneak back downstairs. Perhaps she could catch Týr and have that private chat with him about his mother at the same time. A heavy burden would be lifted from her conscience if she could get that over with.

'My phone's switched off, so no,' Idunn lied, hammering the lift button twice – for the second time. In truth, she had seen that she'd got a message from Alexandra but had decided to ignore it.

'Read it.' Alexandra reached out and laid a hand on Idunn's shoulder. 'Don't worry. I've forgiven you.'

Idunn hadn't been the slightest bit worried. She'd got far more important things on her mind. But Alexandra hadn't finished: 'Do you know why?' She didn't wait for an answer: 'You're just like Dad. Exactly the same. It's not your fault you're the way you are.'

Idunn wasn't going to stand for that. 'We're nothing like each other,' she snapped. 'Not in the least.'

'Yes, you are. You just can't see it.'

Idunn examined her reflection in the lift doors. She didn't look a bit like her father. Her mane of long hair no doubt had something to do with it, but she was sure that wasn't all. Even if her dad started combing his unruly mop and stopped walking around with a five-o'clock shadow, no one would ever mix them up. And she doubted he'd changed at all in that respect.

'I don't mean your appearance – though you do have his smile, actually.'

'When have you seen me smile?'

'Exactly. When have you ever seen Dad smile?'

Idunn couldn't think of an answer to that. She could only repeat what she had said before: 'We're nothing like each other.'

'Oh, really?' Alexandra cupped her chin and raised her eyes to the ceiling as if thinking. 'Let me see. Workaholic: check. Grumpy: check. Likes to be alone: check. Not squeamish: check. Useless at social media: check. No faith in me: check.' She released her chin. 'In other words, exactly the same.'

There was no point protesting, though Idunn strongly rejected this conclusion. She couldn't deny any of it, but what Alexandra didn't understand was the question of nuance. There were different reasons for the character traits they displayed. Fundamentally different. For instance, she didn't like social media because it was so superficial, and she couldn't stand it when people revealed things they would have been better off keeping to themselves. Whereas she was fairly sure that her father wasn't on social media because there was nothing there about fish. In this case, as in all the others, the similarities were purely skin deep.

The lift announced its arrival with a loud ding and they stepped inside. Alexandra pressed the button for the third floor, then met Idunn's gaze in the mirror. 'On the other hand, you and me may be different types but we look identical.' She smiled at Idunn, adding: 'Only you're much older. And it wouldn't hurt you to wear a bit of make-up.'

Never in a million years would Idunn waste time on something as trivial as make-up. She considered pointing out to Alexandra that it was illogical to say that she didn't resemble their father physically yet looked exactly like Alexandra, since their similarity could only have come from him. But Alexandra got in first: 'I'll teach you some make-up tricks when we get to Reykjavík.'

The lift bell rang again as the doors opened. Before Alexandra went to her room, she stooped and kissed Idunn on the cheek. 'Goodnight. You're OK, even if you can be a bit of a cow sometimes. You'll cheer up when you don't have to live alone any more. Don't worry, that was Mum on the phone earlier and I've almost managed to bring her round to the idea. It would help if you'd talk to Dad for me, though. He'll take more notice of you than he does of me. It's fine if you do it tomorrow.'

She vanished into her room and closed the door behind her. Idunn was left standing there speechless. Her sister was even more obtuse than she'd thought. How could she get it into Alexandra's thick skull that there was no way she was coming to live with her? It wasn't a decision that Alexandra and her mother could take unilaterally. It was entirely for Idunn herself to decide and, frankly, she'd rather give up her flat to her half-sister and go and live on the street. Well, almost. She could never actually sleep in the open air, without a toilet or shower.

Once in her room, she took out her phone to check Alexandra's message. She would have to reply to make sure the girl didn't knock on her door and discover that she'd sneaked downstairs again. It seemed this nonsense was never going to end, but perhaps that was hardly surprising when the girl was such an idiot.

The message was brief: *I'm not stupid, if that's what you think. I CAN be a doctor.* Attached was a file that turned out to contain Alexandra's exam results. She'd specialised in the sciences and, despite taking more units than required, had passed all her exams with flying colours six months ahead of schedule. That was a surprise – though not as big a surprise as the actual results.

Alexandra had got top marks in everything.

Idunn might have been holding her own school-leaving certificate.

Chapter 21
Day 3 – Saturday, 25 January

It was easier said than done for Trausti to rejoin the others after Leifur had tottered back downstairs to lie on the sofa. He dreaded meeting Ragga's eye. Now that he had changed his mind, he could expect to have '*I told you so*' thrown back at him, though since Ragga rarely wasted words, maybe she would spare him that. He would just have to read it in her eyes – along with other things that remained unsaid. Personally, he would rather their communication was frank and to the point, even if she did give him an earful. Then at least he would know where he stood and wouldn't be left boxing in the dark, trying to interpret her expressions or behaviour. He had a tendency to over-interpret things, usually to his own detriment. He reminded himself that it didn't matter anyway. His friendship with her and the rest of the group had reached the end of the road. He would stick with them until they got back to Reykjavík but after that it was over. He would say 'See you', then make sure it never happened. He toyed with the idea of blocking them on social media but supposed the decision had already been taken for him in the short term since his phone was dead. Just as well, because otherwise they might interpret his action as meaning that he was planning to break trust with them and throw them to the wolves to save his own skin. Nothing could be further from the truth. He just wanted to forget about them and everything that had happened.

No doubt they felt the same.

The difference between them and him was that they had other friends. He didn't have anyone else. Acquaintances, yes, but no other close friends. Still, it couldn't be helped. He'd managed to make these friends back in the day so he ought to be capable of making new ones. If not – well, he'd just have to go through life friendless like he had as a boy. At least then he hadn't experienced anything like the trouble that had ensued from belonging to this group. A lonely but trouble-free life was probably best.

Ragga was nowhere to be seen when he went downstairs. He followed the sound of Sigga and Ari's voices to the kitchen. Sigga was still in her bathrobe; Ari hadn't yet taken his coat off. They were both clutching mugs of cold coffee – at least, there was no steam coming off them. They shut up when he appeared in the doorway, which implied they'd been talking about him.

'I've changed my mind.' Best get it over with.

Neither made any attempt to hide their relief. Ari reached out and slapped him hard on the upper arm. 'I knew you'd see the light.'

Ignoring him, Trausti looked at Sigga. 'Did you agree straight away?' he asked. 'That it was a good idea?'

Sigga dropped her gaze. 'I was too tired to have an opinion. Still am. I'll just go along with whatever the rest of you decide.'

Ari scowled at her. 'Rubbish. We – that is, you, me, Ragga and now Trausti – are all agreed. And don't try to pretend you're not. Leifur will be on board too when he wakes up. It's the only sensible thing to do. Stop making out you're above all this, it doesn't suit you.'

Trausti intervened to avert the row that was brewing. 'Filling the crate with rocks won't work.'

Sigga abandoned whatever retort she had been about to fire at Ari, and he relaxed as well. 'Ragga has already told us your opinion of that. It was quite lucky, actually, or we'd have got on with it while you were sulking in your room. So, what do you suggest, mate?'

Trausti felt a surge of anger. They had been intending to go ahead anyway, scorning his objections. But he controlled himself and concentrated on trying to conceal the animosity he felt, especially towards Ari. The nightmarish dreams Leifur had described might not have any basis in reality, but if they contained even a nugget of truth, there was only one possible culprit. It couldn't have been Leifur – and Trausti refused to believe it of himself. It was unthinkable, regardless of the state he'd been in. He had to keep telling himself this, had to accept it as fact.

And that left only Ari.

Trausti had no intention of confronting him about it, though. It was vital to keep the peace until he was back in Reykjavík. Besides, he could hardly accuse Ari when all he had to go on was a dream – the shakiest evidence imaginable. Nor was it a good idea to bring the subject up when there was a faint possibility that he might have been the culprit himself. And regardless of who was to blame, they were all implicated in the cover-up. 'Let's find somewhere to bury the body. We can burn the crate. Or break it up and dispose of the bits when we get back to Reykjavík.'

Ari made a face that indicated he thought the idea was OK but not great. Of course, it was hardly a brainwave, but they'd got themselves into such a mess that they didn't have much choice. All that was left were last-ditch solutions. 'Let's do that, then. Can you think of anywhere? Where we won't be spotted?'

Since Heimaey wasn't large, they didn't have many options. It would take time to dig a hole deep enough to ensure the body wouldn't be found, and that would increase the risk of being seen by a passer-by. Regardless of where they dug.

'What about the new lava field?' Sigga turned to the window above the sink. It faced the distant town and the 1973 lava flow at the eastern end of the island, though at present nothing could be seen but darkness. The lighthouse cast its regular beam over the surroundings but the light didn't extend that far. 'I don't think there's anything there except lava.'

'There are tracks running through it.' Ari had always had a problem with accepting Sigga's suggestions but this time he had a point. 'Anyway, I'm not digging a grave in a lava field. You can try if you like, but good luck with that.'

Trausti intervened again as Sigga opened her mouth to make an angry retort: 'There's an area here on the headland, to the south of the house, that can only be seen from the sea. If we dig the grave at night, we should get away with it.'

Ari clearly wanted the last word when it came to the choice of site: 'Or on the beach by the isthmus. It's easy to dig in sand.'

Sigga scoffed at this idea: 'Uh, hello! The road runs straight past. No, the headland gets my vote.' She gave Trausti the ghost of a smile but he maintained a stony face.

'The beach is out of the question. It may be easy to shovel up sand but the sea will dig it up again just as fast. We might as well dump the body in the town square with nothing but a sheet over it.' Trausti didn't return the conspiratorial smile Sigga sent him. He wasn't on her side either. He was on his own from now on.

'We don't have to decide straight away.' Ari couldn't bring himself to admit that Trausti's suggestion was the best of a bad bunch. 'We've got plenty of time. After all, it's not like we can do anything until it gets dark again. Let's just have a think and try to come up with some more ideas, then make a decision this evening.'

Silence fell, giving Trausti the opportunity to focus. 'We're forgetting one thing.' His friends looked at him, their faces showing signs of exhaustion, the light long gone out of their eyes. 'What about the phone calls? The note on the car window? It'll be no use getting rid of the body if someone knows what we've been up to. What if that person's next step is to stop harassing us and go to the police instead?'

While the others' mouths went slack with defeat, Ari rolled his eyes. 'All the more reason to do this tonight. No body, no crime. And stop being such a pussy. We get rid of the body, and if the police come knocking, we say we came here for the funeral and a reunion. We just look confused if they ask anything about a body or a box. We went to the house, sure, but had no reason to go down to the cellar. Got it?' He left no room for objections, but then there probably wouldn't have been any as he had a point. Instead, he yawned and pushed himself away from the kitchen unit he'd been leaning against. 'I'm going upstairs to sleep until lunchtime. If we're going to have another late night tonight, I recommend you have a kip too.' He put down his mug, yawned again and left them. Apparently, the intervening years since they'd graduated hadn't taught him to clear up after himself. He still expected someone else to take care of that.

Trausti stifled the old urge to take his mug, rinse it and put it in the dishwasher. In their student days, he had generally taken on this role as the girls had flatly refused to clean up after Ari, and Leifur had seemed indifferent to dirt and mess. But times had changed. Trausti wasn't going to run around tidying up after Ari any more or indeed after any other slob.

Although he was still in shock after all that had happened, it seemed that one good thing had come out of this ordeal: he had developed a backbone.

Sigga stared at the door Ari had left by, rolling her eyes. 'He's got a peculiar knack of making me want to resist anything he suggests. I'm falling asleep on my feet here but I don't want to go to bed, just because he told us to.' She rinsed out her mug in the sink. 'Is it a skill that has any uses or is it just designed to drive you mad?'

Trausti merely shrugged but Sigga didn't take offence: 'Are you going to lie down?'

'Not right away.' To stop her thinking he too had an inbuilt resistance to anything Ari suggested, Trausti added: 'I'm going to look for a spade. If I can't find one, we'll have to go out and buy one. Or preferably two.'

'Won't that look suspicious? What kind of tourist would buy a spade – in the middle of winter?'

Trausti shrugged again. 'Then we'll just have to hope I can find one. Or we could say our car's got stuck or something. Maybe Ari and Ragga should have thought of that before they brought the body up here. If I can't find anything to dig with, they can bloody well go into town and sort it out themselves.'

Sigga closed the dishwasher. 'I'll come too. To help you look. Not to the shops.' She retied the belt of her bathrobe. 'I'll just run upstairs and change. Wait for me. Don't go out in the dark alone.'

He was no longer sure whether he was more worried about the people inside the house or what might be lurking out there in the dark. But it was pointless trying to give Sigga the slip as the headland wasn't large and there were only a couple of outhouses to search. She would find him immediately. While he was waiting, the phone started ringing. It was the bloody landline in the hall again. The ringing was so unnerving that Trausti felt the skin prickling on his arms. He wasn't usually neurotically oversensitive to this sort of thing and had only once before experienced the same sensation, during a swarm of earth tremors that had hit Iceland when he was in his teens. He hadn't been in any danger, yet that hadn't prevented him from breaking out in a cold sweat, his heart galloping every time he heard the rumbling starting up around him.

The ringing went on and on. Trausti, as the nearest person to the phone, had two alternatives: either let it ring out, knowing that the person on the other end would call straight back, or pick up. The last thing he wanted was to answer, but he went into the hall anyway. He stared at the phone as if hypnotised as another ring tore into the silence. To shut it up, he lifted the receiver, automatically raising it to his ear, though he wasn't expecting to like what he heard.

Instead of saying *hello* as he would in normal circumstances, he held his breath and listened. The caller didn't keep him waiting long:

'*Morons*,' the voice at the other end hissed.

Trausti didn't answer, just listened to the breathing of the caller and the thudding of his own heart.

'*Liars.*'

He stayed silent and concentrated on the voice, ignoring the words and focusing on the timbre and intonation, in the hope of being able to work out the caller's age, sex, any familiar qualities or any other hints that might indicate who it was. But it was no good. The caller was speaking in telegraphese, in single words, which meant Trausti hardly had a chance to focus on the voice before it fell silent. The person was hissing, too, which made it even more difficult. Woman or man – either was possible. Or anything in between.

'*Losers.*'

It was tempting to yell down the receiver at their persecutor to find a healthier hobby and go fuck themselves. But Trausti knew from painful experience that when someone has you in their sights, it's best to keep a cool head. Showing a reaction only encourages your tormentor.

'*You won't get away with it.*'

Although there were more words this time, he couldn't detect anything familiar about the voice. He didn't know anyone who spoke in a hoarse whisper.

'*Who's that outside?*'

Instinctively, Trausti's eyes slid to the nearest window. He could see nothing but darkness out there. His heart beating frantically against his ribcage, he braced himself for the shock of seeing a movement.

'*Bye,*' the voice whispered.

Trausti was on the verge of saying goodbye back, his innate politeness almost getting the better of him, but he managed to bite back the word before it could slip out, and the next thing he heard was the dial tone indicating that the caller had hung up.

Something touched his shoulder, making him jump so badly that he dropped the receiver, which banged against the wall, leaving a mark on the freshly painted plaster.

It was Sigga. She had dressed in jeans and a cable-knit jumper with a polo neck that reached up to her chin. She made no apology for startling him. 'Was that . . . you know?'

Trausti nodded. He picked up the receiver that was dangling from its cord and replaced it. Sigga pushed him gently aside and read the number of the caller from the little screen. Then she took out her own phone and looked it up on the Icelandic directory website.

'Ellidi Jónsson. Lives in the Westman Islands. Not in the same street as Gugga, though.' Sigga met Trausti's eye. 'Do you recognise the name?'

'No. I don't. Any more than the other two who called.'

'I'm going to try calling him back.' Sigga reached for the phone on the wall.

'It won't achieve anything. Except to wind him up and provoke him into making more calls. Anyway, he probably won't answer. I tried earlier and it rang out. It was a different number – but still.'

Sigga didn't let this dissuade her. 'We'll see. Maybe this Ellidi will react differently.' He didn't. The phone rang out. She hung up and turned back to Trausti. 'What did he say?'

Trausti searched his memory but he was too tired to recall the exact words. Not that it mattered whether he got them right, because the contents of the phone calls weren't carefully planned or coded. It was just words intended to intimidate them. That's all. *Why* was the question they should be considering. *Why? And who were these people? And what did they know?* He looked at Sigga. 'Why on earth would a bunch of locals be ringing here at this time in the morning?'

Sigga's face brightened. 'Of course. The calls aren't intended for us. They must have something to do with the people renting out the house or the man who lived here before. The lighthouse keeper.'

'I imagine most people will be aware that he's moved. It's not a big place. And the caller referred to us in the plural.'

Sigga frowned. 'Could it be Ari's friends? The guys renting out the house? I haven't a clue if they're local. Maybe they've found out that Leifur's sleeping on the sofa and are pissed off about it?' The idea was absurd but then so were the phone calls. 'I mean, no one in the islands actually knows we're here. So it's unlikely to be a local calling us.' Sigga suddenly broke off and made a strange face, as if she'd swallowed something inedible.

'What?'

'Oh. No, nothing.'

Trausti wasn't about to let her off that lightly. 'What? Did you tell someone in the town that we were staying here? Someone at the funeral reception?' He'd gone back over the conversation he'd had with Halldóra at the reception but couldn't recall telling her where they were staying. Or that she'd asked.

'Well . . . I . . .' Sigga took a deep breath. 'I may have mentioned it when we were on the ferry. To a crew member.'

'What crew member?' Trausti gritted his teeth. 'What crew member, Sigga?'

'A woman. The young woman working in the shop. When I went to buy a Coke. She . . . She, er . . . was giving me advice about how to deal with seasickness and we got chatting. She asked if we were going to the fishing conference and one thing led to another. I think she was at the funeral too but I'm not sure. It can't be her ringing, can it?'

'It didn't occur to you to mention this before?' Trausti didn't even try to hide his anger.

'I'd forgotten. It wasn't a big deal. Jesus.'

Trausti got a grip on himself. There were so many other things to be angry about. It was hard to imagine why a crew member from the ferry would want to rope a load of people into making nuisance phone calls. It seemed more likely that Leifur was using some AI program to phone in and scare them, though for what reason Trausti couldn't begin to imagine.

'Forget it. Let's go and find a spade.' Trausti cut Sigga off before she could continue making excuses: 'As more than one local seems to know or suspect what's going on here, there's no need to attract even more attention by buying spades in town.'

'Didn't the caller say there was someone outside? Should we wait until it gets light?'

Trausti hesitated. Then, remembering his newly acquired backbone, he shook his head. 'No. There's nobody out there. Let's get it over with.' He wished he felt as confident of this as he sounded.

But it seemed he was right: there was nobody outside. A search of the outhouses achieved little, however. They found a broad snow shovel made of hard plastic that would break at the first thrust into the frozen ground. A plastic bucket with a child's spade that looked ancient. And a rusty garden trowel, suitable at best for planting summer flowers. If they had to bury the body using those, they would need to extend their visit by several weeks.

They would have to buy spades. Another problem; an endless stream of them. Exasperated, Trausti went up to his room and lay down on his bed but couldn't get back to sleep. The echo of the endless ringing from the ground floor saw to that.

Chapter 22
Day 7 – Wednesday, 29 January

Idunn was still in her pyjamas, with unbrushed teeth and hair, when her phone rang. It was lucky she had it switched on. She was in the middle of uploading photos of the woman on the beach from her phone to her laptop. After that, she had been intending to switch her phone off. The police could come and fetch her if they decided her presence was required. Her mother was having one of her major episodes. When she went ballistic like this, it was like a rocket being launched with insufficient fuel. Up, up, up she would go – until she plummeted back to earth, landing with an almighty crash. Then it would be Idunn's job to patch her up again. That meant getting any outstanding jobs out of the way first, hence the need for peace and quiet to work in now, free from continual interruptions. Besides, Idunn reasoned to herself, it wasn't as if she could have any influence on the progress of the investigation at the moment by responding to phone calls or messages.

That wasn't the only reason she was planning to switch off her phone and leave it behind if she got the green light to go ahead with the post-mortem. The truth was, she'd been gripped by an extremely bad idea that she couldn't shake off. If she had her phone to hand, there was a risk she might put it into action. She'd fallen asleep mulling over the idea, dreamt about it, then woken up with it still buzzing in her head. She had even rehearsed the tirade she was planning to deliver; the bollocking she meant to give her father over the phone.

The knowledge that it was a terrible idea didn't make it any the less tempting. She had all the arguments prepared and wouldn't be thrown off her stride. After all, she knew the story better than anyone else, so sheltering behind lies or irrelevancies would be a waste of his time. She was aware that her mother hadn't been telling the truth when she claimed her dad didn't pay her child maintenance. Her mother had done this to fool Idunn into believing her father didn't care about them. Idunn had subsequently discovered that the state provided the payments, then charged them to the person responsible for paying maintenance. This had led her to re-examine everything her mother had ever told her. As a result, she had come to believe that her father hadn't forgotten about her at all and that his lack of involvement in her childhood was entirely her mother's fault. She even suspected that he'd sent her Christmas and birthday presents that her mother had hidden from her. But even if this were true, there was no point in him trying to plead it as an excuse now. Because when he'd been given a chance to re-establish his relationship with his daughter, he'd spurned it.

When Idunn discovered the truth about the child maintenance, she had been so livid with her mother and filled with such a longing to see her father that she had taken out nearly all the money she'd been given in Confirmation presents – enough for an air ticket to the Westman Islands. Instead of going to school next day, she had walked all the way to Reykjavík's domestic airport and caught the first plane to Heimaey. Once there, she had walked from the airport to her father's office by the harbour, with the idea of throwing herself into his arms and declaring that she wanted to come and live with him. She would apologise for ever having believed her mother's lies. But nothing had come of this plan. Her father's secretary had told her he was busy on the phone and asked her to wait. Idunn had sat down and watched as the woman poked her head round the door to tell her father she was there. And she had heard as he told the secretary irritably to get rid of her and say he wasn't in.

When the woman closed the door and turned to Idunn with a look of embarrassment, Idunn had jumped to her feet and rushed out. It was better not to be among strangers when the world collapsed around your ears. She had sat on a bench by the harbour and cried her eyes out. Through her tears, she had seen her father dash out to his car and roar away. Of course, he hadn't noticed the sorry sight huddled on the bench, her nose running, her face puffy from weeping. She had sat there until her tear ducts were empty. Then she had got up and set off on the long walk back to the airport. She had only withdrawn enough money for a one-way ticket, as she hadn't been planning to go home again. How was she to get back to Reykjavík? She'd just hoped the airline would take pity on her youth and lend her the fare.

The first thing she had seen at the airport was her father's car. At the time, she had interpreted this as meaning that he'd decided to fly to Reykjavík to visit his mistress rather than talk to his daughter. But nowadays she was inclined to believe there had been some fish-related emergency that he had prioritised over her. Well, he'd made his choice and he would have to stand by it. No way was she going to let him back into her life. To make sure she never forgot this slight, she had framed her flight ticket to Reykjavík. The frame, crooked and battered now, still hung on her wall. She had made it home again thanks to the kindness of the staff at the check-in desk, who had taken pity on her when she burst into tears on learning that she wouldn't be allowed to fly back on credit. She suspected they had known who she was and subsequently charged the flight to her father. At the time, he had already been in the air. Whereas she had been forced to sit for hours in departures, lonely and humiliated, clutching her free ticket, waiting for the next plane out of there. It might still have been possible to rescue the situation if he'd called her afterwards to apologise and explain, but there had been total silence from his end. She had felt earth-shatteringly betrayed and completely worthless. After that, Idunn had no reason to doubt her mother's constant reminders that he was a mean bastard who didn't give a damn about his daughter.

Given a betrayal of this magnitude, it was frankly unbelievable that he should imagine Idunn would welcome his younger daughter with open arms. The thought made her fingers itch to ring him. She drew her hands back, reminding herself that it was a very bad idea indeed. He was used to dealing with robust criticism in his line of business and knew how to answer back. Her silence and indifference were a far more effective weapon.

So it was that she was sitting with her hands in her lap, waiting for the photos to upload, when her phone rang. She picked it up, ready to put it down unanswered if it was her mother, then saw that it was Karó.

'Are you ready if I swing by and pick you up?' Karó asked.

Idunn surveyed herself in the mirror above the desk. 'Yes, pretty much.' This was far from the truth, but it would only take a minute to pull on some clothes and run a comb through her hair. It wasn't as if she was on her way to a party.

'Dress up warm. It's freezing and we'll be outside.'

Evidently, Karó wasn't ringing to tell her that she'd got permission to go ahead with the autopsy. 'Has something turned up?' Idunn asked.

'Yes. A grave. On Stórhöfdi. Or at least that's what it looks like.'

'Yet another body?' Idunn already had three bodies awaiting post-mortems; if another was added to the list, she'd still be working flat out at the point when her mother came hurtling back down to earth and a major intervention was required.

'Not yet. We just thought it would be a good idea to have you on the spot while they excavate. Just in case. The ground's recently been disturbed. It came to light during the search which began at the crack of dawn this morning.' Karó added hastily: 'But it's not far to go if you'd rather wait and come along later, if we find something.'

They would undoubtedly find something. It was highly unlikely that the group on Stórhöfdi would have taken it into their heads to go planting potatoes in the middle of winter. 'No. I definitely want to be there.' Idunn was already on her feet, raking her fingers through her tangled hair. 'I'll be downstairs in ten. Or less.'

Idunn needn't have bothered combing her hair. The area where the ground had been disturbed was on a slope to the south of the house on the headland. And there was a southerly gale. The elastic band that kept her hair out of her eyes couldn't stop the wind from whipping her ponytail around until it resembled a wild bush. Pulling her hood up was a waste of time as it kept flying off, and if she tied it tightly under her chin, it just filled with air like a sail and then Idunn was in danger of being blown over. The flock of small birds further up the snowy slope seemed indifferent to the weather. So did the tall, slender masts poking up into the sky on the headland, since they were firmly tethered to the ground. They set up an unearthly screeching in the violent gusts, resulting in a composition that was unlikely to be performed on any stage.

'If it weren't for the spades, I don't suppose we'd have discovered it until spring.' Inspector Ína had taken up position beside Idunn to watch the excavations. 'The fresh soil was hidden by the snow but it came to light as soon as a little had been swept aside. We found two identical spades in the house when we searched it, but we assumed they were left behind by the builders. Perhaps they were. I doubt it, though. They had no reason to be digging out here during the renovations.'

The spades had been left beside the snow-covered grave. It was the bright-red handle of one, protruding at an angle out of the drifts, that had caught the attention of the searchers. The tools, which appeared to be brand new, were now in a large bag in the back of a police vehicle, waiting to be sent for analysis, along with the other two that had been found inside the house. Idunn thought there was a good chance they'd find fingerprints, since anyone who left the spades lying around in full view couldn't have been that bothered about covering their tracks. On second thoughts, though, the weather had been so cold recently that whoever had used the spades would almost certainly have been wearing gloves.

Idunn turned her gaze to the island-studded sea. Though the late winter dawn was breaking, there wasn't enough light yet for their jagged shapes to be clearly visible. Still, it wouldn't have mattered even if she'd looked at them when the sun was high in the sky, as no sheep were kept on the outlying islands in winter. So there was no risk of her seeing the animals plunging to their deaths and exploding – if that story was true. She brought her mind back to the present. 'Have you managed to extract any information from Ásta, the woman who crashed her car?'

'Not really. She flatly denies having anything to do with this business. Claims she saw the glow of the fire and climbed down to the beach to see what was going on. But she can't explain what she was doing out there in the early hours. Apparently, she's still a bit confused, so it's hard to get anything reliable out of her.'

'Did she go anywhere near the body of the woman who was sitting on the beach?'

'No. She strongly denies that too. Claims she just went to check out the bonfire, then fled when she saw what was on it.' Ína shrugged inside her bulky police anorak. 'Who knows? Let's hope she'll be a bit more talkative later.'

'What about the dog hairs on the dead woman's clothes? Could Ásta explain them?' Idunn assumed the young CSI would have passed on his discovery.

'No. She insisted her dog never left the car. That can't be right, but I don't understand why she'd lie about it. Perhaps she's muddled up the series of events.' Ína hugged herself as they were buffeted by yet another freezing gust of wind. One of the men digging lower down the slope was almost knocked off his feet by the force of it. 'But I don't imagine Ásta will stick to her story if the hairs do turn out to be from her dog. That'll make it pretty clear that she had some kind of dealings with the group. I sent a CSI to take some samples from her dog for comparison. Maybe the hairs we found were from a completely different animal. A cat, even. All the hairs will be sent to Reykjavík later on today and the attempt to find a match will be prioritised.'

Idunn nodded. Everything was moving in the right direction. She thought of Stefán, the young technician who had been so excited about the hairs, and hoped for his sake that they would prove significant. 'Have you uncovered any other connection between Ásta and the group?'

'No. But apparently she was acquainted with Gugga, the young woman who died in hospital. The one who lived in the house on Túngata that the group were spotted coming out of. They were in contact.'

'Meaning she could be the fifth person Alexandra saw? The one who let them in, perhaps?'

'Not according to your sister. She was asked, remember? She was adamant that Ásta wasn't one of them. Besides, they weren't let in. They broke in. Through the back door. They smashed the glass in the door and reached inside to open it.'

The two women fell silent and watched the flock of small birds that had now settled on the patch of snow between them and the excavations. The birds pecked around but didn't seem to be finding much. Idunn wondered if they were still hoping the old lighthouse keeper would return. He used to feed them when the weather was bad. In fact, he'd set a world record in tagging birds, a record that would probably never be broken. It was remarkable really, to be the only person among the billions on earth who had the stamina to keep at something like that for more than half a century without a break. Idunn couldn't think of any hobby she would be capable of devoting herself to with the same single-mindedness for fifty years. Except perhaps watching TV.

One of the diggers now turned and beckoned them over. At that, the birds took fright and flew up in the air, only to land again a little further off and resume their search for food. The two women set off gingerly down the slope, digging their heels into the slippery snow to get purchase, as neither wanted to lose their footing and start rolling down the hill, to land either in the newly dug hole or in the sea far below.

'Have you found something?' Ína craned her neck to peer down the hole, then immediately straightened up again.

'The ground's frozen, which makes it bloody difficult, but we've got to the bottom. They can't have gone any deeper because we've hit solid rock.' The man wiped the sweat off his brow with the sleeve of his overalls. 'There's nothing here. No body, at any rate.'

The two men had piled the soil into neat heaps in case it needed to be sieved later. But the wind was indifferent to their efforts and brown streaks were radiating out from the heaps across the white snow. The men had been standing in the shallow hole but now climbed out, panting.

The second man laid aside his spade and bent down to examine one of the small heaps of soil. He looked up at Ína and Idunn with a grimace. 'There's something here.' He poked a gloved finger into the earth, extracted something white, then immediately dropped it. 'Shit.'

'What?' Ína moved closer and crouched down beside him. Idunn followed suit. They stared at what appeared at first sight to be a white pebble. It was a tooth.

By the time all the soil had been sifted, twenty-three teeth had been recovered. Only another nine were needed for an entire set – assuming the owner had still had their wisdom teeth. Some of the teeth were held together by silver wire and all either had braces attached to them or showed traces of dental cement. If there had been any question as to whether they were human, the braces removed all doubt.

Idunn examined the teeth. They had been arranged in two rows, one for the upper jaw, the other for the lower. There appeared to be nothing systematic about which teeth were missing; judging by the brackets in the wire, they had all been present when the braces were fitted.

Idunn breathed in sharply through her nose and looked up. Everyone was staring at her, waiting for her to enlighten them with her verdict, but she had nothing startlingly original to impart. Only very routine information. 'In my opinion, the teeth belonged to a woman. The three incisors are quite small; they're usually larger in men. I stress *usually*. They'll need more careful examination.'

Idunn's eyes met Ína's and she realised they were both thinking the same thing. The young woman who went missing from the student residence had worn braces. And had been associated with this group. Idunn cleared her throat. 'I have a theory that the teeth are from the body that was burnt.' She hesitated. 'I also believe that the body is that of a young woman who vanished years ago. Seven years ago, if I remember right.'

No one looked particularly surprised. At first. Then the questions started coming thick and fast, but Idunn could provide few answers. She fielded them by saying that she didn't want to indulge in speculation. Examining the teeth with the naked eye would not provide any information about where the young woman had been since she'd vanished or when she had died. All Idunn could state with confidence was that the teeth had not been removed recently.

What she didn't add was that if the person in question had died years ago, that might explain why the burnt corpse hadn't assumed a boxer's pose in the flames. Bodies typically adopted that position because the muscles contracted in the heat as they rapidly dried out, but that wouldn't happen if the body was already in a desiccated state. If she told them that, they would only start bombarding her with more questions she couldn't answer. One that was puzzling her was why on earth the body hadn't shown more signs of decomposition.

If it was withered enough to have dried out, the person must have been long dead. Unless the body had been placed in a drying cabinet of some kind. If it was seven years since the woman died, there should have been signs of decomposition, even though the body had been burnt. Could it have been kept in a freezer? Or dried out in some way?

'Did the young woman have any connection to the Westman Islands?' Idunn asked.

'No, not so far as I know,' Ína replied. 'There was nothing about it in the old case files. She was from the west of Iceland, if I remember right. But, as I mentioned before, Gugga was from here and they knew each other. In fact, Gugga was one of the last people to see her alive – along with the other members of the group.' Ína turned to her local officers. 'Are any of you aware of any connection the missing student, Gudrún, could have had with the islands?'

They shook their heads.

Idunn was now convinced that her suspicion was right: the young woman who'd vanished from the student residence all those years ago had ended up burning on a pyre at Ræningjatangi. But how she had got to the islands was anyone's guess. Even the connection through her old friend, Gugga, couldn't explain it. Apparently Gugga had moved back to the islands two years ago. Before that she had lived in various places around the country. She could hardly have carted a body about with her every time she packed up and moved. Anyway, it was futile for Idunn to rack her brains over this mystery. The explanation wouldn't be discovered by examining the burnt remains. It was a job for the police.

Chapter 23
Day 3 – Saturday, 25 January

Trausti forced himself out of bed. It was getting on for eleven in the morning and he could only hope that lying flat on his back, practically motionless, for an hour or two counted as getting some sleep. He hastily showered and dressed, then headed down to the ground floor to check the landline. When he'd gone to bed, the bloody thing had rung out repeatedly at short intervals until in the end the calls had abruptly stopped, mid-ring. Instead of being relieved and thanking God for the respite, the sudden silence had sent his thoughts spiralling. Why had the caller hung up before the phone rang out? He couldn't help reading something ominous into the caller's change in modus operandi. What the hell did it mean? He wouldn't find any answer to that by lying in bed.

When he got downstairs, he understood at once what had happened. The telephone receiver wasn't resting in the cradle but dangling from its wire. One of his friends must have got fed up with the constant ringing and taken the phone off the hook. A good solution, as long as it didn't provoke the caller even further. The person's behaviour was already so bizarre that there was a risk it would only make them even more unhinged. God knows what they'd be capable of if riled. Trausti replaced the receiver. The ringing was intolerable enough; it would be even worse if their persecutor came knocking at the door.

'Do you really want him to start ringing again?' Sigga was watching from the kitchen doorway. He noticed that she was wearing a pair of high-heeled clogs. She'd always been annoyed about being tiny and had told him that she could hardly bear to look at herself in group photos because they exposed her self-deception about being averagely tall. For once there were no monogram logos on her clothes. She frowned. 'Just so you know, I'll go crazy if it starts up again.'

Trausti was too tired to give anything other than a polite answer. His new, more aggressive self hadn't found a chance to bloom yet. 'It won't happen. Up to now, the phone calls have always been in the evening, at night or first thing in the morning. Presumably the person behind them has to work during the day, so they can't keep up this nonsense.'

Sigga leant against the door frame. 'It's Saturday. And there's more than one person calling. One of them's bound to have time off at the weekend.'

Trausti no longer believed that there was more than one individual behind the nuisance calls. 'Leifur was awake when I went up to bed this morning. He said he'd read online that it was no big deal to make it look as if a phone call was coming from a different number. There can't be a whole group of locals behind this. It's hard enough to believe that one person would feel compelled to do it.' As he was talking, he felt a growing conviction that he was right. 'It's one person. Who may not even be here in the islands. Let's hope not.'

A look of horror crossed Sigga's face. 'We weren't supposed to be googling. What was Leifur thinking?'

Trausti squeezed past her into the kitchen. He was dying of hunger and caffeine-withdrawal symptoms. Dismissing her fears as groundless, he said: 'I assume he used his VPN. Anyway, there's a world of difference between searching for information about phone calls and googling how to dispose of a body or destroy incriminating evidence. In the unlikely event that Leifur is questioned by the police about his search history, he can just tell the truth about the nuisance calls. It's not like we're committing a crime by letting it get on our nerves.' He opened the fridge and took out a packet of rye pancakes, the butter and a variety of toppings. 'Do you want some?'

Sigga shook her head. 'It's good news, anyway. If someone's ringing from Reykjavík, it's almost certainly the people who rented us the house. Pranking Ari.'

It was hard to picture a group of investors clubbing together to organise a practical joke of this kind. They would be far too preoccupied with other worries at a time of rising interest rates and general market pessimism. 'I doubt it.' Trausti broke off, wondering whether it was wise to continue this conversation. But he felt it would do him good to share the thoughts that had been preying on his mind. 'Remember that note on our windscreen? On the ferry?' When Sigga nodded, he went on: 'It must be linked to these phone calls. It has to be. I can't imagine the people who lent Ari the house going to all the hassle of booking a ticket on Herjólfur just to put the note there. It must have been someone who was on their way to the islands like us. Though of course the ferry was so full that that doesn't narrow it down much.' Trausti put the food on the table and looked at Sigga. 'Did you tell the woman you spoke to on board what kind of cars we were driving?'

'No. Of course not.' Sigga appeared to be telling the truth. 'I'm not Ari: I wouldn't start bragging about the car to strangers. Or to anyone, for that matter.'

It was daylight outside now and the window over the sink offered a view of the distant islands. Outside the window was a wooden deck, divided by a sturdy stone wall from another deck higher up. In different circumstances, Trausti would have suggested taking their coffee outside and sitting there wrapped in blankets. He felt a brief pang at the thought of how fantastic this trip could have been. He had a habit of getting his hopes up and having unreal expectations, which inevitably led to disappointment. But this trip had reached a new low.

He concentrated on buttering a rye pancake. It was too late to salvage the holiday now. 'Where are Ari and Ragga?' On his way downstairs, Trausti had seen Leifur sound asleep on the sofa. He had crashed out again following their conversation earlier that morning. His snores could be heard all the way downstairs now, so there was no question that he was still dead to the world.

'I think they're still asleep.' Sigga rolled up the arms of her white jumper before reaching for the packet of coffee. Obviously, she didn't want to dirty it. Trausti couldn't help wondering whether she'd deliberately chosen to wear this jumper as an excuse not to go anywhere near the crate or the body. 'Let's leave them to it.' She fetched a filter and started making coffee while Trausti carried on making breakfast.

In spite of everything, he couldn't help being impressed by the way the rye pancake didn't disintegrate as he spread it with cold butter. The bread he'd become used to in America fell apart at the slightest touch and, before he knew it, he'd be buttering the plate. This unremarkable Icelandic *flatkaka* was symbolic of how much he was missing his homeland, despite the excitement with which he had originally headed abroad to start his specialist studies. The pure air, the mountains, the rye pancakes, the language, even the cold spells during summer, they were essential for his survival.

These thoughts only emphasised how incredibly important it was that none of this Gudrún stuff should come to light.

His future and happiness depended on them cleaning up every trace, and doing it so thoroughly that nothing linking them to Gudrún's death would ever be found.

As he ate the last mouthful, Sigga pushed a mug over to him and filled it with steaming coffee. 'Come and sit with me. Let's drink our coffee together and try to forget this horrible situation, if only for a moment.' The aroma was so irresistible that he agreed to her suggestion.

They sat down at the dining table, as Leifur was sleeping in one of the living rooms and since it opened through to the other one, they wouldn't be able to talk in there over the noise of his snoring.

'Would you mind getting rid of that box? Preferably by chucking it outside.' Sigga made a face at the cardboard box they'd taken from Gugga's wardrobe, which was now sitting on one of the dining chairs. They'd dumped it there when they returned from their trip to clean the house. 'It reminds me of this whole horrible nightmare. I can't look at it.'

Trausti did as she asked, though he didn't actually take the box outside. Instead, he placed it by the wall under the window, out of Sigga's eyeline.

'Thanks.' She waved at him to sit down. Then gave him a weary smile, devoid of pleasure or mockery. 'This isn't quite how I'd pictured our trip.'

Trausti nodded and sipped his coffee. Noticing that his cup had left a wet ring on the table, he wiped it off with his hand. Sigga reached over and laid her warm fingers over his. 'If only everyone was like you.'

He didn't answer, grimly aware of the irony. After all, he wasn't exactly in demand socially. But he didn't want to discuss that with Sigga. Instead, he looked away and his gaze alighted on the cardboard box. In all the bickering and confusion,

Trausti hadn't given any further thought to what it contained, or considered how to get rid of it. The idea of book-burning made him uneasy, but incinerating the contents along with the wood from the crate would probably be the most effective means of disposal. The textbooks would almost certainly be marked with Gugga's name, so it would be best for them to disappear for good. The diaries too. He felt relief, then was struck by a thought. 'There are diaries in there. Including from the year Gudrún went missing.'

'So?' Sigga said. Which showed that he wasn't the only one who was distracted.

'Maybe there's something in them that will let us off the hook – explain this whole mess. If there is, we'd still have a chance to return that bloody crate to where it belongs.'

Sigga licked her lips. 'Now you're talking.'

Trausti hesitated a moment before opening the box. He could have sworn it had been shut last time he saw it, but now the flaps were loose. Telling himself he must be mistaken, he pushed the thought away. He started taking out one dog-eared volume after another and laying them on the table, making a pile of the textbooks after quickly leafing through them. What they all had in common was that the first chapters contained passages highlighted in yellow, but after that the owner's interest had faded. Before she was halfway through, Gugga's attention had obviously got sidetracked. The same applied to the two exercise books in the box. Gugga had made a lot of notes at first but no more than ten pages had been used in either. The rest were blank.

It was different with the diaries. They were pretty much full of scribblings, as Gugga seemed to have used them for more than just recording the details of her life. They contained countless doodles of the kind that Trausti often resorted to himself when he was having trouble focusing. There were also shopping lists, statements of lofty goals, and calculations that appeared to relate to her finances and almost invariably ended in a minus. She had also noted down ideas about this and that – ideas that had never come to anything. Uncharitable though the thought was, Trausti doubted Gudrún's disappearance had changed much in that respect. Gugga had always been like a cheap firework, going off with a bang, flaring briefly, then puttering out like a damp squib.

Here and there, she had written short descriptions of events in her life, but these seemed limited to things that had broken up the monotony. Sigga pulled over one of the more recent notebooks while Trausti chose another at random. He put it down when it turned out to be from the summer before they'd all met. The next one, dated the same year, proved more interesting. It was from the autumn they had moved into the student residence. He leafed through quickly but when he got to the first entry about the group of friends, it dawned on him too late that it was probably unwise to read her private thoughts. His mother had once caught him eavesdropping when she was talking to his father. At the time, he hadn't taken her warning on board, but now he understood what she'd meant. *Eavesdroppers never hear any good of themselves*. It was certainly true in this instance. The diary had been written only for the eyes of the person wielding the pen.

Gugga hadn't pulled her punches when describing her first impressions of their group. He guessed her opinion must have softened and changed over time, or it was impossible to understand why she had chosen to hang out with them. Ari was a jumped-up prick, Sigga a bossy, vacuous blonde, Ragga boring and judgemental, Leifur a stupid oaf and Gudrún was stuck up. What stung most though was her verdict on Trausti himself. He hadn't been interesting enough to deserve more than one word: *wuss*.

'Did you find anything?' Sigga must have noticed his heightened colour.

'No. There's nothing important here.' He skimmed the final pages but there was no information of relevance. He laid the book on the chair beside him to ensure that Sigga didn't get hold of it. There was no need for her to be hurt as well. Or Ari, Leifur and Ragga, for that matter. It would be best if none of them read it. He wished he hadn't. If they were annoyed with Gugga, it would only increase the risk of them taking rash decisions about how to solve the mess she had unwittingly left them in.

Sigga looked up from her reading. 'Oof. The poor thing. Here she's writing about her mother's cancer diagnosis. She sounds painfully optimistic, given how we know it ended.'

'When was it written?'

'Er . . .' Sigga lowered her eyes to the book. 'The family seems to have got the bad news at Christmas. She writes about it on 23 December, just over a year before her mother died.'

They carried on reading and Trausti soon became used to the snide remarks about him and his friends. They became milder as time went on, and more infrequent too. In the last few pages he actually came across some positive comments – about everyone except him and Gudrún. Apparently, the two of them had still been judged as harshly as they had been at the outset. He longed to ask Sigga if she'd spotted anything about him but bit back the impulse. It was too ridiculous. What did it matter what Gugga had thought of him? It wasn't like he'd ever get a chance to try and change her mind.

Sigga looked up again. 'She writes a lot about her parents, following the cancer diagnosis. Though she's hardly mentioned them before.'

'That's hardly surprising, is it? She's having to face up to the fact that they won't live forever. A fact she probably didn't give much thought to before. No one knows what they've got until they lose it, and all that.'

'There is one thing.' Sigga put down the diary. 'Her dad owned a digger. A mini digger – but still. It suggests he can't have been aware of the body in the cellar.'

'Because he owned a digger?'

'Yes. Think about it. What would we do if we had a digger at our disposal right now?' She didn't wait for an answer. 'Dig a hole, of course, to get rid of the crate. If her father had known, surely he would have dug a grave for the body? I mean, who would want that in their cellar?'

'Nobody. At least, I can't imagine anyone wanting it there.'

'Which implies that Gugga can't have brought it here until after he died. When she moved back to the islands.'

Trausti wasn't entirely prepared to accept this theory, though he couldn't come up with a better one. 'Gugga couldn't have shifted that crate on her own. It's out of the question. Let alone lugged it down to the cellar. I'm surprised Ari and Ragga even managed between them to get it out of there.'

'Actually, they found a couple of barrows in the cellar and used those to carry the crate to the car. Though I gather the stairs were a nightmare.' Sigga obviously realised from Trausti's expression that he couldn't give a damn about Ari and Ragga's struggles. 'Maybe Gugga had an assistant. Maybe she asked someone to help her.'

There were so many problems with this theory that Trausti didn't know where to begin. 'And took the risk that they'd find out what was inside the crate?'

Sigga fixed her gaze on his. 'Or told him. Or her. Perhaps she trusted someone here in the islands. Someone who would keep their mouth shut. Someone who might also know about our involvement. Which might explain the weird phone calls.' She picked up the notebook again. 'Who knows? She may even name her confidante somewhere in these diaries.'

They went through the rest of the notebooks but found next to nothing useful. In one place Gugga had scrawled a reminder to ring her friend Helga on her birthday. Neither Trausti nor Sigga had ever heard of her before. It was impossible to tell whether this Helga was from the islands. A search of the online telephone directory revealed that twenty-six Helgas lived there, so it was a possibility.

None of the notebooks dated from the year Gudrún had vanished. The last entries were from Christmas and New Year, less than a month before that terrible evening. At the time, Gugga's thoughts had mainly revolved around how badly her mother was suffering and how desperate she was to be allowed to die. Trausti wasn't surprised to see his own name crop up in connection with the plan to get hold of drugs that could help put the poor woman out of her misery. He was more surprised when Gugga mentioned Gudrún in this context. She had been studying chemistry, but Gugga thought it was much less likely that she would offer them a helping hand. Though you never knew. In Trausti's opinion, there was no way Gudrún would have reacted well to this request, any more than he had himself. The fact that he'd witnessed Gugga pestering Ari about it too suggested that she'd had to cast her net wider. Perhaps she'd succeeded in the end. Met a pest controller in a bar who could provide her with a powerful poison. When her mother died, Trausti hadn't asked any questions; he hadn't wanted to know the answers.

It seemed the matter was doomed to remain a mystery since the next diary was missing. Yet Trausti was sure he remembered seeing the year on the front of one of the notebooks when he first examined the contents of the box. As he didn't for a moment believe that anyone else had entered the house between their first visit and later that night when they had gone in to clean, it seemed a fair bet that the book had been removed from the box here on Stórhöfdi. By one of his friends. Which one, though? They had all behaved oddly at one point or another during this doomed reunion, as if they had something to hide. The same could probably be said of him but at least he knew for a fact that he hadn't taken the notebook. So it was either Sigga, Ragga, Leifur or Ari. And Trausti was sure it hadn't been out of a desire to read up on Gugga's odd but boring life. The notebook had been taken to make sure nothing in it could negatively impact the thief. And, at present, there was nothing as negative as something Gugga knew that might implicate this person in Gudrún's death. All rivers run to the sea.

Until now he had always believed he would come back home after finishing his studies. But suddenly, he couldn't wait to be on that plane, high above the Atlantic. As far as he was concerned, Iceland could keep its pure air, mountains, rye pancakes, language and cold spells in summer. He was out of here.

Chapter 24

Day 7 – Wednesday, 29 January

The front door opened and Karó and Týr emerged. 'Right, we're finally done here.' Karó pulled up her hood to shield her face from the snow. 'Sorry to take so long.'

The three of them were the only people remaining on the headland; everyone else had gone back to town. The inspector and CSI team had left once it became clear that there was nothing else to be found. They had raked the snow over the entire area surrounding the house but the soil didn't appear to have been disturbed anywhere else.

Týr and Karó had gone inside the house to ring their boss at Reykjavík CID and provide a status update. Idunn didn't envy them the phone call, based on the little contact she'd had with the woman – Erla, her name was – who'd recently returned from maternity leave. Their interaction had been stilted at best, as Erla was a real ballbreaker. So tough and domineering that she reminded Idunn of a human bulldozer. 'How did it go?'

'As you might expect.' Týr zipped up his coat, then tested the door handle to make sure it was locked. 'As far as Erla's concerned, things are moving far too slowly. Apparently, the media have started putting pressure on the police commissioner's office because they're not getting any answers from this end. And the commissioner, in turn, is putting pressure on

Erla, who's not amused. I gather Ína's keeping her cards close to her chest.'

Idunn had no opinion on the subject, apart from being grateful that the media never tried to fish for information from her department. Clearly there were limits that everyone respected, regardless of what happened further down the line. 'I need to stop by a DIY shop. For the post-mortem. I've finally been given the green light.'

They got in the car and on the way back Týr told Idunn about the landline he had spotted in the house, which had turned out to be connected. When he'd examined the screen, he'd noticed that there had been a number of calls made to and from the phone during the group's stay. 'The CSI team must have failed to notice it. No one's mentioned the calls, at least not to my knowledge.'

'CSI missed it? How is that possible?' Idunn knew they'd spent ages going over the house. There were a lot of rooms and the whole place had been teeming with fingerprints. It didn't help that the building work had only just been completed, which meant that any number of workmen had been tramping in and out. As everything indoors was new, every object had been recently handled, during transport and when it had been installed. The property had presented the technicians with a massive headache.

Karó looked round and smiled at Idunn. 'It wouldn't occur to most people that anyone would use a landline nowadays. I don't even have one myself. The group all had mobile phones with them, so why would anyone bother to use a phone that limits you to standing in one place?'

She was right. Idunn did in fact have a landline but hadn't used it for years. No one had rung it since her grandmother had died. 'Who called them? And who did they call? Do you know?'

'No.' Týr pulled into the car park in front of the DIY store. 'But they all looked like mobile numbers to me, as counter-intuitive as that might sound. I'll let Ína know and she can put someone on to it. I'm guessing the phone calls related to the house – checking whether things were working properly, that sort of thing.'

When they entered the shop, neither Týr nor Karó evinced any desire to hang around while Idunn was selecting her tools. Instead, they waited by the counter. She could understand that. People preferred not to know too much about autopsies. This meant she could examine the tools she needed at her leisure, weighing them in her hand and selecting what she wanted. Once she had everything she required, she laid them on the counter.

'Doing a spot of DIY?' The man gave her a friendly smile as he began scanning the items.

Idunn didn't blink. 'No.'

The assistant, realising correctly that further comments on her purchases would not be welcome, addressed himself instead to Týr and Karó: 'I see you're from the police.'

'That's right.' Týr answered for both of them, since Karó seemed distracted. She was peering towards the back of the shop, then suddenly set off in that direction.

'It's all very shocking.' The assistant shook his head, his lips pursed disapprovingly. 'We're not used to that sort of thing here. I hope you'll catch the person responsible.'

'You can rest assured that we will.' Týr shuffled his feet impatiently as Idunn fetched her wallet from her coat pocket. He was obviously dreading being asked any further questions about the investigation. It was always awkward having to tell members of the public to mind their own business.

Idunn held out her bank card. As there had been no time to open an account at the shop, she had told the inspector not to bother; she could pay for the necessary tools herself and claim them back on expenses. 'Here. I'll need a receipt, please.'

While the assistant was busy, Karó reappeared. She was holding a spade just like the ones found on Stórhöfdi. 'Have you sold any spades like this recently?'

The assistant pushed his reading glasses down his nose and peered over them. 'As a matter of fact, yes, I have.'

'Do you remember who bought them?'

'Yes, I remember them very well. It was a couple. Not local.'

'Did they pay by card?'

'No. Cash. Which hasn't happened for at least six months. Everyone here pays by card. Or by phone. Or with their watch.'

If Karó was disappointed by this answer, she didn't show it. 'When was this?'

'On Saturday, just before closing time. That's not the only reason I remember them, though. They were behaving very oddly.'

'In what way?'

'How many people walk around in sunglasses when it's tipping down with snow?'

Idunn automatically thought about people who need to wear sunglasses even on cloudy days due to migraines or over-sensitivity to harsh lighting of the type found in shops. 'Did they put the glasses on when they entered the shop or were they already wearing them outside?' she asked, although she knew the odds were slim that two individuals with the same rare eye condition would be travelling together.

The man shrugged. 'I can't remember. Though I think they were already wearing them when they came in.' He added: 'It was pretty obvious they didn't want to be recognised. They had their hoods up too and avoided eye contact. I thought they were journalists snooping around the fishing conference. On the lookout for new scandals. They were talking loudly to each other about fishing but clearly didn't know the first thing about it. I got the impression they were pretending to be part of the conference. Then they asked if I sold spades and I thought they must have got their car stuck in the snow. There's more than one kind of spade, you see. For different jobs. But they didn't answer when I asked what they needed them for. They just looked incredibly awkward and repeated the question. I directed them to the right aisle and they came back with four spades. *Four.* Then paid for them and left. Nobody needs four spades to dig a car out of a drift. It's not like we're up north, or have any mountain roads to speak of.'

Týr and Karó asked the man to describe the couple but he couldn't provide any details. They showed him pictures on their phones of the group who had been staying on Stórhöfdi and he thought it was most likely to have been the economist, Ari, and the engineer, Ragnhildur. But he warned them that he couldn't be 100 per cent sure.

When it seemed there was nothing more to be learnt from the shop assistant, they said goodbye and left, Idunn with her tools and the receipt in her pocket. He called after them, just as they were stepping outside, that there was one more thing. The couple had also asked if he sold cans. Large cans for petrol. And lighter fluid. He'd had neither in stock.

Idunn pulled off her gloves, removed the plastic visor and mask from her face, and dropped them into the contaminated-waste bin. 'Right. I don't expect to finish the report until I get the results back from analysis, which could take several weeks. If you want it fast-tracked, I'll need an authorised request to cover the cost.'

Inspector Ína was noticeably pale as she removed her protective clothing. She had insisted on being present at the post-mortem, which had delayed proceedings considerably. While Idunn was hanging around waiting for her at the hospital, she had decided to track down the doctor, Breki, and the nurse, Dóra, who had been responsible for looking after Gugga while she was a patient there.

It had been Dóra's day off but Breki had been on duty. At first, the doctor had been guarded, as if afraid Idunn meant to blame the death on the hospital or on him personally. But gradually he had relaxed and become more willing to talk, though he'd been unable to provide much new information. His statement matched what they had already learnt from the young male nurse, Már: Gugga had been in a bad way, in a lot of pain and depressed. They'd had to tailor her medication to take account of her recent spell in rehab which had been only partially successful. Some days she'd been OK, others she had rung the bell incessantly, complaining and begging for stronger painkillers. Breki said he hadn't been aware of any indications that she was planning to take her own life, but guessed she had ended up in hospital as a result of an attempt to do exactly that.

Breki hadn't talked to her much but they'd had the odd chat while he was examining her. He remembered her saying she wanted to move to Reykjavík. When he asked what was stopping her, she'd said she couldn't sell her house. He'd assured her it was no problem getting rid of a house in the Westman Islands. But she had replied that it wasn't the lack of demand that was preventing her from selling. This had stuck in his memory because it seemed such an odd thing to say. She'd also told him on another occasion that she had terrible problems sleeping at home. As insomnia is the enemy of convalescence, regardless of whether the patient's recovering from an addiction or getting over some physical ailment, Breki had tried to find out the reason. He hadn't got anything out of Gugga but he'd wondered if the fact her house overlooked the town cemetery might have something to do with it. She hadn't directly said as much, but she'd hinted that her inability to sleep was related somehow to the dead. Perhaps she'd been referring to her parents, as they had lived in the house, which must have made it hard to push away the memories. If he'd been reading correctly between the lines, he felt that was all the more reason for her to sell up and move. But she had stubbornly insisted it was impossible.

The conversation with Breki had ended there and Idunn had returned to the hospital basement to wait for Ína. It was getting on for four o'clock by then and Idunn had told the inspector to allow for the post-mortem to take two to four hours. She glanced at the clock now and saw that it had lasted three hours. Már, who Idunn had asked to assist her, appeared completely unfazed by the experience. If he was annoyed at having to work overtime, he gave no sign of it.

'Can't we get a preliminary report sooner than that? Listing the main findings?' Ína couldn't conceal her impatience.

'Yes. Of course. As long as I can finish it before I have to start the next post-mortem. I've got two more waiting.'

The report wouldn't have to be long. The inspector was interested in the main conclusions and any facts that were indisputable. There weren't many of those, but Idunn would record the most obvious, which was that all the indications pointed to death from cyanide poisoning.

The moment Idunn had opened up Ragnhildur's body, it had given off a faint whiff of almonds, which was the first clue to what was going on. The second was that the organs, muscles and stomach lining were all a russet colour. Both symptoms were typical of death by cyanide, as was the fiery red colour of the livor mortis. Idunn had read up on the subject and learnt that the poison prevented the uptake of oxygen by the body's cells. As a result, the oxygen remained in the blood, turning it dark in colour, and as the patches of livor mortis were formed from blood, this made them a more intense red than usual. Idunn had subsequently detected foam in the throat, oesophagus and lungs, though, oddly, the mouth and nostrils appeared to have been cleaned out. The only satisfactory explanation she could come up with was that someone had cleared the woman's airways in an attempt at resuscitation. This would be consistent with the bruising on her chest.

The victim plainly hadn't eaten for a long time before she died, as her stomach had contained nothing but fluid. It had given off an odour of menthol, like her mouth, mingled with ammonia, and since no half-digested Ópal menthol sweets had been found in her stomach, it seemed most likely that she'd been drinking Ópal schnapps. Ína mentioned that an empty bottle of the stuff had been found in the kitchen bin at the house on Stórhöfdi. However, Ópal schnapps was black and the liquid in the woman's stomach was pale, suggesting that she couldn't have drunk much of it.

A final, water-tight conclusion would only be possible after analysis of her organs and the blood and urine specimens. The process could take up to two months in the case of suspected poisoning, as Gugga's autopsy at the beginning of January showed. They were still awaiting a final result on that. Even then, some details would remain obscure. And even if the toxicology report proved conclusively that it was cyanide poisoning, the autopsy wouldn't be able to answer the question of whether Ragnhildur had ingested the substance voluntarily, by accident or had been poisoned by someone else. The same was true in Gugga's case.

Idunn and Már had already taken the body back to the cold store, removed the organs that were to be submitted for analysis and cleaned the steel table and all the instruments. Now that there was no longer anything grisly on view, the colour was slowly returning to Ína's cheeks. It was coming home to her that the ghastly ordeal was over and that in time the memories would fade. The brain had a tendency to sweep the worst stuff under the carpet.

Már, in contrast, had no need to forget. He had conducted himself like a trouper, never once changing his expression or colour. Idunn, remembering the course on how to dole out praise that she had been forced to attend after being given a rough ride in a management evaluation, said: 'Thanks for your help, Már.'

'My pleasure.' The young man smiled. 'Highly informative, to say the least.'

Inspector Ína regarded him with a mixture of astonishment and horror, then addressed Idunn: 'I realise you're reluctant to say anything that might later prove incorrect. But I have to ask: if it does turn out to be cyanide poisoning, how quickly would the woman have died?'

Idunn sighed under her breath. 'Quickly, but not quickly enough from the point of view of the victim. It used to be considered a pretty painless death, but that's misleading. The process can take anything from a few minutes up to a quarter of an hour. It depends on the quantity involved, and whether the person has inhaled or swallowed it. The victim's cells lose their ability to absorb oxygen and the consequences are horrific, as you can imagine.'

Weariness and hunger prevented Idunn from elaborating. It wasn't a common way to die, especially if the woman turned out to have ingested the poison. Deaths caused by cyanide poisoning typically occurred in house fires, as hydrogen cyanide gas could form when materials like paper, wool and some types of plastic burned. This method was quicker and more merciful than when the poison was swallowed in the form of potassium cyanide or sodium cyanide. But Idunn realised that if she started complicating matters with an explanation of how there could be more than one compound, she'd be here all night. Since it was impossible to determine at this stage which exact substance had been used, there was no point indulging in speculation.

On balance, though, she thought it more likely that the poison had been ingested than inhaled. It was hard to picture how the latter scenario could have occurred, considering that the bonfire had been out of doors and the smoke wouldn't have been dense enough for the fumes to be deadly.

'Where would someone get hold of cyanide?' Már asked before Inspector Ína could form the question she was obviously impatient to put to Idunn. As he was speaking, he took out his phone and began tapping at it.

'Hard to say. It's used in various industries, I believe. It's also present in nature. And I assume it would be possible to buy it on the internet. Isn't everything available online nowadays?'

'It says here that cyanide gas is used for pest control on board ships.' Már looked up from his phone. 'No shortage of ships here.'

Idunn clapped her hands together as a sign that they were done. 'Right, I need to jump in the shower and I recommend you two do the same. If you have access to a sauna, even better. There's one at the hotel that I'm sure you can use.'

Idunn didn't doubt they would follow her advice. In fact, she'd like to bet that the inspector would set a personal record in the duration of her shower, if not an Icelandic record. She picked up her camera and bag of instruments, then asked Ína if the police station would like to keep the tools she'd bought at the DIY store.

The inspector shuddered. 'No. They can be thrown out as far as I'm concerned. I never want to set eyes on them again.'

Már escorted them to the door and Ína pushed ahead of Idunn to get to her car, in a hurry to put as much distance as possible between herself and the hospital.

'When you asked me about Gugga,' Már said suddenly, 'I forgot to mention one thing she said to me. At least, I don't think I told you. She complained about her friends. She claimed they weren't prepared to help her when she needed them. She seemed terribly hurt. Said they'd left her in the lurch and expected her to clean up after them. I don't know if that's relevant at all.'

'Did she say which friends?' Idunn couldn't immediately see the significance, unless Gugga had been referring to the group who were all now either missing or dead.

'No, she didn't.'

Later, hair wrapped in a towel and wearing a bathrobe, Idunn paused to check her phone before getting in the sauna. She had received the inevitable messages from her mother and Alexandra but didn't bother opening them. She was more interested in the email from her subordinate who had sent her a link to files from the MRI scan of the burnt body. She sat down at her laptop, full of eager anticipation, and started scrolling through the images. She couldn't wait to receive confirmation of her guess that the body was that of Gudrún, the university student who had vanished seven years ago.

But she was wrong.

Chapter 25

Day 3 – Saturday, 25 January

The windscreen wipers laboured away. No sooner had they scraped the glass clear, making it possible to see out for a moment, than the view vanished again behind a wall of white. Still, it wasn't as though there was much to see, apart from the DIY store across the road. Trausti bent forwards over the steering wheel to peer through the falling snow, while Sigga reclined her seat and closed her eyes. Leifur, meanwhile, sat in resentful silence in the back, staring through the side window with a sullen expression that they pretended not to notice.

They had taken Ari's car, although it was smaller, as the crate containing Gudrún's body was still in the back of Leifur's estate. Trausti had offered to drive since Ari had started the day by uncorking another bottle. He wasn't noticeably slurring or unsteady on his feet, but it didn't pay to take any chances in case they were stopped by the police or the car got bogged down in a snowdrift. The aim was to pass under the radar, not draw attention to themselves by having a drunk behind the wheel. He couldn't understand why Ari had chosen to drink when they all needed to stay alert. People deal with stress in different ways, he supposed.

'They've been a long time in there, haven't they?' Sigga had opened her eyes and was staring unseeingly at the roof of the car. 'I bet they've screwed up.'

Trausti thought it more than likely. When they'd parked here, and Ragga and Ari were getting ready to go into the shop, Ari had suddenly asked which of them should pay. He refused to use his own card and Ragga wasn't prepared to use hers either. They argued that since they were the ones going into the shop, it would be only fair for them to use one of the others' bank cards. In the end, it was agreed that they should go to a cashpoint where everyone would take out money and club together to buy the spades, to ensure that no one's name could be linked to the purchase. Trausti didn't need to withdraw anything as he still had enough cash left over from what he'd taken out at the airport. This was lucky, since they spent so long faffing about at the cashpoint that they only just made it to the shop before it closed. If Trausti had needed to withdraw money as well, they'd have been too late.

In the brief window provided by the wipers, Trausti saw the shop door open. Through the film of snow that immediately began to build up again, he just managed to glimpse the others exiting. The next time he could see out, they had reached the kerb, each carrying two spades.

'What the hell's wrong with them?' Trausti waited for the next glimpse to see if he'd been mistaken. 'They've bought four spades. *Four!*'

Sigga sat up, abruptly returning her seat to the vertical. 'What?' Even Leifur snapped out of his bad mood and stuck his head between the seats to peer through the windscreen.

Between each sweep of the wipers, they watched their friends approaching in fits and starts, as if in a film with too few frames. When they reached the car, they didn't open the door but banged on the boot for Trausti to unlock it. There were four metallic clunks, then a slam as the boot was closed.

Ari and Ragga got in the back with Leifur. Their sunglasses looked ridiculously incongruous paired with their snow-covered coats. As they let their hoods fall, snow scattered all over the back seat.

'Right, that went without a hitch,' Ari announced.

'Apart from the fact they didn't have any petrol cans,' Ragga added. 'And they'd sold out of lighter fluid. The guy said no one barbecues with coals in winter.'

They'd been planning to buy an empty can and fill it at a self-service garage, to reduce the number of places where they had to interact with people. But now that Ragga and Ari had already attracted unnecessary attention with their purchase of a ridiculous number of spades, one more place wouldn't make much difference. Sigga seemed to be thinking along the same lines as Trausti: 'Why the fuck did you buy four spades? Didn't you realise how weird it would look?'

Ari looked offended. 'It's no weirder than anything else. The guy who served us was only interested in closing up and going home. You'll thank us when we start digging tonight. The more spades, the quicker the job.'

'I tried to tell him two would be enough.' Ragga brushed a few last snowflakes from her shoulders.

Trausti studied her, trying to interpret her expression. Her face was covered in tiny, glistening droplets. She cut an oddly dreamlike figure, as if some phantom had taken on her likeness. He couldn't decipher her expression at all. What was her game? He simply couldn't read her. Did she agree with Ari that they had sorted it or with him and Sigga that they had drawn unnecessary attention to themselves? 'What do you say, Ragga?' he asked. 'Is the man likely to remember you?'

'It's done now.' Ragga wiped her face and the droplets vanished. She looked like herself again. 'With any luck he'll think we were here for the conference. We pretended to be talking about fishing and I think he heard us. Let's get going before he comes out and spots the car.'

Trausti drove off, the electric engine purring quietly. They pulled in at a petrol station and again despatched Ragga and Ari inside to buy lighter fluid, cans and petrol to fill them with. They adopted the same lame disguises and returned with their spoils, reeking of the petrol that they had loaded into the boot. Sigga then took on the role of navigator, using her phone to pilot Trausti through the streets to the address where Gugga's old neighbour Halldóra lived. Trausti was desperate to pop back to Gugga's house one last time while they still had the key, just to reassure himself that the missing diary wasn't there. None of his friends would admit to having removed it from the cardboard box and their denials had been so convincing that he had started to question his own memory. Had he forgotten to put it back after going through the box in Gugga's room? There was an easy way to find out, but the thought of setting foot in the gloomy house again was more than he could bear. Sending one of the others to do it for him was out of the question too. He didn't trust them. Any of them. Except perhaps Leifur, though his trust in him wasn't based on anything very sound. Besides, there was a risk Leifur would return with another model ship under his arm.

Sigga directed him to turn in to a residential street, then began reading off the house numbers. She indicated the right one and Trausti parked by the kerb rather than in the empty drive. He switched off the engine, then hesitated a moment before opening the door. Once he'd returned the key, they would have no way of re-entering Gugga's place. 'Are we absolutely sure we don't need to get inside Gugga's house again for any reason?'

Sigga and Ari said in unison that they were 100 per cent sure, Leifur was silent, while Ragga expressed doubts. Not about them needing to get back in but about his question. 'Why do you ask? Do you have something specific in mind?'

He did. Quite apart from the diary, any chance of returning the crate with the body in it would be lost. But since neither point was likely to prove popular with the others, he mentioned only the third: 'Something occurred to me. Could there be more recent diaries we should take a look at? It seems likely, seeing how conscientious Gugga was about writing things down. Perhaps we could find an explanation for all this madness. We weren't exactly on the lookout for that the last time we were there.'

'Ragga and I gave her room a thorough going-over,' Sigga objected. 'We opened all the drawers and even checked under her bed. There were no notebooks there and I don't suppose she'd have kept them in her parents' bedroom or her father's workshop. We went through all the other rooms.' Sigga turned in her seat to meet Ragga's eye. 'Don't you agree?'

'Yes. There weren't any other diaries. Maybe she gave up recording things after she moved out of the student residence. Let's just go ahead and return the key.'

Trausti suspected that Ragga's eagerness to drop off the key was related to a desire to prevent them from doing the right thing; in other words, returning the body to where they had found it. But as this was only a hunch, he didn't call her out. Nor did he give voice to his doubts about their claim not to have found any recent diaries in Gugga's room. Or his suspicion that they might have stolen them and squirrelled them away.

'What about the mini digger?' At first, Ari seemed to be talking completely at random. Then he said: 'What about borrowing it? Then we won't need the spades. We can get this business over with as soon as it's dark, then bring it back tonight.'

Ari was obviously drunker than Trausti had thought. 'No. We're not going to steal a digger and go on a joyride through the town. The place is hardly full of diggers, so the neighbours are bound to call the police. It's not like a scooter-sharing service that anyone can use. Besides, it didn't look like it was in working order.' Trausti broke off and hastily got out of the car before Sigga and Ragga could start siding with Ari. It would be best to get rid of the key as soon as possible.

Halldóra seemed surprised, having clearly forgotten who he was. When she finally remembered and understood that he wasn't trying to sell her something, she relaxed. To make the situation even more awkward, she tried to make amends by inviting him in for coffee but he declined with the excuse that his friends were waiting for him in the car.

'Did you find something to remember her by?' The woman wrapped her knitted cardigan around her against the chill.

Trausti, unprepared for this, said the first thing that came into his head: 'No. In the end we didn't like to. We didn't want to remove anything that might turn out to be valuable. But thanks so much for the kind thought.'

'Oh, I'm sure it wouldn't have mattered if you'd taken something valuable. As it is, the state will get the lot. There are no legal heirs and no will.' The woman shook her head, presumably at the injustice of the world and the bottomless pit that was the state treasury. 'It seems such a shame. I expect her parents would have liked everything to go to the church if they'd known what was going to happen. Or the hospital, if poor Gugga had been able to predict the future.'

Trausti nodded, trying to look sympathetic. He had no wish to get involved in a conversation about how Gugga's estate should have been bestowed, especially given the nightmare she had landed her friends in. But now, at least, he spied an opening to find out something that had been troubling him: 'Can I ask you a question? I've been living abroad, so I'm not quite up to speed, but what did Gugga actually die of?'

In return he got a long story. Rehab, a hiking accident, depression, then an error in her medication. No mention of cancer. Yet Halldóra gave every impression of being in her right mind and knowing what she was talking about. It seemed that the misunderstanding about Gugga's health could be laid entirely at Gugga's own door. She had lied to them, presumably to trick them into visiting her. He could only assume that she had resorted to this trick because she needed to discuss something that couldn't be put into writing: the answer to that was obviously the presence of Gudrún's body in her cellar. If he was right, she must have wanted them to help her dispose of it. Because as long as it was down there, she had no way of selling the house. On the group chat she had mentioned that she wanted to move back to Reykjavík, but in order to do so she would need their help. It wasn't hard now to guess what she'd needed help with. It wasn't about money or finding her a job, as they had believed at the time.

If only they had gone to see her in hospital. If only they'd responded positively to her request for help with moving. Or agreed to meet up, as she'd suggested shortly after her father had died. If only. Two short words that contained volumes. If only they'd . . . done this, not that. Everything they had done since the evening Gudrún died seven years ago had been a series of fuck-ups. One fuck-up piled on top of another.

'Are you all right, dear?' Halldóra was regarding him with concern.

'Yes. Sorry, I'm just a bit distracted. I slept badly.' Trausti forced a smile. It was a plausible enough excuse, but when he started fishing for the names of the friends who had allegedly visited Gugga, Halldóra grew suddenly wary and seemed to regret having opened the door to him.

He returned to the car none the wiser and drove his friends back out to Stórhöfdi.

The headland was covered in a layer of freshly fallen snow. Having emptied themselves, the clouds had dispersed, leaving the heavens bright with stars. The area behind the house was illuminated by the moon and the sweep of the lighthouse beam, but even the perfect stillness and beauty couldn't raise any enthusiasm from Trausti. You could have added a school of dolphins to the glittering sea, a pair of swans flying overhead or a pack of sledge dogs in the snowy fields and he wouldn't have blinked. Nothing must distract him from the task in hand, which he was keen to get out of the way as soon as possible.

At his feet lay the wooden crate. After supper, he had got Leifur to help him lift it out of the car and carry it to a sheltered spot behind the wall of the lighthouse. The crate, while lighter than expected, had still required an effort to shift. While they were doing this, Sigga and Ari had organised a barbecue and, although the meat was first class, the sauce perfect and the salad fresh, no one but Leifur had had much appetite. The wine was another matter, though; they had all drunk copious amounts. Including Trausti. He had done so deliberately, to give himself the Dutch courage for what he had to do.

He had refused Ragga and Ari's offer to keep him company. He wanted to be alone while he worked, spared their exclamations of revulsion. Taking a deep breath to brace himself, he stooped to remove the lid from the crate. As he did so, he nearly lost his balance, and realised that the last glass had been one too many. The wine may have given him courage but at the same time it had rendered his movements clumsy and his thoughts blurred. Well, it couldn't be helped.

The sight that met him under the lid was different from the one he had seen in Gugga's cellar. The shape of the body was more clearly defined, and here and there he caught a glimpse of flesh. Only the head was still buried under a layer of the coarse white grit that had previously filled the crate. As he stared down at it, bemused, it dawned on him what had happened: Ragga and Ari had scooped out the grit to lighten the crate. Come to think of it, they couldn't have moved the thing at all if it had still been full of the stuff. Which meant that if Gugga had moved the crate down to the cellar after her father died, she would have needed the help of several people. Could that explain the nuisance calls they'd been receiving from different addresses on Heimaey? Could they have been from different individuals, after all?

The answer wasn't to be found in the crate. Nevertheless, Trausti stuck in his gloved hand and picked up some of the grit still lying on the bottom. As he rubbed the grains between his fingers, it dawned on him that it was probably salt. At no point during his medical degree here in Iceland or his graduate studies in the States had he encountered so much as a chapter, a paragraph, a sentence or even a footnote about preserving a body in salt. All he could fall back on was the well-known fact that foodstuffs were often conserved in salt. The mineral removed all the moisture from anything placed in it, and, without water, nothing – not even bacteria – could survive. And without bacteria and other microorganisms, there could be no decomposition.

From what he could see of the body, it appeared to have dried out, which would fit in with his theory. Whether the person responsible for hiding it there had opened it up and packed the abdominal cavity with salt would soon become apparent. Ari and Ragga had left a thin covering of salt over the body – deliberately, he guessed, so they didn't have to look at the macabre sight while digging the rest of the stuff out of the crate.

Before examining the corpse, he pulled out the plastic bag from under its feet and peered inside, using the torch on the phone he'd borrowed from one of the others. It contained clothes. Afraid that he recognised them, he hastily closed the bag again. The jeans could have belonged to anybody but that jumper had been unique. It had been knitted from left-over yarn, the choice of colours guided by what was available, regardless of whether they clashed. It was unquestionably Gudrún's and, what's more, she'd been wearing it the night of the fateful party.

After pushing the bag back into the crate, he tried to sweep the salt off the body's abdomen. This wasn't easy as it had hardened into a shell. Perhaps Ari and Ragga hadn't left it there to spare themselves a grisly sight but because it was dif-ficult and time-consuming to scrape off.

Eventually, though, he succeeded. He examined Gudrún's stomach. There was no sign of an incision there, but he did glimpse something, just above the navel. He started to scrape the salt off that area too and found an incision running up the torso. The more he saw, the more incredulous he became. He straightened his back, staring at what he had revealed, then started retching. Not from squeamishness, but from shock.

Without pausing to replace the lid, he stormed back into the house. He didn't even stop to take off his shoes but marched into the dining room where his friends were still drinking. Right now, he couldn't give a shit about leaving wet prints on the smart new parquet.

His inner turmoil must have been obvious. The others stopped talking the instant he appeared in the doorway, their mouths falling open in astonishment.

'The body in the box isn't Gudrún.' Trausti hardly recognised his own voice. He had screeched it at a pitch at least an octave higher than normal.

'What the fuck?' Ari's voice also emerged in a falsetto, like a cartoon rabbit. But when he continued, he had it under control: 'What do you think a body looks like after seven years? Of course she'll have changed.'

Trausti clung to the doorjamb and heaved a deep breath. 'The body in the crate . . .' He took another breath, trying to get a grip on himself. 'The body in the crate has a Y-shaped incision resulting from a post-mortem.'

They stared at him uncomprehendingly, then gradually the significance of his words seemed to filter into their alcohol-fogged minds.

'Don't you understand? I recognise the technique. The incision wasn't made by some amateur. The body's undergone a professional autopsy. Which means it can't be Gudrún. We've stolen the body of a complete stranger.'

Sigga began to wail.

Chapter 26
Day 7 – Wednesday, 29 January

'The burnt body cannot possibly be that of the young woman who vanished from the student residence.' Idunn was beginning to repeat herself but it couldn't be helped. Several members of the investigation team, including Inspector Ína, Týr and Karó, were seated around the conference table at the police station. It was Idunn herself who had put forward the theory that the burnt body could be linked to the old missing person case, but now she was claiming the opposite. No wonder most of them needed a moment or two to assimilate this unexpected twist. 'There are various organs missing and the body shows all the signs of having undergone a proper post-mortem. Whereas it goes without saying that the young woman who vanished can't have been autopsied because she was never found.' As soon as Idunn had examined the images from the MRI scan, she had realised that the pieces of metal she'd glimpsed were surgical staples, used to close the Y-incision after a post-mortem.

Inspector Ína's eyebrows shot up. 'Is it definitely out of the question that the person who had been hiding the body all these years didn't do it? Didn't remove the organs as well as the teeth?'

Idunn took a deep breath. What she wouldn't have given right now to be fresh out of the sauna and on her way to eat supper and discuss just about anything else. Even *Love Island*. 'Well, I can't rule anything out, but I regard it as extremely unlikely. It looks like a professional job to me.'

'Couldn't someone who knew how to conduct a post-mortem have done it – but not as an official autopsy?' It was the young CSI, Stefán, who asked. 'Someone who wanted to remove the organs because . . . well, for some other purpose?' He had a lot to learn. He had come along to the meeting with the officer in charge of the CSI team, perhaps for the experience. But instead of listening and learning, he had asked more questions than anyone else. He might have got away with it if the other people present hadn't all been starving.

Idunn smiled grimly. 'There aren't many trained pathologists in Iceland. In fact, there's only one woman. Me.' She paused to let this sink in. 'And I don't go around performing autopsies in my spare time.'

Týr and Karó smiled but Ína was not amused. 'Naturally, no one's suggesting that.'

Idunn's stomach rumbled and she reached for the plate of biscuits. Although she couldn't eat one while she was trying to answer their questions, she felt better for having something edible in her hand. 'I should also mention that the body is old. How old, I don't know. But it could well date from before my time, in which case one of the foreign pathologists who took it in turns to work in Iceland could have been responsible for the post-mortem. It goes without saying, though, that if the post-mortem wasn't performed in a hospital, there's no way a professional would have had anything to do with it.'

'So you're saying that there could be a natural explanation for the post-mortem?' Týr chipped in.

'Yes. In my view. The missing organs point to that conclusion, as does the handiwork.'

'Can you tell why there would have been a post-mortem? Are there any clues as to whether it would have been for forensic purposes or for clinical ones?'

The difference could be significant. The police normally requested an autopsy if there was a suspicion of criminal action; doctors, if they thought it might help explain the progress of a disease or in cases where the cause of death was uncertain. 'No, I can't tell,' Idunn replied. 'Not from these images. And probably not after I've conducted the internal examination either.' She blamed hunger for the fact that she was now going to allow herself to indulge in speculation, although she had been determined not to. After all, that tactic hadn't worked out well so far in relation to this body. 'But if I had to guess, I'd say the autopsy was for clinical purposes. The dead woman had a port-a-cath.'

'A port-a-cath?' The young CSI got in first, though clearly he wasn't the only one unfamiliar with the term.

'It's a port or tube that's placed under the skin and inserted into a large vein leading to the heart. It's used to administer chemo, fluids and so on. This kind of port is never fitted in healthy individuals, which is what makes me think the autopsy would have been for clinical purposes.' Although it was too late now, Idunn added, hedging her bets: 'But that's only a guess and we shouldn't read too much into it. Patients can also die in circumstances that call for a forensic post-mortem.'

Ína had apparently had enough of speculation and was after solid facts: 'Can you tell the cause of death?'

Idunn shook her head. 'No. The MRI shows that the body had no broken bones and there are no visible puncture wounds either, though that doesn't tell us the whole story because of the state the body was in. It's possible something else will come to light when I can finally get on with the internal examination.

But it's only fair to warn you that it's very unlikely I'll be able to say anything definite about the cause of death. Not only is the body badly burnt but all its major organs are missing. In the absence of knife wounds or cuts on the bones, it'll be difficult to provide any firm conclusions.' Idunn wrestled with the temptation to take a bite of her biscuit and managed to resist. 'But, on the positive side, if we can identify the body, we'll be able to refer to the results of the original post-mortem.'

'How quickly can we expect an identification?' Ína corrected herself: 'When is it realistic that we'll have a name?'

Idunn finally bit into her biscuit and pretended to be deliberating while she chewed. She swallowed, then replied: 'We've got some teeth that may belong to the body – but may not. The teeth have remnants of braces attached. We know the young woman who went missing from the university had braces, but she wasn't the only person in the country who did. If the teeth are hers, I haven't a clue how they ended up with this unidentified woman's body.' Idunn paused to catch her breath. 'We don't have any fingerprints. We don't have a date of death, not even a year. Even if I manage to find some undamaged DNA, we'd need something for comparison, and the profiling process takes time. The most likely way we'll solve the problem is by checking all the women who were autopsied during the period when the death is believed to have taken place.'

'Won't that be a lot of work?' Ína didn't sound very optimistic.

The MRI images had removed any question of the burnt body's biological gender, demonstrating beyond doubt that they were dealing with a woman. 'Possibly. But you could say that we're lucky with the gender. Autopsies are performed on about half as many women as men.'

The Wake

Since Idunn was responsible for keeping track of these statistics for the Directorate of Health, she was well placed to know. If the post-mortem had been for clinical reasons, as she believed, about twenty a year were performed on women. It was hard to guess how wide a time frame should be taken into consideration as it was impossible to determine with any certainty when the woman had died. Idunn didn't even know how the body had been stored, but in spite of that she reckoned she could propose a fairly plausible time frame. If the dead woman didn't turn up within those parameters, they could be widened. The port-a-cath would help too, enabling her to eliminate women who hadn't had one at the time of their death and also perhaps to trace the make to a particular year. By that means she should be able to find out which women had been given a port-a-cath and which of those had died. Little by little, she'd be able to narrow it down until she could establish the woman's name.

'I've got a question.' Karó had claimed to be as famished as Idunn before the meeting began, so she must really want to know the answer to this. 'What happens to a body following an autopsy? How could it vanish afterwards?'

Idunn had to acknowledge that this was a good point. All eyes turned back to her. 'It goes to the hospital mortuary, and when all the paperwork and formalities have been taken care of, it's collected by the funeral directors. What happens there, I don't really know, but I assume the body is prepared for the coffin viewing, then buried immediately after the funeral. Unless it's cremated. Though, having said that, there isn't always a coffin viewing before the funeral. I don't know what decides that.'

Ína now weighed in. 'Are you 100 per cent sure the body hadn't been buried?'

'Pretty sure. Bodies in coffins decompose. Whereas this body seems to have shrivelled up or dried out like a mummy. That wouldn't have happened if it had been buried.'

'So, logically, it must either have been removed from the hospital mortuary or from the funeral parlour? Or maybe from the church or chapel?'

'Yes. That sounds plausible. Unless it was dug up again shortly after the funeral. But that seems a bit far-fetched.' Idunn thought for a moment. 'I'm not the right person to hypothesise about how a body might disappear from a funeral parlour, chapel or church, but I imagine it would be harder to steal from a hospital. You couldn't just walk in and remove a body from our locked cold store. Or from any other mortuary in the country. The same applies to funeral parlours. Its disappearance would be reported, not hushed up.' Dismissing any further conjecture on this subject, Idunn pointed out: 'The body on the bonfire showed signs of being naked but with something spread over it, like a blanket or clothes. But there's no trace of anything similar underneath it. When bodies are laid out in coffins, they're dressed, not naked. Just in case that's significant.'

'The person who stole it could have undressed it,' the young technician blurted out, apparently without meaning to say it aloud. He turned bright red and shut up again.

This had gone on long enough. Idunn laid her hands flat on the table and said with finality: 'I can access documents relating to all the post-mortems in Iceland via my computer. So I think I'd better call it a day here and start the hunt for our woman. But first I need to eat.'

The three of them were seated in Slippurinn, a restaurant down by the harbour. They'd got window seats as there were few diners there that late on a Wednesday evening. Týr and

Karó gazed out at the ships moored to the docks, something Idunn avoided doing as far as possible. The harbour, the boats and anything else related to the fishing industry reminded her too powerfully of her father. She wanted to savour her meal and a moment's respite from work. She'd been so hungry when they sat down that she'd ordered three courses. Now, it looked as though she would have to admit defeat in the middle of her dessert. Which was a shame.

It was a long time since Idunn had eaten so well. She rarely dined out in Reykjavík and wasn't much of a cook herself. Preparing meals for one was so depressing that as a rule she made do with whatever was nearest the front of the fridge, as long as it didn't require any particular effort involving the cooker. But that didn't mean she didn't appreciate being cooked for by somebody else, particularly when the food was prepared with such artistry.

She pushed away her half-finished dessert and reached for her water glass. She'd had to exercise restraint when the waiter brought their main course and asked if he could offer them wine with it. Luckily, common sense had prevailed, as she was planning to work late tonight. The sooner this case was solved, the sooner she could go home. The forecast was good, with no storms in the offing. Even the Hellisheidi mountain road was passable again, and Ína had implied that they would be flying home tomorrow. The search of Heimaey was as good as complete and, apart from the teeth in the hole on Stórhöfdi, they had discovered nothing but rubbish that had no relevance to the case – including a robot vacuum cleaner with a flat battery, which had been found in the snow beside the road to Stórhöfdi. How it had got there was anyone's guess.

Karó asked to be excused and disappeared in the direction of the toilets. That left the two of them alone together;

Týr contemplating the harbour, Idunn trying to pluck up her courage. It was now or never if she wanted to tell him what she had discovered about his mother's murder. Idunn decided to take the plunge.

'There's something I need to tell you, Týr. You probably won't thank me, but I feel you have a right to know.'

'What?' He looked at her, his contented expression giving way to surprise and puzzlement at her tone. The scar on his forehead seemed even more conspicuous, though this might just have been Idunn's imagination.

'It's about your mother. And your father. Your biological parents.' Without hesitation or tripping over her words, Idunn told him what she had learnt. As briefly as she could, she summed up the inconsistencies between Týr's father's description of the incident and the evidence of his mother's wounds, explaining how no part of his account fitted with the injuries or the blood stains in photos from the scene. Idunn was in such a hurry to blurt it all out that her account would not have been considered admissible in court, but Týr seemed shaken, nonetheless. 'I'm terribly sorry,' she added, 'but I don't think this will be enough to warrant reopening the case. It's a horrendously convoluted process, and the fact your father's dead complicates matters even further. He's not here to bear witness. He can't change his statement or retract his confession. It would be too easy for the prosecution to claim that he would have corrected his statement later and to insist that the confession carries more weight than the description of the incident by a man in a highly charged emotional state.' Idunn wanted to reach over the table and lay a hand on Týr's clenched fist but didn't dare. 'I hope there's some value for you in knowing that your father almost certainly didn't commit murder and wasn't responsible for the attack on you.'

She fell silent and studied Týr's face in the hope of seeing some sign that she had done the right thing. Týr looked as if he'd been turned to stone.

He ran his hands through his hair, leant back in his seat, then rubbed his fingers down his face. 'I . . . er . . .' He blew out a breath. 'So, what now? Who did kill her?'

'I don't know, I'm afraid.' Out of the corner of her eye, Idunn saw the door of the toilets opening and added quickly: 'There's a faint chance that the old case files contain the names of some other possible suspects, but I didn't notice any. I think you should be prepared for the fact that you'll probably never get any answers.'

This was the worst way Idunn could ever remember ending a conversation. But she had no time to rectify the situation before Karó came back and sat down. At first, Karó didn't seem to notice that the mood had changed, but when Týr just sat there in silence, staring into space like a zombie, she grew suspicious.

'Has something happened?'

Týr didn't answer, just stood up and announced that he was going back to the hotel. He settled his part of the bill. After he had disappeared downstairs, Idunn sighed and broke the silence, imparting the gist of the conversation to Karó, since she was already aware of the story and could be trusted. Her reaction wasn't what Idunn had been hoping for. She'd taken it for granted that Karó would reassure her and praise her for doing the right thing, however difficult, but she couldn't have been more wrong. Instead, Karó appeared shocked and asked whether it wouldn't have been better to protect Týr from this information. Sometimes ignorance was bliss. The example Karó chose to illustrate this didn't make Idunn feel any better. Karó started talking about NASA's decision not to inform the crew of the Columbia space shuttle that they would die on re-entering the Earth's atmosphere, on the grounds that there was nothing the crew could do to influence the course of events. Just as there was nothing Týr could do with the information Idunn had given him – apart from feeling bad and wasting time impotently brooding on what might have happened.

'Are you interested in space, Karó?' Idunn couldn't think of anything else to say. She didn't want to discuss her decision. She'd made a mistake, but there was no going back now.

'Yes and no. I'm mainly interested in disasters. They happen in space like anywhere else.' Karó's attractive brown eyes widened. 'Look, sorry – I shouldn't have used that example. Týr will get over it, of course he will. And in the end he'll be glad he knows. You did the right thing by telling him. Definitely the right thing.'

This did nothing to alleviate Idunn's feelings of guilt. She was conscious of a knot in her stomach as they worked out the bill and walked the short way back to the hotel, and when they entered reception, the knot only tightened. There was Alexandra, surrounded by kids her own age. She stood up, smiling from ear to ear, and announced that this was her sister, then explained to Idunn that these were her friends. Feeling dazed, Idunn shook hands with each young woman in turn, their names going in one ear and out the other. Then she stood there like an idiot, listening to Alexandra telling them proudly what her sister did for a living and that she was here for a murder investigation. She was a pathologist who conducted autopsies. Idunn got the impression from the other girls' reactions that they had heard it all before.

Perhaps it was because of the business with Týr or because Idunn was feeling a little chuffed at hearing the pride in her half-sister's voice, but she didn't object when Alexandra told her friends that they were going to live together in Reykjavík. She even managed to bite her tongue and keep her frozen smile in place when Alexandra added that her friends must come and visit. They could sleep in the living room.

In a voice that sounded rather shrill, Idunn excused herself, saying she needed to go up and work, then she scuttled into the lift that Karó was holding open for her. Alexandra called after them cheerfully that she'd see them at breakfast.

Not until she was in her room did Idunn allow herself to groan. Then she sat down with her laptop and got to work.

It wasn't long before she had identified a potential candidate for the burnt body. She perked up a little – until it dawned on her that this meant she was unlikely to be going home in the morning.

Chapter 27
Day 3 – Saturday, 25 January

Four mobile phones lit up the inside of the crate. Trausti had brushed the grains of salt off the face, then scraped off most of the hard white coating. The others took in the sight, mute as the awful truth filtered in. The only sound was a pathetic whimpering from Sigga. At any other time, it would have been barely audible up here, but for once the wind had dropped, the sea was calm and the birds were asleep or had fled south to warmer climes. The clear, starry sky was accompanied by a frost that the others didn't seem to have registered yet. Trausti was the only one wearing a coat; his friends had rushed out into the night without a thought for the weather.

In the bright glow cast by their phones, the shrivelled face of the corpse was clearly visible. The skin looked leathery, the scalp was bald and the cheeks had sunk, unless the dead woman had already been emaciated when she died. Her tooth-less mouth hung slightly open, as if it had stiffened like that after she drew her last breath. The woman was nothing like Gudrún, but then she had presumably looked quite different when alive.

'How . . . ?' Ragga began hoarsely, but left her question unfinished. It didn't matter, as now that she had broken the ice, the others rediscovered their tongues.

'It's not Gudrún,' Leifur said to himself, expressing what they were all thinking. He was in the habit of voicing his thoughts aloud, as if to reassure himself that he had come to the right conclusion.

'You said it, Leifur. It's not her. Like I told you.' Trausti ran his torch beam down the body from head to foot. He pointed out the plastic bag containing clothes that had been stuffed down by the feet. 'But for some reason, Gudrún's clothes are in the crate. Her bracelet too. And probably her teeth. And hair.' Trausti indicated the bag full of hair that he had picked up when first examining the contents of the crate in Gugga's cellar. The torch beams from the four phones followed his gesture.

'No. That's impossible.' Ari was still in denial. Although he'd been forced to concede that the woman lying in the crate was a stranger, he wasn't going to agree to anything else without a fight. It would be typical of him to reject every new detail until he was finally forced to confront the truth. 'Why would Gudrún's clothes be in another woman's coffin? Not to mention her teeth?'

Trausti bent and picked up the bag of clothes. There was no need to argue about it when they had visual proof. 'See for yourself.' He handed it to Ari, then plucked out the bag of hair and held it up. He couldn't face the thought of fishing the teeth out of the corpse's open mouth, so he left them where they were.

While Ari was struggling to open the bag without dropping his phone, Ragga seized the chance to finish the question she had started to ask earlier: 'How could this happen? Some woman we've never seen before!'

'I don't suppose we'll ever know.' Trausti wasn't angry any more. He felt drained and exhausted. 'We'll just have to accept that this is the situation, and work out what to do. Find the least bad solution. Because there aren't any good ones that I can see.'

Sigga teetered in her high heels on the uneven surface of the snow. She had stopped crying. 'What? What solution?' she demanded. 'There is no solution. This is a fuck-up. A total fuck-up.'

Trausti didn't contradict her, but allowed Leifur a chance to speak:

'Let's put the crate back,' Leifur suggested. 'Then get the hell out of here. I don't know about you but I have no idea who this woman is and there's no reason why the police should ever connect her to me. They can find the crate as far as I'm concerned.'

'I returned the key, remember? So we can't.' Trausti filled his lungs with the frosty air, then released it slowly in a cloud of steam. 'We could stick the crate in the garden behind her house. It might not occur to the police that anyone other than Gugga or her parents put it there.' No sooner had he finished speaking than he realised the stupidity of this plan. The cellar floor must be covered in salt. What's more, the garden was overlooked by the house next door and the neighbours couldn't fail to notice the sudden appearance of the crate. It wouldn't take the police long to work out that someone other than Gugga or her parents had moved it and that it had been down in the cellar before. Whether suspicion would fall on Trausti and his friends was another matter, but were they willing to take that risk?

'We could break in.' Leifur wasn't ready to abandon the idea. 'Isn't there a back door? We could buy a crowbar and force the lock. Return the crate to the cellar and put all the salt back inside it. Then everything would be the same as before.'

'We're not going to buy a crowbar,' Trausti said. 'It's Sunday tomorrow and the shop is bound to be closed. Besides, the man working there would really start scratching his head if we bought a crowbar in addition to the four spades. You might as well ask straight out if he stocks burglary kits. And, given our luck, we'd almost certainly be spotted.' He rubbed his eyes, wishing he was back in the States. The worst hospital shift in the world would be a step up from this nightmare.

Sigga's breathing had grown ragged again but she postponed her next bout of crying long enough to snap at Ari and Ragga: 'Why did you have to bring that fucking box here? If you hadn't done that, we'd be fine. Not in . . . in deep shit like this.'

This was neither the time nor the place to start losing their tempers over what couldn't be undone. They had too many other things to worry about. In any case, Sigga's reproaches were like water off a duck's back. Ragga didn't appear to take them personally and Ari was preoccupied with the contents of the bag.

'Let's put the lid back on the crate and go indoors,' Trausti said. 'There's no point freezing out here any longer.' The phone torches were switched off. Ragga and Leifur replaced the lid. All it would need was one strong gust of wind to blow it out to sea but they'd just have to take that risk.

They went and sat in the dining room and Leifur fetched alcohol and glasses which he banged down on the table. Far from objecting, they all helped themselves, Trausti included.

'Why are you still holding that bloody bag, Ari?' The moustache of beer foam on Leifur's top lip was so thick it almost touched his nose. 'Put it back, man.'

Although Ari's face was partly concealed by his glass of wine, they could see that the blood had risen to his cheeks.

Whether it was due to the alcohol or the heat in the room or Leifur's words was impossible to tell. Ari dropped the bag on the floor by his chair. 'I'll do it later.'

'Can I see the clothes?' Ragga held out a hand. 'I want to be sure that they're Gudrún's.'

'They are. I've already checked.' Ari made no move to pick up the bag.

Ragga stood up, grabbed it herself and slapped it down on the table, where she proceeded to pull out one garment after the other. The others watched in silence as she spread them out as if dressing an invisible doll. When she had finished, it looked as if Gudrún had been lying there, but her body had vanished into thin air. No one tried to deny that they were Gudrún's clothes. At least, the garish jumper was definitely the one she'd been wearing the evening she disappeared. The jeans and black socks were too nondescript for Trausti to be sure, and the white T-shirt and bra would have been hidden under her other clothes.

'Oh my God!' Sigga shuddered and took a slug of wine. 'Take them away.'

Ragga peered into the empty bag, then straightened up and contemplated the table. 'Notice something?' They studied the clothes, shaking their heads. 'There aren't any knickers.'

'So?' Ari shrugged. 'Haven't they just been lost? Unless the person who took the clothes wanted to hold on to them? I mean, it wouldn't exactly surprise me if the person who kept her body in a crate was a pervert too.'

Leifur's brows drew together in a frown. He stared down at his beer for a moment, then said: 'Did you take them, Ari? Have you got them in your pocket?'

Ari's look of outrage was a little overdone. 'What the fuck's wrong with you? No. Of course I haven't.'

Judging by their looks of puzzlement, Sigga and Ragga were in the dark, but Trausti knew exactly what Leifur was insinuating. If the dream he'd described had any basis in hazy memories of that fateful night, it was only too plausible that Ari would have wanted to dispose of the knickers. Even after all these years there could be traces of his DNA on them if he had exploited Gudrún's drunken state and forced himself on her. Once again, Trausti's habitual inertia smothered the voice inside him – the voice that told him to side with Leifur and demand to search Ari's pockets. His inertia told him that none of this mattered any more. Since this message overrode his better instincts and avoided rocking the boat, he chose to obey it. He pushed away the thought that his lack of backbone might have something to do with his fear that any DNA could equally belong to him.

But Leifur wasn't ready to give in. 'Gugga was naked from the waist down when I saw her lying in bed. She wasn't wearing jeans or knickers. So why were her jeans in the bag but not her knickers?'

'Naked from the waist down?' Sigga was disconcerted enough to forget that she was in shock. 'What are you talking about?'

Leifur didn't answer her, just continued to glare at Ari. 'Ask him.'

Ari looked ready to explode with fury, but instead of going off the deep end, he resorted to diversionary tactics. 'If it's true and you were perverted enough to look under her bedclothes, isn't there another question we should be asking ourselves?'

'You're the fucking pervert.' Leifur, less cunning than Ari, resorted as usual to childish insults.

Ragga cut across him: 'What question is that, Ari?'

315

'Could we have been mistaken about Gudrún's condition that night? Could she have got dressed and gone out, after all? If she was dead, and naked below the waist, as Leifur the pervert claims, and if her body was spirited away, how come her jeans ended up with the rest of her clothes?'

Sigga was so relieved that she clapped her hands loudly together. 'Yes! Exactly! Gudrún wasn't dead. She was only sleeping.' She paused, then went on pensively: 'Could she have killed the woman in the crate? In cahoots with Gugga?' Seeing the disbelief on the others' faces, she rushed on, firing out words like a machine gun. 'Maybe they stole the woman's organs. Gudrún had debts everywhere. Credit card, overdraft; she even owed her brother and sister. She was in deep shit. Don't you remember? People can do all sorts of crazy stuff to save their own skins.'

She tailed off under the incredulous stares of her audience. No one bothered to comment, since her theory was patently ridiculous. Trausti didn't know whether to laugh or cry.

Ragga turned to him. 'Do you want to answer that?' Apparently, the imaginary black-market trade in organs was his department, nominally coming, as it did, under the heading of medicine.

'There's no market in Iceland for the organs of murder victims.' Trausti held up a hand when Sigga opened her mouth to disagree. He directed his next words at Ari: 'Gudrún didn't go anywhere that night under her own steam. Whoever removed her from the bed must have wrapped her in her duvet and her jeans just got tangled up in it.'

'And her knickers,' Leifur chipped in. 'They must have been in the bed too.' He shot Ari another look of hatred.

Trausti took a deep breath. 'Let's stick to the point. I've got a suggestion.'

Ari sounded relieved. 'Let's hear it.'

'We stick to our original plan – bury the body here on the headland and burn the crate. The clothes, the hair and all the rest too. Then we go home on the ferry we booked tomorrow morning, as planned.' It was with disbelief that Trausti heard himself proposing this. He put his capitulation down to his inertia. If he'd had a few days to recover from the shock, think things over and weigh up the options, he might have kept his mouth shut now. But he had to head back to the US on Monday at the latest. Sometimes the worst option was making no decision at all. And this was one of those times.

What finally put an end to the discussion was the phone starting its infernal ringing again. Trausti felt the sound reverberating through his body, making his hands shake and his heart beat faster. From the panicked look on his friends' faces he could tell he wasn't the only one agitated by the mysterious caller. But no one said a word; instead they got to their feet, emptied their glasses and prepared to go and dig a grave. It didn't cross anyone's mind to answer the call, and since they couldn't bear the noise of its ringing, there was nothing for it but to leave the house. Even Sigga jettisoned her heels and pulled on a pair of flat shoes as a sign that she had abandoned her plan to get out of digging.

The faint echo of the repetitive phone calls had long ago fallen silent, replaced by the grunts of those wielding the spades. It was typical of them to overlook the fact that the ground was frozen, making it hard to dig. They sweated as they shovelled, then shivered as they took their turns at resting. The attempt to all dig at once was quickly abandoned, as they kept clashing spades with each other. At best, only two could work at the same time. It would have been enough to buy two spades, as Ragga had told Ari in the shop.

'Shh!' Sigga suddenly flapped her hand at Ragga and Ari who were standing in the dishearteningly shallow hole, which still only reached to mid-calf. Leifur had nipped to the loo and Sigga and Trausti were on their break. 'Shh!'

Ragga and Ari leant on their spade handles, glad of the chance to catch their breath. Ari looked up and asked irritably: 'What?'

'Can't you hear it?' Sigga raised her chin, as if she thought this would help her hear better. 'There's a crunching sound somewhere nearby. Like footsteps in the snow. Listen.'

Trausti's ears could detect nothing but the muffled lapping of the waves far below as the sea licked at the perpendicular cliffs. 'I can't hear anything.'

Ragga freed her spade from the frozen soil. 'It must have been Leifur. It would be just like him not to bother going inside but to piss in the snow the moment he was out of sight.' She started digging again – if that was the right word. The job mainly consisted of hacking at the frozen earth as hard as they could with the sharp edge of the spade. From time to time, they were able to shovel up half a spadeful of loose snow and fling it out of the hole. They would be here all night if things continued at this rate.

They had been hoping to get below the frostline soon, ignoring Ragga's assertion that outside built-up areas they might have to dig to a depth of two metres before they hit frost-free soil. If she was right, they wouldn't manage it before sunrise, even though dawn came late at this time of year. But they struggled on regardless, such was their desperation to consign their secret to the bowels of the earth.

Behind them, they heard a noise that Trausti recognised: it was the sliding door to the upper deck opening. Shortly afterwards, there came a clearly audible crunching of snow, heralding Leifur's return. Sigga immediately tensed up, as here was proof that the sound she had heard couldn't have been made by him. She scanned the surrounding headland in the dim moonlight, hugging herself. 'Did you see anyone about, Leifur? I heard footsteps in the snow.'

Leifur gaped at her, nonplussed. 'No. Who would be out here?'

This did nothing to allay Sigga's fears and she kept peering around, though she was careful never to look at the body. It lay on the ground a little way off, where they had dumped it after taking it out of the crate and carrying it to what they had agreed was the best site for the grave. This was as far south on the headland as they dared go before the slope became too steep. It seemed unlikely anyone would ever tamper with the ground here. No one would build another house or raise more masts this close to the edge of the cliff.

Trausti, concerned that his friends were getting jittery, hastily asked Leifur if he could do an online search on his phone without leaving a trail. When Leifur assured him he could, Trausti asked him to find out how deep a hole they would need to dig to be on the safe side.

The cold seemed to have no effect on the speed at which Leifur could tap away at his screen. The search took a while, but after several attempts he seemed to glean something useful. Sticking his phone back in his pocket, he said: 'Burying the body one metre down ought to do. But that means a metre's depth of soil on top of it, so we'll have to dig twenty or thirty centimetres deeper to allow for the body as well.'

'Where did you get that from?' Trausti wanted to be sure that the information didn't relate to another country with different soil or climatic conditions.

'An Icelandic site about grave digging. It said there needed to be a minimum of one metre of soil on top of the coffin.'

'That's not the same. Coffins are heavier. Much heavier than a body on its own.' Trausti remembered how frustrated his mother used to get when alternating freeze and thaw conditions brought her autumn bulbs up to the surface of her flower beds, though admittedly they hadn't been planted nearly as deep. But there was a lot more at stake in ensuring that a body stayed below the surface than a few bulbs. 'Did it say anything about why that depth is sufficient? Were they talking about burials in a built-up area or in the countryside? Could it be affected by the cycle of freeze and thaw?'

Leifur rolled his eyes. 'No. Of course it didn't. It was just a short piece about what graves should be like. Not a PhD thesis. Anyway, aren't all cemeteries in towns or villages?'

'One metre will be enough. More than enough.' Ari had been listening. 'I'd have thought half a metre would do. I mean, what's going to happen? No one's going to start tampering with the ground out here. I can promise you the landlords aren't going to amuse themselves by digging holes all over the property. No chance. They're not the type.'

Trausti hadn't a clue what kind of people would do something like that in Ari's book. He'd had enough of wrong-headed decisions. He told them about his mother's bulbs but none of them showed any interest or seemed to understand the relevance. He tried again: 'What about animals? They can sniff bodies out and dig them up. Maybe that's why burials have to be at least one metre deep. We should probably aim to go deeper.'

'What animals? Sheep? Are you joking?' Sigga had revived. She jabbed him with her elbow. 'As far as I know, the only animals they have out here are sheep, in summer. Unless you're afraid a puffin will accidentally burrow down to it?'

'Let's swap places. That'll soon cure you of this one-metre nonsense.' Ari stepped out of the shallow hole and handed Trausti his spade. 'I've freed quite a lot of soil.'

Resisting the urge to point out that Ari still had ten minutes of his turn left. Trausti took the spade. Ragga, meanwhile, carried on chipping away at the frozen ground and didn't exploit this chance to stop early. Her forehead was glistening with sweat. At first, things went well and Trausti chucked one spadeful after another onto the side. But after he had shovelled up all the soil Ari had loosened, the job became more difficult. He drove the spade repeatedly into the iron ground. It felt as if it was deliberately resisting him, trying to make his life as hard as possible.

The other three watched in silence from the sidelines. Leifur produced a bottle from his pocket, which he must have fetched when he nipped away to the loo, if he had actually needed to go at all. Perhaps it had just been a pretext to fetch more booze. Trausti could understand that. He wasn't much of a drinker himself but at this moment he would happily have drunk himself into oblivion. After all that had happened, numbing his brain could only be an improvement.

Leifur handed the bottle to Sigga. She took a swig from the neck, then passed it on to Ari.

'Ópal schnapps? What the hell's wrong with you, man? Why didn't you bring out the brandy?' Ari waved the bottle away in disgust.

'Shut the fuck up,' Leifur growled. Plainly he hadn't forgiven Ari and still harboured suspicions about the missing pair of knickers. Although dreams weren't reliable as evidence, Trausti thought, there was no denying that they could leave a residual bad feeling. He was also of the opinion that dreams didn't appear out of nowhere – each contained a seed that had originated in reality.

'Fetch your own piss if Ópal's not good enough for you,' Leifur added to Ari.

Trausti braced himself to have to listen to a quarrel. He rammed his spade into the ground with all his might and groaned when he heard a clang. It could mean only one of two things: either the spade had clipped a stone or it had hit rock. He hacked at a different spot. The same metallic clang. To make matters worse, Ragga was experiencing the same thing.

They had got down to the bedrock. It would be futile to waste any more time on this botched attempt. The grave was barely half a metre deep, far too shallow to serve its purpose. Even Ari must see that they couldn't leave the body under a thin covering of soil. It felt as if they were being dogged by bad luck.

Before they set off back towards the house, mentally and physically shattered, they agreed to put the body back in the crate. Leifur and Sigga had wanted to leave it where it was until they had come up with a new plan. The others thought this was absurd. Although few if any people had a reason to pass by this isolated spot, they couldn't afford to take the risk. It would be just their luck if the Met Office chose this moment to send a crowd of scientists to take measurements from their equipment.

It was as if a black cloud was hanging over them. Nothing worked out. It wasn't only the soil that was thin here; Trausti's habitual subservience had worn thin too. He was beginning to think they didn't deserve any better. As he picked his way up the steep, icy slope, carrying the legs of a stranger's corpse, it dawned on him that they had forgotten to bring the two unused spades back with them. They'd chucked the teeth, still held together by their braces, into the shallow grave, on the grounds that it would be no good trying to burn them, so he supposed they could console themselves that their efforts hadn't been entirely in vain. Afterwards, they had shovelled the soil back into the hole and spread snow over it to make the dark patch less conspicuous. You never knew – the sight of a black stain on the pristine white headland might rouse the curiosity of a passing fisherman. In the ensuing argument about who should carry the body back to the car, the extra spades had entirely slipped their mind. Trausti decided not to mention them. Lugging the body up the slope was hard enough without having to talk at the same time.

He also omitted to mention the trail of footprints that he had spotted out of the corner of his eye when they got back to the house and lowered the body into the crate. The tracks led to the parking area in front of the house and appeared to have come from the gate. It was too dark for him to see that far, but light enough for him to register that there was no sign of any footprints leading back the same way.

Chapter 28
Day 8 – Thursday, 30 January

The mini digger was working away in the glare of the floodlights. These had been set up by the CSI team, as the excavation was a fiddly job and the bucket of the digger a clumsy tool for use in a confined space. Since the sun hadn't yet risen, the locals couldn't fail to notice from the blaze of lights that something was afoot in the cemetery. Drivers and pedestrians on their morning commute paused to watch; some were curious enough to enter the cemetery to ask what on earth was going on. They were all turned away without explanation. Nevertheless, it must have been clear to passers-by that the police weren't simply there to assist with the digging of a new grave.

Idunn, who was standing in the middle of the floodlit area, couldn't help grimacing ironically at the futility of her attempt to pass under the radar. Here, she was about as inconspicuous as an actor under a spotlight at the National Theatre. But her presence was essential, so it couldn't be helped. Besides, she knew her father was already well aware that she was in the islands.

As a child, she had always been afraid of the cemetery. It was impossible to ignore; the conspicuous white arch of the gate, with its illuminated cross, was like a scream for attention. After she had learnt to read, the inscription filled her with even more dread: *Because I live, you shall also live.* She had interpreted it as a cryptic message, meaning that the dead in the cemetery had permission to return to haunt the living. For a moment or two she wished she could travel back in time and whisper in the ear of her younger self that she had nothing to fear. Not from the dead, at any rate; the living were another story.

The headstone that had marked the grave was now lying flat on the ground a safe distance from the excavation site. Either side of the hole were the gravestones of the woman's daughter and husband. Idunn had repeatedly read the inscription on the headstone to reassure herself that it was the right grave before the digger operator tore into the soil. Locating the correct spot wasn't her responsibility, but she couldn't control the impulse: there were some things she had to see with her own eyes before she was convinced.

Clearly, she wasn't the only one who didn't trust other people to do their job properly. 'You are absolutely positive that the burnt body is the woman who's supposed to be buried in this grave?' It was the third time Inspector Ína had asked.

'Yes. As sure as I can be.' Idunn could have added that it wasn't inconceivable that she'd made a mistake. Individuals weren't quite as unique as people liked to imagine when you couldn't rely on a comparison of DNA, irises, dental records or fingerprints – all of which were absent in this case. Time constraints had precluded DNA profiling, while the victim's eyes and fingerprints had been destroyed by the fire. And the teeth were missing, of course.

Ína raised her eyes from the grave to Idunn. 'You do realise that's not what I was hoping to hear? I wanted you to answer with an unequivocal yes; that you're 100 per cent certain. That's the answer I was after.'

Idunn shrugged. Ína's wish couldn't be granted. 'There's a good chance that the coffin will be empty. I can't say any more than that.' She could understand the inspector's anxiety. As soon as Idunn had contacted her yesterday evening, Ína had asked the judge to fast-track a warrant granting them permission to exhume the body. She had followed this up energetically first thing this morning, and before most people had stood up from the breakfast table the warrant had been issued. It had helped in this instance that there were no close relatives whose permission needed to be sought. Idunn had also composed a memo in record time, laying out her grounds for believing that the burnt body was very probably that of a woman who had died seven years ago – a woman who should, by rights, have been resting in the graveyard in the Westman Islands. The case was unquestionably linked to the investigation that was currently under way there. The woman, whose name was Marta Bjarnhédinsdóttir, was the mother of Gudbjörg, who had recently died in hospital from an overdose of opioids. The same Gudbjörg, or Gugga, who had belonged to a group of friends who were all now either dead or missing, and, furthermore, had been linked to the young woman who'd vanished from the student residence seven years ago.

The digger operator raised the bucket and clambered down from his seat. He came over to Idunn and Ína. 'I'm so close to the coffin lid now that the rest will have to be done by hand. It shouldn't be too hard. There's only a thin layer of earth left.'

They moved over to the edge and peered down into the open grave. Here and there the coffin lid could be glimpsed through the soil. Idunn sent up a silent prayer that she was right. The vicar was standing a little way off and she would rather not have to admit to him that they had disturbed the peace of the dead in his cemetery for no reason.

The digger operator and his mate set to work shovelling the rest of the soil off the coffin. Idunn zipped her coat up to the neck and pulled her hood over her head as the wind gathered strength. Ína was made of sterner stuff and stood there with her coat flapping around her. Now the digger engine had been turned off, it was easier to talk and Idunn seized the chance to ask how things were going. 'Have you prised any more information out of the car-crash woman yet?'

Ína sighed. 'No. Two female officers went to talk to Ásta at the University Hospital yesterday but I gather she's still claiming not to know anything about the people we're investigating. She insists her dog was in the car the whole time and that she herself didn't go anywhere near the body on the beach. But I got a message from forensics earlier confirming that the hairs found on the body are a match with her dog's. So she must have approached the body or touched it. Unless she's lying about the dog and it was running around the site off the lead, which would be a pretty odd thing to lie about. If the burnt body does belong to Marta, as you claim, there's no question that Ásta has to be involved on some level. She not only knew the daughter, Gugga, but she was present at the scene when the body was burnt and Ragnhildur died.' Ína smiled at Idunn. 'And here was I, hoping the whole thing could be blamed on outsiders.'

It was a matter of indifference to Idunn whether those involved in the case were locals or not. All she cared about right now was seeing proof that the coffin was empty, so that she could get on with her work.

It would be empty. That was a safe bet. The woman's post-mortem report had been entirely consistent with what Idunn had deduced from the MRI scan of the burnt body. The port-a-cath was the same make and shape. The same organs were missing as had been removed during Marta's post-mortem.

Her estimated height checked out too, and there was an old, healed fracture in her arm in the same place, containing the same screws as had been put in to hold the bones together. The woman had lost her teeth as the result of a squamous cell carcinoma that had rampaged uncontrollably through her mouth, so that was consistent too. The post-mortem report mentioned a set of dentures but their absence wasn't significant. They would have been returned to the family following the autopsy, in case the relatives wanted an open coffin for a viewing. They could later have been removed by whoever stole the body or else they could have fallen out by accident. By Idunn's estimation, the body hadn't been burning long enough for them to have melted. There was more: the MRI scan showed that the same part of the corpse's tongue had been missing as had been removed from Marta due to her cancer. Her upper lip had also been removed, but the body was too badly burnt for that evidence to be used for comparison.

A photograph of the Y-incision from the post-mortem and the position of the staples that had held it together also seemed to fit with the evidence of the MRI. These incisions were typically done the same way, though not according to a template, and they weren't sewn or stapled together according to a set procedure either. In other words, close observation revealed subtle differences. All of which meant that it had to be the right woman.

The purpose of the post-mortem was yet another argument in favour of the body being Gugga's mother, Marta. Despite her advanced cancer, there had been some uncertainty about her cause of death. According to her prognosis, she should have had a few years left, but her death had occurred with suspicious suddenness – she had been alive one moment, dead the next – so her doctor had requested an autopsy. There had been

symptoms suggesting poisoning, and the results of the toxico-
logical analysis and an internal examination had confirmed
this: Marta had died from ingesting potassium cyanide.

As all those who knew her had agreed that she had wanted
to put an end to her suffering, the conclusion had been that
she'd died by her own hand. Her quality of life had been
severely impaired and when people can't face going on any
longer, it's not unheard of for them to take fate into their
own hands. Where or how she had got hold of the poison had
never been established. Her husband and daughter had both
steadfastly denied any involvement and the police had seen no
reason to pursue them further. Their phones and computers
had been analysed but no evidence had been found that they
had searched online for ways of procuring the substance.

Given that Ragnhildur, the young woman found dead on
the beach, had very probably succumbed to the same or a
similar type of poison, there was a good chance that this old
case would now have to be reopened. It was an uncommon
cause of death, and this more or less ruled out the possibility
of a coincidence. The question of how the two deaths were
related was a job for the police, however. It wasn't immediately obvious. The bodies had been found practically side by
side and the two women had almost certainly died the same
way. Nothing unusual about that – until you took into account
that they'd died seven years apart.

The vicar came over, his face sombre. 'This is a bad business. I've never heard of anything like it – disturbing the peace
of the grave like this. I don't know what to think.'

'I couldn't agree more.' Ína gave him a subdued smile. 'Did
you officiate at the woman's funeral?'

The vicar nodded. 'Yes.'

'Was it a private affair?'

'No, not at all. It was well attended. She had a good reputation in the town. Used to sing in the church choir. The place wasn't completely packed but there was a good turnout.'

'Did you notice anything out of the ordinary? Such as the coffin being suspiciously light?'

'Well, obviously I wasn't one of the pallbearers myself, so I wouldn't know about that. But I can't remember anything odd or suspicious. It all went as smoothly as you'd expect with a standard funeral.'

Idunn interrupted at this point. 'What about the viewing of the body? Did it take place in the church.'

'Yes, it did. On the morning of the funeral. But the body wasn't stolen then.' The vicar added: 'I've spoken to the funeral director. He remembers it and says he closed the coffin himself after the viewing and that there was no question of it being empty. He said it was completely impossible that the body could have disappeared while the coffin was in his care.'

'There aren't many other possibilities.' Ína smiled at the vicar again. 'After the viewing, I take it the coffin remained in the church?'

'It didn't happen on our premises,' the vicar said quickly. 'I simply can't see how it could have. Coffins aren't left lying around unattended in the church. There's always someone coming or going, preparing the funeral. If the coffin does turn out to be empty, all I can think is that someone must have dug it up and removed the body. I just can't picture it, though. The cemetery is in a very conspicuous position in the town.'

Ína frowned. 'The widower owned a digger. Didn't he run a small business hiring out his services?'

The vicar smiled. 'Yes, but he could never have driven his digger into the cemetery without being noticed. Not even in the middle of the night. Trust me. He worked for us, clearing snow, but he charged for each job separately. And there was no snow on the ground when his wife was buried, so his digger wouldn't have been in the cemetery or in the car park by the church. Besides, he wasn't at work because he was burying his wife. Gaui has been digging the graves for us for more than twenty years.' He indicated the digger operator who was now busy clearing the last of the earth from the coffin by hand. 'He dug the hole and filled it in again once the coffin was in the grave and everyone had gone home.'

Gaui looked up on hearing his name. He opened his mouth as if to say something, then went back to his work.

They lapsed into silence and watched as Gaui and his companion cast the loose soil up onto the sides of the hole. Not long afterwards, he climbed out and came over to them to report that the coffin lid was now accessible. They approached the hole and surveyed the results of the men's labours. 'What now?' Gaui asked Inspector Ína, who was in charge of the operation.

'Can the upper half of the lid be opened? If the woman's in there, there's no need to lift the entire coffin out.'

'Yes,' Gaui said. 'We've dug deep enough for you to be able to get at the screws.' He glanced at his co-worker. 'But for God's sake give him a chance to get out first.'

It wasn't as if Idunn was about to jump into the hole then and there, still in her coat, and undo the screws to throw open the lid. She waved to the CSI team, who came over and started setting up screens around the grave to make sure that no unauthorised personnel would get an eyeful of the contents of the coffin. Hopefully there would be no contents for them to see. If Idunn was right, there would be no corpse in there.

While the CSI team were positioning the screens, she dressed in protective overalls and gloves, and donned a plastic visor. Before lowering herself into the hole, she thought it right to warn Ína: 'If the coffin isn't empty, it won't be a pretty sight.' Once down there, she set to work loosening the screws, hampered by the visor that kept misting up. When she was done, she glanced up at her audience. 'Right, no reason to hang about.' She gripped the edge of the lid and had to work it back and forth for a minute or two before she eventually succeeded in prising it off.

No sooner had she done so than she heard Ína's blurted: 'Fuck!' Her ears caught the word before her brain even had a chance to register what her eyes were telling her.

In the coffin was the body of a woman. The improbably well-preserved hair had to be a wig, and between the withered lips there was a glimpse of false teeth. The rest was as you'd expect: the corpse resembled nothing so much as a leather-bound skeleton. Idunn's theory had been wrong.

'You said this wouldn't happen.' Whether deliberately or not, Ína had apparently forgotten or misinterpreted Idunn's earlier caution.

Idunn didn't answer. She was staring at the body, trying to get her bearings. Then she noticed something strange, especially given that the coffin had been open for the viewing. It appeared that the woman's shirt or dress had been placed on top of her body, whereas you'd expect her to be wearing it. Idunn reached out and tried to peel the rotten fabric away from the flesh. This proved tricky, but she was able to pull enough away from the skin to see that she had been right: the body underneath was naked. Then she noticed something else that filled her with relief. Twisting round to look up at Ína again, she said: 'This isn't Marta Bjarnhédinsdóttir. This is a completely different woman.'

*

The few souls who had lingered to watch the activity in the cemetery were eventually rewarded for their patience. The lid was closed, the screens taken down, and the digger recommenced its work until it was possible to hoist the coffin out of the grave. After which, it was transferred to the hospital mortuary. The curiosity of the passers-by was easy to understand, as coffins were generally conveyed to the cemetery, not away from it. Idunn had no need to turn her head to satisfy herself that the spectators were now trooping into the cemetery to see from the headstone who it was that had been exhumed. In their place, she would have done exactly the same.

The small hospital mortuary where bodies were processed had probably never been busier than over the last few days. The fridge was becoming quite full by the time the latest cadaver had been placed inside. It was now resting in the company of the two young people from the group of friends – Leifur and Ragnhildur – but the ninety-five-year-old woman had been removed. The average age of the bodies in there had probably never been lower.

The hospital's super new X-ray machine had come in very handy for determining the identity of the body in the coffin. It didn't take long as Idunn's suspicion had proved correct. With the assistance of the Identification Commission, she had been able to access the medical records of Gudrún, the girl who had gone missing from her university residence seven years earlier. Although there wasn't much information to go on, there were a few details that could be used for comparison. Gudrún had had her appendix removed as a child and had broken her collarbone in her teens. Idunn's preliminary examination of the body had revealed a scar from the operation, and X-rays from the new machine showed a healed fracture in exactly the right place on her collarbone. Idunn had also spotted an indecipherable tattoo on one ankle and Gudrún's father had confirmed to a representative of the Identification Commission that his daughter had had a little penguin tattoo there. Armed with this information, Idunn had been able to trace the outlines of a bird on the badly decomposed flesh. A DNA test would be necessary to provide the final incontrovertible proof, but in the meantime they must surely have enough to go on to demonstrate that Idunn was right. Anything else was unthinkable.

It was hard to imagine the distress Gudrún's family must be going through. Were they relieved to finally know her fate or desolate that they could no longer cling to the tenuous hope that she might still turn up alive? Personally, Idunn thought she would always prefer certainty to uncertainty. But it was one thing to talk about it, another to experience it. She had never had anything like this happen to her and never would. Children were out of the picture in her case and, perhaps even more sadly, so was love. She would always be alone. Suddenly she realised that her desire to get home to the solitude of her flat wasn't as strong as it had been over the last few days. She reminded herself that there was no point being melodramatic about her situation. She wasn't pitiable in the great scheme of things.

The man she spoke to from the Identification Commission turned out to have talked to Gudrún's father over the phone. Apparently, her mother had died five years ago. He said the father hadn't believed him at first, but once he'd been convinced that this wasn't some kind of horrible hoax, he hadn't been able to stop talking about how terrible it was that his wife had died without knowing what had happened to Gudrún. He had broken down and wept over the phone, in between offering to send Gudrún's brother to identify the body. The representative from the Identification Commission had eventually managed to get through to him that this wouldn't be necessary or desirable. If it was Gudrún, it would be better for all concerned to remember her as she had been when she was alive.

'What do you want to do with the coffin?' Ína nodded at the large casket that was propped against the wall in the examination room.

'Send it to Reykjavík. With the bodies.' Idunn finished washing her hands. 'If things carry on at this rate we'll need to hire a cargo plane to convey them all back.'

There was a light knock on the door, then a hospital employee poked his head through the crack: 'There's a man out front asking to see you.'

'Who is it?' Ína obviously had no intention of letting just any Tom, Dick or Harry walk in. And no wonder, since although the coffin was closed, there was a lingering smell in here that might be too much for the uninitiated.

'Gaui. He said you'd asked him to come and have a word.'

'Tell him to wait for us in the corridor.' Ína watched while Idunn collected up her instruments. 'Right, let's hear what he has to say.'

Once the coffin had been brought to the hospital and could be examined under proper lighting, Idunn had noticed a detail she had missed while bending over it down in the grave with her visor misted up. The varnished surface was scratched around the screws, not only around those fastening the upper lid that she had loosened, but also those securing the lower lid, which she hadn't touched. She observed moreover that the crosses customarily placed over the heads of the screws were missing. It was possible that the damage had been incurred during the exhumation, but it was more likely that the person responsible for swapping the bodies had inflicted it when opening the coffin after the undertaker had closed it. It went without saying that the person would have been in a hurry.

The grave digger was sitting in a chair, turning his knitted hat over and over in his hands. One of his knees was jigging up and down. When they appeared, he immediately sprang to his feet. 'I didn't touch the body.'

'You?' Ína folded her arms across her chest. 'You're not under suspicion. Why would you think that?' She explained why she had summoned him. Strangely enough, he didn't seem any the less agitated on learning that she was only interested in knowing whether he or his assistant could have scratched the coffin around the screws in the process of digging it out.

'I need to tell you something that might be important. I hope not – but it might be. I don't want to be suspected of tampering with the coffin.' When Idunn and Ína showed no signs of interrupting, Gaui went on: 'I was a friend of Geir – Marta's husband.'

'OK,' Ína prompted. 'And?'

'He . . . er . . . he . . . When Marta died, he asked if I'd do him a favour. He asked if he could fill in her grave himself. Stand in for me. It was his way of saying a last goodbye to her. I agreed. He knew how to operate the digger and it didn't occur to me for a minute that he might have anything else in mind. I found it strange, of course, but there are so many things we don't understand, especially when it comes to grief. Geir was in such a state after losing her. He never got over her death and just became more and more unstable. Like, towards the end, he became totally obsessed about whether his wife's brother had sold the family farm. I'd never heard him mention any wish to visit it before, let alone inherit the place. He just became really, really odd.'

Idunn couldn't care less about old farms or any other strange behaviour the man had exhibited in the years following his wife's death. All she was interested in was the burial itself. 'Did you watch him do it? Fill in the grave, I mean?'

'No. He wanted to be alone. To be left in peace. So I took myself off home.'

Idunn and Ína exchanged glances. Witnesses would hardly be needed now. It was Geir, husband of Marta, father to Gugga, who had swapped the bodies in the coffin after it had been lowered into the grave but before the grave had been filled in. But the million-dollar question was: how had he come to be in possession of Gudrún's body? Assuming she had been dead when he encountered her . . .

Chapter 29

Day 4 – Sunday, 26 January

Trausti had woken up feeling miraculously restored. If the phone had kept up its ringing while he was asleep, he had remained oblivious to it. He had gone straight to bed after the grave-digging fiasco instead of staying up drinking with his friends. It would have done his head in if he'd had to listen to any more of their crap: their suggestions had become more and more outlandish and impractical with every mouthful of booze. But there was no denying that he was curious to know what new plan they had hatched, if only because he wanted to know how unworkable it was. He couldn't wait to break it to them that he was having nothing to do with it. He'd had the whole situation up to here. He was heading back to Reykjavík, then catching that flight to America, even if it meant making his own way to the harbour on foot and swimming to the mainland.

Downstairs the place was a tip, littered with empty bottles and dirty glasses, some still half full. Two of the dining chairs were lying on their backs as though they'd taken an active part in the revelry and got so pissed that they'd fallen arse over tit. The others had obviously been hungry because there were all kinds of leftovers spread out on the table: doughnuts with bites taken out of them or the icing licked off, and a tray of posh French cheeses – presumably provided by Sigga or Ari

– that had melted after sitting there too long at room temperature. Which must account for the unpleasant smell. They were almost untouched, whereas Leifur's crisps and cheap dips seemed to have been hoovered up, judging by the empty packaging in the middle of the table, surrounded by crumbs.

There was absolute silence. Apart from the quiet gurgling of the coffee machine he had just switched on, there wasn't a sound. No snores, no movement. The peace would probably last through to the afternoon, since the state of the place suggested they'd been up half the night. That was fine; Trausti wasn't in the mood for company. As soon as the coffee had dripped through the filter, he filled a mug and carried it outside onto the lower deck and sat down. He hoped the fresh, crisp air would clear his head and that he could distract himself with the spectacular view, but it was no good. All he could think about was whether his friends had thrown the body over the cliff during the night. Getting to his feet, he walked round the back of the house and saw that they hadn't. The crate was still there. His relief was mingled with disappointment. If they'd done it, the matter would be out of his hands. He would be able to stop obsessing about it and focus on his own plans instead.

On his way back up to the deck he scanned the snow for any more mysterious footprints but the wind, which had picked up in the early hours, had obliterated all trace of human presence. Even the tracks they'd made yesterday when carting the body back and forth had vanished. Theoretically, then, someone could have done a circuit of the house in the night, peering in all the windows, and nobody would be able to tell. The thought left him strangely unmoved. It was a matter of indifference to him now whether the person responsible for yesterday's footprints was the same as the nuisance caller.

Last night he had felt so panicky over their presence that he'd thought at one point he was going to have a heart attack. But it seemed the latest shock had pushed him through some kind of barrier to where nothing mattered any more. He'd achieved a Zen state that nothing could disturb, but in spite of this he nearly jumped out of his skin when he rounded the corner of the house. He'd been expecting to see a row of empty seats on the deck but Ragga was now sitting there.

'I didn't mean to startle you.' She was looking astonishingly perky, considering the evidence he'd seen in the house of last night's piss-up. She'd pulled a coat on over pyjama trousers and T-shirt, but had no socks on her trainer-clad feet. With her ruffled hair and make-up-free face, she resembled a younger version of herself. In her hand was a steaming mug of coffee.

'I wasn't expecting anyone else to be up this early – not after seeing the state of the dining room.' Trausti vacillated between taking a seat beside her and going back up to his room.

'I gave up and went to bed. Not that long after you.' She smiled at him and patted the seat beside her. 'I need to talk to you. I should have done it earlier but that can't be helped now.'

Trausti's curiosity was piqued and he sat down. 'So you've no idea what brilliant plans they came up with for dealing with the body?'

'Nope. Not a clue. I need to talk to you about something different – though it's related to all this.' She paused and took a sip of coffee, gazing at the islands rising out of the sea on the horizon. 'It was me who steered the planchette on the Ouija board. And it was me who went to see Gugga in hospital.'

Trausti seemed unable to feel surprise at this news. It was as if he'd lost the capacity to be shocked after everything that had happened. Right now, he felt he wouldn't be surprised if a sheep wandered over and started contributing intelligent remarks to the conversation. 'And?' he said flatly.

'I should have confided in you but I didn't know if I could trust you. You see, Gugga told me something about the evening of the party and I needed to think about it. I didn't know what to do, and believe it or not, I was trying to protect you.' Ragga warmed her hands on her mug. 'I don't know where to begin. The whole thing has gone so disastrously wrong.'

Trausti wanted to fast-forward to the point where she told him how she meant to mix him up in all this. He could see now that in all these desperate twists and turns, each of them was out to save their own skin. None of them had been motivated by a desire to protect any of the others; all they cared about was themselves. 'Start at the beginning,' he said. 'That's the best place. Isn't it obvious?'

And so he learnt that, according to what Gugga had confided in Ragga, the surreal party at the student residence and the bizarre state they had all been in that night were easily explained. Gugga had been so keen that the party should go with a bang that she had put a microdot of LSD in the cupcakes she'd provided and insisted that everyone ate. *One per person. And no giving yours away.*

Trausti had been wrong. He hadn't entirely lost his capacity to be surprised. Even flabbergasted. 'What's a microdot?'

'Do you remember the little red stars on top of each cake?'

He wasn't particularly interested in cakes, let alone in how they were decorated, but he did recall the small red star that had topped the white icing on the cupcakes; perhaps because the decoration had been so minimalist. 'Wasn't it made of fondant? Just an innocent cake decoration?'

'It was acid. LSD. Maybe mixed with sugar, I don't know. I doubt Gugga knew herself. She'd spotted them for sale on a dealer's Facebook page while she was searching for cannabis. Anyway, she bought some for later use and spiked us with the bloody stuff. That's why our memories of the evening are so confused. It was chaos. Not fun-chaos like Gugga had planned but deadly chaos.'

Trausti's jaw dropped. At the time it had crossed his mind to wonder if there could have been something in the punch, but he had never dreamt that it was LSD, let alone that the cupcakes were the culprits. There was no point asking if Gugga had been out of her mind: the answer was obviously yes. 'Did Gudrún die from taking acid, then?' He couldn't remember ever reading that LSD could be life-threatening, only that it increased people's tolerance of alcohol, which could put them at risk of alcohol poisoning. Then again, he had heard stories about hallucinations leading people to their deaths, for example by walking out into the traffic in the belief that they could stop cars with the power of their minds. 'Did she have a bad reaction to it or did she injure herself while she was off her head?'

'Neither. That wasn't what killed her.' Ragga drew her feet up underneath her on the chair. 'Not according to Gugga, anyway. But she lied. To me. To all of you. So who knows?'

'What did she believe had happened?'

Ragga leant her head back and closed her eyes briefly before resuming the tale: 'I don't quite know how to tell you. It's so fucked up. Were you aware that Gugga was trying to get hold of poison for her mother? Proper poison. Not just drugs.'

Trausti nodded. 'Yes. I couldn't avoid knowing; she kept pestering me about it. Ari too. But we refused to listen. At least, I did. And I'm sure Gudrún refused.'

Ragga met his eye. 'Actually, Gudrún gave in.'

A few snowflakes began floating idly to earth. Trausti tried to follow one of them with his eyes but soon lost sight of it.

'Gugga must have been lying to you. Gudrún was even less likely than me to get mixed up in something like that.'

'I'm only telling you what Gugga told me. I don't know what's true and what's a lie. According to her, Gudrún got access to some poison in the university lab and stole a little for her. I think she said it was cyanide. The stuff the Nazis used to kill themselves with when they were caught.'

When Trausti didn't respond, Ragga kept talking: 'Gugga claimed Gudrún still had the poison the night we held the party. She hadn't handed it over yet. All Gugga could think was that Gudrún must have been so out of it on acid that she mistook the powder for cocaine and snorted a line to perk herself up. And dropped dead as a result.'

Trausti tried to get his head around this. He couldn't possibly buy the story: there were too many details that wouldn't stand up to a moment's scrutiny. 'That's complete bullshit. Gudrún wasn't into drugs. No way would she have snorted the cyanide she herself had stolen, let alone because she'd experienced a sudden craving – for the first time in her life – for cocaine. It just doesn't stand up. Gudrún wasn't the type to steal chemicals from the lab to please Gugga either. Or to stop her nagging. I just don't believe it.' Then he added: 'Besides, how could Gugga have known what Gudrún got up to in private? Are you telling me she found her lying face down on her desk with a half-finished line of powder and a rolled-up banknote in front of her? Then – what – did she move her to the bed? We all agree that we saw Gudrún in bed, remember?'

Ragga looked hurt, as if she'd assumed he would swallow the story whole. 'I'm no fool, Trausti. I asked her about that. It turns out Gudrún had money troubles. She stole the cyanide in return for payment. She owed her brother and he needed the cash urgently. He was planning to take time off in the spring to prepare for his entrance exams for a dentistry degree or something. Apparently Gugga's father was prepared to pay generously. Gugga claimed she was acting on his behalf.'

Ragga paused for breath, before continuing: 'If that's true, it must have been because he was desperate to fulfil his wife's last wish and, at the same time, to make sure the poison couldn't be traced back to him or Gugga. That's why the stuff was still in Gudrún's room: she was supposed to be paid in cash and Gugga's father wanted to withdraw the money in several batches to avoid arousing suspicion. The full amount was meant to be ready the following day.'

Two gulls now appeared, soaring up into the air in search of food, then swooping down in the direction of the sea and vanishing from sight. A simple life with no complications, Trausti thought. Short – but straightforward. Hatch. Eat, sleep, procreate. Die. 'What was that bullshit about cocaine, then?' he asked. 'How could Gugga justify believing anything so far-fetched?'

'She claimed she'd gone into Gudrún's room to see the cyanide. Maybe she was planning to steal it. Who knows? Gudrún was lying there, dead, with foam at the corners of her mouth. The powder had been poured into a little heap on the bedside table. Gugga swept it up, put it back in the bag and shoved it in her pocket. Then, later that night, she dragged us into Gudrún's room, telling us that Gudrún was being *a bit strange*. That's why we all piled in there.' Ragga paused and met his eye. 'What else was she supposed to think in the circumstances? That Gudrún had decided to kill herself? Because she was in debt?'

Trausti still wasn't buying it. 'No one's going to get me to believe that Gudrún decided to snort some cocaine to perk herself up. She just wasn't the type.' He didn't comment on the suicide theory as he wasn't in a position to judge. 'Anyway, go on. What happened next?'

Ragga related how Gugga had woken early next morning, and, sober now, had gone to check up on Gudrún and realised that she really was dead. She'd rung her father in hysterics and explained what had happened. At the time, he had been in Reykjavík, visiting her mother at the University Hospital, so he'd jumped in the car and raced over to the student residence. After taking a look at Gudrún, he had gone to Gugga's flat where he had sat and stared at the wall for what felt like ages, then buried his head in his hands. According to Gugga, he had been working out what it meant and racking his brains for any way to prevent him and his daughter going to prison for their part in the girl's death. If they hadn't offered to pay for the poison, Gudrún would never have had it in her possession, regardless of how she had ended up taking it. And since Gugga had tried to rope some of her other friends into their plans, they were bound to report the fact when the police started investigating.

Gugga's father had two choices, both bad. One was to ring the police and go to prison, along with his daughter. That would leave his wife alone to cope with her illness, which would make her sufferings even worse – if that was possible. The poison would be confiscated and she would be denied the long-desired release. The alternative was to cover up the death and make sure no one ever found out.

It seemed Trausti and his friends weren't the only ones who had made bad decisions – over and over again. Gugga's father had opted for a cover-up and taken matters into his own hands. Wrapping Gudrún in her duvet and sheet, he had carried her out to his car and hidden her in the boot. Then he had driven straight to the harbour at Landeyjahöfn on the south coast, caught the ferry to the Westman Islands and taken the body down to his cellar, where he had built a crate for it and filled it with gritting salt, which he had in large quantities thanks to his snow-clearing business. This done, he had hurried back Reykjavík. Shortly afterwards, Gugga's mother had died as a result of taking the cyanide. Voluntarily, unlike Gudrún.

If Gugga was to be believed, she hadn't asked her father what he had done with Gudrún's body until years later, when he was lying on his deathbed. There was a tacit agreement between them never to mention it. According to Gugga, he'd suffered a complete breakdown after her mother's death and she hadn't wanted to bring up any difficult subjects for fear he would lose it completely. So it wasn't until then that she'd learnt about the crate in the cellar; the crate that would make it impossible for her to move when she inherited the house. She had been frantic at the news, unable to deal with it alone. The crate was the reason why she had tried to persuade her friends to visit her in the islands after her father died, in the hope that they would help her dispose of both crate and body. When they didn't respond, she had pretended to have cancer. At the time, she had been at the University Hospital in Reykjavík and hoped that if she told them it was urgent, they might be more willing to visit her there than they had been to trek all the way over to the Westman Islands.

This made-up sob story had worked on Ragga, who had duly gone to see her.

Ragga paused for breath. 'But she was lying. The body wasn't Gudrún's. So perhaps none of what she told me was true. Perhaps she just wanted to drag us into some other crime involving a body. For all I know, Gudrún may have gone for a swim while off her head on acid, drowned and been washed out to sea.'

'Why the fuck didn't you tell me this?' Trausti didn't have the energy to judge the plausibility of Gugga's story. They would almost certainly never discover the truth now. As far as he was concerned, it would join the other questions to which he had no answers: *where was Madeleine McCann? Was there life on other planets? What happened to Malaysia Airlines flight 370?* There were any number of unsolved mysteries in the world and he could live with the fact. 'If I'd known all this, I might have acted more sensibly. We all might.'

He was staring at Ragga with a mixture of incredulity and contempt. She blushed and dropped her gaze. 'But according to Gugga, that wasn't all she had seen,' Ragga added after a little pause. 'She claimed Gudrún was naked from the waist down and her legs were splayed apart. It was obvious she'd been raped, but Gugga didn't know who had done it.'

Trausti's blood ran cold. Leifur's dream had been rooted in reality after all. Desperately, he retorted: 'And you thought it might have been me? You're not serious?' He couldn't hide his shock and indignation. 'You know me. Is there anything in my character that screams *rapist*? Christ, Ragga.'

'Don't forget about the LSD. For all I knew, it might have driven you crazy. I realise now that Gugga was probably making it up, but I couldn't know that at the time. You slipped away from the party at one point and mentioned that you'd checked on Gudrún. I was afraid there would be evidence on the body that wouldn't only result in a conviction for rape but for murder too. Whoever raped her would be blamed for her death, that's for sure.'

The recollection of his visit to Gudrún's room was as unbearable as ever. Trausti shrank away from thinking about it and also about the implications of having been off his head on acid. Would he be able to use diminished responsibility as a defence? Could a drug like LSD bring out characteristics that someone had never possessed before? Or did it merely unleash traits that a person normally kept under control when sober? What did that say about him? He cleared his throat. 'Everyone left the party at some point,' he said desperately. 'It wasn't just me. Ari and Leifur did too.'

'I don't give a shit about Ari and Leifur – but I do about you. I realise now that of course you didn't rape her. After all, you're the one who wanted to call the police. To do the right thing. But I couldn't have known that before we got here. That's why I fiddled with the Ouija board – to see your reactions. Specifically, yours, Leifur's and Ari's. But now I suspect Gugga lied about the rape, just like she did about the rest.'

Trausti took a deep breath while he tried to get his head around the fact that it had been Ragga who had started the ball from hell rolling. 'Did you tell Leifur and Ari to go down to the cellar when they were looking for something to remind them of Gugga? Was that planned too?'

Ragga shook her head, her eyes still downcast. 'No, I didn't. The visit to the house was as much of a surprise to me as it was to the rest of you. It just happened. I should have told you, all of you. I was going to. You have to believe me. But then there was one fuck-up after another and I . . . just went along with it. It became harder and harder to admit what I knew.'

Trausti couldn't sit still any longer. He sprang to his feet in his agitation and chucked his coffee away, marring the white surface of the snow. It had gone cold and tasted bitter – like this trip. 'What on earth did you tell Gugga? That you'd dispose of the body for her? Throw it off the cliff, as you and Ari were planning?'

'No. I said I needed to think about it. But before I could make up my mind, I heard that Gugga had been transferred to the hospital here on Heimaey. Then suddenly it was Christmas and I wanted to forget about it. I kept delaying, wondering if I should tell the rest of you, or just Sigga, or none of you.' Ragga sought out his gaze. 'Next thing I knew, Gugga was dead.'

The gulls reappeared, one carrying something in its beak, the other giving chase. They fought an aerial battle over the titbit until the successful fisher dropped it and it fell back into the sea with both birds in hot pursuit. Even a simple life had its complications.

Yet again, Trausti found himself at a loss. Eventually, rousing himself, he said: 'I'm going to wake the others and tell them to get on with the clean-up. They can have a rest later if they like, but we need to get the house in order and decide what to do about the body. This madness has to stop.'

Leifur had disappeared. His car was gone but his phone was lying under the dining table. Sigga said she'd seen him at around 4 a.m. when she went to bed, and Ari said he'd followed her example shortly afterwards. Leifur had been the only one still up; he'd insisted on finishing his beer. Sigga and Ari were so hungover they could barely respond to the simplest of questions. Clearly, this wasn't a good moment to share Ragga's revelation with them. They wouldn't be capable of taking it in. Ragga seemed to agree because she didn't raise the subject.

Ari was unshaven and red eyed, his short hair sticking up in the air. He had dragged on his trousers and a bathrobe, and had a towel wrapped around his neck as if to keep warm. But in spite of this he was shaking, either from a chill or from being extremely hungover. Sigga was no better, her mascara smudged and her hair a tangled mess. Her shirt was hanging out of her trousers and she kept complaining that she couldn't find her belt. She had eaten so many snacks yesterday evening that she'd had to take it off. It must be downstairs somewhere. Judging by the state she was in, her missing belt was the least of her problems.

Trausti bit back the urge to scream at them to take a cold shower, then bloody well get their arses moving. What was wrong with them? Their friend Leifur was missing. They should be worried about his well-being, or at least the possibility that he had gone rogue and decided to go to the police. But screaming wouldn't do any good. Plainly, they wouldn't be any use until they'd slept it off. Their relief was palpable when he suggested this, and they tottered back upstairs, each clutching a can of Coke from the fridge.

Trausti extracted Ari's car keys from his coat pocket. 'I'm going out to look for Leifur. Do you want to come along?'

Ragga nodded. Neither of them said much as they got in the car and set off. Trausti guessed she was thinking the same as him, wondering whether Leifur had been so drunk that he'd driven off the road, crashed his car and was now lying injured somewhere. Or whether he'd caught the first ferry back to the mainland. Or, worse, gone to the police and told them the whole sorry tale.

None of these conjectures turned out to be correct. After hunting high and low they finally spotted his car, parked behind a large industrial building on the outskirts of the town. The building had a relief sculpture of a bottle of malt soda on the front, and the roof had been designed to accommodate the neck of the bottle. Next to this was painted in big letters: *Karl Kristmannsson Agent and Wholesaler*. They couldn't begin to imagine what Leifur had wanted there – unless the giant bottle of malt had caught his eye and he had fallen asleep in the car after discovering that it was only a decoration.

But Leifur wasn't in the car. They explored the vicinity but couldn't see any sign of their friend. The building and car park were situated to the northwest of the airport, on the town side. In the end, they gave up their search of the area and did a circuit of the town, but drew a blank. Nothing. Leifur was nowhere to be seen. The fact that his car was parked near the airport made them think he must have caught a flight to Reykjavík, leaving behind his belongings, his phone and his car. Neither of them wanted to mention all the empty parking spaces in front of the terminal, which would have spared him the need to make a long detour on foot around the runway. Or to scuttle across it. It was preferable to imagine that he was so drunk he simply hadn't been thinking straight.

They drove back out to Stórhöfdi in perplexed, anxious silence, made some fresh coffee and took it outside again to drink on the deck. Trausti couldn't help feeling a bit like a passenger on the *Titanic* just before the ship had its brush with the iceberg. It seemed as if no matter what they did to try and salvage their situation, their destiny was already determined.

Ragga took a sip of her coffee. When she spoke, she didn't look Trausti in the eye. 'Do you think Leifur could have raped Gudrún? That he ran away and left us in the lurch because of that?'

Trausti shook his head. 'No. I don't believe that. I think he simply snapped. Decided he had to get out of here or risk going crazy. Can't say I haven't felt the same. But who knows why he left? He was drunk, so I doubt it was a carefully considered decision.' He changed the subject. 'Did Gudrún's brother ever get the money?' He felt this was important: Gudrún had sacrificed her life for the cash, after all.

Ragga looked at him blankly. 'No. I very much doubt it. Gugga didn't mention it and it didn't occur to me to ask. Why? Do you know her brother? Is he a dentist?'

Trausti shook his head. 'I haven't a clue.' He just hoped the money had found its way to the brother. At least one of the people whose lives Gugga had destroyed deserved to get something good out of it. But instinct told him that it hadn't happened in this case.

Chapter 30
Day 9 – Friday, 31 January

Idunn closed the door stealthily behind her. She headed down the corridor, pulling her suitcase as quietly as she could, and held her breath when the lift dinged to announce its arrival. Nothing happened. The doors closed without Alexandra sticking in an arm to prevent them. As the lift descended, Idunn thanked her lucky stars that her escape had been successful and she was on her way home at last. Without once having crossed paths with her father. Oddly enough, this hurt a little. She was allowed to hate him but he had no right to return the sentiment. That wasn't how it was supposed to work.

The doors opened to reveal the reception area. It was deserted. Again, Idunn felt a wave of relief. She rang the bell to conjure up an employee, asked him to store her suitcase for her, then settled her bar tab and paid for Alexandra's room. When the receptionist enquired whether the young lady was still in her room, Idunn had to admit that she had no idea. This taken care of, she hurried outside to wait for her lift. Apparently, the search-and-rescue team had combed the island from end to end but no more bodies had been found. Divers had dragged the seabed off Stórhöfdi and Ræningjatangi but drawn a blank there too. As a result, there was no reason for Idunn to be kept kicking her heels in the Westman Islands a moment longer. A plane was being sent to pick her up along with the CSI team, Týr, Karó and the three bodies. Just one more meeting – then she would be free.

While she was waiting for her lift, she sent her mother a message suggesting they go out to supper together the following evening. With any luck this would help appease her mother. Idunn was expecting to have to work all weekend, since in addition to the tasks relating to this investigation, she knew she had one autopsy for medical reasons awaiting her, and very probably a couple more in the pipeline, since the midday news had reported a fatal accident on Hellisheidi, in which two people had been killed. Still, even she had to eat like other people. The only difficulty would be finding a restaurant with a table secluded enough to spare the other diners from having to listen to her mother fast-forward through the million questions and accusations she had been bombarding Idunn with by text ever since she got here. Idunn was braced for it to be a tricky reunion.

A police car drew up outside the hotel with Karó behind the wheel.

'Any news?' Idunn asked.

'Yes, plenty.' Karó pulled away again. 'They're going to run through the latest developments at the meeting. But before that, Ína asked if you could accompany me and her to the hospital. She's going to interview Ásta and thinks you should be there in case you can pick up on something that doesn't fit the facts.'

Idunn thought it more likely that Ína wanted her along as an additional justification for having grounded her on the island. Still, she would soon be free to go home. The case was close to being solved, and had reached the stage where things started happening fast. So much new information had emerged at that morning's meeting that Idunn still hadn't digested it all.

Little of it would be of any practical use to her when she embarked on the post-mortems, but there were details here and there that should make her job easier. At least she hoped so. Most significant of these was the hypothesis about how Gudrún had come to die at the student residence seven years ago. It would be difficult to prove the cause of death so many years after the event, but at least Idunn now knew enough to search for traces of potassium cyanide in the body that had been exhumed. It was the same poison as had been responsible for bringing about Gugga's mother's death, according to the old post-mortem report. The two women had that in common – as well as having shared a grave, so to speak.

The information about Gudrún's death had finally been prised out of Ásta, who had been airlifted from Reykjavík yesterday evening and transferred to the hospital here on Heimaey. Inspector Ína hadn't wasted any time; she had been her first visitor in her new sickroom, with Karó tagging along. Under the vigilant eyes of a nurse, they had been allowed to conduct an informal interview. The one Idunn was headed to now was the formal follow-up, according to Karó. On the drive, Karó explained that although the police had failed to get anything out of Ásta while she was in Reykjavík following her car crash, now that she was back on her home turf, forced to look the local inspector in the eye, it would be hard for her to go on refusing to speak. It was inevitable that she would cross paths with the inspector regularly – in the bakery, at the supermarket, while walking her dog or travelling on the ferry. In a small town where it was next to impossible to avoid people, it was better to come clean, rip the plaster off in one go.

In a small town it was also easy to renew old acquaintances. Karó told Idunn how, according to Ásta, she and Gugga had been in the same class at school before Gugga left to attend sixth-form college on the mainland. They hadn't been particularly close friends but neither had they been enemies. When Gugga moved home to the islands, they had run into each other and picked up their old acquaintance. Apparently Ásta had pitied Gugga, who was socially isolated and battling various demons. She had started dropping by regularly to cheer Gugga up, with mixed results.

Karó parked the car behind the hospital and they met up with Ína at the staff entrance. Waiting with Ína was Már, the nurse who had assisted Idunn with the autopsy on Ragnhildur. He was here now to ensure the well-being of the patient in case Ína or Karó became too pushy when questioning her. They exchanged brief hellos, after which Idunn followed the trio through various white-painted corridors to Ásta's room. The woman's eyes widened when they walked in and Idunn read fear in her face – presumably the fear of a person with something to hide when approached by the authorities. It probably didn't help that she was lying in a bed with the three of them looming over her like inquisitors. Ásta seemed to find Már's presence comforting as her eyes kept shifting to his during the conversation. But then of course he was the only one with no agenda other than ensuring the patient's well-being.

Much of the interview was a recap of what Karó had already told Idunn during the drive there. But hearing Ásta's story first hand provided more detail and gave Idunn a chance to study the woman's demeanour while she was talking. For the most part, Ásta seemed to be telling the truth, and yet Idunn couldn't help feeling there was something missing from her narrative. But as she had nothing to go on apart from intuition, Idunn kept her mouth shut and let Ína and Karó do the questioning.

In a hoarse voice, Ásta continued: 'As I told you, I once went round for a visit and found Gugga in a real state, not just drunk but on some drug as well. I didn't ask her what she'd taken but it was obvious she was extremely high. She started rambling on about the night Gudrún vanished from the student residence.' Ásta stopped and took a deep, painful breath before continuing. 'Gugga kept blaming herself, saying it was her fault. Gudrún had died because she'd stolen some poison for Gugga's mother. But I didn't know what to believe because later Gugga backtracked and started playing down her responsibility. She claimed her friends had been involved too as they had all been taking LSD that evening, Gudrún included. She didn't explain in any detail, just said that one thing had led to another and for some unknown reason Gudrún had taken some of the poison and died. I thought Gugga must be hallucinating or making it all up and said so. But she insisted it was the truth and in the end she dragged me down to the cellar to prove it. She showed me a crate and said it contained the body of her mother, preserved in her father's road-gritting salt.'

Ásta seemed a little surprised that the three women listening to her didn't so much as raise an eyebrow at her story. But then she wasn't aware that the investigation had already uncovered the link between Marta's body and the case. The only person in the room who would be looking astonished by this story was presumably Már, but Idunn couldn't gauge his reaction as he was standing behind them. Then again, maybe he had seen and heard it all in his work as a nurse and had lost the capacity to be surprised by anything.

'Did Gugga open the crate?' Ína asked.

'No, I didn't see the contents, so I can't vouch for what Gugga said. She could have been talking rubbish.'

357

Karó jumped in at this point: 'Did you ask her how her mother ended up in the crate?'

'I did, in case Gugga's story was more than just a drug-fuelled delusion. But what she told me . . . it was so strange.'

'Go on,' Ína prompted.

Ásta closed her eyes as if to help her remember, then opened them before speaking. 'Gugga told me her father had removed Gudrún's body from the student residence because he was afraid of the devastating repercussions it would have for her, himself and his wife if it was found. But he had no idea how to get rid of it. She said all he could think of was to take it home to the islands and hide it temporarily in his cellar. He wanted to be able to concentrate all his attention on his wife now that she'd finally been given the chance to put an end to her suffering. Gugga also told me that a few days later, her mother went ahead and took the same poison that had killed Gudrún. Neither Gugga nor her dad ever told her about the terrible thing that had happened because of the way they'd got hold of the poison for her.'

Idunn knew that Gugga's mother's death had prompted an inquest, as she had been expected to live for several more years – if you could call that living. She'd had nothing to look forward to but more chemotherapy and more surgery, in which her mouth, cheeks and throat would be whittled away until there was almost nothing left, followed eventually by death. Her post-mortem had revealed that she'd been poisoned. Gugga and her father had been investigated by the police, but had got away with it. After all, it couldn't really be described as murder since it had been no secret that Marta had wanted to die. Since no evidence had been found to connect father and daughter to the poison, the investigation had been dropped.

When Ásta resumed, her voice was even hoarser than it had been when they'd entered the room and Idunn could only hope the nurse wouldn't intervene to stop the questioning just as things were getting interesting. 'Anyway, eventually Gugga's mother's body was released for transport to the islands for burial. By then, her father had realised that Heimaey was one of the worst places in the country to dispose of Gudrún's body. All he could think of was the lava field, but although he owned a digger and would be able to excavate a deep enough grave, the activity was bound to attract attention and he wouldn't be able to explain himself. The island was just too small for him to be able to operate anywhere without being seen. He ruled out the sea as well, since the odds were too great that the body would turn up again, either in a fishing net or washed up on the shore. He was at his wits' end – just days away from completely losing it, Gugga said.'

Idunn could well imagine that having a dead body in a crate in your cellar could do that to a man.

Ásta picked up the story again: 'But if Gugga was telling the truth, he had the idea of hiding Gudrún in his wife's coffin. Of switching the bodies. He couldn't face having Gudrún's body in the cellar a moment longer and was afraid he'd go mad, knowing it was there.' Ásta broke off to point to a glass of water on the nightstand that she couldn't reach herself. Már squeezed in to pick up the glass and help her take a sip.

'What was the plan for his wife's body?' Karó asked, as soon as Ásta had swallowed the water.

'Apparently, his original plan was to transport the body to the mainland and bury his wife in secret at the remote farm where she grew up. There was a small family graveyard there and at some point she had mentioned that it was where she wanted to be buried. The farm now belonged to his wife's brother, who only used it as a holiday house, so the plan wasn't all that bad. Until Gugga's father found out that the brother had sold it and it was now being rented out to tourists year round. So that plan went to shit. Her words, not mine.' A bout of coughing interrupted Ásta's account, but once it was over, she carried on. Her voice was even weaker now, though, and Idunn was sure their time would soon be up. 'After he heard this, her father became so depressed that he ended up in a state of total apathy, according to Gugga, and before he could tie up the loose ends, he died, leaving Gugga to clean up the mess.'

Ásta went on to describe another detail Gugga had shared. Apparently, her father had taken measures to ensure that if a decision was taken to exhume his wife at any point due to lingering suspicions about her cause of death, it would be hard to identify the body in the coffin. The inquest had made him nervous that the police might take this step, far-fetched as it seemed. That was why he had removed Gudrún's teeth, hair and clothes before swapping the bodies. He had stripped his wife's body too, intending to dress Gudrún in her clothes, but hadn't finished the job. He'd had to work fast, hampered by the lack of space down in the grave with the coffin, and in the end he'd made do with spreading his wife's funeral clothes over Gudrún's body, putting her wig on the girl's head and pushing her dentures into the girl's toothless mouth. This done, he had replaced the lid and buried the coffin, before taking his wife's body home, wrapped in a sheet. He had carried her down to the cellar, laid her in a homemade coffin together with Gudrún's belongings, packed her in with gritting salt, then closed the lid and never opened it again.

Idunn badly wanted to jump in at this point but stopped herself. Ásta wouldn't be able to answer anyway, but as a forensic pathologist Idunn knew that the missing teeth and hair wouldn't have fooled anyone conducting an examination of the body if it had been exhumed. It would have been clear immediately that the body in the coffin hadn't undergone a post-mortem and therefore couldn't belong to Gugga's mother. But then judging by the other details of Gugga's father's plan, the man had been no genius, or else he'd been in such a state that any semblance of reason or common sense had evaporated.

Ásta told them she'd found the story so grotesque that she had reeled out of the house after hearing it, unable to decide whether it was a drug-fuelled fantasy or the truth. She had avoided Gugga for the next few days, while trying to work out what to do. But before she could make up her mind, Gugga had come to grief on Heimaklettur, perhaps deliberately, perhaps not.

'Why didn't you come to us?' Ína asked sternly. 'Did it never even occur to you to notify the police?'

Ásta licked her cracked lips. 'I thought about it, but I hesitated because I didn't really believe the story could be true. Not only that but it would have ruined our friendship if you or someone from the police had gone round to her house after Gugga had trusted me with her secret. She was all alone in the world and I didn't want to take the risk of alienating her until I'd had a chance to think it through. For all I knew, the crate could have contained old Christmas decorations. I wanted to go to the police, believe me. I just needed to talk to her first and get the facts straight. I never got the chance, though. Even when Gugga was moved back to the hospital here, it was impossible to have a private conversation with her. Whenever I visited her, the nursing staff were constantly in and out of the room.'

Ína turned her head to Már. 'Is this true?'

Már shrugged: 'I wasn't here twenty-four seven, but it sounds likely. She was in a very bad state and needed a lot of attention.'

Ína turned her gaze back to Ásta: 'What about after she died? Notifying the police couldn't have jeopardised your friendship at that point, could it?'

'No. But I thought it best just to wait and see what happened. I thought the crate would have to be opened eventually. And I was afraid to go to the police in case you treated me as an accomplice for failing to report it immediately.'

Ásta went on to swear that she'd played no role in the deaths of the people on Stórhöfdi, nor had she had anything to do with lighting the bonfire with the body on it. She was adamant too that she hadn't gone anywhere near Ragnhildur's body on the beach and she couldn't explain the presence of the dog hairs. This raised doubts in Idunn's mind about the truth of the woman's account, though she kept these to herself. Ína and Karó seemed to accept Ásta's explanation of why she had been on her way to Stórhöfdi the night she crashed her car. When Gugga had told Ásta the story of the crate, she had also told her about the friends who had been with her the evening Gudrún had disappeared. She was so hurt by them not coming to her aid that she had lied to two of them that it was Gudrún's body in her cellar on the Westman Islands, in the hope that they would help her get rid of the crate. Then she would be able to sell the house and realise her dream of moving back to Reykjavík.

Ásta had been working in the shop on the ferry when the group of friends travelled out to the islands. One of the women had got into conversation with her, hoping for tips on beating seasickness, and had mentioned that they were on their way to a funeral and also that they were going to stay on Stórhöfdi. As soon as Ásta had heard how they knew Gugga, she'd realised who they were. Afraid they would be tempted to do something foolish about the crate in the cellar, she had tried to warn them off. She'd put a note under their windscreen wiper on the car deck. She knew which one it was because she'd seen the woman getting out of the car when they'd boarded. But it had been like water off a duck's back. She'd found the note lying on the deck after the car had driven away. Next, she had gone out to Stórhöfdi late on Saturday evening to push the same kind of note through their letterbox, but had been forced to retreat when she heard them talking behind the house. She'd been on her way there to make another attempt in the early hours of Monday morning. That's when she'd spotted the bonfire, pulled over and gone to see what was happening. All she could remember after that was running back to the car, and some vague memory of encountering a robot vacuum cleaner, which must have been a hallucination. She denied that she'd ever made calls to the landline of the house on Stórhöfdi or persuaded anyone else to do so.

At this point Már intervened to stop the interrogation. A good call, in Idunn's opinion as a medical professional, although she would have liked to see Ína press Ásta a bit harder in relation to various aspects of the story.

Once back in the car with Karó, Idunn asked: 'Did you believe Ásta's story?'

Karó shrugged while reversing out of the parking spot. 'Yes and no. Some parts but not others. On the whole, though, I found her very convincing. As soon as she's feeling better, she'll be interviewed again. A number of times, I expect. And if she's on the mend, there won't be a nurse present to make sure she's not distressed. That'll make it easier to follow up on any points that need more explaining.'

Karó parked outside the police station and they went inside for the meeting. Týr was already sitting at the table. He avoided Idunn's eye, perhaps still upset with her. There was little she could do to remedy the situation but that didn't stop her feeling wretched about it. She took a seat diagonally opposite him to avoid any awkwardness. Then reached over for a plastic cup and helped herself to coffee that turned out to be lukewarm.

Inspector Ína, who had pulled up at the same time as Karó and Idunn, appeared with a steaming mug of her own and got straight down to business: 'We believe we've made a considerable amount of progress in the investigation. Admittedly, it's still not clear who killed who among the group that attended the funeral, but with any luck that will be clarified to some extent by the post-mortems. And no doubt the evidence collected at the scene will shed further light on things once we've had the results back from analysis. For example, I've just learnt that fingerprints have been found on the belt in exactly the places where Leifur's killer would have held it while strangling him. Apparently it's a woman's belt and there are also any number of smaller prints that must have belonged to the owner. The suspicious prints are much larger, probably male.'

Idunn wondered if she should comment on the assertion that the post-mortems would help clarify matters. They would almost certainly determine the cause of death, but the circumstances surrounding the victims' demise were not to be found under their skin. However, she thought better of interrupting at this point and took a sip of the vile coffee, allowing Ína to continue. Over the years, her rule of never holding up a meeting unless it was absolutely necessary had saved her quite a few precious hours when you totted them up.

Regrettably, not everyone observed this golden rule. The young CSI Stefán coughed and asked: 'What about the people we're still looking for? Won't their statements be important too?' He smiled self-consciously. 'Assuming they're telling the truth, of course.'

Ína smiled grimly. 'That brings me to the big news.' It was easy to see from the faces around the table who was in the know and who wasn't. Some, like Idunn and Stefán, looked baffled, while others smiled rather smugly. Idunn understood why when Ína continued, and also why she herself had at last been given permission to go home. 'I got a phone call earlier informing me that the second car the group was using has been found. It had driven off the mountain road on Hellisheidi and rolled over. There were two passengers inside, a man and a woman. All the indications are that they were the missing members of the group, though we have yet to receive official confirmation.'

Stefán beamed but the smile was quickly wiped off his face when Ína glanced at him and added: 'They were both dead. It looks as if they ignored the signs warning that the road over the mountain was closed when they got back to the mainland last Monday. Which turned out to have been a foolish decision.'

Idunn blew out a breath. So much for that. There would be no witnesses now to explain what had happened, which meant the case would never be satisfactorily solved. The police could infer some of the details and come up with reasonable theories to explain how each of the victims had met their end, whether it had been murder, accident or suicide, and possibly also who had committed murder. But the conjectures would always be subject to doubt. No court would pass judgement in this case, except in the unlikely event that the car-crash woman, Ásta, was charged with perverting the course of justice.

Idunn locked gazes with Týr. Instead of looking away, he maintained eye contact and she thought that perhaps, like her, he was wondering whether the conclusion would be as erroneous as it had been in his mother's case. Would Idunn's successor as pathologist one day examine photos of her post-mortems and think: *Hang on a minute, how on earth could she have missed that?*

In front of the air terminal was a memorial to the 1986 Reagan–Gorbachev summit in Reykjavík. Idunn had forgotten it existed. There were two doves symbolising peace, commemorating the end of the Cold War. She couldn't remember if the summit had made much impression on her as she had been a small child at the time. Nor could she remember if she had ever known why the memorial had been erected here, in front of a tiny air terminal in a town that neither of the leaders had ever visited. She walked over to the artwork in the hope of finding an explanation but without success. In the end, she concluded that the artist, a local called Grímur Marinó Steindórsson, must simply have wanted to celebrate the peace agreement. But the ends of all wars had one thing in common: it was never long before hostilities broke out again somewhere in the world. Humans were impossible.

Could the same perhaps be said of her? Should she have replied to her father and offered him an olive branch? Made her peace with him and put an end to their own private cold war? She stared at the air terminal, feeling a stirring of the old resentment and anger. The building was a painful reminder of the way he had humiliated her when, as a kid, she had walked in there with her tail between her legs and no air ticket home. No, there was no chance of burying the hatchet in this case.

Idunn took a deep breath and reminded herself that she was going home. She would no longer have to be on edge, thinking about him all the time. Cheered by the prospect, she walked towards the entrance and, catching her reflection in the glass doors, smoothed down her coat and squared her shoulders before going inside. Her cheerful mood didn't last. The other members of the team seemed to have boarded already but there, a little way off, stood Alexandra with her luggage, beaming and waving at her.

'I'm ready. I hurried over to be sure I wouldn't miss you.'

Idunn had gone straight from the meeting to the hospital, accompanied by two members of the CSI team, where she had organised the transport of bodies and coffin to the airport, then watched as they were loaded onto the plane. After that she'd got a lift back to the hotel to fetch her case. When Idunn asked if her sister had left, to her relief the woman on reception had confirmed that she had. Idunn had assumed that Alexandra must have had a change of heart, made it up with her parents and gone home, thereby sparing Idunn the necessity of being mean to her. But of course she wasn't so lucky. 'You're not coming to Reykjavík with me,' she said firmly. 'I was hoping I wouldn't be forced to spell it out to you but there it is. You're not coming to live with me and that's final. Go home.'

Alexandra opened her mouth but seemed unable to find any words. Idunn thought she saw tears in her eyes, and she sighed under her breath. 'I mean it, Alexandra. Go on. Go home.' At that moment the phone rang in Idunn's coat pocket and she fished it out, glad to be interrupted in the middle of this awful conversation. She answered without checking the number, turning her back on Alexandra.

'Hello, Idunn. It's your dad here.' Now it was her turn to be lost for words. 'I know you're angry with me but I need to have a word with you about Alexandra.'

Idunn automatically glanced round and saw that her sister was tearfully gathering her bags together. She moved away so the girl wouldn't overhear. 'I've nothing to say to you. If you need to talk to her, I'm sure you've got her number.'

'She won't answer my calls. I wanted to ask you—'

Idunn cut him short. 'You don't get to ask any favours of me. But I want you to tell me something: why did you run away when I came to see you that time? When I still thought you cared about me?'

It was his turn to be silent. Idunn, determined not to let him off the hook, kept quiet too, long enough to compel him to speak: 'Something came up. Nothing you need know about. Except that I wouldn't have gone if it hadn't been serious.'

'A fishing crisis, was it? Or just some excuse you invented so you didn't have to take me in?' Idunn's anger was rising with every word. 'What was so urgent that you couldn't even come out and say hello? *Hi, Idunn, I've got to go. I'm sorry.*' Idunn was surprised by the emotion in her own voice. She'd believed she would be able to adopt an icy tone with him that could be interpreted as meaning: *I don't give a shit about you.* Instead, she sounded like a hurt child. The same hurt child who had been forced to crawl back to Reykjavík all those years ago.

'Let's have this conversation another time, Idunn. Not now. I rang to ask you not to take Alexandra with you. She belongs here. At home.'

'Don't worry, I don't want her with me.' Now Idunn sounded more the way she wanted to: cold and devoid of feeling.

Her father couldn't hide his relief. 'Thanks. Thank you. She's got some foolish dream about studying medicine. Like you. But as I'm sure you'd be the first to agree, her mother and I feel that the life you lead isn't exactly a desirable one.'

Idunn was brought up short. 'What do you mean?'

'Don't take offence. I'm hugely proud of you. But you must have to work round the clock. No husband. No kids. That's not the life I want for my daughter.' Apparently realising how crass this sounded, he corrected himself: 'My younger daughter.'

Idunn stared into the middle distance, not knowing whether to laugh or cry. Her father and his new wife were afraid that Alexandra would turn out like her. Her rage boiled over again but instead of biting her father's head off, she turned and looked round. Alexandra had left the building and Idunn was alone. Phone in hand, her father still on the line, she ran outside after the girl.

Idunn called, loud enough to be sure both her sister and her father could hear: 'Alexandra! Alexandra! Come back. I've changed my mind. You're welcome to live with me.'

Her sister looked round and seemed at first to think that Idunn was saying this to mock her. But when Idunn beckoned, her face split in a radiant smile and she started eagerly retracing her steps. Idunn put her phone back to her ear and said in an acid tone: 'Don't you dare ring me again.' Then she hung up, braced to experience a wave of regret at her rash decision. It didn't come.

Alexandra dropped her cases, flung herself at Idunn and hugged her stiff figure tightly. 'Thank you! Thank you! You won't regret it.' Then she released her and smiled. 'Wow! We're going to have a wild time. Wild!'

Idunn doubted that. But it would be all right. It would have to be all right.

They returned to the terminal and Idunn informed the staff that there would be an additional passenger on the flight. She wrote her sister's name on the form she was handed. After that, they went through the gate and out to the plane.

On the way up the steps, Alexandra prodded Idunn's shoulder. 'There's just one thing. I'm now 100 per cent sure there were five of them. Not four.'

Idunn shook her head. 'Four. There were four of them.'

'Nope. Five.'

'Four. And not another word about it.' Idunn wanted to savour the feeling of being on board the plane and on her way home at long last. She fastened her seatbelt, closed her eyes and gave a contented sigh. As the plane took off, she watched the scenic island until it vanished from view, probably for the last time. Or at least for a very long time.

Alexandra poked her shoulder again and Idunn looked round. 'Five,' the girl insisted. 'There were five of them.'

This didn't bode well for the flight. Or for their living together. Idunn reminded herself of her sister's words: it would be wild. Not that she had any faith in this prediction.

At least it would be something, though. Something other than the monotonous, lonely existence she had now put behind her.

Alexandra smiled at her. 'Seriously. There were five of them.'

Chapter 31
Day 5 – Sunday Night/Monday Morning – 26/27 January

After drinking coffee with Ragga on the deck, Trausti had got down to the cleaning, working on autopilot like the robot vacuum. He put on one dishwasher load after another, threw out the leftover food from the dining table, cleared away the glasses and plates and washed the bed-clothes Leifur had been using on the sofa. He also packed Leifur's bag and stowed it in his room where his own luggage stood ready.

Among the belongings Leifur had left behind was his phone, which had been lying under the dining table beside one of the chairs that had been knocked over. Images of Leifur standing outside the police station in Reykjavík, mustering up the courage to go in and tell all were driving Trausti crazy. He was sure that if he could reach Leifur, he would be able to talk his friend out of the idea. But the theme of this trip seemed to be that nothing was going to go their way. Another thought entered his mind: could the owner of the footprints or the caller have done something to Leifur? Was he still on the island, after all? But then he remembered Leifur's car and couldn't fit the detail of it being driven away into a scenario of that kind.

Trausti picked up the phone. He used it to look up the ferry website and tried to book a new ticket back to the mainland as theirs had expired. But it seemed he wasn't the only person who'd had this idea: there was a whole fishing conference on its way back to Landeyjahöfn and all the remaining crossings were booked up that Sunday. The same applied to the flights. He was stranded in the islands for another day. That was the point at which he had surrendered to fate. Like running water, he would choose the path of least resistance. In this case, that meant waiting and letting the others decide what to do, without interfering.

They had cobbled together a plan over a subdued supper. Ari and Sigga had still looked hungover when they'd emerged late in the afternoon, despite having had a chance to sleep it off. They'd both tried to act as if nothing was wrong but they weren't fooling him or Ragga. No one thanked him for cleaning up the place, or even mentioned it. Normally, he would have been hurt by this but now it was a matter of indifference. He was too numb to let it get to him. It didn't occur to him to clear the table after supper, though, any more than it did to the others. The dining table remained as they'd left it and the kitchen was a tip, although hours had now passed and night had fallen once more.

Once they'd decided what to do, Trausti had retired to bed. He wanted to be properly rested when the time came to put their plan – if you could call it a plan – into action. The other three had been entirely responsible for shaping it. He hadn't contributed at all, just listened in silence. After dismissing various other proposals, they had agreed in the end to burn the body together with the timber from the smashed-up crate, the books, the clothes and the hair. Trausti didn't remind them of the model ship he had come across in the utility room. It had been lying, half submerged, in the sink where either Leifur or Ari must have set it afloat the evening before while drunkenly messing about. The craftsmanship was too fine to be sacrificed to the fire, he thought. Which was stupid, considering that they were about to burn a human body. But he couldn't help how he felt.

They had concluded that the most suitable spot would be the beach on the eastern side of the neck of land that connected Stórhöfdi to the main island. There was the least risk that the glow of the fire would be spotted there as it was some distance from the nearest house or farm. They had even displayed a modicum of common sense by immediately ruling out the headland: the site of a lighthouse is, by its nature, visible for miles around. Trausti had also silently agreed with Ari that it was out of the question to take the body to Reykjavík with them and dispose of it there. Admittedly, Ari had only been concerned not to dirty his new car. No doubt he'd have thought differently if they could have used Leifur's, but Leifur had taken the keys with him when he flew back to the mainland – if that's where he'd gone.

Neither Trausti nor Ragga had said a word about the secret she had confided in him. He'd felt it wasn't his place: it was Ragga's story, therefore it was up to her who she chose to tell. When Trausti woke up from his nap, Sigga and Ari were still puzzling over how the body could have ended up in Gugga's cellar, so it was obvious that Ragga hadn't enlightened them while he was asleep. He didn't care if they never found out what had happened. What did bother him was the realisation that all three had started drinking again. The situation hadn't got out of hand yet, as they had only opened one bottle of white wine and a few beers. But peering through the green glass, he thought the bottle was empty.

'Want some?' Sigga had drawn her hair into a large bun and was wearing her polo-neck jumper and jeans, both bearing the logo of the same fashion house. She didn't seem to have found her belt yet, though, as she had to hitch up her jeans when she rose to fetch a glass and, presumably, another bottle.

'I'll pass.' Trausti was quite numb enough without making the effects worse with booze. 'Shouldn't we get on with it? The body will take time to burn, you know. Have you looked into ferry tickets?'

Ari drained the rest of his glass. 'Yup. I've booked us onto the ferry at half past nine in the morning. That should give us enough time. But, by all means, let's get on with it.' He stood up, revealing that he had dressed for the occasion, for once. Well, almost. A smart shirt collar was visible at the neck of his thick jumper. Usually, Ari was immaculately turned out, but now Trausti noticed that his collar was sticking up at a ridiculous angle, as if Ari had deliberately pulled it up to his ears. It made him look more like a bad Elvis impersonator than a banker. His formerly shiny banker's shoes had also taken a beating. They were now scuffed and dusty, mirroring their owner's decline.

Trausti suddenly sniffed the air. He was worldly wise enough to work out what had been going on. 'Were you smoking a joint?'

Sigga gave him a dopey smile. 'That was me. Don't worry. It was nothing.'

'Was that one of the joints you took from Gugga's jewellery box?'

Sigga nodded and Trausti shuddered at the memory. The powder in the bag could have been the remnants of the cyanide that had set the whole tragedy in motion. In as steady a voice as he could muster, he asked: 'Where's the other stuff? In the plastic bag?'

'The amphetamine or coke, you mean? I got rid of it. Ari threw a fit like Ragga when I brought it out.' Sigga's glazed eyes met his. 'I poured it down the sink. The bag's in the bin. Go and check, if you don't believe me.'

He didn't trust her, so he did just that. He knew that, although she was no addict, Sigga had a penchant for taking drugs when drinking. She had told him back at university that because it took so little booze to get her drunk, a tiny hit of coke or amphetamine helped clear her head. The small Ziploc bag, empty but for a faint film of dust clinging to the plastic, turned out to be in the bin, as she had said. Trausti felt a surge of relief. If Sigga had snorted that up her nose instead of pouring it away, she'd be dead by now – assuming it was the cyanide. At least that danger was past. But his hopes that the group would stay reasonably sober were dashed when Ari stuffed a half-empty brandy bottle in his coat pocket and Sigga did the same with Leifur's second bottle of Ópal schnapps. Trausti let this pass without comment, though. Each of them had to find their own way of getting through the night. In his case, it meant shutting down all his feelings.

Ari had to resign himself to getting his car dirty after all. Since there was no question of trying to carry the body and crate down the hill, they tipped back the seats in his car and crammed everything into the boot: crate, books, petrol can and lighter fluid. They shoved in the robot vacuum too, though it wasn't destined to go on the bonfire. Then they lowered the door of the boot, though it was impossible to close it completely. When Ari and Sigga got in the front, Ragga and Trausti volunteered to walk, as neither wanted to crouch in the back with the crate. Ari drove off, his erratic course suggesting he was much drunker than Trausti had realised; not fit to be behind the wheel. Given their luck so far, Trausti feared it was almost inevitable that Ari would veer off the road and plunge into the sea, but it was too late now to run after the car and stop it.

They spoke little as they trudged down the hill in the dark. When Trausti asked why Ragga hadn't let Ari and Sigga in on Gugga's secret, she just shrugged. Then, after a moment or two, she said it was because of Ari. She would tell Sigga one day when they were alone. But if Gugga was right that Gudrún had been raped, Ragga had no intention of discussing it with the suspected rapist. Besides, she couldn't take any more right now. Trausti could understand that.

In the event, Ari didn't drive off the road. He even managed to park successfully. They all helped to carry the body down to the shore. Once there, they took it in turns to smash the crate to pieces using rocks, as none of them had had the foresight to bring any tools. When it had been reduced to kindling, they built a pyre from the wood splinters and stuffed the books in among it. Then Ari and Trausti laid the naked body on top of the pile while Sigga fetched the clothes and carefully draped them over it. Seen from above, it would look as if it were fully dressed. After that, she brought over the bag of hair and emptied it over the lot, but a breath of wind whisked the locks away and scattered them over the beach.

It would have been impossible for them to collect up all the hair; it was too dark on the beach and the strands had dispersed over too wide an area. If the body burned up, leaving nothing but bones, they would be able to dispose of them in the sea and be fairly confident that they would sink. Nothing lasted forever in the ocean and in time all trace of the dead person would disappear for good. There was no need to worry about the ashes: people were always lighting fires on the country's beaches, and although it was against the law, in practice the police wouldn't bother investigating such a minor infringement.

Ari sprayed lighter fluid over the body, then turned to the others. He regarded them in silence. They all got the message: if they wanted to stop this, now was their chance. When no one spoke, he held out his hand. 'Has anyone got a light?'

Sigga fished a lighter out of her pocket with a glance at Trausti, remarking: 'If I hadn't smoked that joint, I wouldn't have a lighter on me. So stop looking so disapproving.'

He didn't reply. She was both right and wrong. Wrong that he was disapproving – he couldn't give a damn. But right that she'd saved them a trip back to the house to fetch a lighter. It simply hadn't occurred to any of them.

Ari held the lighter to the body and a river of flame ran flickering over the pyre. They all watched the fire as if hypnotised, each lost in their private thoughts. No one said: *What the fuck are we doing?* No one ran down the beach to fetch sea-water to put out the blaze. It wouldn't have worked: the body was a mass of flame now. But they would have to be ready to splash more petrol on the fire as soon as it began to die down. Since there was no need for them all to keep watch, they split up. Trausti and Ari undertook the task of going back to the house, loading the car and tidying up. That way they would be able to get out of there as soon as the fire had done its job and the bones were in the sea. No one wanted to linger a moment longer than necessary.

Ari was usually the last person to volunteer for housework but it seemed that even he thought it preferable to watching the flames consuming the corpse. Trausti tried to persuade his friend to let him drive up the slope, on the grounds that Ari wasn't in a fit state, but he wouldn't listen. Instead of standing there arguing, Trausti got in the passenger seat, trusting to fate again. It was only a short way. During the drive back up onto the headland, Ari proved more talkative than Ragga had been on the walk down. But his cheerfulness rang hollow. He seemed wired, in a state of wild elation. Trausti answered in monosyllables, unable to fake nonchalance. The car stank of lighter fluid from the empty containers lying on the floor by Trausti's feet, so he opened the window and stuck out his head. It was a relief to get out of the car and start work on the tidy-up, in spite of his resolve never to clear up after those slobs again.

Instead of helping, Ari thought only about his own stuff. He went up to his room and came back down with his suitcase which he dumped on the floor in the dining room. Then he fetched a vacuum cleaner. Manoeuvring the car closer to the front door, he began to hoover and clean the boot. Trausti, speechless at this behaviour, decided he was damned if he was going to lift a finger himself. They could just leave the house looking like a tip. The only bedding that had been washed, dried and folded was Leifur's. Still, that was Ari's problem. He would have to apologise for the mess to his colleague who had lent them the house. It would serve him right for being so selfish. But as Trausti seethed at his friend's behaviour, he was struck by a sudden thought that made him momentarily forget his anger: *why had Ari – of all people – apparently thrown a fit when Sigga brought out the little bag of what she had believed to be cocaine?* Ari used to dabble in various recreational drugs himself in the old days and didn't seem to have changed much, at least not when it came to booze. Trausti had seen him taking regular nips of brandy while he was cleaning his car, though he hadn't commented. He wasn't about to let

Ari drive back down the hill in that state, let alone all the way to the ferry, but that argument would have to wait.

Stealthily, Trausti opened Ari's suitcase. He rooted around inside until his suspicions were confirmed: there it was, Gugga's diary from the year Gudrún had gone missing. The spiral-bound notebook Trausti knew he'd seen, which should have been in the cardboard box. Opening it, he searched for entries relating to Gudrún's disappearance. There weren't many but there were enough to confirm what Gugga had told Ragga. And a little more besides. Gugga blamed herself for having disturbed her mother's final rest, for the fact she was stuck in a crate in the cellar of the family home instead of lying in the cemetery. Gugga expressed deep regret for all the mistakes she had made, but in such a self-pitying manner that it undermined the credibility of everything she had written. So the body now burning on the beach was Gugga's mother, not Gudrún. Gugga had deliberately lied to Ragga, since if she'd told the truth, her friends would never have agreed to help her. They'd had to be tricked into believing that the body was Gudrún's.

'Looking for something?' Ari was standing in the doorway, holding the vacuum cleaner, his face blank.

Trausti was so startled that he dropped the diary and it fell back into the open suitcase. His rage flared up again. 'Why didn't you say anything? And why did you take the diary?'

Ari put down the vacuum cleaner without taking his eyes off Trausti. His expression was hard to read. He was smiling but his eyes were hard. 'Oh, come on. I just wanted to know if she'd written anything about me. In case she'd misunderstood something she saw.'

'Do you mean in case she'd *misunderstood* the fact that Gudrún was raped?'

'Something like that.'

Trausti took in his old friend's ice-cold demeanour. 'How do you know what she saw?'

'I visited her. At the University Hospital. Twice, in fact. After she sent that message. I thought she was dying and might need to unburden her conscience. I wanted to persuade her not to go to the police – for all our sakes. The second time, I took her some CBD pills she'd asked me to buy for her on my first visit. I know, I should have told you. And we should have done what she asked, but . . .'

'So you raped Gudrún?' Trausti was amazed that he was able to get the words out of his mouth without screaming them so loudly that he'd wake up everyone on the island. He had never been a violent person but right now he longed to punch Ari's teeth out. He was outraged. After all his agonising over whether he could have done something to Gudrún himself, it turned out that it had been fucking Ari all along.

'Raped? No. Had sex with her? Yes. There's a difference.'

Trausti breathed hard through his nose. His indignation knew no bounds. 'You absolute cunt. You're not fooling either of us. She was totally out of it that night. Incapable of giving her consent. You can try and kid yourself that it was OK but, please, don't bullshit me.' Before Ari could protest, Trausti asked about something he suspected, though he hoped to God it wasn't true: 'Did you give her that powder? From the bag? Were you trying to bring her round? I'm guessing it's more fun to have sex with someone who's actually conscious.' The whole thing was clear now. Gudrún wasn't into drugs and, even if she had been, she would never have deliberately taken a substance that she knew to be a deadly poison. Ari had to have been responsible.

'Don't talk shit. I gave her some of the stuff from that bag after we'd slept together. She seemed like she needed it. But it was an accident. How the fuck was I supposed to know what it was? It looked like the real McCoy to me. I'm bloody lucky that I rubbed it on her gums before I took any myself or I wouldn't be here now. She immediately started having some kind of seizure. It was only then that I realised it wasn't some party drug.' Ari took a step closer to Trausti. 'Anyway, why the fuck are you bringing this up now? You're not going to the police, I know that. We're all equally guilty. But Gugga was the guiltiest of all. Everything we did that night was because of her. Did you know she'd spiked the cupcakes with acid?'

Trausti didn't answer. There was no point. He violently rejected everything Ari had said, apart from the fact that it was too late to go to the authorities.

Ari, reading Trausti like an open book, went on: 'I knew it. You're not going to squeal. Anyway, what about you, mate? I seem to remember you going into her room not long after me. Leifur as well. What did you two do to her? Grab your chance, did you?'

Trausti felt the blood rising to his cheeks and lowered his gaze. This was something he couldn't bear to remember, let alone discuss. He knew that he had gone to see if Gudrún was OK but he had never been able to remember why. He just knew that he had failed her so badly he couldn't face thinking about it. But now, suddenly, it came back to him what he had been doing in her room. He knew exactly why he'd gone: Ari had sent him. He'd been behaving a bit oddly, asking if the doctor shouldn't check on the patient since she was off her face. Perhaps he had been hoping that Trausti could do something for Gudrún. Or perhaps he'd just wanted to get more people involved. And Trausti had obeyed. He'd been in such a state that he'd had to support himself with a hand against the wall as he staggered along the corridor but eventually he had made it to her door. Gudrún was lying in a darkened room. Her breathing was laboured, foam was oozing from her mouth and her whole body was shaking and convulsing. But instead of doing the right thing and calling the emergency number, he had shushed her in a kindly way and spread the duvet over her. Then he had returned to the party, reporting to the others that she was asleep. Then he, the medical student, had sat down and carried on drinking.

He'd had a chance to prevent her tragic demise and the ensuing shitstorm. If he'd called an ambulance at the time, he wouldn't be in this mess now. Gugga would doubtless have got into trouble but it would have been nothing in comparison to the present nightmare. At least there was a minor consolation in knowing that if the bag had contained cyanide, an ambulance wouldn't have made any difference; Gudrún's fate had been sealed the moment Ari forced her mouth open.

At that moment the front door was flung wide and Sigga burst into the dining room, panting and crying hysterically. 'Ragga! Ragga! She's had a heart attack.'

Trausti didn't need to hear any more. He was out of the house and sprinting down the hill as fast as his legs would carry him, immune to the sound of Sigga's screams from the house behind him. The situation was too urgent to worry about her. He stumbled and fell twice on the way but got up immediately and kept on running.

The fire was still burning on the beach, casting an orange glow over the surroundings and lighting up Ragga's motionless body, lying a short way off. She was dead by the time he reached her, bloody foam dribbling from her mouth and nostrils down to her chin. The foam smelt of menthol and he guessed at once what had happened. Sigga hadn't poured away the cyanide powder she had mistaken for cocaine. Instead, she had dissolved it in the Ópal schnapps and offered Ragga a drink, not for a moment suspecting that she was writing her friend's death warrant. Presumably she'd only been trying to perk her up.

Drunk, high and panicking, Sigga hadn't made the connection between Ragga's sudden illness and the schnapps. Victims of cyanide poisoning didn't die instantly, although it worked relatively fast. As a result, Sigga had believed a heart attack was to blame, not accidental poisoning.

Ragga's body was still warm and Trausti tried in vain to massage the life back into her. Every time he pressed on her chest, more foam oozed out of her mouth, until in the end he had to give up. He screamed his lungs out at the sky, then took her in his arms and propped her up against a boulder. Putting on his gloves, he wiped the bloody foam from her face and out of her mouth, squeezing the last remnants from her nose. He wanted her to look as decent as possible – not that it mattered now.

After a long moment, he turned away, picked up the petrol can that was lying on the stones nearby and splashed the remains over the burning body on the pyre. Then he hurled the can out to sea, not caring when it failed to sink. He slowly retraced his steps up the hill, tears pouring down his cheeks. The whole situation had finally reached its nadir.

He was only halfway there when Ari's car appeared, coming towards him. It was hard to see through the windows in the blinding glare of the headlights but he thought they were both inside. The car stopped beside him and the driver's window slid down. 'Get in. We're leaving.'

Trausti bent down and peered in. Sigga was sitting in the passenger seat, a vacant look in her eyes, her body shuddering with sobs. 'Let me drive, Ari,' Trausti said.

'Fuck, no. Get in.'

Trausti shook his head. He tried to make eye contact with Sigga. 'Sigga, Sigga,' he said. But she just stared into space.

'Get in the fucking car or you can walk.' Ari tightened his grip on the wheel. 'I mean it.'

'Only if I can drive.'

'Last chance. Do you want a lift or not? Jesus. Stay here, then. You're no fucking better than Leifur was.'

There was something wrong about Ari's use of the past tense for Leifur. The collar of his shirt had sagged and Trausti found himself staring at the evidence Ari had almost certainly been trying to hide. 'What's that on your neck, Ari?' There were red marks that looked to him like scratches running down Ari's neck into his collar.

Ari raised a hand automatically to his neck, trying to pull up his collar. 'I cut myself shaving.'

This was a blatant lie as his cheeks were still covered in dark stubble. Trausti suddenly remembered the two chairs that had been knocked over in the dining room and Leifur's phone lying under the table. Peering through the window into the back seat, he saw that Ari had brought his own luggage, along with Sigga's and Trausti's, but hadn't bothered with Leifur's. Yet Leifur's case had been standing next to the others'. It was obvious why he'd left Ragga's case behind – the dead don't need luggage. 'Where's Leifur, Ari?' Trausti demanded. 'It was just the two of you downstairs when he disappeared. Did he accuse you of raping Gudrún? Did you do something to him?'

Ari didn't need to say anything; Trausti could read the answer in his face. 'Get in the car, you stupid prick,' Ari snapped. Beside him, Sigga sat sobbing hysterically. She seemed unaware of her surroundings or what was being said.

When Trausti shook his head, Ari scowled at him, then reached into the back and tossed out Trausti's case. The robot vacuum cleaner tumbled out with it, accidentally activated by the fall. Ari flung one more 'fuck you' in Trausti's face, then slammed the door and accelerated away.

Once the tail lights had vanished from view, Trausti set off on foot. Behind him, the robot stuttered and skidded on the icy tarmac, its wheels spinning. Glancing back, Trausti saw the robot detect the edge of the tarmac, reverse and change direction. He turned and started walking in the direction of town, dragging his case. The robot would have to fend for itself. No doubt it would make it to the bottom of the hill in the end.

Trausti met only one car on his desperate solitary walk to the ferry. The woman at the wheel was grimly focused on holding the car on the icy road but the dog in the back seat set up a furious barking when it spotted Trausti and started scrabbling at the windows. The car kept going towards Stórhöfdi but Trausti was too dazed to wonder what business the woman might have out there or whether the bonfire was still burning on the beach. When he finally made it to the town, he walked down to the harbour and spotted Ari's car, the only one queuing for the ferry. The last thing Trausti wanted was to encounter the others again, so he slipped round the corner of a building and lurked out of sight. Since there would be no way of avoiding them on board, he would just have to wait for a later ferry.

The weather was windless but bitterly cold. Trausti had a choice between skulking there, shivering, or taking a seat in a café and risk having to cope with people. He decided to hide, but soon realised he'd freeze to death if he didn't get indoors somewhere. All he could think of was Gugga's empty house. He walked the short distance to her street, went round into the garden, broke a pane of glass in the back door and let himself in. He no longer cared about leaving obvious signs that he'd been there. Unless there was a miracle and the body burnt to ashes, they were done for anyway. A break-in wouldn't make much difference at this stage.

There was a deathly hush in the house. He had come here purely in search of warmth. He sat down in the living room and stared at the clock on the wall, waiting for the interminable minutes to tick by. He wanted to cry but for some reason he couldn't. It was as if something inside him had shrivelled up and died, leaving him strangely numb. Every now and then, his gaze flicked to the photos of Gugga and her parents on the shelf, and his rage briefly flared up, then subsided again. Gugga may have set all these terrible events in motion but he had to face up to his own responsibility. He couldn't blame the dead for the foolish decisions he and his friends had made over the last couple of days, not to mention seven years ago. The only innocent person in this whole tragic tale had been Gudrún. Though, on second thoughts, her decision to steal the poison for Gugga had been the first step on the road to the mess they were in now. But he had only himself to blame for his fate. He had connived in the disastrous decisions the others had made and been too feeble to act when he should have insisted on doing the right thing.

When it was time to leave, Trausti stood up and glanced around the sitting room for the last time, then hurried past the cellar door on his way out. With utter futility, he wondered about the existence of some other dimension in which Leifur and Ari had never gone down there and everything had turned out OK. But however hard he tried to picture that scenario, the end was always the same. The body would have been found eventually and they would have been dragged into the investigation. They would have been in trouble, regardless of how they had acted, and there was a certain comfort in that thought.

Down at the harbour he went to buy a new ticket for the ferry. He still had a bit of cash left in his wallet. Behind him, two men were engaged in a passionate discussion about a handball game that had taken place the evening before and he found himself genuinely envying them. The young man in the ticket office, obviously assuming the three of them were travelling together, grinned and said 'Go ÍBV,' as he handed Trausti his ticket and change. Evidently the local team had won. Trausti managed to squeeze out a smile before taking a seat and waiting for the gangway to open. The two men sat down beside him and started a conversation, apparently convinced he was a big handball fan after hearing what the ticket guy had said to him. He managed to answer yes and no in the right places, though not much more than that. They didn't seem to mind.

When Trausti finally boarded, he realised that he had no plan beyond getting back to the mainland. His flight to the US wasn't until after 5 p.m., but he had no idea how he was going to get to Keflavík in time. The ferry was calling at Landeyjahöfn, which was more than two hours' drive from the airport. The mountain road over Hellisheidi was still closed, according to his new friends, and he had no phone on which to check whether there were any buses going to Keflavík from the port. He sat at a table in the saloon on board, gazing out of the window, and hoped the soothing influence of the sea would stop him from laying his head on the table and crying his eyes out. For Gudrún, who had paid for Gugga's stupidity and Ari's deviance with her life. For Leifur and Sigga, who had been completely in the dark about all the goings-on. For Ragga. Even for Gugga. For everything he had lost and for what was to come.

Fate hadn't exactly been on his side. Particularly not in the last few days. But he couldn't be unlucky forever. He pricked up his ears when he heard an older couple at the next table talking about passports and flights to the Canary Islands. He had nothing to lose. Turning to them, he introduced himself and asked if they were by any chance on their way to the airport. It transpired that they were and, moreover, that they had nothing against giving him a lift. In fact, they were eager to help, apparently under the impression that he had been attending the fishing conference and had missed his ferry the day before. Once again, all he had to do was say yes and no in the right places.

Trausti caught his flight. He wasn't stopped at check-in as he had feared. He wasn't stopped at passport control or on his way out to the plane. He settled into his window seat towards the back of the plane, listening to the booming of his heart, terrified that the police would come storming on board and drag him off at the last minute. To make matters worse, he didn't have a clear view of what was happening at the front.

Only when they finally took off could he relax. He gazed out of the window at his native land, now spread out below him, and thought he would never see it again. Not as a free man.

As Iceland finally vanished from view, the tears began to slide down his cheeks.

Epilogue

Idunn hammered away at her keyboard, averting her eyes from her pink-lacquered nails. Whenever she caught sight of them, she felt they were the fingers of a stranger. The manicure was down to Alexandra, who had nagged at her until Idunn had given in. Some of her colleagues had raised their eyebrows when they noticed the pink varnish and one of the women had asked if she'd met someone. The glare Idunn shot her had hopefully nipped that idea in the bud. Since then, everyone had tactfully avoided commenting.

Idunn resolved to buy some nail-polish remover on her way home. She may have capitulated to her sister in this instance but she had to be allowed to be herself or their cohabitation wouldn't work. It was fragile enough, though up to now they had got on OK. In fact, Idunn had been surprised to find how little she missed being alone. She'd even got used to Alexandra's constant chatter during TV programmes; oddly enough, her uninvited commentary seemed, if anything, to improve the offerings. Now and then, though, it would get too much for Idunn and, reminding her sister that she was here in Reykjavík to study, she would chivvy her to do her homework. Though, in truth, Alexandra had taken her by surprise there as well. She was quick to absorb information and her good marks were clearly no accident. If she carried on like this, she had every chance of sailing through the entrance exam to study medicine. Which would mean that Alexandra wouldn't be going home any time soon, and Idunn's home office would continue to be co-opted as a bedroom.

Things had gone more smoothly than Idunn would have dreamt possible, if you discounted the reaction of her mother, who had freaked out at the news. *How could you? I knew you were trying to insert yourself back into your father's life, you ungrateful bitch! What next? Are you going to disown me?* Fortunately, though, her mother had still been so exhausted from the tantrum she had thrown about Idunn going to the islands in the first place that she had deflated like a burst balloon. At that point, Idunn had seized the opportunity to remind her that her father's relationship with Alexandra's mother had begun long after their divorce. Besides, Alexandra couldn't be held responsible for his behaviour. This made little impression on her mother. It was only when Idunn mentioned that her father was furious at the arrangement that her mother calmed down and even cheered up a bit.

Idunn pressed 'Send' on the email she had been writing and reached for her phone. She stared at it for a while, wondering whether to ring Týr or Karó. Týr had sent her a report of the investigation's preliminary findings, which she had just finished reading. Was he hoping to hear back from her about it? Or had he simply been acting on orders, in which case he might have no desire to talk to her? There was only one way to find out.

'Hello. It's Idunn.'

Týr greeted her in a neutral tone, sounding neither especially pleased nor annoyed. He asked if she'd read the report and was satisfied with the conclusions. She replied that she hadn't spotted any mistakes or misrepresentations of the facts.

There were still a few unanswered questions but she had every confidence that the investigation team would deal with them. Týr wasn't so sure, citing staff shortages and other urgent priorities. They had managed to establish fairly conclusively that the banker, Ari, had killed Leifur, the man who had been strangled. Ari's fingerprints had been on the belt and his DNA had been found in the traces of skin under the victim's nails. Leifur, in turn, had left scratches on Ari's neck. In addition, it seemed highly likely that Ari had smuggled opioids to Gugga in the CBD capsules she'd had with her in hospital.

The analysis of the capsules' contents had finally come through, proving that some of them had indeed been swapped with opioids. An orderly at the University Hospital remembered a man bringing Gugga the capsules and had identified Ari from photos. Ari's fingerprints had been on the bottle, though it was impossible to establish how he had sourced the opioids. As a result, the circumstances of Gugga's death remained obscure. Perhaps Ari had slipped her the opioids, perhaps she had ground down her own pills and hidden the powder in the CBD capsules. Since neither she nor Ari was alive to tell the tale, it was unlikely the mystery would ever be solved.

Ari was dead. His body was one of those in the car that had skidded off the road on Hellisheidi and subsequently been buried in snow. With him in the car had been the second woman from the group – Sigrídur, known as Sigga. They had ignored the signs warning that the mountain road was closed, driven round the barrier and ventured into hazardous conditions in an inadequately equipped vehicle. A high concentration of alcohol had been measured in Ari's blood and there had been an empty brandy bottle beside him; it was hardly surprising he'd crashed. Although the sequence of events would never be entirely clear, it was believed that he had lost control of the car in a fit of panic when the passenger beside him started to choke and convulse. He hadn't died instantly but had been badly injured in the crash and, as the road had been closed for a further forty-eight hours, during which time there had been a heavy snowfall, the car had been buried under a drift and he hadn't been found until Thursday evening, more than seventy-two hours after the crash. It might have been possible to save him if help had arrived quickly enough, but he had died of his injuries, hanging upside down in his seatbelt. A death that was neither quick nor merciful.

The woman in the passenger seat had died some time before him from potassium cyanide poisoning, as in the case of her friend Ragnhildur, whose body had been found sitting on the beach in the Westman Islands. She had apparently imbibed the poison by drinking Ópal schnapps, a bottle of which had turned up in the car, containing a solution of the substance. It was believed that the schnapps had been chosen because the smell and taste of menthol hid the almond odour of the poison. A small bag containing traces of cyanide had been discovered in the bin at the house on Stórhöfdi, though they had found Sigga's full fingerprints on that, rather than Ari's. Gugga's prints had been on it too, as well as partials from Gudrún and Ari. The police were fairly certain that this was the substance that had killed Gudrún at the student residence seven years earlier.

It was impossible to establish beyond doubt how Sigga had come to die like this. Her fingerprints on the bag suggested that she had mixed the deadly Ópal drink herself but it was hard to see why. Had she been intending to take her own life or to poison the others? If it was the latter, her friend Ragnhildur had obviously walked into the trap. Perhaps Sigrídur had intended to do both – murder her friend, then take her own life. It would never be satisfactorily explained. The results of tests made in connection with her post-mortem revealed that the woman had been drinking and smoking cannabis shortly before her death, so it was possible she had just forgotten and taken a swig from the bottle by mistake. Another theory was that the driver, Ari, had poisoned the schnapps. He'd had the sense not to drink it himself and could have used gloves when he handled both bottle and plastic bag. Idunn was inclined to this view, as it was clear that he had murdered Leifur and possibly Gugga as well. It beggared belief that there could have been two murderers in the same group of friends. But then it was the most bizarre case Idunn had ever worked on.

'What's bothering you most?' Týr asked.

'Minor details. I don't understand why Ari bought four tickets for the ferry that morning if he'd already murdered Leifur. There would only have been three of them left, as he must have realised.' Idunn regretted choosing this example. The ticket purchase could easily be explained away by saying that Ari hadn't wanted to betray his action to the two women, so he had pretended to assume Leifur would be coming with them. 'The phone calls are bugging me too. All those endless night-time calls to the house on Stórhöfdi. Did you never get to the bottom of them?'

'Yes and no. The owners of the numbers have been interviewed but they deny having made any calls. They were all senior citizens, from the local retirement home, or else patients at the hospital. Forensics are going to check whether it could have been a trick, as I understand it's easy enough to hide behind a fake number when making calls. What's more, there are no signs that these calls were made from the phones Inspector Ína has been able to examine – apart from one. It's possible they've been deleted, but there weren't thought to be any grounds to confiscate the phones to check. If it was the owners of the phones, it could be written off as nuisance calls. Just a bunch of old people getting together to harass strangers out of boredom. It wasn't considered worth following up in the report. For their sake. After all, they have nothing to do with the murders. Maybe I shouldn't tell you, but one of the people concerned is Ína's own mother. Who knows whether that played a part in her decision to leave this business out of the report.'

Idunn wasn't convinced by this explanation, though she didn't say as much. The people must have had a reason to make countless nuisance calls to the same number in the middle of the night. Unless they resented the automation of the lighthouse on Stórhöfdi and the conversion of the keeper's house into a holiday let? Nostalgia for the past could take on unlikely forms.

'What about the dog hairs? I'm still wondering whether Ásta was being completely honest with us.' Idunn couldn't shake off her doubts, though the bulk of the woman's statement had been confirmed by the notebook or diary that Gugga had kept. It had been found in Ari's luggage, along with a woman's underwear in his trouser pocket, which turned out, on analysis, to contain Gudrún's DNA and traces of his own semen. The police had been unable to explain why he had taken the knickers with him when none of her other clothes had been found, though it was thought that they had probably been burnt on the bonfire.

'Isn't that in the report?' Týr sounded surprised. 'They must have forgotten to include it. After all, it's only a draft. Anyway, the presence of the hairs has been accounted for.'

'Oh, how?'

'You remember that Ásta's dog was injured in the car crash and sent to be operated on?' When Idunn said she did, Týr continued: 'It turns out that the hospital mortuary facilities are also used for operating on injured animals as there's no separate veterinary hospital in the islands. The dog was operated on using the table where you performed the post-mortem. The two hairs must have been left behind when the table was washed down afterwards.'

Idunn was momentarily lost for words, but quickly recovered. 'Didn't it occur to anyone to tell me about this earlier? Like the inspector or the nurse who assisted me, for example?'

'Maybe they don't own pets or haven't had to use the service. Anyway, Ína had much bigger things on her mind than an injured dog.' Behind Týr, there was an outburst of angry shouting. Idunn guessed this was his boss, Erla. The woman had an extremely odd management style, in Idunn's opinion. You'd have thought she'd learnt it from studying pirate captains, where every order had to be accompanied by a curse. 'Look, I'd better go,' Týr said. 'I'll add the detail about the origin of the dog hairs. I gather there are a number of other things still to be included.'

'Like what?'

'We haven't yet interviewed the only surviving guest from the party held at the student residence the night Gudrún died. Apparently he's studying in the States. I understand they're hoping that the recent events will loosen his tongue about that evening. But I expect he'll stick to the story he told at the time, now that there are no other witnesses left but him. He's not exactly in any danger of being caught out in a lie. That's why we haven't rung him yet. We need to have everything straight beforehand, so we're well prepared.'

'Is there any chance he'll be prosecuted for Gudrún's death?'

'No. Not that I can see. The guy probably just had the bad luck to be present at the party. No one's going to pursue him now because he didn't report her death at the time. We don't have any conclusive evidence that he even knew about it. He doesn't seem to have been as close to Gugga as the others, if her diary is anything to go by. She barely mentions him and when she does it's to call him a total wuss. But one thing's clear, he was lucky – it probably saved his life that he's doing graduate studies in America and so couldn't attend the funeral. The guys at the station are joking that if anyone makes a film about the friends' fateful trip, they could call it *Four Funerals and No Wedding*.'

'One more thing, Týr, before I ring off,' Idunn said, ignoring the tasteless joke. 'I want to apologise for what I said to you about your mother's murder. I shouldn't have told you.'

Týr was silent and the yelling in the background rang in Idunn's ears. When he finally spoke, his voice sounded friendly and sincere: 'Look, you did the right thing. I was just knocked sideways. I'm sorry if you thought I was angry with you. I'm not at all. I'm just still trying to get my head around it. Wondering what I should do or whether I should just let things lie.'

Idunn was so relieved that it was all she could do not to let out a sigh. 'You know where to find me if you do decide to look into it further. I'm ready and willing to help.'

They rang off and Idunn sat there for a while, unsure what to do. She always found it hard to let go of cases – that was nothing new. As with any job, she had the feeling there were things she could have done better. But the unsettled feeling was particularly strong this time. There had been so many autopsies and she'd been working under such time pressure that she was afraid she'd missed something. Alexandra was partly to blame for this niggling feeling, as Idunn could still hear her voice echoing in her head as she insisted that there had been five people outside Gugga's house that day.

Idunn contemplated her pink nails and released a long breath. Her sister must be misremembering, because the report couldn't have been clearer in that respect. Four people had arrived in two cars; two had been found dead in the islands and two in the car on Hellisheidi. The owners of the holiday let had talked of accommodation for four, and four bedrooms had been used. Money had been withdrawn using four bank cards. Four people had turned up to the funeral. Four phones had connected to the Wi-Fi at the house on Stórhöfdi during the days the group was staying there. The same applied to the 4G network. There had even been four spades.

Nevertheless, Alexandra's voice continued to reverberate in her head: *there were five of them.*

What rubbish. And that nurse she'd been so impressed by – the young man who'd assisted with the post-mortem. It was perfectly possible that Inspector Ína hadn't been aware that the mortuary examination room doubled as an animal hospital, but the nurse should have known. He had actually been there with her when she'd found the hairs, which would have been the perfect moment to inform her. Idunn looked back at her phone, wondering whether to ring him. Or would that be too petty of her? He might have been responsible for cleaning up after the operation on the dog and been ashamed of his sloppiness.

Her phone beeped and she saw that the message was from Alexandra: *I've just booked us a massage and spa treatments for Sat. Need a credit card number to confirm. Can you send me your card details?* This was followed by a series of emojis:

toasting champagne glasses, hearts, smiley-face kisses, fire-works, a shower head, a white coat and a thumbs-up. Idunn had no idea whether the sequence itself meant anything. Although she didn't use emojis herself, she wondered if they included a symbol for 'fuck off'. But instead of searching for one, she reached for her wallet. Resistance was useless.

She took out her credit card and typed in the information. Sending one's card details electronically wasn't recommended but she suspected that once Alexandra had got her mitts on her card, there would soon be little left for potential hackers, anyway.

Idunn sent the message, then turned to the window, catching her own reflection in the glass. The sight caught her off-guard. She was smiling. What's more, it wasn't a polite rictus or one of the other pale versions of a smile that she usually adopted. It was a broad grin of happiness, yet the face was definitely hers. For the first time in many years, she was looking forward to leaving work and going home.

Idunn realised she was in too good a mood to tear a strip off anyone, so it was probably best to forget about calling that nurse. She'd forgotten his name, anyway. She closed the report on her computer screen and decided to stop thinking about it. The case was more or less closed, at least on her side. It was time to turn her attention to new tasks.

Már looked in on the old man who had been brought in that afternoon. He was constantly in and out of hospital, his health steadily deteriorating. Már had been waiting for him to reappear. He went over to the monitor the man was hooked up to and saw that everything looked normal. Turning back to the bed, he made sure that the old man was sound asleep. He was lying on his back, his mouth wide open, and although his breathing was heavy, it was regular, so he was obviously in the land of dreams.

Már picked up the old man's phone from the bedside table, opened it and went straight to the call log. He scrolled down the few calls the man had made since he'd last been admitted to hospital and quickly found what he was looking for. Then he began to delete the calls to the number on Stórhöfdi. They had only been answered once. That done, Már put the phone back on the table, smiling to himself. He wouldn't have to endure any more sleepless nights on account of this one phone that he hadn't managed to clean. The phones of the other patients he'd used behind their owners' backs were all clean, as were those belonging to the residents at the retirement home where he sometimes took night shifts.

It had all been so easy, better than he could have hoped. He had secretly used the old people's phones while they were asleep, muted the sound, then repeatedly rung the house on Stórhöfdi to torment those bastards. Sometimes he had borrowed the phones so he could keep it up throughout his night shift, then returned them before their owners woke up in the morning, having deleted the calls from the log. When people noticed that the phones had been muted, this was invariably attributed to the patients' senility, even when the old people insisted they hadn't done it. But he'd twice had a narrow escape. The first time, the orderly who'd been taking the night shift with him had entered the room of the old man who was now lying in front of him, meaning that Már hadn't had time to delete the calls from the log. The second time, he had unwittingly used the phone of a woman who'd turned out to be the police inspector's mother. But he'd got away with it.

Luck had been on his side. Just as it had when Gugga was transferred from the University Hospital in Reykjavík to the islands, a mass of broken bones. By then he'd been living on Heimaey for more than a year, knew who she was and had developed a good relationship with her at the hospital, despite having to fight back a violent urge to smother her with a pillow. For years he'd been convinced that she and her friends hadn't told the whole truth about the disappearance of his sister, Gudrún. This wasn't some baseless suspicion; he had a reliable source. One of the cops who had worked on the investigation after she went missing had told his parents this in confidence, and Már hadn't been able to forget it. It made no difference that the investigation had been closed without coming to a conclusion or proving the friends' role in Gudrún's disappearance.

Of course, he'd been careful not to tell Gugga about his relationship to her missing friend. He'd said he was from Reykjavík rather than the west of Iceland, to reduce the chances of her making the connection. It worked, but then she'd had no real interest in talking about him, only about herself. He had long ago come to the realisation that the less there was going on in people's lives, the greater their need to discuss it in detail. But this time it was to his advantage. It had proved easy for him to persuade her to confide in him about what had happened the night Gudrún had vanished. He had given her the painkillers she craved and exploited her resulting high to winkle the story out of her. The following night, she had regretted unburdening herself to him like that, but he had assured her that she needn't worry; he was bound by patient confidentiality. He'd added that the main thing was that she was genuinely sorry for what she had done.

That was a blatant lie, of course. Gugga's regrets were mainly for herself; for the way that terrible evening and her own foolish decisions had destroyed her life. This wasn't enough for him. The punishment inflicted on her by fate didn't balance out the damage that he and his family had suffered, let alone the torment his sister had gone through. Gudrún had died, his parents had hardly experienced a moment's happiness after she vanished, his mother had gone to her grave never knowing what had happened to her daughter, and he himself had been forced to change direction in life. He'd failed his entry exams for the dentistry degree, having been forced to go out and get a job instead of being able to concentrate exclusively on revision. He'd enrolled in a nursing degree instead. The course and job suited him well and he didn't regret his decision. On the other hand, he resented having been forced to make this U-turn and abandon his dream of starting his own dental clinic in his home town in the west. But, above all, he couldn't forgive Gugga for having caused his sister's disappearance and death. For that, she would have to pay.

It was clear to Már that Gugga's fall while climbing the Heimaklettur rock had been no accident: she'd planned to kill herself. She had even hinted as much during their chats when she was unable to sleep at night. Since Gugga didn't want to live, he reasoned that it wouldn't be such a heinous crime to give her a helping hand. He had built up a stock of the strongest opioids in the hospital pharmacy by reducing the other patients' doses or giving them different, milder painkillers that weren't monitored. Then he had ground the pills down, stolen Gugga's bottle of CBD capsules from her bedside table and emptied some of the capsules out, filling them with the opioids instead. When she eventually took them, her fate would be sealed.

Már checked on the old man again, then left the room. He spoke to the orderly who was on duty with him, then went into the nurses' station. All was quiet and he could afford to take a rare break. As in other hospitals, there was always a lot happening and the pressure was often considerable, even at night.

Már opened Facebook and looked up Gugga's friend, Ásta. She had also known about what had happened at the student residence. When the local inspector and the Reykjavík detective had interviewed Ásta in hospital, Már had volunteered to observe and make sure they didn't push the patient too hard. As a result, she hadn't said one word about him. Their eyes had met frequently during the interview, and he'd tried to convey to her in no uncertain terms that she was to keep quiet. At one point he had even drawn a finger across his throat to frighten her into obeying. Not that this had been necessary.

It was Ásta who had got in touch with him. She'd said that Gugga had confided in her that he knew her secret too and she'd wanted to ask his advice about what to do. He'd persuaded her to leave well alone and she had been very relieved. It was obvious that she'd been thinking along those lines herself but hadn't been able to come to a decision. Like most people, she had jumped at the chance to do the wrong thing when it was handed to her. When they'd encountered each other again at Gugga's funeral, she had pointed out the friends who had been at the party the night Gudrún vanished. She'd spoken to one of the women from the group on the ferry, and whispered in his ear that they were staying on Stórhöfdi. She was going to do her best to make them hurry home again, in case they were planning to tamper with the body in Gugga's cellar. Ásta wanted the body to be found and the case to be solved, for the sake of Gudrún's family. She hadn't a clue that she was speaking to Gudrún's brother, any more than Gugga had before she died.

He had found the group of friends too carefree and cheerful – bearing in mind that they could have informed the police about his sister's disappearance at the time but had chosen to keep their mouths shut. There was no sign that they'd suffered for their sins in the way that Gugga had.

He couldn't leave it at that.

Már checked Ásta's latest update on Facebook but couldn't see any sign that he should worry. He had probably got away with it. The police investigation was as good as over, his sister Gudrún had been found and her fate had been laid bare. Gugga's death wouldn't be looked into any further since it was clear what part she had played in what had happened to Gudrún. Who cared how someone like that had met their end? The deaths of the others had nothing to do with him. He hadn't needed to lift a finger. He had tormented them with phone calls at night, but they themselves had seen to the rest. It was quite incredible, really.

Már opened his email and began to compose a resignation letter to the HR department at the hospital. Although he was happy enough in the islands, it wouldn't pay to stay here much longer. It was too risky. He'd had a narrow escape when Gudrún's body had been found and his father had volunteered him to identify her. Luckily, the policeman on the line had been in such a hurry to refuse the offer that his father hadn't had a chance to mention that Már was living in the islands. He'd had another close shave when he'd obeyed the impulse to lay flowers on Gugga's mother's grave, after discovering that Gudrún was buried there. He'd run out of patience while waiting for the body in the cellar to be found and the whole thing to be revealed. The vicar had seen him and come over to ask if he'd known Marta. He'd thought quickly and said he was doing a favour for a patient, as Gugga was still in hospital at the time. The vicar had taken this at face value. In the end, it would emerge that Már was Gudrún's brother and questions were bound to be asked. So it was better to move on. There was no shortage of demand for nurses.

He sent the email, then sat back in his chair with a smile.

If you loved *The Wake*,
we know you're going to love…

A masterclass in tension from one of the world's
finest crime writers

THRILLINGLY GOOD BOOKS
FROM CRIMINALLY
GOOD WRITERS

CRIME FILES BRINGS YOU THE LATEST RELEASES FROM
TOP CRIME AND THRILLER AUTHORS.

SIGN UP ONLINE FOR OUR MONTHLY NEWSLETTER AND BE THE FIRST
TO KNOW ABOUT OUR COMPETITIONS, NEW BOOKS AND MORE.

VISIT OUR WEBSITE: WWW.CRIMEFILES.CO.UK
LIKE US ON FACEBOOK: FACEBOOK.COM/CRIMEFILES
FOLLOW US ON TWITTER: @CRIMEFILESBOOKS